Connecticut: Small, but Scary

Twenty-one carefully curated tales set in Connecticut span the gamut from dark fairy tales to possessed objects, from *Dungeons & Dragons* games that overlap into real life to aliens among us. Kids on bikes ride through these pages, confronting themselves, nature, and the general weirdness of Connecticut in the '80s and '90s.

Meet bullies, saviors, ghosts, weirdos, and sweethearts, dreamed into existence by some of the most innovative horror writers of Connecticut, and a chosen few from elsewhere.

Horror over the Handlebars
A Yankee Scares Anthology of Connecticut Horror Stories

Gevera Bert Piedmont

John Opalenik

Editors

Horror Over the Handlebars: A Yankee Scares Connecticut Horror Anthology

© 2024 Gevera Bert Piedmont/Transformations by Obsidian Butterfly, LLC

This is a collected work of fiction. All events portrayed in this book are fictitious, and any resemblance to real people or events is purely coincidental. All rights reserved, including the right to reproduce this book or portions of this book in any form without the express permission of the authors and the publisher.

Introduction © 2024 John Opalenik
Cover art © 2024 Amanda Opalenik
Transformations by Obsidian Butterfly LLC
www.ObsidianButterfly.com
Transformations@ObsidianButterfly.com

Paperback ISBN: 978-1-963760-03-3
Ebook ISBN: 978-1-963760-04-0

"Forever Children" © 2024 J.P. Behrens.
"Many Deaths Before Dying" © 2023 Warren Benedetto.
"Ouch" © 2024 Sasha Brown.
"Out There" © 2024 Tom Deady.
"You Couldn't Steal a House in the Eighties" © 2024 Agrimmeer DeMolay.
"Omnivision" © 2023 Michael Gore.
"P.E.T.E." © 2024 Dale W. Glaser.
"Between Sharp Teeth and Lady Slippers" © 2024 T.L. Guthrie.
"No Rider in the Flesh and Bone" © 2024 Charles Montgomery.
"Below the Surface, We Can Only Imagine" © 2024 Matt Moore.
"It Happened Deep in the Woods" © 2023 Tom Moran.
"The Withering" © 2024 Kurt Newton.
"Incident at Elderhill Farm" © 2023 John Opalenik.
"Doug's House" © 2024 Judith Pancoast.
"Biker Gang" © 2023 Gevera Bert Piedmont.
"Fluke" © 2024 Joe Russell.
"Nathan's Night at Norwich" © 2024 Rob Smales.
"The Ghost Girl of Rocky Neck" © 2024 Benjamin Thomas.
"The Crimson Staircase of Tryethelone" © 2024 Margret A. Treiber.
"19 Miles from Millstone, June 17th, 1988" © 2024 M. Tyler Tuttle.
"A Home for His Fears" © 2024 Anne Woods.

Table of Contents

Introduction
John Opalenik 7

Omnivision
Michael Gore 9

19 Miles from Millstone, June 17th, 1988
M. Tyler Tuttle 22

No Rider in the Flesh and Bone
Charles Montgomery 39

The Crimson Staircase of Tryethelone
Margret A. Treiber 52

Below the Surface, We Can Only Imagine
Matt Moore 62

Biker Gang
Gevera Bert Piedmont 82

A Home for His Fears
Anne Woods 97

Ouch
Sasha Brown 111

Forever Children
J.P. Behrens 114

Nathan's Night at Norwich
Rob Smales 119

You Couldn't Steal a House in the Eighties
Agrimmeer DeMolay 146

The Withering
Kurt Newton 153

P.E.T.E.
Dale W. Glaser 159

The Ghost Girl of Rocky Neck
Benjamin Thomas 170

Out There
Tom Deady 181

Many Deaths Before Dying
Warren Benedetto 191

Fluke
Joe Russell 202

Doug's House
Judith Pancoast 224

It Happened Deep in the Woods
Tom Moran 239

Between Sharp Teeth and Lady Slippers
T.L. Guthrie 255

Incident at Elderhill Farm
John Opalenik 268

Introduction

John Opalenik

"We were all kids on bikes once."

That line led to the anthology you're holding now. Bert and I were at adjacent tables at an author event on the Connecticut shoreline and we were talking about what we were working on. Bert was looking to begin a series of Connecticut-based horror anthologies, and I said that I was writing a story involving three teenagers riding their bikes to an old farm at a forest's edge to play paintball when they stumble upon something they shouldn't. When I went into a bit more detail about what happens in the story, Bert jokingly said, "We've all been there."

When I replied, "We were all kids on bikes once," it clicked that coming-of-age horror would be an ideal theme for the first volume of the then-untitled Yankee Scares anthology series. Stories centered around that age where we're just starting to gain more freedom and often find out that the world is much bigger and darker than we thought would be equal parts nostalgic, terrifying, and relatable.

Then came the question, "Why Connecticut?" which is a valid question, since Connecticut often occupies many identities. It's part of New England, which has its own brand of the old and spooky, but it's also knocking at the door of the Mid-Atlantic region. All the while, the vast Atlantic Ocean is looming. To me, that's what makes it such a unique backdrop for this anthology and for the volumes of Yankee Scares that will follow.

In many ways, the theme expanded while also staying true to itself as the project grew. Initially, the anthology was meant to drip with '80s nostalgia, and I'd like to think it still does. But the classic image of "kids on bikes" has evolved but never gone away. Coming-of-age horror can include stumbling into a monster on a shoreline bicycle ride just as much as it can speaking to a potential monster in the disorganized anonymity of a chatroom in the early '00s. Expanding the theme in that way also forced us to confront another type of horror, the fact that the early '00s was twenty years ago and therefore can be deemed nostalgic.

What follows are twenty-one stories, both wonderful and strange, where the difficulties of coming-of-age come face-to-face with the weird, wondrous, and horrifying. A bullied girl gets back at her tormentors with the help of a creature washed up by Hurricane Gloria, a young man meets the (ghost) girl of his dreams, teenagers playing *Dungeons & Dragons* go on a real-life adventure, and we confront a VCR-related horror more terrifying than getting your favorite tape stuck in the machine.

With all of that, I invite you to the sidewalks, cul-de-sacs, shorelines, suburbs, cities, and forests of Connecticut.

John Opalenik
March 29, 2024

Omnivision

Michael Gore

Delivering the evening paper was torture to Justin, even if it was only thirty houses on two streets. Every night he had to roll the papers and cram them into those cheap orange plastic bags, load them in his canvas sack, and then walk to each house with the strap cutting into his shoulder. He tried to use his bike at first, but he could never balance well enough, so walking it was. Every step over the course of the hour it took him, which was right before he had to cook dinner, he thought of the Panasonic Omnivision VCR *with remote*. All his friends were obsessed with Nintendo, but Justin loved his television. A game might have red and green eight-bit brothers who challenged your skills, but there were no funny situations with perfect families that you could pretend to be a part of. Like the Seaver family. *Growing Pains* might have been a new show, but man, they were an ideal family. Mike was so damn cool, and the dad could solve anything. Justin just knew the mom would cook whatever he wanted and give him plenty of hugs. The last hug Justin had was two years ago before Mom died. If he just had a VCR, he could watch *Growing Pains* over and over and truly feel like he was a part of *their* family.

When his route was done and the bag was hung in the garage right next to his black cherry BMX bike that his dad "found" in the trash one day, Justin would always head inside to wash the black ink off his hands, which never seemed to fully fade, as the next day another coat would be added to his pudgy fingers. Being a little after five o'clock, it was time for him to make dinner for Lou, his older brother, and himself. Dinner was supposed to be Lou's job, but after being threatened with a steak knife one night (which resulted in a four-inch-long scar along his left thigh), Justin promised to make dinner every night his father was working and *never* tell that he had made dinner, *ever*. If Mike Seaver was

☽ Omnivision ☾

his older brother, they might have a few fights, but they would end in family talk and hugs, not a scar. Most of the nights it was TV dinners, mac and cheese, hot dogs, and other easy-to-make things, but lately Justin had been branching out to cooking real food. Tonight, he was going to try and make a paprika chicken recipe he found in Dad's *Reader's Digest*—the issue with that long article about the Titanic that his dad made both of them read. Justin couldn't care less about the boat, but he fell in love with the recipe. It was a special night, after all: the season finale of *Growing Pains* was on, and Justin couldn't wait. A fancy dinner beforehand would make for a perfect evening.

At eleven years old, Justin felt he was already a man, slapping on an apron, using knives and a gas stove—that was something only adults did, after all. The raw chicken was slimy and felt funny to Justin; before he put them in the pan, he squeezed the tenderloins through his fists and let it shoot out like the water-snake toy he loved playing with as a kid. Tossing them in the pan, he couldn't believe the sizzling and popping like mini grease fireworks. As he watched it cook, he licked the chicken goo off his fingers. It didn't taste too good, but the garlic salt and paprika that mixed in with the slime made him keep licking. When the chicken was done (which he could only tell by cutting them all in half), Justin was proud of himself. He had sautéed chicken, and it looked pretty good! Placing the bright orange strips next to a plop of sticky chicken-flavored Rice-A-Roni on the plate, he felt a wave of pride he had never felt. *It was going to be a good night.*

Grabbing a New Coke out of the fridge, Justin picked up the plate, took a deep breath, and walked down the hallway to Lou's room. The door had a poster of Iron Maiden sloppily taped to it; the picture of the skeleton/robot/muscle-monster-thing (or whatever the hell it was) always scared the shit out of him; he never looked at it, and he even moved his bed to a different spot in his room so he wouldn't see it through his door at night. With his hands full, he lightly kicked the door twice and yelled, "Dinner is ready, Lou. Made something new." For a split second he giggled at the rhyme, but then the door opened so fast it made him jump. Justin had a habit of not looking at Lou, just like he didn't look at that monster on the poster. Holding out the plate, he stared at it over daring to look at his brother's zit-covered face and spiky, jet-black hair. Sometimes he wondered if Lou was so mean because his entire face was made up of a million little red mountains filled with pus.

☽ Michael Gore ☾

"Where the fuck is the barbecue sauce?" Lou barked as he yanked back the plate and Coke at the same time.

"Oh, it has a lot of seasoning; you shouldn't need any on . . ." Justin knew better than to talk back, but he was so excited about the meal, he simply forgot. The foot hit his stomach flat, the toe of the shoe right over his belly button and the heel right above his crotch. It wasn't so much the impact as the thrust behind it that was the worst. It sent him flying, completely leaving the ground. Justin landed on his ass first; his back slammed the ground next, and then his head in one fast succession that sent bursts of pain through his body. Crying was quick and easy for him, but this time it came instantly. Lou marched down the hall in his massive black boots and stepped squarely on Justin's chest. At the same time he crushed Justin's chest, Lou said, "I'll fucking get it, you pussy." Two quick pops happened in concert with *pus* and *sy*, like tiny twigs snapping, one after the other, to the word. Justin felt them inside his chest, but also eerily heard the noise in his ears, as if his brain was telling him, *Oh shit, you hear that?*

As he heard the fridge door open, he took the opportunity to roll on his side, pushing the front of his body against the wall for protection. As his cheek stuck to the yellow linoleum floor, he stared at the flower-print wallpaper, bracing for what might happen next. The pain was unlike anything he'd ever felt, but he knew if he hadn't moved, Lou would step on his chest again. Thankfully, this time as he passed, it was just a steel-toe-tipped kick to the ass. When the door slammed shut, Justin fell onto his back and sucked in a breath for the first time. It felt like Freddy Krueger had jammed his rusty blades right into his chest, then twisted. There was no question that his ribs were broken. Over the course of the next ten minutes, he cried and did his best to slow his breathing to stop Freddy from jabbing him over and over again. The pain did not get better, but he had to get up and find some of Dad's aspirin in the cabinet, fast.

Justin pictured himself as John Rambo getting ready for his final fight, for he would certainly have to fight against the pain and get up. And that is just what he did, but the tears never stopped falling and Fred never stopped jabbing. After taking four aspirin, Justin fell into the stool at the counter right in front of his plate and sobbed. The crying was making the pain worse. Staring at the beautiful meal he had just cooked next to the glass of soda losing its fizz and knowing there was no way he could eat it, Justin once again thought about the Seavers. They never had

☽ Omnivision ☾

to eat alone; Mike would never hurt Ben like this. *Why couldn't I just have a family like that?* One where there were family dinners, where the dad would play basketball after eating and then watch television together. Putting his head down on the counter, he enjoyed the coolness against his skin, but he had to be careful not to get too close to the edge; that sucker was sharp and had hurt him before. Within a few seconds, Justin passed out.

☾ ☆ ☽

"Come get my plate and bring me another Coke, fucktard!" The scream woke Justin from a dream of playing hoops with Mike and Dr. Seaver. For a beautiful split second, he forgot that there was a cold dinner he was unable to eat in front of him and that he had a few broken ribs, but the second he breathed, his reality filled his lungs. Lou yelled a second time, but Justin did not get up. He simply couldn't. The door slamming open and the stomping of the boots would normally scare him, but with an empty stomach and pain that was too hard to handle, Justin hoped Lou would just end all of this for him. As the steps got closer, he braced for just that to happen.

"What is wrong with you? Why didn't you eat? That shit was good; you need to make it more." This was rare for Lou, who was normally raging in any conversation unless Dad was in the room.

"Justin, fucking answer me."

Justin tried to sigh but winced and cried before whispering a reply.

"Ribs . . . you broke my ribs. Can't breathe . . . or talk. Hurts too much," he said in a wheezing whisper. Hearing Lou take in a massive breath as he set down his plate, Justin felt a pang of jealousy for how easily air filled his brother's lungs.

"You got to be kidding me," Lou said, clearly annoyed. Suddenly he felt hands spin him around and two fingers start jabbing his ribs all over. The scream he let out was unlike anything that had ever come out of his mouth before.

"Shit," Lou said in his own whisper as he tried to keep Justin from falling off the stool. He wanted Lou to finish him, to just stab him with a knife like he'd threatened so many damn times and end all of this, but instead his brother backed away, pointed a finger at him, and yelled.

"You fucking let Dad know about this, and you are dead. Seriously dead. A few ribs won't kill you. Clean up the kitchen, ice that shit, and keep your mouth shut." Lou reached across him, took Justin's plate and soda and walked back to his room. *There was the Lou I knew.* It took him nine times longer than normal, but he cleaned the dishes and the counters, then grabbed frozen peas and went into the living room to ice his ribs and watch television. It wasn't a second too early; it was only ten minutes before the season finale of *Growing Pains*. At least he could disappear into their happy lives for a few minutes. Just as that thought ran through his head, the doorbell rang.

Justin wanted to cry. He didn't want to move, but he knew if he didn't get the door by the second ring, Lou would throw a fit. Moving with extreme care, but fast as he could, pain shot off like black cat fireworks, rapid-fire explosions all through his chest. In the kitchen, ten steps from the door, the bell rang again. Justin mumbled half a dozen swears and hurried his pace. Pulling aside the curtain, he saw a man in a frumpy brown suit and a small matching hat holding a large briefcase. The guy was the epitome of a door-to-door salesman. He hadn't seen one of those since he was really little, when he used to be home with Mom and Lou was in school, back when things were okay. Justin just wanted him to leave, so he opened the door, preparing to tell him he was not interested, but the mustached man spoke first.

"Evening, son, are your parents home? I have a deal they simply can't pass up!" The sun was just starting to set behind the man. *Why the hell was he coming out so late?* This thought briefly flashed in Justin's head, but then the pain spoke up and told him to get rid of the man fast so he could lie back down.

"We don't want any," Justin said as he started to push the door shut, but then the man said three magic letters that made the pain not so bad.

"A VCR? A kid like you could tape all his favorite shows. You'd never have to miss another, and you could watch them over and over. Hell, you and your brother could watch one show while taping another, ain't that a thing?"

Justin pulled the door open a bit wider, gave the guy a suspicious look—*how did he know I had a brother?*—but didn't respond.

After an awkward moment, the man kept talking. "I can have you set up in five min'. I'll even install it and give you a tutorial. You'll have it working before *Growing Pains* even starts! Best part, you alone can afford the payments; just give me your weekly pay from your paper route and in two months, it's all yours."

The voice was so soothing and convincing, Justin stepped back and the man walked right in. Justin eyed the suitcase, won-

Omnivision

dering how a VCR could fit inside. It seemed impossible. There were also a lot of other questions swirling in his head, but things were getting cloudy, and he just didn't care. *He was getting a VCR.*

Sitting in awe, Justin watched the man as he expertly wove a wire behind the wooden frame of the television, plugged in the device and sat it on top. As the orange and green screen lit up, Justin felt a smile, bigger than any he'd had since Mom died, cross his face. The man knelt down and pushed some buttons and within a few seconds, the time displayed. It was three minutes before *Growing Pains* was to start. *I need blank tapes*, Justin thought at the exact second the man pulled out a pack of three VHS tapes, tightly wrapped in cellophane, with red and white writing and some logo he had never seen before blazoned across the packaging. Using his finger as if it were a knife, the man sliced open the side, pulled out a tape, slipped it out of its sleeve, and slid it into the machine. The sound it made while entering, the clicking and churning noises, was so beautiful.

"Now, son, listen here," the man said in a serious tone as he sat down on the coffee table—something his father would have been furious with. Justin looked at the clock; less than a minute to go, but just as he was about to speak up, the man put up a finger and kept talking.

"'*Pains* is taping; you can watch it and fast forward through the commercials. I need you to hear me first. There are some important rules to owning a VCR."

The fear of missing a show was a fear deep inside Justin's chest, but he sat and stared at the man, wondering how the VCR could record if the television was off.

"A VCR is controlling time. You can rewind time to experience the best moments and even fast forward through the boring parts. It is power. Use it wisely, especially those tapes. Those are from my private collection; you can't get those in stores, and you only get three with a purchase." With that, the man stood up, flipped his hat on in a gesture that seemed unnatural, and then winked at Justin.

"Just need a handshake, son. I don't do paperwork; a handshake seals the deal. I'll come to collect the first payment in one week's time. This is a golden opportunity. Don't mess it up."

Without thinking, mostly wanting the man to just leave, Justin put out his hand. The man grabbed it, almost crushing his bones. Justin could feel a slight tingle of static electricity whirling

Michael Gore

around their hands as the man held his, pumping up and down a bit too long. When the man let go, there was a tiny static shock that hit the tip of all five fingers, all in a row, in quick succession, *zap, zap, zap, zap, zap.* As he stood there looking at his fingers, he heard the door gently shut.

Not even a few seconds later, the pain in his ribs returned with a fury, which took him by surprise as he had forgotten all about the broken bones the entire time the man was there. This caused a wave of confusion in his head; pain and anger mixed with the pure joy of having his own damn VCR. Holding the remote, he looked at it in awe. *It is all mine.* Doing his best to ignore the pain, he lay back down on the couch, grabbed the bag of peas that had fallen on the floor, placed them on his chest, and closed his eyes, the remote still in his hand. He could rest. The television schedule no longer needed to control him. *He* controlled television.

☆

"What the hell is that?" Lou's scream woke Justin from a dead sleep. He jumped up, pain shooting through his body. Ignoring it, he stood up to get between Lou and the VCR, as Lou was known for destroying things Justin loved. Lou stood in front of him, his face scrunched up in disgust and curiosity at the new machine. Justin steadied his breath—*Christ, my ribs hurt*—before trying to explain.

"I bought it with my paper route money. It's mine, but if you aren't a dick, you can use it, too. Just . . . just ask, please, okay? It's expensive." Hearing the words come out, Justin was proud of himself for, sort of, standing up to Lou. Unfortunately, Lou stopped looking at the machine and turned his gaze to the wet stain on Justin's shirt where the peas had melted. Instantly, Lou shot out his arm, his finger pointing hard, and jabbed it right into Lou's chest. Justin could feel the rib move inside of him as Lou pulled back and called him a donkey dick, one of Lou's favorite terms ever since seeing *Weird Science* the year before. As Justin crumpled into a ball and fell to the floor, he reflexively squeezed his hands, forgetting he still had the remote in his right hand. Just as his knees were about to hit the ratty old brown carpet, he froze in midair, in an impossible position.

Panicking, Justin worried he was having a stroke like his uncle did, or some sort of mental break causing him to hallucinate his virtual floating stance, but when he turned his neck, which was difficult, it felt like he was fighting massive weights. He saw Lou

☽ Omnivision ☾

frozen in midstride, one hand reached toward the VCR. *A VCR is controlling time.* It was impossible . . . Fighting the stiffness of moving, he looked at the remote. Sure enough, his thumb was on the pause button. *No way.* With a bit of effort, he pushed his thumb down, and he instantly fell to his knees, all the pain shooting through him. The pain was so intense, he instantly hit the pause button again, shutting off the hurt, all sound, and their movement.

Laughing out loud, he slowly moved each limb until he was able to fight against whatever force kept them frozen. It took some practice, but after what seemed like ten minutes, he was able to move freely. Feeling comfortable, he made his way over to Lou to examine him and see if he was conscious or completely frozen. Lou looked like some sort of wax figure, perfectly still and lifelike, his arms reaching out to the VCR. It was absolutely insane. Lou's eyes were wide open, yet when Justin moved his hands in front of them, there was not the slightest reaction. This made Justin laugh more. He had not gotten this close to Lou in years. Standing near his face, knowing Lou couldn't do anything to him . . . the punch was fast but not that great. It would have been liberating, had Lou moved at all, but his face felt like a steel beam. Shaking his hand, Justin cursed and then laughed. His knuckles were going to be bruised, but it was worth it. Reaching out with one finger, he poked his brother's face. It was hard, as if his brother were a statue. Justin's jaw dropped in wonder.

After settling in with his new reality, Justin built up the courage to try the rewind button. Sure enough, that worked as well. As he lightly pushed it down, he felt an invisible force trying to pull him backward to recreate all the steps and actions he had just done, but he was able to fight against them as he watched Lou walk backward, then reenact the jab, only this time to empty air and then march in reverse right out of the living room. Once Lou was gone, he hit pause and thought for a moment. *How far can I rewind . . .? What if . . . Mom?* Looking down at his ribs, he wondered if he could go back far enough to stop them from being broken; that would be a start, but that was *before* the salesman came, so would it work? Could he fight against time and these forces to keep the VCR, or would the man simply pack it up? Wait, even if he did, the man would just bring it again. *Rewind.*

Staying seated on the couch, Justin watched the clock spin backward and the sun outside start to rise again. He felt like a god. After a few moments, the salesman walked backward into the room, but as soon as he was in front of Justin, the man stopped and turned toward him. The world kept moving around them as the man fought the forces as well.

"Son, be careful. Time is power." The man walked out of the room, pushing against the rewind, yet time kept going backward. He was leaving the VCR there; he was letting Justin rewind further.

)) ☆ ((

Paused in the moment after the moment his ribs were crushed, Justin felt free and calm. The world was silent, and there was no fear of his brother slamming into the room to hurt him some more. Time was stopped. There was no wind, no noise at all; the Earth was shut off. Lying still on the couch, enjoying the silence, he thought about how he could sleep without the fear of being woken up. He could sleep for as long and as deep as he wanted. Being more tired than he was excited to play with this new power, he held tightly to the remote and slipped off into a dreamless sleep. When he awoke, everything was exactly the same, and he had no clue how long he'd slept, but it didn't matter, did it? Getting up, he walked around the house, looked at the food on the counter that was consistently staying warm, and then looked at Lou. His brother was half inside the fridge, looking for the damn barbecue sauce he'd forgotten. For some reason, Justin was scared to go back further than he did, but he also did not want to relive the moment his ribs broke. Looking at the food some more, he realized he wanted to eat the damn meal he'd cooked, and he hit rewind.

Within seconds, Lou had walked backward to his room, the door shut, his ribs were no longer broken, and the other plate was back on the counter. Hitting play, he instantly jabbed at his ribs. They were better. *This is insane*. This time, Justin grabbed the barbecue sauce along with the plate and brought it down the hallway. Lou was still an asshole, but Justin did not end up on the floor; instead, his brother accepted the food and let him be. He couldn't help but smile and laugh while enjoying the ability to take deep breaths. Sitting down in front of his plate, he smiled, picked up his fork, cut a big bite of chicken, and greedily put it into his mouth. It was absolutely delicious. Looking at the remote, which he purposely set far back from his plate to make sure he got nothing on it, he smiled and thought about how life was going to be better. Taking his second bite, he heard Lou's door fly open. Justin nervously grabbed for the remote, but Lou was already

☽ Omnivision ☾

there. His brother was upon him so fast it was almost as if the tape had skipped.

"That was fucking delicious. Give me your plate and make this more often, ass wipe." Just as Justin grabbed the remote, Lou came up from behind, hunched over Justin, and clamped down around both of his wrists. This was a move that Lou loved; he called it the "Puppet Master" because he could control Justin and make him do whatever the hell he wanted. Thankfully, Justin was able to hit pause, freezing time once again, but Lou's grip was too tight, and his brother was practically on top of him. He couldn't maneuver his way out of it as Lou was stone-hard again. Justin had to push rewind, but his grip on the remote was so awkward that he had to adjust it to try and get his finger on the correct button.

Of course, that's when he dropped the remote. It clanked on the counter, teetered on the edge, then fell to the linoleum. With a loud crack, the battery compartment door shot off, and two batteries spilled out. Justin was stuck.

Lou's body was solid, like a marble statue carved by some sick artist to be a torture device. The hands around his wrists were clamped so tight that his fingers were starting to fall asleep. No matter which way or how hard he pulled, he couldn't loosen the grip, not even in the slightest. When he pushed back against Lou, it was like trying to move a pillar. Over the next ten minutes (at least he thought it was that long; there was no time after all), Justin screamed and thrashed; he kicked, he pulled and yanked and moved every possible way. Lou did not budge an inch; his grip did not change. The only change was that the skin on Justin's wrists was starting to tear open.

Settling into a slow sob, resting his head on the counter, Justin's mind started to race. *Was the rest of the world frozen? What happens if I die? Did I kill the world? Wait, how long will it take me to die? I'll starve to death; it will take days. Days of Lou keeping me locked in the Puppet Master position, his face and chest smashed up against my back and head. I won't even know how many days, let along hours, it will be, because nothing will change. I don't even know how long I've been sitting here. I can't do this, I can't, I can't.*

After sulking for a few more minutes, Justin tested how far he could move his head. If he slammed it back into Lou's face, then down on the sharp edge of the brown linoleum counter, he could kill himself. It could work. He could break his nose and cut his face enough that he'd bleed to death, and if the impact didn't kill him, it would at least knock him out long enough that he wouldn't have to live through the pain of the position he was in and the eventual starvation. All he wanted was to not feel the pain of his ribs anymore; now he was in more pain and contemplating his own death. *Fucking Lou.* The thought of dying was terrifying, but the pain in his wrists and the growing claustrophobia were stronger.

Justin sang the *Growing Pains* theme song through a sobbing cry as he slammed his head back into Lou's stone face. Lou's nose felt like a steel point, and it did the same damage, cutting a deep gash into Justin's scalp. The pain made the tears come harder, but he couldn't stop. Slamming his face forward on the edge of the counter—that damn sharp counter—did its job. Justin's nose snapped and popped just like his favorite cereal. The blood poured quickly as fireflies zipped in front of his vision. If he were standing, he would have fallen to the floor. As he rested a second, the pain started to seep in; it was awful and he wanted it to stop, but there was only one way to stop it. *Slam back, slam forward, pause, orientate, slam back, slam forward, slam back, slam forward.*

As Justin faded in and out of consciousness, blood flowing freely from the lacerations on the back of his head and the cuts and slices on his face, he thought of the Seavers. The images were fractured and confusing, but they made him smile. Playing basketball with Mike, dinner with the family, Dr. Seaver giving him advice and so many damn hugs. It was wonderful; it was what a family was really like. When enough blood had finally drained out of him to put him into a deep sleep, Lou's hand suddenly let go, but Justin didn't feel it.

☆

"What the mother fuck!"

Lou jumped back. There was blood everywhere—all over the counter, the floor, even on his face. But he had absolutely no clue what the fuck was happening. He had just grabbed Justin's hands like he always did. After several long seconds of panic, Lou grasped Justin's shoulders and shook him, but his brother slid off the chair sideways and landed on the floor with a sickening thud. *Was he dead?* Lou bent over and shook his brother some more. Justin's face looked like it had been chewed on by Cujo. Even the back of his head had massive cuts. *What happened? Did . . . did I do this? Holy shit, I have to fix this.*

☾ Omnivision ☾

As Lou rolled Justin over onto his back, there came a knock at the door that made him scream. Looking over his shoulder, Lou saw a man's silhouette through the dingy curtain. "Go the fuck away!" Lou screamed in a panic, not knowing what else to do as he contemplated putting pressure on the wounds. *But which one?*

The knocking came again.

With pure rage, Lou jumped up, grabbed the handle, swung the door open, and screamed at the intruder to leave, using half a dozen swears. When the man hardly reacted, Lou calmed himself down and stared at the guy in the hat, who was looking beyond him into the kitchen. Lou looked back himself and saw the remote control on the floor. He hadn't noticed it before, and in fact, he had never seen that remote. Batteries were scattered on the floor next to it, but the oddest part was that the blood had encircled it, without touching it, as if the remote were pushing the blood away. As he started to contemplate this, the man spoke.

"I guess he didn't know that all VCRs un-pause after a while so it doesn't cause stress on the tape." The man raised an eyebrow and laughed lightly.

Lou looked at him with pure confusion and rage boiling up, and he kicked the door. The man raised a hand and pushed a button on an identical remote. Lou planned on tackling him, but when he got through the door, the man was gone. He'd simply vanished. Like a maniac, Lou ran down the driveway looking for him, but there was nothing, not even a car pulling away. *I'm losing my mind.* Running back inside, he didn't notice the remote on the floor was gone, the clearing of blood filling in.

An hour later, after forcing himself to call for an ambulance, Lou found himself handcuffed, sitting in a hospital bed, waiting to have his mental state examined. Just as the doctor walked in, the *Growing Pains* season finale started on the television hanging from the wall.

☽ ☆ ☾

Michael Aloisi (writing as Michael Gore) *is a national bestselling author of more than a dozen published books, including the official biographies for film legends Tom Savini and Kane Hodder and* A Life with Ghosts *(Simon & Schuster) about famed Ghost Hunter Steve Gonsalves's favorite haunted locations.*

In the fiction world, Michael has written several novels, including Mr. Bluestick *and* Pieces *(cowritten with Rebecca Rowland), which was picked as an "Essential Read" by Rue*

☽ Michael Gore ☾

Morgue Magazine. Under his pen name, Michael Gore, he has released three horror short story collections, including Do Not Open *and* Skeletons in the Attic. *His books have been turned into a reality show and a documentary film, and they have been translated into several languages. With a BFA in film directing and an MFA in creative writing, Michael runs Dark Ink Publishing.*

Visit AuthorMike.com to learn more about his books and other projects.

19 Miles from Millstone, June 17th, 1988

M. Tyler Tuttle

Rot hung dank and cloying in the air as Mollie and Grace made their way up the crumbling stone stairs of the abandoned manor house. Grammy's basement smelled like this—the musty, sickly sweet stench of concrete and carpet left too long in the damp; generations of animal fur and cigarette ash and cracker crumbs left in corners by sticky hands. Grammy would have another fit if she knew what Mollie was up to. But that—according to Grace, anyhow—was exactly what made it fun.

Mollie looped her thumbs in her backpack straps and stared up at the enormous stone building. She never knew this patch of woods hid such a mammoth. Mollie's pulse thudded as she tilted her head back, trying to see where the stone ended and the sky began. The building plunged into the shadows of the vast green canopy overhead, like there was no separation between shadow and stone.

"This is perfect!" Grace grabbed her by both shoulders and shook her. Mollie tried to hide how much that spooked her, but Grace had eyes only for the building and its great gray doors.

"What d'you think it was?" The trees and the stone swallowed Mollie's voice like a hungry cat. "A castle?"

"Nah." Grace's whole body was alight with fascination as she drank in the decrepit stones. Sweaty curls popped out from her frizzy blond braids. "This whole place was supposed to be an adventure park." Now she turned her freckled grin on Mollie, and Mollie's face burned. "I thought everybody around here knew that. You never heard of the Hall of the Mountain King?"

"No." She scuffed at the dirty stone with the tip of one OshKosh sneaker.

"It woulda been like Disneyland, only a lot spookier." One of Grace's front teeth was just a little longer than the other, but not in a you'd-have-trouble-eating-an-apple way. In a nice way. "Haunted houses. Trolls everywhere. But they only built *this* thing before it happened."

After a long pause, Grace glanced her way, and Mollie dutifully asked, "Before what happened?"

"A little girl died."

Mollie shivered.

Grace's eyes danced. "Right here. Maybe right where we're standing. A whole bunch of stones like this fell down and walloped her right on the head, and then everybody said the land was cursed and ran for it." She laughed, and Mollie tried to laugh along with her, trying not to imagine the heavy stone bricks falling on top of her. She wasn't brave like Grace.

Grace was thirteen, not even a whole year older than Mollie, but she'd been a celebrity at St. Felicitas Middle School from the moment she walked in the doors. Sometimes Mollie didn't know why Grace hung around with her. Grace was from California; Grace had been all over the world; Grace was all blond curls, freckles, and lanky limbs built for soccer. Mollie was a pale, runty sixth grader with Coke-bottle glasses and hair the color of mouse fur, and the furthest she'd ever been from Norwich was fifty miles southwest to New Haven.

All they really had in common was a bus stop.

Mollie sighed. "Grammy never takes us to adventure parks. Not even the carousel."

"Well, this isn't any old adventure park." Grace shrugged out of her backpack and stooped to examine the door handles.

A hush of wind made Mollie turn back to the woods. Black oak trees towered above spindly sassafras and lonely beeches. Wild huckleberries clumped low to the ground, the fruit green and sour in the early summer heat but promising good pickings in September. Tangled in with the berry bushes were some kind of bramble Mollie couldn't name. She and Grace had struggled through the darn things, ripping their jeans and snagging their shoelaces on the thorns. Now that she stood on the other side, Mollie could still feel the brambles tugging on her clothes, like that itchy-icky squiggle of walking through a spiderweb.

"Help me with this, would you?" Grace scowled at the door. Mollie dumped her backpack and stood beside her, trying not to think about falling rocks or forest curses. She stood where Grace told her to, gripped where Grace pointed, and together they heaved on that door with as much strength as they could.

☽ 19 Miles from Millstone, June 17th, 1988 ☾

A big *CHUNK* rang out as some dust or gunk or what-have-you clogging the doorway broke free. The door swung open in complete silence.

The gaping darkness waiting for them was exactly the color of a ripe huckleberry.

A metallic click, and then a small beam pierced the darkness. Grace laughed when Mollie jumped. "Did you forget a flashlight?"

"No." Mollie's blush came back in full force as she dug through her backpack and unearthed a flashlight the length of her forearm. Neither Grammy's torch nor Grace's dinky pen light did much to puncture the gloom.

"C'mon," Grace whispered. "I'll tell you the rest of the story once we're inside."

"The rest of what story?" Mollie couldn't tear her eyes off all that blackness.

"The little girl?" Grace giggled. "You didn't think that was the end of the story, did you?"

Mollie wanted to run. Turn her back on that creepy dark and sprint all the way back to her bike, all the way back to Grammy's if she had to. But Grace took her hand in her paper-soft palm, and Mollie forgot how to argue.

The doors opened onto a vast, dusty foyer. A few sticks that might once have been chair legs, some shredded fabric, and a panel of glass, long-shattered, twinkling at their feet, separated this large room from a smaller one tucked to the side.

"The ticket booth," Grace whispered.

Ahead stood a massive wall of wrought-iron fencing. Twenty people could've stood shoulder to shoulder across the space, maybe more. Squinting, Mollie made out the rusty hinges of gates—ten of them side by side, as if people lined up here to be shoved through the gates like cattle.

Mollie shivered. "I don't like this place."

"Well, I *love* it." Grace's voice rebounded into the depths of the darkness. Grace tugged at one of the wrought-iron gates. The rusty hinges disintegrated; the metal grated against itself with an awful screech. Mollie cringed, but when Grace pulled the smaller gate open and beckoned, Mollie crept forward to follow.

"So . . . " Grace cast her flashlight beam up into the corners, down to the chipped tile floor. A gentle whirring sound, Grace's flashlight or something on her shoes, rustled along with the dead leaves on the ground. "The rest of the story. See, what

M. Tyler Tuttle

made the little girl's death so sad was that her parents loved her very, very much. But they loved each other too—true love, the real kind, not the kind from kids' books, y'know?" Mollie nodded, but she doubted Grace saw. "The Hall of the Mountain King was supposed to be this big water ride, one that splashed into a big pool at the end, but when the little girl died, they hadn't put any water in it yet. It was just this big, bottomless pit. So the mom and dad cried and moaned, 'No, we can't live without our perfect daughter!'"

Grace's voice grated with bad humor, like she was making fun of the poor parents. But Mollie could understand that kind of love, feeling like if you lost someone, you'd have to go on and lose yourself, too.

"What did the parents do?" Mollie asked.

Grace held her flashlight under her chin. "They went to that pit . . . " The pale beam made her green eyes glow like tiny, menacing ghosts. "They peered over the edge . . . and then . . . " She leaned close to Mollie's face. "They threw themselves in! BAM!"

She stomped her foot, and a tile shattered beneath her sneaker.

At that exact moment, a door slammed behind them with a shriek of stone.

Mollie screamed and dropped her flashlight. It rolled across the tiled floor, casting dizzying whorls of light that skittered across Mollie's vision like frantic fireflies. The flashlight hit the wall, rebounded, and rolled to a slow, slithering stop.

Grace was watching her oddly. Amused. Blushing more than ever, Mollie scurried to pick up her flashlight. She was only halfway across the room when Grace said, in an entirely different voice, "Wait. What's that?"

Illuminated in the dim beam, a metal plaque hung loosely from the stone wall by one corner nail, like the others had long rusted away. Letters the size of Mollie's palm spelled out:

THIS PLACE IS NOT A PLACE OF HONOR.
NO HIGHLY ESTEEMED DEED IS COMMEMORATED HERE.
NOTHING VALUED IS HERE.
WHAT IS HERE WAS DANGEROUS AND REPULSIVE TO US.
THIS MESSAGE IS A WARNING ABOUT DANGER.

Mollie squinted at the letters, trying to make them make sense around a dread that she didn't understand coiling in the pit of her stomach. She read the words out loud, stumbling to sound

19 Miles from Millstone, June 17th, 1988

out "esteemed," "commemorated," "repulsive." She didn't know what all the words meant.

But she knew "danger."

"Grace," Mollie whispered. "I think we should leave."

Grace stepped closer to the sign, running her fingers across the letters as she mouthed the words to herself. Mollie heard it again—that whirring, like the ancient electric fan Grammy plugged in on hot nights or the prickle-tingle static buzz Mollie both heard and felt when she turned off the heavy box television in the basement and touched the still-warm screen. A shiver ran up the back of Mollie's neck.

"Grace," she said again. "Let's go."

"Shh." Grace scooped up Mollie's flashlight and shone it further into the gloom, making crisscrossed beams with her penlight.

"I don't like this place." Mollie knew she sounded like a baby, but she couldn't help it. "I want to go home."

"Don't be such a wuss." Grace strode into the darkness without any doubt Mollie would follow. And of course, Mollie followed—Grace had both flashlights. "Come on, I think we're almost there."

"Almost *where*?" Without the flashlight in her hand, the shadows felt darker, thicker somehow, like she could reach into them and scoop out handfuls of black sludge.

They passed the skeleton of a gift shop, empty clothing racks like bony fingers squashing the flashlight beams into dull, dusty glimmers. Next was a small cafeteria, with long rectangular tables carved out of some dark, sweet-smelling wood, and elegant, decaying dining chairs. Ripped tapestries hung on the wall, and old portraits watched them disapprovingly as they tiptoed through the dust. Mollie felt their eyes on her back as she eased past. Grace trained the larger light on the portraits. They all wore the same long, white coats, standing out bright against gaunt cheekbones and sunken gray eyes.

"They all look so sad," Mollie whispered, but Grace was already vanishing. Mollie followed the dancing flashlight beams into what her Grammy might have called a *grand foy-ay*, an enormous room with majestic stone columns and a curved double staircase in the middle, now crumbling with age. The stairs clung to the curved walls in an upside-down U, a dusty hallway at their center. Mollie sucked in a relieved breath—grimy windows as tall as her house lined the walls, letting in weak afternoon sunlight.

☽ M. Tyler Tuttle ☾

Grace knelt halfway up the stairs where the old wood had caved in on itself in a massive, rotten pile. Mollie snatched her flashlight but Grace didn't look up, too caught up in scratching around in the rubble. More portraits lined the stairs, and Mollie could feel their eyes on the back of her neck everywhere she turned. The portraits' gaze itched.

"What are you looking for?" Mollie scratched the back of her neck.

Grace stood and wiped her hands on her denim overalls. "The end of the story."

Mollie couldn't help her alarm. "The bottomless pit?"

Grace shot her a look that made Mollie feel very young and very stupid. "No." She rolled her eyes up to the ceiling, sighed, and offered up a rueful smile. "There's one last bit to the story, okay? It's dumb, but it's something my dad's been telling me forever, and now that we've moved back to Connecticut, I just had to see if it was here." She pointed one finger in Mollie's face. In the low light, Mollie could just make out her chipped blue nail polish. "Don't make fun of me, all right?"

"I won't." Mollie held up one hand. "Scout's honor."

Grace narrowed her eyes, but Mollie gave her look for look until Grace finally laughed and dropped her voice to a stage whisper. "All right, so you know how I said the parents were oh-so-in-love? Not storybook love, but the real deal?"

Mollie held herself very still. "Yes."

"Well . . . " The expression on Grace's face was confusing now, mostly intrigued and curious, but something else, too. A little manic, a little frightened. Her green eyes were just a smidge too wide when she said, "The mom and the dad loved each other and their daughter so, so much that they never wanted to leave this place. Not now that they were all together, y'know? So, some people say they're still here." Mollie must have made some kind of horrified face because Grace added quickly, "Not like ghosts. Like—guardians. They guard what it was that brought them here in the first place." Grace licked her lips. "They guard true love."

Mollie tried not to look at Grace's mouth. "How can somebody guard true love?"

"My dad said there's a statue," Grace said. "If you find the statue, you can tell it things, and it'll help you out. You know Stella and Duke, in the eighth grade?" Mollie nodded. Her mouth was very dry. "Well, the other kids told me Stella'd been pining over Duke for ages, but he never looked sideways at her. She came

☽ 19 Miles from Millstone, June 17th, 1988 ☾

here and talked to the statue, and the next day Duke asked her to the Laurel Formal." Grace's eyes were very bright. "If you whisper someone's name in the statue's ear, they become your true love forever."

Mollie's face burned so red they wouldn't need flashlights anymore.

Either Grace noticed or she'd said more than she meant to, because her face went pale, and she backed up a hurried couple of steps. The girls stared at the floor, at the portraits, at the gaping hole in the stairs—anywhere but at each other.

"All right then," Mollie said, as if her heart wasn't pounding a thousand miles an hour. "Let's find your statue. And then we're going home, okay?"

"Deal."

They clambered back down the stairs and passed into the hallway beneath them. The deeper into the building they explored, the dirtier it got, with a dank, metallic scent Mollie could almost taste. They had to pause more than once to blow their noses and cough and wipe their streaming eyes. They moved through what Grace confidently said had been an employee locker room, then another room full of giant vats that Grace declared used to be for laundry. Once, out of the corner of her eye, Mollie thought she saw something blinking red, but by the time she turned it was gone—and more importantly, she had bigger problems, because her legs tangled in something brushy and sharp, and she fell hard on one knee.

"It's those damn briars," Grace said, the same way Grammy might say, *It's those damn squirrels* whenever sunflower seeds went missing from the feeders left out for robins and goldfinches. Indeed, grown in through one of the broken windows, the heavy black briars from outside had spread out through the darkened hallways like a torn, thorny blanket.

Mollie had never heard someone her own age swear before. She felt very grown-up as Grace helped her back to her feet and didn't even wince when Grace prodded at Mollie's scraped knee, even though it hurt an awful lot. It was *those damn briars'* fault.

Before long, they needed the flashlights again. With each room they passed through, it felt like they delved not only deeper but down, descending into the very bowels of the Earth. This room was a manager's office, said Grace. This one was where the ride designers worked on their blueprints. Grace passed her

☽ M. Tyler Tuttle ☾

flashlight across a dusty, tattered piece of paper labeled *MEMO RE: THREE MILE ISLAND—IMPORTANT!* Grace declared it to be the plans for a canned amusement park. The girls paused in a long, rectangular room filled with heavy metal barrels. It stumped Grace for almost a solid minute before she said, "Aha! Supplies—for the kitchens."

But nowhere did they find a statue.

"If it's close to the pit, shouldn't we be looking outside?" Mollie suggested. They climbed over black briars constantly now—they seemed to grow thicker as the light grew dimmer. Mollie scratched the back of her neck again, then her cheek. The dust was really getting to her.

"No." Grace chewed on her lower lip. "Stella told me the statue was inside, and this is the only building on the property." She glanced at Mollie, then frowned. The flashlight nearly blinded Mollie when Grace shone it in her face. "Hey, are you okay? You're all red."

"What?" Mollie blushed again as Grace took a step closer.

"Like—really red, Mol." Grace reached out to touch Mollie's cheek, but Mollie backed away, nearly upending herself over the brambles again.

"It's probably the briars," she said hastily. "Grammy says I've got summer allergies."

"Are you sure you're okay?"

In her haste to get away, Mollie lost her balance again and walked straight into the wall—and *through* it. An explosion of dust fell around them both as Mollie's pinwheeling arms ripped a mealy, crumbling piece of fabric off the wall. A bramble-choked hallway lurked just beyond.

The dark at the end of that hallway was so thick, so viscous, that it felt like a living thing. A sound, so soft Mollie almost missed it, drifted to her on a musty, incongruent breeze: a soft pull of air, like a gentle inhalation.

She was immediately sure she wanted nothing to do with whatever hid in the shadows.

Grace stepped up beside her. "I think you found something."

The shadows swallowed Grace's voice and gobbled up the flashlight beams. The briars grew so thickly that there was barely room to walk single file. In the distance, a tiny red light blinked on—then another, then a third—then disappeared into the dark-

☽ 19 Miles from Millstone, June 17th, 1988 ☾

ness again. Mollie squinted and rubbed her eyes. For a moment, it looked like the briars were moving.

"Maybe we should leave this part alone," Grace said.

"Yeah. We probably should."

At the exact same time, they took a step forward. And another.

Grace took the lead, and without thinking about it, Mollie took her hand. Grace's fingers were hot and sticky with sweat, and she clutched Mollie's hand so hard it hurt.

It took Mollie a few minutes to realize what felt so wrong about this hallway. Beneath the brambles was the smoothest, cleanest black surface Mollie had ever seen. It wasn't the dusty, cracked tile of the manor building's entrance, nor the fractured wood of the foyer. This was solid metal, flawless and frozen, and their shoes scraped coldly against it.

Mollie's senses played tricks. She couldn't shake the feeling of eyes on the back of her neck, like something or someone lurked just beyond the reach of their lights. Once, she could have sworn she heard a soft blip, like a machine powering on, and a few seconds later, the sounds of their footsteps echoed louder, coming from every direction at once. The girls froze, and it took long seconds for the ricochets of their footsteps to fade.

Mollie felt it then—an odd hum, a reverberation—pressing against the soles of her feet and past them, deeper into this cavern.

"Did you feel that?"

"I don't know if this is such a good idea anymore," Grace said.

"Should we go back?" Even as she said it, she knew they couldn't. The statue had to be just beyond this, Mollie told herself. That tremble beneath their feet—that was power. It had to be good. It had to be real. It had to be real, or she'd panic, and if they panicked, whatever else was down here would find them.

There's nothing else down here, Mollie wanted to say, but her mouth was too dry. *It's the guardian of true love.*

They moved faster, nearly running, Mollie's hand clutched in Grace's sweaty palm. Gray light seeped in before them, getting brighter, closer, with every step. Anticipation and dread bubbled in Mollie's stomach. The light called to her, like something that had been waiting for her all this time was just beyond the next doorway—

☽ M. Tyler Tuttle ☾

And then the hallway ended. They stumbled into an enormous, circular room, wide as a soccer field. Everywhere Mollie looked there were briars, briars as thick as her waist. The last of the setting sun filtered in through an elegant stained-glass skylight in the center of the ceiling. Greens, blues, and the occasional red dappled the black metal floor. A jumble of furniture stood at the room's heart while concrete spread out like moss into every distant nook and cranny.

Grace let out a soft gasp, laughed, and turned Mollie in a full circle under the skylight. Mollie could see the pattern now, intertwined vines dotted with red flowers and vicious, wicked thorns. Grace twirled, letting go of Mollie's hand to raise her arms to the ceiling, grinning like she danced under a summer rain.

As soon as Grace released her, sense and sensation flooded back into Mollie like a sucker punch. The smell was awful, that horrible metallic stench paired with putrid vegetable rot, like someone had chewed up a mile of moss and spat it back out all over the walls.

Mollie stared at the room, trying to make sense of her dread. Some frantic, buzzing alarm roared in the back of her head, but Grace was laughing, too loud in this enormous space. The skylight dribbled the room with a dim, ethereal glow; it stained the walls with sickly color.

Gone were the paneled wooden facades of the manor entrance, the painted industrial walls of the lower rooms. This room was a cavern, a gaping hole beneath the earth, but there was nothing natural about it. It was a carved dome of solid rock, a perfect semicircle made of what seemed like miles-thick concrete.

The skylight stood in the dead center, and beneath it was a set of ancient bedroom furniture. A dresser, two chairs, a fabric-covered mirror, all exquisitely carved from the same wood. An enormous canopied bed frame, a tall wardrobe, a writing desk. The pink cushions on the couch had begun to rot, but they were vacant of dust, sitting plush and plump as if some busy maid had just scurried through and straightened them on her way out.

Mollie's stomach sank further and further with every second. There were rugs on the floor, elaborately woven carpets—the kind her Grammy would use a comb to clean, not a vacuum—old and fading but conspicuously free of dust. She turned, squinting at the bed. Someone had cleaned the bedposts and drawn the curtains—new, not as faded or as full of holes as the rugs and the

☽ 19 Miles from Millstone, June 17th, 1988 ☾

cushions. Everywhere she looked, it was all the same: ancient, crumbling, but meticulously—lovingly—clean.

She heard that whirring again, that mechanical sound, and red lights blinked from behind her, beside her, from every angle—winking on and off again like a hundred iridescent eyes.

"Mollie." Mollie didn't notice Grace had stopped dancing until she spoke. Something in her voice drove a spike of ice directly into Mollie's heart. Something was wrong. Something was very wrong.

Her friend stood by the bed where she'd pulled the canopy to one side. Something long and pale stood out in sharp relief against the dark bedspread. No, not a bedspread, Mollie realized—brambles. A thicket, a nest, a warren of briars, dug through and over and around and under every piece of furniture and sprawling inky black across the entire room.

She was halfway to the bed when she spotted it—the dying sunlight reflected off the beady black eye of a camera lens tucked into a corner of the great wooden bookshelf. She froze, and a small red light blinked into being just beneath the lens. She heard it again, that faint whir like a whisper of machinery, and her blood turned to ice as the camera turned, ever-so-slightly, in her direction.

The ice in her veins turned to fire. "Grace, we need to leave." She grabbed her friend's arm at the elbow. Panic turned her voice into a babble. "Right now."

"Get off me." Grace wrenched her arm away, the motion pulling the canopy all the way open, and Mollie's gaze fell on the prone body of a sleeping girl—

Right as she opened her eyes.

Mollie screamed. Grace jumped away from the bed with a yell. The girl on the bed didn't move but her eyes followed them across the room, a mild sort of disinterest in her gaze, like they were late bringing her breakfast. The girls froze, Mollie with her arm outstretched in front of Grace's chest, pushing her back toward the entrance.

"Who are you?" the girl asked, and all thoughts of leaving this horrible place fled Mollie's mind. Her voice was lower than she'd been expecting, throatier, and younger. She couldn't have been much older than Mollie and Grace. She watched them only with her eyes, and it took Mollie a moment to realize that this was because she couldn't move.

) M. Tyler Tuttle (

She was fully grown over with briars: they clung to her head like spindly hair, wrapped around her frail torso like a gown, plunged into her chest and arms like the IV tubes that had tethered Mollie's mother to life in the hospital. No, Mollie realized, the briars tore *out* of the girl like some horrid, ravenous beast. They didn't come from outside of the building. They came from the girl, and scratched forth into the world as some black, clawing disease.

"What happened to you?" Mollie found herself asking.

The girl on the bed closed her eyes. She drew in one long, ragged breath. "A great many things. A great many things have happened to me."

Another whir, a click—red lights blinking. Mollie watched as another camera turned toward the bed, toward the girls. A second followed suit, then a third. Mollie felt their presence like a looming parent, a forbidding hand on her shoulder.

Grace scrabbled at Mollie's arm, tugging on her sleeve. "Mollie," she whispered.

"Are you hurt?" Mollie asked the girl. "Do you need help? What are you doing here?"

The girl smiled. She was a thousand years old and an infant. "There's nothing you can do to help me now." Her voice wasn't sad, just determined. Truthful. "The best you can do for yourselves is to go."

"Let's go," Grace said. "I'm sorry, I— "

"No." Mollie shrugged Grace away and took a step toward the bed. "We can't just leave you here." Sweat beaded on her forehead, and she raised one arm to wipe it away. The girl on the bed tracked the movement with her eyes—so too did one of the cameras, lens glinting dully as it refocused on Mollie. "Come with us." She swallowed hard. "We'll—we'll get you help."

The girl smiled again, and this time there was something fractured in it. "There's nothing you can do for me. There's nothing anyone can do for me. And if you don't leave now, there will be nothing anyone can do for *you*."

Mollie's heart stuttered. Grace's voice, ghostlike, warbled beside her. "What does that mean?"

Now the girl's eyes were dark pools of sadness. "Step into the light."

Mollie stepped. She and Grace stood beneath the skylight and stared down at the girl. She raised one delicate, exhausted eyebrow and, like they'd planned it, Mollie and Grace turned

☽ 19 Miles from Millstone, June 17th, 1988 ☾

to each other. They looked—really *looked*. And Mollie, suddenly, could see it.

A red rash climbed up the side of Grace's neck, past her jawbone, and into her nostrils. Where her skin wasn't sheened with sweat, it was flaking. As Mollie watched, a patch of white blossomed on Grace's cheek and sat there, a fat white spider in a web of red.

"What's happening to us?" Grace choked on her words. Whatever Mollie saw in Grace must have been obvious in her, too, because her friend's eyes had filled with frantic tears, and she clutched at the collar of her white shirt like it had grown too tight.

"Eight years ago," the girl said, her voice so raspy and brittle that Mollie had to lean in to hear her, "I found something I was not supposed to find."

"What?"

"My father worked in a very dangerous place," the girl said urgently. "They called it Millstone."

"Millstone?" Grace shot Mollie a worried look. "Isn't that where your mom used to work? You know, before— "

"The power plant?" Mollie asked.

She nodded, just the scantest movement of her chin. "So you know."

"Know what?" Grace repeated. "You know what?"

Mollie shook her head. "It's a nuclear power plant. Mother said—Mother said her job was dangerous, that she helped keep people safe. She kept inventories."

"Then she would have known what went missing." The briars growing out of the girl's chest stretched when she inhaled. "I was with my father that day. He used to let me play in his truck when he was done at work. There were all sorts of useful things in there: his tools, his models. I used them as toys. I pretended I worked at Millstone too—my factory was a huckleberry patch behind our house, as tall as I was." She laughed, a choked, bitter sound. "The best part was that if I brought his tools into the thickest part of the thorns, they all glowed in the dark."

The girl swallowed, and her face contorted in pain—she coughed wretchedly, unable to move from her supine position. Automatically, Mollie reached for her to help her sit up, but the girl's eyes flashed into hers with fierce determination.

"No," she said. "Don't come any closer. Don't you understand? Something happened to me that day. Something was different. I don't know what it was he brought home, but it was something that never should have left the station. By the time my father found me unconscious in the huckleberry bushes, *these*— " She jerked her chin savagely at the thorns burrowed in her chest. "—had already started pouring out of my mouth."

Mollie's hand flew to her own lips.

Not a moment later, retching split the air, and she turned to find Grace doubled over, vomiting onto the smooth metal floor. Mollie rushed forward and pulled her friend's braids away from her face. Grace was crying; the tears carved crevasses down the flaking skin of her cheeks.

"Mollie," Grace cried. "Mollie."

"Everything's gonna be fine." Mollie whirled back to the girl on the bed, who watched them like the end of a sad movie. "What happened after that?"

"Daddy brought me back to Millstone. He thought they would help me." Her eyelids fluttered closed. "Instead they brought me here, and every day they watch what I've become. They like it, I think. They want to know how it works, this thing growing inside me. I've told them over and over I don't know."

Red, blinking lights crowded every inch of Mollie's peripheral vision.

"They're watching you now." The girl's baleful black eyes found Mollie's again. "They've been watching you since you stepped foot in the building."

"What do we do?" Mollie whispered.

"Go," the girl said. "Maybe your mom can help you."

A hot lump formed in Mollie's throat. "My mom died."

"I'm sorry." It truly sounded like she meant it. "She died at the plant?"

Mollie shook her head. "Ovarian cancer." She hated the way those words felt in her mouth, the warped *o*, the stagnant *v*. The girl on the bed watched her with such knowing sadness that it felt like a fist reached deep inside Mollie's chest to crush her heart.

Beside her, Grace took one massive, shuddering breath, tears still leaking from eyes squeezed shut. Mollie rubbed her back. "We're getting out of here," she said to Grace and to the girl. Before she could think better of it, she closed the distance to the bed and reached for the girl's arm. Her fingers burned when they closed around her bony wrist; the second Mollie's hand touched the girl's skin, every camera in the room whirred and

☽ 19 Miles from Millstone, June 17th, 1988 ☾

spun at once to center on the place where the girl stopped and Mollie began.

She tugged. The arm on the bed didn't even move. The black briars grew around and over and through it like an endless, clutching snare. Mollie's eyes filled again with hot, sticky tears. She couldn't look the other girl in the face.

"It's too late for me," the girl whispered to Mollie. "You've already stayed too long. You have to go. Now."

"I'll come back for you," Mollie said, already hauling Grace up, throwing her friend's arm over her shoulders. "I'll—I'll find help."

The girl smiled. "No, you won't."

The cameras tracked Mollie's every move as she staggered under her friend's weight. Grace was barely coherent, and Mollie dragged more than led her back down the bramble-choked hallway and into the guts of the deserted building. Everywhere Mollie looked was another blinking red eye. Her heart pounded; every breath was loud, painful—shattered glass in her lungs—and only Mollie's panic kept her stumbling through the abandoned manor house. By the time they exploded out of the hallway beneath the grand double staircase, Grace's weight was too much for her; Grace collapsed to her knees against the wall as Mollie fell face-first into thick black briars. She thrashed her way out and gripped Grace's chin with bleeding hands.

"Grace!" she shouted, over and over, until her friend fixed bleary eyes on Mollie's. "You have to get up. I can't carry you."

"Did we find the statue?" Grace's voice was a reed, a single blade of grass.

"What? What statue?"

"The guardian of true love," Grace whispered.

"Grace, c'mon, you've got to get up." Mollie tugged on her arms like she'd pulled at the girl on the bed, but Grace's limbs were just as unresponsive. Mollie shot to her feet and screamed. "Help! Somebody help us!" All around her, inescapable red lights blinked on and off, on and off. "I know you can see us," Mollie sobbed. She fell to her knees beside Grace. "I know you see what's happening."

Mollie was crying now. She tugged at Grace's arm again like a dumb animal, a doomed and frightened rabbit trying to tear its way free of a trap. All at once, the tears overwhelmed her until she was coughing, nearly retching, her body folding over on itself like that would help it escape.

☽ M. Tyler Tuttle ☾

Hot, sticky fingers touched her cheek.

"Mollie." Grace smiled. Her chapped lips ran with blood. "Were you gonna whisper my name in the statue's ear?"

Mollie just clutched Grace's other hand in both of hers and cried.

"Go home, Mol." Grace's voice was swollen, thick. She tried to smile again, but only half her mouth twitched. "Get out of here."

"I'll get you help," Mollie whispered as she climbed to her feet. "I promise."

Grace waved a hand at her, a shooing gesture; her eyes drifted out of focus. Her head drooped to the side; her chest heaved with labored breaths. The last Mollie saw of her friend, as she turned and ran full tilt toward where they'd entered the building, was Grace's face turned up to the ceiling, her eyes wide and misty. The very last of a brilliant red sunset pierced through the dusty windows to paint rainbows on her patchy, sloughing skin.

Mollie ran. Every step hurt. Her breath tore at her chest, and any second now she knew she'd start coughing again, lose her strength entirely, and fall to the ground in a gasping heap like Grace. Every camera she passed—she could see them everywhere now, poking out of bookshelves, tucked into corners, lurking above crooked doorways—turned to track her progress with lazy, fluid motion. Mollie's ears roared, buzzed, whirred. Her head spun, and she squeezed her eyes shut and ran full out, sprinting over the cracked tile floor of the entryway, through the rusted metal gates. She didn't stop running when she saw the enormous wooden doors, closed and menacing, and plowed right into them with the full force of her small body. It was—just barely—enough.

The doors opened the smallest crack, and Mollie tumbled through it, falling to her hands and knees on the stone steps of the crumbling manor. Now she coughed. She hacked. She retched. Something fell out of her mouth to drop to the stone with a wet smack. A twig—curved and black, with sharp, wicked thorns.

Mollie couldn't remember where they'd left the bikes. She didn't know if it mattered. But something drove her to stand up, to take one step, to take another, until she plunged into the black oaks and the spindly sassafras and the lonely beeches, stumbling through the huckleberry bushes and the brambles and the briars and the briars and the briars and the briars and the briars.

19 Miles from Millstone, June 17th, 1988

M. Tyler Tuttle (they/them) *is a writer, journalist, and wandering pit demon from Baltimore, Maryland. Tyler holds a degree in creative writing and English from George Washington University in Washington, DC, and is a graduate of The Loft's Year-Long Novel Writing Project in Minneapolis, Minnesota. Tyler's work has been published in* Cosmic Horror Monthly, Wooden Teeth, *and multiple philanthropy journals, and has been considered for the Halifax Ranch Fiction Prize (semifinalist, 2021), F(r)iction Magazine's Short Story Contest (finalist, fall 2023), and "Best Original Script" at the Great Salt Lake Fringe Festival (winner, 2022). You can catch up with Tyler online at TheHighwayMFA.com or @mtylertuttle on Twitter and Instagram, where they will be documenting their journey as an incoming MFA candidate at the University of Alaska, Fairbanks. If you look closely—and if you're very, very lucky—you'll find them meandering through the wilderness with their dog Piglet or dancing in a field somewhere, pretending to be Stevie Nicks.*

No Rider in the Flesh and Bone

Charles Montgomery

Tommie still remembered that Christmas, fresh snow on Greenwich ground. When he came down the stairs, a mountain of presents waited beneath the tree. They all faded away, like a bad special effect, when Tommie saw the cherry-apple red Schwinn Sting-Ray Lowrider peeking from behind the tree. He remembered knocking over his older brother, as well as other boxes and parcels, to get to the bike.

He named it BigRed, and it was love at first ride.

Tommie tricked the bike out as you only could a banana-seated Schwinn. He added a sissy bar, thumb-operated bell, colorful spoke wraps, handlebar-grip streamers, and even toe clips. The latter earned Tommie some grief at school. He didn't care.

Tommie loved that bike, and wherever he went, the corner of the block or to the city dump to forage for adult magazines, he would hop on BigRed to get there. The family dog, Billie, often tagged along several feet behind.

As time passed, classmates began to tease Tommie for riding the Schwinn. He didn't let it show, but it did bother him.

Tommie took longer and longer rides, more for fun than anything else. BigRed became less a means to get from point A to point B and more a tool for exploring the world. The Sting-Ray, unfortunately, was a fixed-chain one-speed. This made it super for wheelies, but not great for long distances.

During his first year of junior high, Tommie saw student after student move from their childhood bikes on to ones that were more suitable for ranging farther and farther afoot ("Afoot? Abike?" He laughed at himself when he thought of that).

Tommie looked at BigRed a bit differently.

That summer, Tommie watched Lance Armstrong come in thirty-sixth in the Tour de France. That wasn't great, but it was

☽ No Rider in the Flesh and Bone ☾

better than the year before when no one from the USA had even finished. The idea of long-distance riding began to take hold in his mind.

As Tommie set his mind to long-distance biking, he started riding the Kensico Reservoir Loop.

Well, he rode the part on Lake Avenue, which was the start of several longer loops. This section was ideal as it wasn't too strenuous and because one of the trails it led to dipped into New York. That seemed cool. Tommie could say he had visited multiple states if he finished that loop. The Sting-Ray, however, was not the bike for a long trip with elevation changes. So he stayed on the relatively flat section.

Tommie decided to buy a new bike. In the December snow, he began planning for spring. He hoped to bike across the US eventually but knew he'd have to start smaller. He scoured *Bicycle Magazine* and *Bike Magazine* for information on trails, tours, bicycles, and assorted kit.

By the time the snow started to melt, Tommie had a plan. Eventually, he found an older Cannondale touring bike in the back of *Bike Magazine* for two hundred and thirty dollars. That would be a good start!

Tommie called the owner and made arrangements to buy the bike.

When the Cannondale arrived, Tommie parked it in the garage, against the Schwinn, both leaning against the wall. The next day, Tommie took a closer look. The new bike was in decent shape, but the derailleur had been damaged during shipping, and the bike probably needed a new seat. Tommie picked up a seat and derailleur at the bike shop and, using BigRed to prop up the Cannondale, swapped them onto the new bike.

Done, he picked up both the bikes, propped the Schwinn against the wall, and took the Cannondale for an inaugural spin. He was sure to cruise past his school. Maybe his classmates would see that he had moved to a grown-up bike.

The Cannondale sped where the Schwinn had labored. Just getting on a seat that allowed hunching over the pedals gave Tommie velocity and power he could only have dreamed of on BigRed.

Returning home satisfied, he propped the Cannondale back up against the Schwinn and went inside the house.

The next day, he went into the garage and saw that the dog had knocked the bikes over. The Cannondale was on the ground,

Charles Montgomery

with the Schwinn lying halfway on top of it. He picked them up and dusted them off.

Feeling nostalgic, he decided to spend a few minutes on BigRed doing stunts he had perfected over the years. Rolling into the driveway, Tommie pushed hard on his pedals, pulled back on the handlebars, spun the front wheel into the air and leaned back. In the air, something subtle shifted. The balance of the bike changed. For the first time in several years, he found himself flat on his ass, the bike flipping backward onto him.

Tommie laughed and kicked the Schwinn to the side. It had been a long time since he had blown a wheelie! Maybe it was another sign that it was time to move on to the new bike.

He put BigRed back in the garage and was surprised when the dog growled as he passed.

The next day, he took the Cannondale for another spin, this time on the Putnam Lake Loop. Slightly less than twenty miles long and essentially flat, this was great for a trial run—just to make sure that everything was humming. "The Cannon," as Tommie now called it, ran great.

When he got back, Tommie noticed Billie lurking uneasily on the lawn, something hanging out of her mouth, looking like she had lost a fight with another dog.

Tommie laughed. "Here, girl," Tommie coaxed Billie toward him. She had small scrapes on her face and several patches where her fur had been pulled out. Looking closer, Tommie saw that the thing hanging from Billie's mouth was a piece of plastic streamer from the handlebars of BigRed. Tommie shrugged. The dog was always doing something stupid.

When Tommie put The Cannon in the garage, Billie stayed on the far wall away from the Schwinn, and slunk through the kitchen door. It was odd, but Tommie didn't think too much of it. By the time he went to sleep, Billie had taken her normal place at the foot of his bed.

That night, Tommie awoke with a start. He heard panting from the dog and a mysterious scraping sound. He swung his legs out of bed. The mystery would be cleared up once the light was on. He put his feet down, took a step, and immediately plunged, face-first, to the floor. Reaching down, he felt intersecting steel bars and a chain. Swearing, Tommie carefully pulled his legs out of whatever had ensnared him. On hands and knees, he made his way to the door and turned on the bedroom light.

It revealed BigRed on the floor by the bed.

☽ **No Rider in the Flesh and Bone** ☾

"Who the hell put my bike in my room?" he wondered aloud. "Did that stupid dog drag this thing in?"

His shins hurt, with several bruises emerging, as well as some scuffing on the heels of his hands where he had taken the fall.

The dog crouched in the corner, making herself as small as possible.

Pissed, Tommie grabbed the bike by its handlebars and pulled it across the room, out the door, through the hallway, into the kitchen, and through the door to the garage. With a grunt, he tossed it against the wall.

"Piece of shit," he swore, slamming the door, turning off the garage lights, and returning to his room to yell at the dog and go back to sleep.

If someone had been in the garage, they might have seen something unbelievable. BigRed bounced, eventually wobbled to its wheels and tipped over to lean against the Cannondale on the wall.

The next day, planning to take a ride on the Grant Road-Mamanasco Pond Loop, Tommie entered the garage to find the bikes fallen over again. Somehow, a pedal on the Schwinn had damaged the derailleur on the Cannondale. There would be no riding The Cannon, at least for today. Tommie wondered if the dog might have knocked the bikes over while chewing on the streamers on the Schwinn. That dog was out of control!

With The Cannon out of commission, Tommie decided to take BigRed on a spin just to keep his legs fresh. It was a short trip, about twenty miles, out to Babcock Preserve, then back. BigRed could make it, and so could he.

Beginning on Railroad Avenue, Tommie slowly pedaled past Babcock Reserve and stopped at Round Hill Road to eat lunch and take a few hits from a joint he had taped under the bike seat. He wasn't in the mood for a longer ride, at least until he had The Cannon ready to go. He had gone about ten miles and that was more than enough on the old Schwinn. Tommie was happy that the road back would be a moderate to very slight downhill.

To the right, planes took off from the Westchester County Airport—buzzy little planes zipping up from and down to the tarmac.

As he began to descend, a tremor ran through the bike's frame, and it began to speed up. That didn't make sense. The road was relatively flat and Tommie was putting no pressure on

Charles Montgomery

the pedals. Tommie decided to stop and make sure everything was okay. He applied the hand brakes. Nothing happened. When he squeezed the hand brakes harder, they wouldn't budge. They were stuck open.

The bike accelerated.

Tommie felt his legs moving faster. His feet inside the toe clips weren't applying any pressure to the pedals. In fact, the pedals were pulling his feet and legs. The pedals spun faster and faster. Tommie tried to slow his feet, but the power in the pedals was too great.

Fighting the speed of the pedals' rotation, he pulled his feet out of the toe clips.

This was a mistake—the rotating pedals beat at his calves and feet, scraping and bruising them. He was forced to pull his legs upward and push his feet up and over the front of the pedals, with his feet on either side of the front wheel. This contorted his body into an L-shape, and steering became precarious.

In this ludicrous position, barely in control of his balance, Tommie passed Babcock Preserve. This was good news. Tommie knew the road would turn upward for a stretch, and he could try to regain control of . . . of whatever was happening.

Tommie was surprised when the road sloped slightly upward, but the bike did not slow. His legs were burning from the unnatural position he held them in, and he felt sweat, or tears, stinging his eyes.

The bike raced along.

Ahead by Home Farm Road, Tommie saw a low, flat, grassy spot and decided it was time to end this wild ride. Then he could figure out what was wrong with the bike. With ten feet to go before the patch, Tommie yanked the handlebars hard to the right and, using his arms as best he could, pushed away from BigRed, which slammed into the curb.

It seemed he was in the air forever, though it was only an instant. Then the grass came up at him with amazing speed. The impact knocked his breath away as he put down his left shoulder to roll to a shaky stop.

Tommie lay on his back, stunned and staring at the sky. For a long moment he listened to little planes buzz in the distance. Finally, he got up and looked at BigRed. It had a few tufts of grass in the spokes and some jammed under the banana seat, but other than that, it seemed fine. Trying to move it, however, he discovered that the impact had bent the forks backward. Turning

☽ **No Rider in the Flesh and Bone** ☾

the handlebars caused the wheel to hit the frame, and steering was impossible.

Shaken, and with the bike only capable of pointing straight ahead, Tommie could not ride. So it was that, two hours later, he arrived home, walking his bike. Every time he changed direction, the tire hit the frame. Tommie had to jerk the front up and point it in the direction he wanted to go.

He hated BigRed.

He would get rid of it.

The next day, still walking BigRed, he took a trip to the public dump on Holly Hill. He padded past the entry gate, walked the bike in, and tossed it onto a pile of assorted scrap metal. Maybe it could be recycled.

Tommie walked back home, begged a loan from his brother, and went to the bike store for a new derailleur. That evening, he installed the derailleur on The Cannon. Satisfied, he went to sleep and dreamed of all the rides that would now be possible.

The next morning, after breakfast, Tommie entered the garage from the kitchen and prepped The Cannon for a ride. He opened the garage door, with Billie next to him. They both jumped back at what they saw.

BigRed stood in the driveway with a note on it.

Tommie. I was at the dump last night and saw your bike standing there. It looks like someone stole it, crashed it, then dumped it. The forks were badly bent. I banged them as straight as I could, but you're probably going to have to get new ones.

The note was signed by his next-door neighbor.

The dog retreated into the garage and cowered by the kitchen door.

Tommie cautiously approached the bike.

Nothing happened. Everything was normal. Yesterday seemed like a bad dream.

Tommie put the dog in the kitchen and, grabbing BigRed firmly, propped her against the garage wall. *Maybe this was a good thing*, he thought. Someone might buy BigRed, even with the banged-up forks. He could make a few bucks and put it into The Cannon.

The next day, Billie came into the house scuffed up with bloody gums from chewing BigRed's banana seat and tires nearly into shreds. Tommie gave up the idea of hanging onto BigRed, even just to sell. Once again, he headed to the dump, this time

Charles Montgomery

being sure to attach his own note to the sissy bar, "For recycling or trash."

Walking home, he imagined he saw BigRed out of the corner of his eye, but it was only a younger kid on a Schwinn of his own. Tommie laughed to himself a little shakily. *That freaking bike was possessed or something.*

The next day was gorgeous, and Tommie decided to celebrate his official move from kid to road cyclist. It was time for a complete loop.

He pulled The Cannon out of the garage, relieved to see Billie acting normally. He headed toward the Kensico Reservoir Loop. It was a glorious day for a ride, and The Cannon surged beneath him.

The first part of the loop was on Lake Avenue, a narrowish two-lane road with bike paths and thick trees on either side, guardrails going both ways.

Tommie was passing Hope Farm Road when he heard a bicycle bell chirping behind him. He pulled over toward the guardrail to allow the rider to pass, interested to see who was moving so fast. Instead, he felt a massive thump against his back tire, causing it to swerve to the left. That sent the front of The Cannon rightward toward the guardrail. It was only extremely quick reflexes that allowed him to avoid a spill over the guardrail and into the thick trees lining the road.

Surprised, Tommie turned his head to see who had hit him. His sweat chilled. Thirty feet behind him, with no visible support, BigRed wobbled upright on the side of the road.

BigRed?

Slightly bent forks, mangled seat, flat tires, and tattered handlebar streamers.

It was definitely BigRed.

Tommie began, still looking backward, to slowly pedal forward.

BigRed followed.

He stopped.

BigRed stopped.

Alarmed, Tommie hopped on The Cannon and pedaled as fast as he could go.

Seconds later, he heard the bell and was thumped from behind. Again, he barely kept his balance. When he stopped and dismounted, BigRed was fifteen feet behind him. She slid forward

☽ No Rider in the Flesh and Bone ☾

and back, maybe two feet each way. It was like a cat swaying before pouncing, or a bull pawing the arena floor.

BigRed began to move.

Tommie dismounted and jumped over the guardrail to the edge of the trees on the side of the road. BigRed, empty pedals spinning, raced up to Tommie. She paused, then began smashing into the side of The Cannon's back wheel. This was no good. The Cannon's spokes were far more flimsy than BigRed's, and if enough of them were broken, the bike would be unrideable. Tommie inched toward the guard rail, causing BigRed to stop and turn toward him. Tommie approached the Cannondale and so did BigRed. Tommie reached over to grab the Cannondale, hoping to drag it over the guardrail, but BigRed was too fast. BigRed hit the Cannondale just as Tommie grabbed it, managing to smack the back of Tommie's hand. Tommie raised his hand to see a smear of wheel rubber on its back and a bruise already forming. He stood between the guardrail and trees, confused. None of it made sense, but BigRed was clearly trying to hurt him.

Fuck that crazy bike! He'd have to get away from her, maybe even take the long walk home. Or get to one of the few houses scattered on the other side of Lake Avenue and call his parents. They'd stop whatever the hell was going on.

Stepping back behind the tree line, Tommie beat his way through thick brush, swearing quietly whenever a bramble caught him. Negotiating his way over a tree that had fallen, he tripped and caught his pants on a branch on the downed tree. It ripped a hole just under the front-left pocket of his pants. *Shit, Mom is gonna kill me!*

He laughed. He had to get past his homicidal bike before his mom would have a shot.

When he got far enough down the road, he headed back the few feet to the guardrail and peered back up the road to the right. BigRed was no longer bashing The Cannon, instead pointing down the road toward Tommie. The bike knew which direction Tommie had traveled. Tommie took a step over the guardrail, and BigRed began moving the wrong way down the bike lane toward Tommie, ignoring The Cannon. Tommie waited until BigRed was near, then hopped across the guardrail, back behind the edge of the trees. While this expanded the rip in his jeans, it also gave him an idea.

He would lure BigRed far enough down the road that he could double back, get a good lead, and then run across Lake

☽ Charles Montgomery ☾

Avenue to one of the houses on the other side. He would reach a phone and safety. BigRed couldn't do anything while Tommie was protected by trees, and running up the driveway would get him to a house. Simple.

He dipped deep into the forest, where the ground was still thick with puddles, and headed back up Lake Avenue. There was no avoiding some of the water and mud, and it wasn't long before his shoes were soaked and his jeans muddy. Slogging on, he made it past the spot The Cannon still lay in the bike lane, and continued on a bit more.

He came back out to the guardrail and looked to his left. He was slightly surprised to see that BigRed had come partway up the road, either to get back to the new bike or sensing where Tommie was. It wasn't clear which, but the bike was adapting.

Tommie steeled himself and jumped over the guardrail. He took a quick look toward BigRed, who was already steaming toward him. He sprinted across the two-lane road, reaching the opposing bike lane and putting both hands on the guardrail. Then, he made the mistake of turning to check on BigRed.

BigRed was already there and blasted into his right hip, sending him sliding along the guardrail. Both of his palms were lacerated by the guardrail edge. While BigRed backed up to take another shot, Tommie grabbed the guardrail again, sliced-up palms screaming with pain, and somersaulted over it.

He went headfirst into the dirt, banging against tree roots as he landed. Getting up and wiping dirt from his face and eyes, he celebrated. The fucking bike had given him a pounding, but now he could just walk between the forest and guardrail and about a quarter mile up the road to a house. He had won!

Stupid bike, he thought, *try to kill me!*

He traveled up the side of the road, and when he came to the driveway, he stepped out and looked back down the road. BigRed twitched and began to glide toward him.

He ran, faster than he ever thought he could, up the driveway and to the door of the house. He rang the doorbell for fifteen seconds. Looking back over his shoulder, he saw BigRed perched at the end of the driveway. The bike stood stock still.

He turned back to the door and pounded twice. Just as he was about to pound a third time, with his fist still in the air, the door opened, and a woman's eye regarded him from beyond a short chain that still held it secure. Slowly, he lowered his clenched fist.

☽ No Rider in the Flesh and Bone ☾

Relieved that he had found a savior, words began to rush out from him between deep sobs.

"Oh, thank God," he heard himself say, "my bike is trying to kill me. My red one, not the new one, the good one. It followed me up the road, and it ran into my other bike, and then I jumped over the guardrail and then . . ." He paused as he saw that the eye visible through the crack in the door was watching him with a mixture of fear and disgust. The skeptical eye looked him up and down. He became uncomfortably aware of what he must look like—bleeding, covered in mud, clothes torn and stained.

And the ranting, there was also the ranting.

Tommie took a deep breath. "I just need to come in and call my parents. They'll come and get me, and then I can deal with that stupid bike." Tommie pointed back to BigRed at the corner of the driveway.

He was pointing at nothing. BigRed had vanished.

While his head was turned, the woman spoke. "I'm sorry, I'm here alone. You're not making sense. I . . . " She slammed the door shut. Tommie heard the sound of a deadbolt being turned and a handle being locked.

Tommie freaked and began sprinting to the trees on the uphill side of the driveway. He saw BigRed moving fast, remnants of the handlebar streamers nearly horizontal at the speed. But BigRed wasn't moving toward Tommie. Instead, she was heading toward the spot where the driveway met the road. She was trying to intercept him!

Tommie adjusted his path to the left, across the lawn and toward the yard's tree line. As he arrived there, so did BigRed, smacking into his right hip. Tommie fought through the impact and rolled into the trees.

He was safe!

BigRed, stymied by the trees, patiently waited in the bike lane and moved parallel to any moves Tommie made. This was a waiting game, and BigRed seemed ready to wait until nightfall, the next day, whenever.

Remembering every detail about this stretch of road, Tommie decided to continue up to the Merritt Parkway, where it crossed under Lake Avenue. He could find help there. Lake Avenue crossed the Merritt on an overpass. If Tommie stayed on the ground as Lake Avenue kept rising, BigRed would have to continue on Lake Avenue or lose Tommie's trail. She certainly couldn't follow Tommie on the ground. Tommie drew a deep breath, said a short prayer, and started fighting though the underbrush.

He staggered through the trees until he approached the Merritt, from which he could hear the sounds of heavy traffic. Breaking through the final trees, he found himself on the south side of the Merritt, with Lake Avenue above him. Looking to his left, across the traffic, he saw Exit 29. It looked like safety. He could put out a thumb or flag down a car. Hell, he could *jump in front* of a car if he needed to.

Careful to avoid traffic on the Parkway, Tommie crossed the southbound two lanes and scrambled into the median. He clambered south down the median until he was directly opposite Exit 29. A short wait for a break in the traffic and Tommie found himself at the exit, looking to the right to avoid traffic. He shot across the lanes, taking one last look.

His blood froze in his veins. On the Lake Avenue overpass, above Merritt Parkway, BigRed stormed northward at breakneck speed. Tommie knew that the next intersection on Lake Avenue was Old Mill Road North and was only two hundred feet from Exit 29.

BigRed was still coming. Tommie slumped to the ground, sniffling. While he waited, he picked up the thickest stick he could find.

Seconds later, moving quickly, BigRed steamed around the corner. The bike braked to a stop as though pausing to consider what to do.

Tommie jumped to his feet, waved the stick in the air, and screamed, "Come and get me, you piece of shit!"

He waited until the bike was nearly upon him, then, gathering what strength he still had, leaped to his right and jammed the stick into BigRed's spokes. The stick went in and was wrenched from Tommie's hands, knocking him down and causing the bike to flip, sissy bar over front wheel.

Tommie looked back at the Parkway behind him as the bike twitched and jumped, finally working the stick loose. Tommie quickly found another stick.

The bike heaved forward as Tommie scrambled backward on his butt, hands on the ground behind him and heels scrabbling to keep him moving. The bike lurched again, and Tommie scrambled again. He looked quickly over his shoulder—he was past the Old Mill Road off-ramp, getting close to the Parkway—cars whizzing past him, honking, as they exited the Parkway.

☽ **No Rider in the Flesh and Bone** ☾

Waving the stick at the bike as it advanced, Tommie watched the southbound lane. Just as the bike began to speed up, Tommie saw his opportunity and, tossing the stick toward the front wheel, hoping to slow BigRed down, raced across a short break in traffic, car horns wailing around him.

The bike, undeterred, moved toward Tommie, who allowed himself a short smile.

The car hit the bike with a surprisingly quiet thump. BigRed bounced into oncoming traffic, where it caught under the bumper of a work van headed north toward New Haven.

Tommie gasped, feeling fresh hope.

The van's driver swerved back and forth across both northbound lanes, wedging BigRed even deeper under the chassis. It looked like something from a Big Truck Rally, with sparks flying out both sides of the van as it careened up the highway. As Tommie watched, pieces of the bike, some identifiable, some not, bounced out accompanied by a hideous screeching as what remained of the bike scraped along the asphalt. After what seemed an endless amount of time, one final knot of mangled metal bounced to the verge of the road.

Tommie watched as the driver, now out of his wrecked van on the other side of the Parkway, surveyed the long trail of debris. Occasionally, to add insult to injury, a car smacked into one of the smaller parts of the shattered BigRed. Tommie stood at the off-ramp as the driver stood by the van. From these different angles, they contemplated the wreckage of BigRed. It was done. The frame was mangled beyond recognition, and nothing Tommie could see could conceivably be put back together.

Tommie limped away before anyone could ask him any questions.

It felt like a long walk, considering it was only several thousand feet, back to The Cannon. It was still in the bike lane. Pushing it upright, Tommie saw damage to the spokes, scratches, and a loose chain. With trembling, sore, and cut hands, he put the chain back in place and slowly pedaled home.

The ride seemed to take forever, but he finally made the last turn to his house, the lawn and driveway straight ahead.

In the driveway, sparkling, with a full banana seat, ape hangers with red, white, and blue tassel streamers on the handlebars, a four-foot sissy bar, and laced spokes, stood a brand-new Schwinn Sting-Ray.

☾ **Charles Montgomery** ☽

It was pointed toward Tommie, swaying slightly in the wind like a slow snake.

Tommie stopped his battered Cannondale and dismounted. The bike dropped from his nerveless fingers.

He knelt and cried like a baby.

The next day, Tommie arrived at school, scratched and bruised, but on a Schwinn.

☾ ☆ ☽

Charles Montgomery *spent his youth indoors, primarily at the request of neighbors. He worked in computers and the internet while living in Silicon Valley, yet managed to leave without much money. He spent seven years in Korea, teaching in the Translation Department at Dongguk University. He retired to Spokane with his wife, where they bought a suicidally ideated house and acquired several "volunteer" pets. He is working on a series of short stories about his Korean experience, several of which have been published. His work can be found at https://www.descendingcat.com/home-2/fiction/.*

The Crimson Staircase of Tryethelone

Margret A. Treiber

My heart pounded as I struck the asphalt. I gasped as the road tore the flesh off my knee with the precision of a cheese grater. I lay in the middle of the road, panting and gazing upon the scarce, dried-brown leaves of the mid-December trees. The sun trickled through the bare gaps where the fallen had once clung to life on now-empty branches.

"Ow."

After several moments, I gathered the strength to stand. Pulling my bike up by the handlebars, I wondered what happened. There weren't any wet leaves on the road, yet the brakes didn't stop me.

I was pulled from my reverie by the barking of Sharon's dog.

"Shut up, Cody!" Kyle yelled. "Sharon, why do you bring your stupid dog everywhere?"

"He just follows me," Sharon replied. "And he's not stupid. He found my missing bracelet yesterday. Sniffed it right out when he knew I was looking."

"That's stupid," Kyle replied.

"No, you're stupid," Sharon rebutted.

I hopped on my bike and tested the brakes. They weren't working. I coasted over to Kyle. "You broke my bike, Kyle."

"No!" Kyle folded his arms. "I only rode it."

Sharon nodded. "You probably broke it yourself to blame us, weirdo."

"You said you were testing it, and then you broke it and pretended you didn't." I felt tears forming as the cold breeze poked at my scuffed knee. "You did it on purpose. You're just mean."

"No, we're not." Sharon crossed her arms. "You think you're so great. We don't get special parties or presents."

Cody added a few barks.

Margret Treiber

"What?" My head felt hot and was throbbing. "What parties?"

"Stop lying, you stupid weirdo." Kyle kicked my bike. "Go home! Nobody wants you here."

"Yeah, go home!" Sharon said.

Cody remained silent.

I sniffed and peddled away, snotty and tearful. The sounds of the dying leaves rustling in the wind echoed my frustration and misery. A leaf blew into my face, nearly blocking my view.

"Goldie . . . " the breeze whispered my name as I brushed the fallen foliage away.

"What?" I gasped. But as I questioned the sound, the air became still and quiet. A single duck quacked as it flew south. It was late in the year for it to be there. I wondered if it had been separated from its flock. Was it alone, like me?

Upon my arrival home, I saw my mother making dinner through the kitchen window. I rolled my bike into the shed and locked it inside.

"I hate my life." I limped up the wooden staircase to my back door, pulling the door open and stepping inside, shaking off the chill. The sound of the evening news played through the small black-and-white television perched on the counter by the phone and answering machine.

After hanging my jacket in the coat closet, I stepped into the kitchen, sticking to the edges in an attempt to avoid my mother's gaze. I almost made it around the corner, through the serving pantry, when my mother spoke.

"What happened to your knee?"

"I skidded. My brakes didn't work." I wiped the snot from my nose on my sleeve.

"Let me see." Mom handed me a paper towel, and I wiped my face.

She grabbed another paper towel and some alcohol and wiped the wound. "It's not too bad. It should be okay in a day or two."

"Sharon and Kyle broke my bike." I gazed down. "Nobody likes me."

"That's not true. I like you." She grabbed another paper towel and wiped my face.

"That's not what I mean. Everyone thinks I'm weird, and they all make fun of me."

☽ The Crimson Staircase of Tryethelone ☾

"You're not weird. You just need to find friends who appreciate you for who you are."

"I try to." The smell of the broiling roast momentarily distracted me. "But *everyone* picks on me. I hate it here. Can't we move back to New Jersey?" I walked over to the fridge, pulled out the jug of fresh apple cider from the local farmstand, and poured a glass.

"Just give it time." Mom started peeling potatoes. "We've only moved to Connecticut a couple of months ago. Come on, you must like something here."

"Besides the Pez, no," I scoffed. "When you said we'd be near the Pez offices, I thought I'd get all the candy I want."

"You'll rot your teeth *and* your brain. You need to use moderation."

"Tell that to the people who pick on me *all the time*! They don't use moderation. I don't know why you and Dad brought me to this stupid place!"

"Goldie Bennett! That's enough." Mom shook her head and returned to preparing the potatoes. "Don't you have homework to do?"

I frowned and stomped my way out of the kitchen. "Fine!"

Instead of doing my homework, I went to the basement to play *Mario*. I was terrible at the game, but it was a suitable distraction from my post-move woes. I'd been playing for about an hour when my mom called me to dinner.

"Your father is working late, so it's just us." She handed me a plate, and I served myself from the counter next to the stove. Once my plate was full of roast beef, mashed potatoes, and creamed spinach, I sat at the butcher-block table.

Mom switched the television off. She filled her plate and joined me at the table. "Stop sulking."

"I'm not sulking," I scoffed. "I just hate it here."

"Too bad. This house is twice the size of our old one, and your grandfather paid it off before he died. Your father has a great job here that covers everything we need. Now we can afford to pay for your college. There is nothing wrong with this place. It's only a couple of hours from where we used to live. It's almost the same in most ways. What do you hate?"

"The people. They're jerks."

My mother sighed. "You hated everyone when we first moved to New Jersey, too."

"No," I replied. "I hated Beth. She stole my eraser the first week, and even though it had my name on it, she convinced the teacher it was hers. But she went to Catholic school in the fourth grade. They're all like Beth here. They think they can take everything, and it's okay because they're rich."

"They're not all rich."

"We're the only ones that don't belong to a country club."

"We have a pool." Mom motioned to the backyard. "We don't need a country club."

"We have a stupid above-ground pool, and I don't want to go to the country club anyway. I want to go back to New Jersey!"

"Nobody wants to go to New Jersey." Mom shook her head. "You're impossible."

I rolled my eyes and returned to the plate. Despite my misery, I was hungry, and my mom's roast was irresistible, caramelized just so with a slight layer of perfectly seasoned fat that melted in your mouth. And the mashed potatoes were like heaven.

Just as I polished off my last forkful, my father pulled in. He stepped inside, dropped his briefcase on the kitchen counter, and kissed my mother.

"Sit and eat," Mom said.

"What we got?" Dad sat down and poured a glass of soda.

"Roast beef," I answered.

Dad filled his plate and began to eat.

"How was work?" Mom asked.

Dad held up his finger as he finished chewing. "Mmm. Good. Almost forgot!" He jumped up, walked over to the counter, and popped open his briefcase. "Here!"

He handed my mother a flyer and sat back down at the table.

"Oh, the company holiday party!" My mother grinned. "Next weekend? That's not much notice. Do we need to bring anything?"

"No," Dad replied. "They just told us. But it's fully catered. They're even planning on serving rib eyes for the grown-ups."

"I want steak!" I interjected.

"You get steak all the time," Dad replied. "You can have hotdogs and burgers with the rest of the kids."

"I'll sneak you some." Mom winked at me. She always had my back.

"Miri," Dad growled. "Both of you behave."

☽ The Crimson Staircase of Tryethelone ☾

"We will," I said. "It's the other people who always start stuff."

My father frowned and exchanged glances with my mom.

"It will be fine." Mom collected my empty dish and put it in the sink. "It'll be fun."

☾ ☆ ☽

The weekend quickly arrived. I was ready. Holiday parties were fun, and although my father was at a new company, I had never been disappointed by one of his company parties.

I changed into my favorite yellow outfit, a baseball shirt and jeans with matching socks. The particular shade of yellow made it special, like lemon sunshine. It took me a few trips to the mall to find the exact matching components.

As always, my mother had overprepared. The backseat was crammed with towels, emergency changes of clothing, and various wet wipes—just in case. There was barely room for me.

I wedged myself in, eager and full of anticipation.

The sun had begun to set. It was nearly dark by the time we arrived at the catering hall, which was on the outskirts of town, surrounded by undeveloped land. As we pulled up, the bare trees seemed to lean in menacingly.

There were only a few cars in the parking lot, and there was no sign of any festivities.

"Are we early?" Mom asked.

Dad shook his head.

"Maybe they're all just running late," I suggested.

My mother checked the flyer. "It says today." She checked the address and looked at the numbers above the building's door. "This is the place. Goldie, grab the bag."

"Ugh." I climbed out of the car and heaved the oversized bag over my shoulder.

My parents exited the car and tried the front door. Stepping inside, we found ourselves inside a dark, empty catering hall.

As the door closed behind us, a dark foreboding overtook me. "Maybe we should go home."

"Yeah," Mom agreed. "Let's go."

I reached for the door with my free hand, but it wouldn't open. "Uh-oh."

"What?" My father reached for the handle and unsuccessfully tried to force it open.

"I'm sure there's a fire exit." My mother pointed to a red glow from the back. "There's the sign."

☽ Margret Treiber ☾

We followed the light, which led us to a long, dim hallway ending with an open door. The illumination came from the other side.

"Are those stairs?" I peeked my head in and saw the slope. "We're not going there." I turned and looked for another way out.

My mother nodded. "I agree. There's got to be another way out of here."

I took that as my cue and ran back to see if I could find an alternative exit. But as I ran back down the hallway, the dim lighting started to flicker, and I found myself back where I started—in front of the red-glowing door. "Do I have to keep carrying this stupid bag? It's getting heavy."

Nobody answered.

"Dad?" I turned to my father, but he was gone. "Mom?"

Realizing I was alone, I assumed they either went searching themselves or I was at a different door. I ran back the other way in hopes of returning to them.

Again, I was standing at the crest of the crimson staircase.

Five more attempts later, I was winded and panting before the abyss.

"Maybe they went down there." Sighing, I gazed into the red maw of the concrete descent into the unknown.

The first step was the hardest. My heart pounded, and I almost slipped. But when nothing happened, I took the next step and the next. Soon, I was on a landing that led to another set of stairs.

"I'm gonna die." I considered going back up, but the steps above me had gone black and seemed more dangerous than my downward option.

I continued down until I was standing before another door. Exhaling, I tried the knob, and it opened.

Flickering torchlight assaulted my eyes. I gazed around to find robed individuals facing a stage of some kind. After a moment, I recognized some of them from my father's office. Examining them closer, I also noticed Kyle's and Sharon's parents. They stared blankly at the stage where a man in a loincloth waved a knife around and chanted.

I gasped, and the room turned to stare at me.

"Welcome!" the man on the stage greeted me. "Come closer. We've been waiting for you."

I decided to be brave and approached the stage, still clutching my mother's bag of stuff. "Where are my parents?"

☽ The Crimson Staircase of Tryethelone ☾

"They're fine." The man smiled. "We sent them home. The invitation was only for you."

"They were promised rib eye," I said. "I don't even see any burgers here."

"A necessary deception. I assure you they have been compensated."

"I'm hungry and want to go home!" I stomped my foot in protest. "Now!"

The man didn't even acknowledge my demand. "Bradley, how's the alignment?"

"Hold on, Gary." A rustling sounded from the left of the stage. In the dim light, I could make out the shadow of a man fumbling a large, folded paper. "From what I can tell, we're set." A small light danced around in his proximity. "It would be easier if we had some light."

"That would ruin the ambiance," a female voice replied.

"Well, Marlene, if we get this wrong, it's not on me."

"You told us you could read the star charts," Marlene replied. "You *are* the astronomer."

"Yeah, but I didn't say I could read in the dark," Bradley whined.

"Enough!" the man on the stage bellowed. "Bring her!"

Two of the larger robed figures stepped forward and grabbed me by each arm.

"No!" I screamed as I struggled against their grasp. I gripped the bag as if it would somehow save me. "Let me go!"

My heart pounded as I kicked and squirmed as the two people dragged me onto the stage. "Mommy! Daddy! Help me!"

But my parents didn't appear. Instead, I was deposited before Gary. The overstuffed bag slipped from my hand and fell to the stage.

"This will only hurt a little." He held the knife and began chanting again.

"Wait!" Bradley waved the star chart. "Time check."

Gary sighed and looked at his watch. "Six-twenty-three."

"Okay." Bradley held up his finger. "We need to wait two minutes, or we get Anassinlone."

"Which one is that?" Marlene asked.

"Anassinlone?" Bradley responded. "Some kind of duck god. It says it's the protector of aquatic fowl or children or something. It's like some seabird with a saddle or something. We need perfect timing because if we wait too long, we get Šulak the crap monster. We don't want that."

"No, I don't want the crap monster," Marlene complained. "You said six-twenty through six-forty-five was Tryethelone."

"Yeah, but I didn't anticipate daylight sav—" Bradley paused, looked at his watch, and shook his head. "Never mind. I'm overthinking this. Please proceed."

"Fine." Gary again raised the knife and began his incantation.

> *In this hidden hall where fortunes intertwine,*
> *Beneath the stars that silently shine,*
> *We call upon the ancient dispenser of fines,*
> *To bring forth Tryethelone, divine.*
>
> *Golden Tryethelone, hear my plea,*
> *Master of riches, from land to sea,*
> *By coin and gem, we summon thee,*
> *Grant abundance and prosperity.*
>
> *Let the chains of poverty break and fall,*
> *As we offer this spirit, this child's all,*
> *On this sacred ground, we stand tall,*
> *Awaiting your presence, at your beck and call.*
>
> *By this incantation, with words so true,*
> *We invoke your power to see us through,*
> *Bless us with wealth, in forms old and new,*
> *Tryethelone, to you, our loyalty, we renew.*

A deep rumbling sound echoed through the room. Before I could react, Gary grabbed my arm and sliced the palm of my hand with the blade he had been waving around. Blood splattered the stage.

"Ouch!" I yanked my hand away and kicked Gary in the shin.

The rumbling turned into shaking. The shaking grew stronger, making it challenging to stay balanced. I grabbed the bag and swung it, striking Gary in the knee and sending him stumbling backward. Running to the edge of the stage, I planned to jump down and make for the exit.

"He's here!" cried Gary. "Tryethelone! We fed you the blood of the unwanted child. Now, bless us with your riches!"

☽ The Crimson Staircase of Tryethelone ☾

A dark, amorphous form started to materialize next to Gary. It was several times his size and took up most of the space on the stage. I climbed down and ran toward the stairs. A man dove for me, but he missed. He slammed to the ground with a thud and then whimpered.

"Goldie," the form hissed. "Come to me."

A chill shot up my spine. While the whole situation was terrifying, I was more upset by the assertion that I was unwanted. Tears welled up in my eyes as I realized that, indeed, nobody liked me.

"I . . . why?" was all I could get out.

The form reached out a tendril that brushed my cheek. "Goldie . . . I understand."

Suddenly, the trembling increased, and it felt like the place was going to cave in. The others ran for the exit. I followed.

Out in the parking lot, I saw my parents' car. As I ran for it, I noticed them inside, unconscious.

"Wake up!" I shouted. I flung the back door open and jumped inside.

As my parents stirred and regained consciousness, I watched the building disintegrate into a pile of debris. A loud screech sounded from above, and I saw a form floating up toward the clouds. My father's disheveled, robed coworkers meandered around the parking lot, seemingly baffled and in search of answers. I wondered if they all made it out.

"Worst holiday party ever," I complained.

My mother was the first to return to her senses. "I don't know what that was, but I didn't get any rib eye."

"Me neither," Dad added.

"The Ground Round?" Mom suggested.

"I want the roast beef!" I replied.

As we drove off, I saw the form assume an aerodynamic shape and take to the sky. It seemed to match our direction halfway to The Ground Round. I could have sworn I caught it flapping away out of the corner of my eye.

☾ ☆ ☽

"Will you please do something about all those ducks in the pool," my father bellowed as he stepped inside the house.

"Talk to your daughter," my mother replied. "She keeps feeding them."

☽ **Margret Treiber** ☾

"Goldie." My father sat next to me at the kitchen table and took a deep breath. "Could you do something about the ducks, please?"

I turned to him and smiled smugly. "Nope. And tell Gary that Anassinlone wants more bread."

☾ ☆ ☽

Also going by the moniker of "Ew! It's Margret," **Margret "The Margret" A. Treiber** *has been voted "most likely to display awkward and inappropriate behavior in public" by a random group of drunks downtown.*

Besides being odd and writing speculative fiction, Margret serves as editor-in-chief for the speculative humor magazine Sci-Fi Lampoon. When she's not writing or working at her day job corrupting technology, she helps her birds break things for her spouse to fix.

Her fiction has appeared in a number of publications. Links to her short stories, novels, and upcoming work can be found on her website at the-margret.com and on Amazon at https://www.amazon.com/Margret-A.-Treiber/e/B0052U63BI/.

01110011 01101001 01101110 01100111 01110101 01101100 01100001 01110010 01101001 01110100 01111001 00100000 01110011 01111001 01101101 01110000 01100001 01110100 01101000 01101001 01111010 01100101 01110010

Below the Surface, We Can Only Imagine

Matt Moore

Dylan beats me and Rubén to where the trees end. He spreads his arms wide in victory and shouts, "See? Told ya!"

I reach him, legs burning.

Rubén catches up a second later, sucking wind.

Dylan—picked last in gym class since we were kids—isn't even breathing hard.

We're standing on the edge of a flooded quarry about the size of a Little League infield. Below us, the rock face goes straight down fifteen feet to the water, which reflects the August evening's purple-pink sky. Trees grow right up to the cliff's edges. If we'd been fifty feet to either side, we'd have gone past without knowing it was here.

Rubén wipes sweat from his face. "*Now* you gonna tell us how you found this place?"

"Sure." Dylan's grinning, enjoying leading us on. "When we get down there."

If I had to choose between being with that girl from Madison I dated or getting in the water, it would be tough. The summer's been a scorcher. Today topped ninety-five, brutal weather to be working at Parks and Rec, still repairing from when Hurricane Gloria blew through last fall. Rubén works the grill at a burger stand on Route 1. At least Dylan, learning how to fix up old houses, works inside.

And I wish John could see this. It's a crushing weight he's not here.

"So how do we get down?" I ask. We could jump, but the rock face is too steep to climb back up.

And who knows how deep the water is.

Dylan goes back into the trees. "This way."

☽ Matt Moore ☾

Three weeks ago, Dylan said he'd found one of the lost quarries but wouldn't tell us where it was until half an hour ago when I picked him up from work. He's helping renovate an old saltbox-style house on the shore. Hurricane Gloria stripped its cedar shake and blew out windows. Now it's got vertical plank siding and an additional build-out from the sloping back roof. I'd been thinking how different it was from the other old houses around it when Dylan got in the back seat and said, "Go north to Conklin Island Road."

But he won't tell us *how* he found it. That means a story. I hope it's a good one and not some bullshit like getting laid at the office Christmas party where his mom works part-time as a receptionist, or beating up some New Haven kid, or a whacked-out Vietnam vet trying to sell him a gun on the town green.

If John was here, Dylan would have told us by now how he found this place.

That thought is a gut punch. So is never knowing why John went swimming without us. He died alone.

☾ ☆ ☽

"No talking," Mrs. Carmady tells us as she leaves the room. I remain facing the blackboards we'd been forced to clean. I hear her go down the hall. It's almost four-thirty, and the middle school is almost empty. "Going to try your parents again," she'd said, but we all know she's going for another smoke.

"Man, I have to get out of here," the small kid—Dylan, I think—whines.

I stare at him. *Be quiet.* My first week of seventh grade in a new school and I'm already in trouble. This short, bony sixth grader isn't going to make it worse. Hell, if I hadn't skipped third grade, I might be in classes with him and his big mouth.

The quiet kid who's always sketching, Rubén, also in seventh, stares, too.

The last guy, John, another seventh grader, looks out the window. Maybe he doesn't care.

"I was going to go to a girl's house," Dylan says.

"Shut up," Rubén whispers.

"I was gonna get lucky," Dylan tells him.

"'I was gonna get lucky,'" Rubén mocks. "Shut. Up."

"You shut up."

There were twelve in here an hour ago doing detention for a stupid food fight. A mix from richies down to poor townies like Dylan. I don't know how it started, but I didn't want any part of

☽ Below the Surface, We Can Only Imagine ☾

it. I almost got kicked out of school last year for fighting when I put a kid in the hospital. To keep me from getting expelled, my dad moved us to the southern part of town so I would go to the other middle school. *You need a fresh start*, he said. But when I saw three rich kids in their Izod shirts and Jordache jeans had Rubén down on the cafeteria floor, smearing vanilla pudding on his face and telling him, "We're making you white!" I had to step in. Just one would have been a fair fight, even if Rubén isn't that big. I don't know him, don't owe him anything, but three-on-one is bullshit. So I pulled them off. I wanted to start throwing punches. Put them down. Make them bleed.

That's when teachers flooded in, breaking it up, and marched us to the principal's office. "Call your parents," we were told. "They can pick you up at four." My dad drives a New Haven bus doing a noon-to-eight shift. I called home and told the sound of a still-ringing phone when to come get me.

It was a quarter of four when the first pissed-off parent stormed in. More came, furious at their kid for getting detention, furious for needing to leave work early, furious at Mrs. Carmady for giving their kid detention.

Now it's just us four. Do Dylan, Rubén, and John also have parents they can't reach?

"I really shouldn't be here," Dylan moans.

"I'm here because of the Spaz," Rubén whispers, looking at me.

"Spaz saved your ass, didn't he?" It's John. I don't know him, but everyone in town knows about his dad. How his family goes back generations, and his dad used to own a lot of land until he got arrested for selling it to housing developers in some shady deal. "And I was outside Principal Craig's office when he talked to Dylan. You should have heard the story Dylan told. How it wasn't our fault. Richies started it. Don't know if Craig believed him, but we're lucky we just got detention."

"You're welcome," Dylan tells us.

"Who's talking?" Mrs. Carmady calls from the hallway.

I face front.

"Who?"

We're silent.

"If no one tells me," she threatens, trailing nicotine as she moves to the front of the room, "you all do detention tomorrow."

We don't say a word.

☽ Matt Moore ☾

"Rubén?" Mrs. Carmady asks. "Dylan? It's not like you two to be in detention."

I guess it's common for John. Maybe she thinks it's common for me because I'm big.

"The phone rang!" Dylan points at the wall-mounted handset that connects to the office. "Well, it didn't really ring but made a *pftz!* sound that wasn't that loud, and we didn't know what to do, and then John said maybe we should answer it in case it was the office saying one of our parents was here or had called, but we're not supposed to get out of our chairs, but we also didn't know when you were coming back so— "

"Okay, Dylan." Mrs. Carmady holds up a hand, either convinced or not wanting to hear more. "If we can't reach your parents, a teacher will drive you home."

"I don't live too far away." John stands. "I usually walk."

Dylan slides out of his seat. "Yeah, me too. My mom's probably in market capital venture takeover meetings all afternoon— "

"You two can go," Mrs. Carmady tells them, and they do.

Dylan's voice fades down the hall, describing how hot the girl he's going to see is.

Me and Rubén, hating it, ask for rides.

☾ ☆ ☽

Dylan leads us through the woods to a fifteen-foot-wide trench cut four feet deep into the bedrock, lined with a thick layer of dead leaves. One direction slopes up into the forest, the other down toward the quarry.

"Access road," Rubén explains.

We hop in and follow the declining slant, the walls growing taller and shadows deeper. They're about twelve feet high when we reach the water's edge, ten feet up the trench from its opening into the quarry. A light breeze flows in, a relief from the woods' clinging, humid air.

"Check it out." Rubén grabs a length of chain, brown with rust, hidden among the leaves. My eyes adjusting to the shadows, I make out other rusted tools—a shovel blade, the head of a pickax. What we don't find are empty beer cans, cigarette packs, or condom wrappers.

Rubén circles the chain over his head and flings it out into the water. "So, we're here," he says to Dylan. "Start talking."

Dylan pulls off his shirt. His job must be working him hard. He's put on some muscle since our last swim—after graduation and just before John died. God, has it really been two months?

☽ Below the Surface, We Can Only Imagine ☾

"Lee Wallace told me," Dylan says.

So, it's bullshit. Lee Wallace—like John—is one of the five kids who drowned this summer in our town's quarries. A richie in Dylan's class, he bragged about kayaking all over the town's rivers and lakes. In the spring, word around school was Lee had found some of the lost quarries. Something about rain from the hurricane filling in dry creek beds, and flash floods carving new ones. No one could figure why he hadn't been wearing a life vest when his body was fished out of the small quarry in the north part of town.

I peel off my sweat-soaked clothes, staying silent and not taking the bait. If he was here, John would be asking questions to dig into Dylan's story. Sometimes it opened the door for Dylan to make the stories more outrageous, and we'd laugh along with him. Other times, John tripped Dylan up until Dylan admitted it was bullshit. And, in that way John had, John made sure Dylan knew he didn't need to make up those stories for us to like him.

But Rubén can't resist. "Rich kid boat-boy friends with a poor townie?" He strips down to his trunks.

Dylan points to rocks sticking out of the water. "I'll tell you *that* out there."

Rubén gives me a grin like *Enough of this shit*. I motion for him to keep cool. Maybe I can poke Dylan. "Did you want to learn to kayak?"

"Stop!" Dylan pounds a fist against his leg. It's something John used to do. Dylan stares at me, mouth a thin line.

I hold his gaze, like John would, hiding my surprise at Dylan's sudden, violent outburst. His stories are supposed to be fun.

Dylan keeps staring. "You wouldn't be here if it wasn't for me. You here just because it's a place to cool off? Do you give a shit about *me*?"

That hurts. Me and Rubén haven't seen him much this summer. John was the one to make the calls. Get us to where we needed to be. I took that on, and should have done more. But Rubén is taking painting lessons and doing his usual, dating someone new each time we talk. I went out with that girl from Madison for a few weeks. We all have jobs, and Dylan is working crazy hours. He's working for Evelyn Greer, whose name townies say like they just swallowed flat beer. She came here six years ago and started buying houses from old folks, fixing them up, and selling them at prices no townie can afford. Hurricane Gloria

Matt Moore

gave Evelyn another business line. Richies got big, fat insurance checks from the companies up in Hartford, but plenty of townies found they didn't have enough coverage. For months, blue tarps hung across damaged roofs and plywood covered broken windows. And in came Evelyn with a low-ball offer they had to take. Now townies like Dylan are turning those houses into richies' homes.

What's worse, Evelyn's twenty-year-old son, Eric, is a real pain in the ass who loves giving townies shit.

But what really hurts is in a week me and Rubén are headed to college, leaving Dylan here. Alone.

"I'll tell you." Dylan points to the water. "Out there."

Rubén chuckles. Not a good sign, but he's cool.

Dylan piles dead leaves over his clothes. "Better stash 'em. Someone might come along and fuck with them."

"Who else would find this place?" I ask.

"Ghosts of dead miners?" Rubén laughs.

"So many questions." Dylan is loving this. He wades into the water.

I cover my clothes even though looks like no one's been here. There are no houses nearby. Dylan had me park on a deserted stretch of Peddlers Road and we walked—then ran—half a mile here.

Still, I'm nervous. There's been a lot of fights this year. Usually, it's townies and richies. Richies acting like they own everything and treating us like dumb, poor hicks. Too many expensive cars with Reagan/Bush bumper stickers. Demands for cops to clear out the dozen Vietnam vets who hang out on the town green. Another big box store opening while family-owned places shut down.

But sometimes it's two groups of townies, neither willing to back down. Especially when it's us. What keeps us close since that day in detention is we're the only children of single parents. I got my dad, the other three their moms. No big brother to look out for us. No set of parents to gang up on a teacher or principal. To say nothing of Dylan's motormouth. Rubén's *I'm gonna get your girl* swagger. Me as the big spaz. And John carrying the blame for his dad—townies hate him for selling the land; richies hate him for getting caught.

If someone comes, I can't get in a fight. I hate how much I like making people hurt. I hate the guilt after. And if they're richies, they might go to the cops. Then I don't go to college. I

☽ Below the Surface, We Can Only Imagine ☾

can't do that to my dad. And he never knew and never will, but I can't do it to John, either.

☾ ☆ ☽

I grab the rebound—

An elbow smashes my nose. I stumble, tears squirting, and go down on my ass.

"Think your nose is on the rag, Spaz."

Standing over me is some richie—and his name might be "Rich." It's tenth-grade gym class, but this asshole has to throw a cheap shot. I feel blood flowing over my lips. I don't wipe it. I'm up *gonna-kill-you!* quick. Screw college. Screw my dad. I'm going to put Rich down. Put him in his place.

But then John's in Rich's face. "The fuck?" John slams a fist against his own leg. Like he wants to hit someone, so he picks himself. "Only way richies win is to play dirty?"

I'm furious that John's between me and Rich.

"We make the rules." Rich pokes John in the chest. "Play how we want."

John shoves Rich. Rich starts to turn away all *Yeah-whatever*, then spins back with a sucker punch. But John ducks it, and counters with a liver shot that drops Rich. The gym teacher is a blur of flailing limbs separating them. John lets himself be moved. Rich is holding his ribs and breathing like puke might follow as the gym teacher pulls him up.

"You're both going to the office!" he yells, dragging them to the hall.

A few of the jocks keep playing, but I step aside, letting myself cool off. I get why John got in Rich's face. He started the fight so he could end it. He's taking the punches, blame, and consequences that should've landed on me. That could've gotten me kicked out of school.

Watching him get dragged off, I swear I'll never put him in that spot again.

☾ ☆ ☽

Me and Rubén follow Dylan out into the water. There's that first bit of shock at the cold, but after a few seconds, it's heaven. It's too dark to see below the surface, so I walk slowly, wondering if the ground will turn left or right, corkscrewing down like the other quarries.

"Race ya!" Dylan shouts, just like he did back in the woods, and dives in.

Matt Moore

Again, we follow. Darkness presses in. Cool and peaceful. My friends' strokes are gentle whooshing. I let it soothe my frustration. Dylan's got a story to tell. I'll let him tell it. Maybe it's his way of dealing with what happened to John.

I wonder what it was like being alone and going under, knowing it's over, but it won't be quick.

There are three quarries in our town. The big one's on its western edge, a smaller one a mile north near I-95. The third is up in the northern part of town where not a lot of people live and maybe a mile from here. Most people—well, townies—take pride that granite used to build places like the Statue of Liberty's pedestal, the Brooklyn Bridge, and Grand Central Station was mined here. We sometimes joke our town motto should be *Half of New York, New York is built on Trenton, Connecticut*, but we don't want the attention. Or tourists.

In the 1950s, the quarries shut down and slowly flooded. For us townies, not welcome at richies' pools and the town beach a place for moms and their kids and not teenaged boys, they became where we'd hang out and cool off after work. Technically trespassing, but cops didn't bother us unless someone complained.

Then, a few months ago, kids started drowning in the quarries. It happens now and then, but not five in a summer.

The first was a nineteen-year-old girl named Mandy Jones. Everyone knew she was crazy. Dropped out at sixteen. Went topless through drive-throughs. Walked around the green yelling, "I want to buy drugs!" Arrested for spray-painting profanity on churches. She was found just after dawn in the big quarry. Her death surprised nobody.

Next was Cara Dumphrey, just before graduation. She had a perfect GPA and was probably going to be valedictorian. We had some classes together. Hard to think she'd be dumb enough to go swimming by herself at the small quarry in the north part of town. Except she'd been shy and overweight with the nickname "Caca Dump Free." Maybe she didn't have friends to go with.

After Cara, cops said the quarries were off-limits.

People talked. Undertow, some said. Hurricane Gloria flooded basements, washed out roads, and caused rockslides. Maybe it knocked something loose below the water.

A week after Cara, it was John in the quarry near I-95. We can't imagine why he'd go by himself and risk getting caught. We should have been there. We could have saved him.

☽ Below the Surface, We Can Only Imagine ☾

Lee Wallace, two weeks after John in the small quarry. It was after he died that Public Works dumped mounds of dirt and gravel to block the old roads going to the quarries, and cops began regular patrols.

Then Carlos Reyes a few weeks ago. All-state wide receiver and regional wrestling champion. A jock who wasn't an asshole. He worked with Dylan. Sneaking into the big quarry could have gotten him in trouble, so hard to figure why he did it.

It was after Cara that us townies started talking about the legends of other, smaller quarries somewhere out in the woods, lost and forgotten. There are sleepover stories about them being haunted, or a brutal killer like Jason Voorhees who slaughters anyone who gets in the water, or a Loch Ness Monster–type thing deep underwater. When the dirt piles blocked roads after Lee, we started looking. But Trenton is huge. Thirteen miles north to south, same as Manhattan, and fifty square miles. I checked old maps at the library. Rubén talked to his granddad, who'd worked the quarries, but his granddad just said, *Don't look. Best you don't find it.* Rubén said it was his granddad's Alzheimer's talking.

Somehow, it's Dylan who found one.

He beats me and Rubén to the rocks. He scrambles up, arms wide in another victory. "Yes!"

I climb up. The rocks make a space ten feet square. We find spots to sit. The breeze is cool on my damp skin. I drink in the quiet and enjoy this moment. A week from now, Rubén will be living with his aunt in New York City to go to art school. I'll be in Providence going to URI. The first one in my family to go to college. My dad insisted. I already lined up a job. I'm splitting an apartment with two other guys to get started on state residency and its lower tuition. My dad wanted me there in June, but I needed to spend this summer with the guys, especially after John.

☾ ☆ ☽

Me and John sit on some rocks above the water line, back in our clothes that stick to our slick skin. Rubén is swimming a slow backstroke. Dylan's thin enough to float on his back, arms out. The sun's gone below the lip of the quarry, but the stone still holds the sunlight's warmth.

There are other groups here in the big quarry. Police tape from when they pulled out Mandy Jones's body is caught in the rocks. Not far away, some townies are hanging out and playing the *Top Gun* soundtrack for the third time. One of them—Hector—works with me at Parks and Rec, and when me, John, Rubén, and

☽ Matt Moore ☾

Dylan arrived, there was that *How's this going to go?* vibe. Me and John stood up front, me terrified it would get physical, but I spotted Hector, we nodded, and that was it.

"There's this awesome place at Eighty-Eighth and Twelfth," Dylan is telling Rubén, "where there's a tattoo shop right in the bar so you can get inked while you drink—which is the name of the place! Did I say that?—and people make stupid decisions when they're drunk." Dylan is describing all the cool bars his cousin, who lives in Brooklyn, has snuck him into. Dylan's never mentioned this cousin before. Even if it's just stories, the bars sound pretty cool. One has girls dancing on the bar top. Another lets underage kids drink because they have a dozen exit doors to run out in case the cops come in. Rubén isn't saying anything. Maybe he's thinking. He just told us he's been accepted into a New York art school and is going there in the fall, not the one in New Haven. Or maybe the silence is to encourage Dylan to make up something even more wild. Dylan should be a writer or something. Something creative. Maybe a comedian.

"I wish you and Rubén weren't headed in opposite directions," John says. "I wonder when the four of us will get to hang out again."

"Thanksgiving," I tell him like he's asked the sky's color. "Christmas. If Rubén and I have the same spring break, maybe you get Dylan to play hooky for a few days and we all take the train to NYC." *Money on a ticket you should be saving*, I can hear my dad saying. *A week of missed shifts at work. Of not doing homework.*

"And next summer?"

I know what he's asking. To keep in-state tuition, I have to keep living in Rhode Island. "I'll come back. Visit my dad. Or you guys come see me."

"And Rubén?" He's speaking quietly, but I doubt Rubén could hear us over Dylan's bar talk and Kenny Loggins's "Playing With the Boys." "Think he'll come back to Trenton?"

"Yeah."

John grabs a small stone—flat, round. He flips it over like he's studying it. "I think Rubén is going to find some artsy types, cool spots to hang out, get himself a hot girlfriend, and never leave Manhattan. He's done with this town."

"Does that mean he's done with us?"

John tosses the stone in the air, judging its weight. "High school's almost over. Things gotta change."

☽ **Below the Surface, We Can Only Imagine** ☾

There's a lot in those three words. I can't imagine my life without these guys, but I've also thought about how I drifted away from my friends when I changed middle schools. Two years later, when we all started as freshmen at Trenton High, we'd talk if we were in the same class or wave passing in the hall, but that was it. We never hung out. They were in one group, and I was in another.

Is that going to happen again? "His mom and granddad are here."

"Plenty of dental hygienists jobs and nursing homes in New York and Jersey." John launches the stone. It skips six times. The record is eight that John hit a few weeks back.

I want to tell John he's wrong. I can't. Rubén has always dreamed of living in New York. Going to college is my dad's idea, but I want out of Trenton. Who I am here. How I'm seen. I have an A-minus average and took three Advanced Placement courses this year, but everyone knows me as "Spaz."

"What about you and Dylan?" I ask.

"We'll do fine. A couple of guys at the garage are cool. Maybe hang out with them." John's turned his after-school job at the gas station into something full-time, finally convincing the boss he's not a crook like his dad and letting him work on cars. It's always pissed me off how John has to carry what his dad did because his dad's not here to carry it himself.

Dylan's lined up a job with that bitch Evelyn Greer. We don't hold it against him. The money should be good, and working construction might help his reputation as a small, weak kid. Right now, he's talking about a tavern at Fourth and Madison where they keep the lights low since it's got a great view of the Statue of Liberty.

"We're always gonna be friends," I tell John.

"Always. But life keeps ticking on. For me and Dylan. Rubén the famous-artist-to-be. You gotta go to college. You skipped a grade. You got a brain. You can't let these people pull you down." He eyes the other group, whose argument about skipping "Take My Breath Away" because it's a pussy song might turn into a fistfight.

☾ ☆ ☽

"Check that." Rubén points across the water at a square hole in the rock face. There's enough light to see it goes at least ten feet deep. The surface of the water is five or six feet below its top, so there's no way to know how tall it is, but it's as wide as a truck.

"That's how Lee found this place," Dylan says. "Tunnels connect some of the quarries."

"Underground?" I ask.

"Keep them secret."

A hidden network of underground tunnels beneath Trenton is a story Dylan might tell.

"So," Rubén says, "you're gonna make me ask? Fine. Why'd Lee tell you?"

"I need a place to kill Eric Greer."

Rubén chuckles. "Shoot him with that gun the Vietnam vet had?"

Dylan is motionless. "I'm serious."

"No," I say, wanting to pull this back, "you're not."

"The fuck do you know!" Dylan shouts, voice echoing off the surrounding rock. "I mop the floor. The fucker shows up with boots smeared in dog shit. He parks his car in my driveway and says to wash it. Blasts music in the other unit when I'm trying to sleep. I told Evelyn, and it just made it worse."

"And you didn't tell us?" I ask. "All summer? Wait until we're about to go and 'Hey, I'm gonna murder somebody!'" But I'm stuck on what Dylan said about the other unit. Dylan lives in a duplex with his mom. The other unit is empty last we'd heard.

"Like *you* would do something?"

I get it: John, who was staying, would. And John wouldn't be afraid of a fight.

"Um . . . quit?" Rubén says.

"I can't! Guess who owns the other side of my house."

My stomach drops. I get it. "Evelyn Greer."

"Evelyn Fucking Greer," Dylan says. "Ever wonder why I work for that bitch? Ever ask? She says my mom and me haven't kept our side in good shape. It's hurt the value of her side. I gotta work it off. I'm getting paid shit! Evelyn says if I quit, she'll put a lien on our side. And what do you think Eric would do? I'm stuck here. I'm alone."

Maybe this isn't bullshit.

"And Lee was cool to tell you his big secret?" Rubén scoffs.

"No," Dylan says. "I paid him off."

"You don't have the money—"

"It took everything I had. I'm broke."

"And how the hell would you even get Eric out here?" I ask.

"Easy. We're friends. I listen to him bitch—about his mom, this town—and agree with him. When he cuts down on someone,

☽ Below the Surface, We Can Only Imagine ☾

I do, too. When he cuts down on me, I smile and say, 'Yeah, good one.' I wash his car. I mop the floor again. I tell him he's cooler than you two." Dylan moves to a gap between two rocks. "Way cooler than John."

A flash of anger hits me.

Above the trees, the first stars are out.

Dylan, on all fours, straddles the gap. "He'll come because no one knows about this place. Like it will be his." He reaches elbow-deep into the narrow gap. "His mom's got property. Now he does, too. He'll think I'm sucking up." He pulls out a baseball bat. "Because I picked him over you." He reaches in again and removes a three-foot piece of one-inch metal pipe. He lays them side by side like they're on display.

Dylan's stories are funny and make him look cool. They don't have him showing he's got weapons stashed here. The bat would float, but it would be tough to swim out here with that pipe. He wants us to think he's serious.

"I don't believe," I tell him calmly, "you really want to do this. There's some cruel and fucked-up people in this town. You're not one of them. Come on, what's going on?"

Dylan stares at me. "I killed Cara Dumphrey."

"Yeah, right," Rubén giggles. "She drowned."

"I did." He picks up a small, flat stone.

I'm hating this. "Why?"

"We were dating."

Rubén bursts out laughing. "You and Caca? A senior—"

"Yeah! I knew I'd catch shit if I told you." He turns the stone over, looking at it. "We went swimming at the small quarry. Early, so no one would be there. She said she was going to college for the summer semester. Would be leaving in a week. We should break up." He tosses the stone in the air like John used to. "I yell at her. Tell her I hate her. Tell her I wish she was dead. And she goes under the water and doesn't come up. No waves, no bubbles. Gone."

Rubén hums the two-note theme from *Jaws*.

"So she did drown," I say.

"That's what I thought." Dylan tosses the stone sidearm, and I count six skips across the purple-black water before losing it in the darkness. "An accident. Or maybe she did it on purpose. I didn't tell anyone. Then something happened." Dylan grabs another stone. "I got smarter. Read faster. Do math in my head. Figure things out."

☽ 74 ☾

More bait, but whatever this is, Dylan needs to tell it. "How'd that happen?"

Dylan keeps looking at the stone. "Something's here. In this quarry. Something deep. It's been waiting. The hurricane let it out."

"Oh, fuck off with that ghost story shit." Rubén turns to dangle his feet in the water, back to Dylan.

"Your granddad ever talk about why the quarries closed?"

Rubén sighs for effect. "My granddad said it wasn't going bankrupt or they took all the good stone out or whatever. He said in the secret ones, the small ones like this one, they were digging for something else. But they were going too deep, too fast. Men got hurt. Killed. Started killing each other. Then, they killed the owners. Stashed their bodies in a pit, and everyone just took off."

"What were they looking for?" I ask.

"I dunno. Granddad's got Alzheimer's. But it's just a story." He jerks a thumb at Dylan. "Like his."

"It's like this town." Dylan tosses the stone in the air. "Workers die, but, hey, the owners get profit. Workers kill each other just to get a little ahead. Townies lose their homes, but richies get an investment. I give it a life; it gives me a little something back."

"And it's here?" I ask. "*This* quarry? No one drowned here."

"Yet." Dylan turns the stone over and over. "But it's in all of them. In the water."

The full moon hangs low, caught in backlit branches.

Quarry stories are kids' stuff, but the bat and pipe are real. And he's talking murder. I poke at his story. "Don't sound too broken up about killing Cara."

"I didn't mean to. And it hurt. What I said to her. I tried to tell myself she's just some richie bitch. But she was nice. And lonely. And unhappy." He pounds a fist on his leg. "I wish it didn't happen, but it did. So I go to work for Evelyn. Eric starts giving me shit. And John dies. Because I'm smart like Cara, I figured out Eric did it."

Rubén says, "Wait— " as I shout, "What?" We're both on our feet.

"I told John about Eric making my life hell," Dylan explains. "John must have told Eric to leave me alone. Eric killed him. Made it look like another drowning."

"And you didn't tell us?" My voice echoing. "You wait until now? Make us drag it out of you?"

☽ Below the Surface, We Can Only Imagine ☾

Rubén crosses his arm. "You're making this up. It would have been more believable if you said what Caca sounds like when you fuck. Is it 'Oh! Oh!' or 'Oink! Oink!'"

"Are you sure?" I demand. "About Eric?"

Dylan shrugs, his reflection in the water a perfect duplicate. "Makes sense."

"You didn't tell the cops?"

Dylan's still sitting, still looking at the stone. "That's a richies' way."

"You don't know for sure?"

"I think he killed Mandy and Carlos, too."

Me and Rubén, still standing, look at each other.

"Mandy hung around with Eric. Stupid bitch called me 'the white Ethiopian.' Maybe things went bad. Maybe that's why Eric's so batshit crazy. And Carlos wouldn't take Eric's shit, so Eric killed him."

Eric is about my height, six feet, with a medium build. Not huge. While I'm "big boned," Carlos is college-scholarship big, six-foot-two and a star wrestler. I don't see Eric winning that fight.

Rubén sits back down. "This is your worst story ever. 'Super-evil quarry monster,'" he chuckles, trying to imitate Dylan, "'turned me into a badass killer.'"

I think about my dad telling me, *"The devil made me do it" is bullshit* when I tried to make excuses for fighting. *Good people don't make deals with the devil. Good people tell the devil to fuck off. The devil can't make you do anything, but it lets bad people do what they always wanted.*

I hate it John's not here. He'd have Dylan telling us the truth by now.

"If I'm going to kill Eric," Dylan says, "I needed to figure it out. Pieces of a plan. First, I'd need someplace no one knows about. That meant Lee. I said I wanted kayak lessons, but keep it quiet. It's richie stuff. We meet for a lesson at the small quarry. I take his kayak out, wearing his vest, and tip over. I yell for help. He swims out to help me. I didn't know if it would work, but I start muttering how I wish he was dead. Down he goes. Just like Cara. That's why he didn't wear a life vest. I had it. By the end of that day, I knew where this quarry was." He tosses the stone. Moonlight catches seven silver rings.

I finally sit. "You're saying you killed Lee, too? Cara was an accident, but you meant to kill Lee?"

"I needed what he knew."

☽ 76 ☾

"You said you paid him."

"Yeah, for lessons."

It's not what he said.

"Richie boat-boy wouldn't sneak into the quarries," Rubén says, "when he could go to a lake or someplace cops *aren't* patrolling."

Rubén's right. Plus, if Dylan had a girlfriend, he would have bragged about it, even if he didn't say it was Cara.

But if this is a story, he'd say he fucked Cara silly before they went swimming. Threatened to beat the shit out of Lee for the location. Carlos was the coward, and Dylan confronted Eric. And somehow he knows about this place. Knows its history. Maybe John learned about it from his dad and only told Dylan as a sign of trust. Now Dylan's using this place in his story, fitting everything else around it.

"You kill Eric, Evelyn's still a problem."

"Eric has Evelyn wrapped around his finger. When he's dead, I will be able to, too. She'll be a wreck. Maybe I can talk her into giving me the company."

"So your plan is he comes out here." I motion to bat and pipe. "You hit him with the bat? Or is it the pipe?"

"Not me." Dylan stands, picks up the bat, and holds it out like he expects me to take it. "He's meeting me here at nine." I look to the ramp, suddenly worried someone will be there in the shadows. It's empty. I have no idea what time it is. My watch is back with my clothes. I picked up Dylan around 7:30. Twenty minutes to drive here. How long through the woods and out to these rocks?

Above, the trees are silver-black in the moonlight.

"Get in the water and hide behind the rock." Dylan still holds the bat out. "I'll call him out here. If I can't get the water to take him, we beat on him."

I stand. "Why wouldn't the water take him? Don't you tell it who to take?"

"Haven't you been listening? He killed John in a quarry. Mandy and Carlos, too, I think. Maybe he can do what I can. And if he knows I can, too, do you think he'll let me live?"

"What if I knock you out and throw you in? Tell the water to take you to test it?"

Dylan just stares. "First punch you've thrown in years is at me? Knock me out before running off to college? Maybe you've always wanted to hit me?"

☽ Below the Surface, We Can Only Imagine ☾

I take the bat like I'm giving in. When Dylan offers the pipe to Rubén, I swing the bat at it, knocking it away. It clangs against the rock. I hurl the bat up and over the quarry's edge into the woods. "We're not doing this."

Dylan glares at me. "You're going to leave me here with that piece of shit?" He looks at Rubén, who gets to his feet. "Both of you? Running off to college. Like richies? He killed John!"

I look to Rubén for support, but he can't meet my eyes. "And what if Eric doesn't show?" I ask Dylan.

"We'll find another way," Dylan says. "Another time. The next time you're home. Or will I never see you again?"

Shit. I think I get it. "Dylan, I'm leaving town, not you. I'll call. I'll come back to Trenton to hang out. I want you to come to Providence. Imagine the stories about going to college parties. You don't need to do this to prove we're your friends."

Dylan doesn't move. "Eric said he'd be here."

"So, you're a killer now?"

"Guess I am."

It's like I don't know who Dylan is anymore. Like my friend was emptied out, and someone new poured in. I won't be a part of this, whatever "this" is. Either he's lying to test our friendship or hasn't told us what he's been going through all summer and now expects us to ambush Eric. I move closer, chest to chest. A narrow, scrawny chest back in June. Now Dylan looks like he could play football.

Or wrestle.

"We're leaving, or I make you leave."

"No," Rubén says. He's got the pipe.

"You believe this?" I ask.

Rubén chuckles. "I don't know. But I'll beat on Eric. Not to kill him. I don't need that. But hurt that shit? Yeah."

"Why?"

Moonlight catches tears on his cheeks. "I've never done anything that means a shit. We gotta talk our way outta something, it's John or Dylan. Square off? You and John. I'm just sketching in my book. You guys are like brothers, but I've always been looking to New York." Rubén slams the pipe against the rock. The impact rings off the stone surrounding us. "I gotta do something. Can't just leave like 'Later, guys.'" He looks at Dylan as Dylan is struggling to free something else from the gap. "I think you're full of shit. And I give you a lot of shit. But if Eric shows, I'm with you."

☽ **Matt Moore** ☾

"He's bigger than you two," I tell them both. "Even with that pipe, you get one swing to end it."

"We had a bat," Dylan reminds me.

"If he gets that pipe from you, he'll kill you. Or you could slip and bash your head."

"So you do believe me?" Dylan finally frees whatever it is in the gap.

I don't answer because I don't know. "It sucks what he's doing, but it's not worth killing over. And if he gets away, he's going to the cops."

"My mom will say all of us were at my place tonight." Dylan stands, hauling up a heavy coil of rusted chain. It looks long enough to wrap around someone a few times.

The suddenness of how real this might be makes my head spin. "Cops will believe Eric over some townie."

"So we make sure he doesn't get away." Dylan drops the chain at his feet. The metal clanging echoes all around.

How did he get it here? It's way too heavy to swim out here. Or did something bring it up from deep below the water for him?

No. That's crazy.

Rubén swings the pipe like he's taking someone's head off. "You staying?"

My heart pounds. This split between us is a physical pain.

I'll go to my car and wait. When Eric doesn't show, Rubén will give up and swim in. Dylan, too. We'll figure out what's next.

But if I run into Eric on the access road or in the woods? If it's real? I could try to talk to him like John. Tell him to leave Dylan alone. He won't listen. I'd probably just make it worse. Maybe end up in fight. And then it's me going to jail.

I turn three-sixty, looking for another way out. There's none. The cliff is too steep.

"No," I tell Rubén and go to the edge of the rock. "I'll wait at my car."

The moon's reflection in the still, open water is huge.

"I need the Spaz!" Dylan shouts.

My friends lose any way this goes. Dead. In jail. Even if they get Eric down, they're not cruel like me. Not cruel enough to hurt him. Make him bleed. Finish it. And I don't want them to be. Don't want them to know the guilt, and worry their whole lives about a visit from the cops. Not when I can stop it.

I can't fix this like John, so I'll fix it my way. Stop them from ruining their lives or getting killed. I'll grab that rusted pickax head

⟩ Below the Surface, We Can Only Imagine ⟨

back on shore, and wait in the shadows of the access road. Narrow. High walls. Nowhere to run. Do what they can't. And I won't tell them. If Eric doesn't show, I can't let Dylan think I bought into his story. How far will he go next time? And if it's true, I'd rather they think I abandoned them than know what I did. Maybe someday, if we stay friends, I'll tell, but not now. I don't want anyone to know. Not when I'm close to getting out.

I jump in, swallowed in silent darkness. I think about John again. What it had been like to be alone.

What if he wasn't?

What if Dylan did talk to John about Eric, but just them? The ones staying behind. Dylan suggested they go swimming, to hell with the cops saying the quarries are off-limits. When Dylan asked John for help, John said "no." Like Trenton, like graduating from high school, things were changing. Dylan needed to stand up for himself.

Would Dylan, feeling betrayed, say the words like he had with Cara, and then John was gone?

No, that's insane.

I surface.

A stone whizzes past my head. I count nine skips.

Rubén, pipe in hand, stands next to Dylan.

All of this is insane. Dylan keeping secrets all summer. Secret underground tunnels. John going swimming alone.

Or does it all make sense?

"What are you waiting for?" Dylan asks.

What did Dylan say? *Pieces of a plan.* What if there are more pieces?

Mandy. Crazy, short-tempered, unpredictable. Like Dylan is being.

Cara, the smart one to plan it out.

John, who got us to the right place at the right time, like getting on the rock when Eric is about to show up.

Lee, who knew about hidden quarries.

Carlos, strong and athletic. Maybe Dylan talked him into sneaking into a quarry after work to cool off.

No. Dylan's a storyteller. A pretender.

A liar.

Maybe we've never seen who he really is.

No. That's crazy. And why would he start with Mandy? Unless he stumbled across her at the quarry. Maybe she teased him? Maybe she was the first one he wished dead, not Cara. But

Matt Moore

he hadn't started working for Evelyn, hadn't gotten shit from Eric. Unless going to work for Evelyn was part of the plan. An incomplete plan he needed Cara to help with.

No, insane.

Dylan motions toward shore. "It's a short swim."

There's a missing piece of that plan, isn't there? Carlos could wrestle, but knowing how to fight isn't enough. And you can't just wish someone dead. You have to be cruel. Vicious. Want to see them hurt. Bleed. Suffer. Dylan isn't, not yet. But he wants to be.

"You'll be fine."

Did he know I'd leave and get back in the water?

I tread water, wondering how far down it goes. What rusted-out, abandoned equipment is down there? Does light reach that deep? Has that chain Rubén threw hit bottom yet? How many bodies, just bones now, lie beneath?

"What are you waiting for?"

How many more will there be?

"Afraid I'll say 'I wish *you* were dead' for leaving me?"

Above, the full moon is the brightest thing I've ever seen.

Matt Moore *is an Aurora Award-winning author, poet, and columnist. Exposure to Poe and Star Trek while still in grade school firmly set in him the belief that fiction should both thrill and make you think. His horror and dark science fiction have appeared in a number of online and print markets including* The Drabblecast, On Spec, Cosmic Horror Monthly, Leading Edge *and* Polar Starlight, *as well as several "Year's Best" anthologies. His (now out-of-print) short story collection* It's Not the End and Other Lies *was published in 2018. Matt has been an Aurora Award nominee ten times across three categories, a Friends of the Merrill finalist, twice long-listed for the Sunburst Award, has been a frequent panelist and presenter, and was cochair of a local reading series for five years. He lives in Ottawa, Ontario, but was raised in small-town Connecticut. He's thrilled to return home, even if just on the page, to add to the rich tapestry of New England's legends and ghost stories. Find Matt at mattmoorewrites.com.*

Biker Gang

Gevera Bert Piedmont

As Hurricane Gloria pummeled Connecticut, Hyssop stood outside under her mom's apple trees. Fruit flung itself from the branches like a weapon, embedding in the mud at her feet. Her dad's wind sculptures rang and crashed, depending on what materials he had used: shells, metal, sea glass. The cacophony cut through the howl of the hurricane.

Gloria, her first hurricane, didn't impress Hyssop. A tall, thin, gangly girl, she had been hoping it would be a *Wizard of Oz* situation and blow her away to some better place. The Storm of the Century, Gloria was forecast to fling boats a mile inland, tear down houses, and drown people and pets.

It was fine for Hyssop to be outside in the midst of a hurricane as long as there were no allergens. Wheat, peanuts, and dairy didn't lurk in the yard waiting to attack. If a tree crashed upon her, it would be a welcome change to go to the hospital for a broken bone instead of gasping for breath from anaphylactic shock.

A terrible noise broke through the competing sounds of wind sculptures and hurricane: bicycle bells and playing cards flapping against spokes. Hyssop slid to the other side of the apple tree, into the wind. As skinny as she was, the tree wasn't thick enough to hide her. Gloria plastered her against the rough apple bark, and Hyssop had no choice but to fling her arms around the scaly trunk. She pressed her cheek to the tree and forced her eyes open, watching the street.

Because of her life-threatening allergies, Hyssop didn't go to school anymore. Someone eating a peanut butter sandwich for lunch could kill her. The other eighth graders saw Hyssop as weak, as prey. A loose group of them with sporty bikes, mostly boys with a couple of girls, hunted Hyssop for fun. And they were out in the storm, just like she was.

They knew better than to enter Hyssop's yard. But they had slingshots and air rifles. They had broken several of the wind sculptures, and Hyssop understood the warning: *that could be you.*

Hyssop clutched the tree as Gloria blew fiercely against her back, molding her thin jacket and T-shirt to her ribs and shoulder blades. Her sleeves were blue against the brown bark. Three bikes skidded to a stop before Hyssop's home. The kids on them were so drenched Hyssop couldn't tell who they were, their hoods plastered to their heads and their jeans black with water. One was wearing glasses, so she thought maybe that was Charlie. They turned their bikes to face Hyssop's house, so she knew it wasn't an accident they paused there.

Gloria's wrath blew off their hoods and ripped the playing cards from the wheels of their bikes. A piece of glass detached from a wind sculpture and flew into the street, smashing. Charlie, if it was Charlie, winced, but one of the others started shouting Hyssop's name. They must be able to see her blue sleeves.

She clenched her fists and stayed still. Her pulse hammered in her wrists.

The bikes crowded closer to the front fence. "Hyssop! Come play in the storm."

Even when she was younger, she had never played with any of these kids. They would drown her like an unwanted puppy if she came out.

The old slatted wooden fence had never been very straight, and now it was serpentine, like the back of a dragon, in the wind. If Gloria knocked it down, would the kids take it as a sign to invade?

The front door opened. "Hyssop? Are you outside?" her mom called.

The bikes wheeled, and their riders pedaled off into the storm.

☆

Hyssop, mounted on her basic banana bike, the woven red basket filled with collecting bags, headed to the beach the morning after the storm. Her father, part of the town's public works department, was out removing downed trees and debris from the roads. The power was out in swaths across town. Her mom let her off from doing schoolwork when regular school was out.

☽ Biker Gang ☾

Hyssop avoided the streets where she thought the other kids might be. Today, fallen trees and wires blocked many roads and made her route meandering. But after a storm, all sorts of cool stuff would be washed up on the beach that her dad might use in his sculptures.

The wind was still blustery and the waves crashing high when Hyssop locked her bike to the rack. Some of the dunes protecting the beach were a different shape. The waves had come way over those dunes during the past few days. The path between the dunes had silted over, and Hyssop picked her way carefully, her Converse high-tops filling with sand.

"I might even be too early," she told a wheeling seagull, staring at the wrecked beach. The waves were fierce, frightening even. Enormous pieces of driftwood, lumber, and general trash littered the beach far above the usual high tide mark. The area stank. Dead fish and parts of critters were strewn among the debris. The seagulls chattered and fought over these delicacies.

Usually, the smells of the sea invigorated Hyssop, but today, she raised a hand to her face and grimaced. This was bad. The noise of the fighting seagulls pierced through her eardrums. She wanted to put two fingers up her nose and her thumbs in her ears. There might be many treasures on this stretch of beach, but she didn't think she had the will or the stamina to search them out.

She pinched her nose once and then let it go. The stiff wind made it run, dribbling onto her lip. Hyssop wiped with her index finger and then picked her way across the sandy disaster, head down. She found a good, long stick and used it to turn over things she didn't want to touch, searching for sea glass and shells, making her way to the tide pool to see if any interesting fish had gotten trapped in there.

Scoring a few perfect shells and unusually colored pieces of glass for her father, she squirreled them into her bags. The seagulls realized she wasn't a threat and calmed down, except when she got too near a choice bit of dead thing, of which there were far too many. Lots of crustaceans. Hyssop figured every day, the high tide would recede, leaving more fragments. In a few days, her father could come down to the beach with her. He would make it into a biology lesson and count it as school. Or art. The eighth-grade lesson packages the middle school sent over were so very boring.

☽ Gevera Bert Piedmont ☾

Around the corner was the tide pool, where Hyssop had been coming all her life. Every high tide brought new fish, like a living aquarium. Hyssop hoped the massive storm surge had washed in extraordinary fish. At the far end, waves still crashed over the rocks.

She put down the collecting bags and leaned over the pool. She could see to the sandy bottom through the stirred-up water. Black mussels, starfish, and sea urchins clung to the rocks. Darting silver fish, killifish, swam in a school as if being chased. Hyssop held her breath to see what was behind them, hoping for a small shark or something unusual but saw nothing. She eased around the side of the pool on slippery bladderwrack-covered rocks, using her stick for balance.

And there *was* something unusual, about three feet in, clinging to an empty section of rock close to the sandy bottom. A sea anemone, Hyssop thought, but she had never seen one like this before. Or was it a cluster of several similar anemones?

It was black, or an extremely dark purple, and hydra-shaped, thick trunk on the bottom, tentacles on top. But it had several trunks; it was hard to tell how many, and at least a dozen long whips.

Leaning on the stick, hoping it would take her weight, Hyssop crouched and studied the hydra-shaped anemone. It was about the size of her two hands together, with her palms as the trunks and her fingers as the tentacles.

Those thick whips didn't move listlessly in the water like the top of a normal anemone did. They moved like octopus tentacles, autonomously, with purpose. The trunks seemed more like legs, and as she watched, one of them shifted and aimed the body, and the mass of tentacles, in another direction.

Toward the school of killifish. The tide pool was about thirty feet across and three to four feet deep, and the trapped killifish were circling, trying to find a way out. They blundered toward the black hydra, and its tentacles reached out, stretching thinner and longer, and in a moment, they ensnared half of the school. The little fish struggled, but the tentacles drew them in, getting shorter and fatter, bringing the fish toward the center stalk, where some sort of mouth orifice pulled in the struggling, living fish and consumed them under Hyssop's amazed gaze.

The various thick trunks—feet, they really seemed to be feet—moved about as if getting more comfortable while the tentacles stretched back out into the water and gently waved.

☽ Biker Gang ☾

The hydra was larger now, no longer the size of Hyssop's thin hands. Maybe the size of her dad's hands.

She wished for a Polaroid instant camera. She had to bring her dad to see this. Hyssop stood, and her shadow fell on the hydra. It moved again, crawling slowly out of her shadow.

Weren't anemones stuck in place once they grew to a certain size?

Once more, Hyssop crossed the bladderwrack to return to the sand and her collecting bags. Near her treasures, half under a piece of driftwood was a dead fish on top of a plastic bag. Hyssop pursed her lips and then used her stick to lever off the driftwood. The smell that wafted out was unpleasant and also served to summon the seagulls. Wrapping the slimy fish in the plastic bag before she could think too hard about what she was doing, Hyssop started back across the slippery seaweed toward the hydra. A seagull dive-bombed her, trying to get the fish, and she waved the stick at it.

The hydra was where she had left it, and Hyssop was careful not to let her shadow fall on it. Still, she felt as if the creature knew she was there. She unwrapped the dead fish from the plastic and let it fall into the water near the black anemone. The corpse drifted about a foot from the hydra, seesawing down into the tide pool.

Shifting on one of its thick feet, the hydra thinned its tentacles, extended them, and grabbed the fish just before it hit the sandy bottom. The fish was larger than the hydra.

Hyssop settled on her haunches, leaning on the stick.

The tentacles tore off pieces of the soft dead flesh and pushed them into the orifice in the center until the remains were small enough to eat whole, including the bones. The hydra did another settling stomp and shook its tentacles. It was now about twice as large as it had been when Hyssop had found it. She no longer believed it was an anemone.

"I'll see you tomorrow," she told it.

On the way home, a series of fallen wires and branches forced her to detour, and yet another closed road led her even further away. Hyssop wanted to get home, tell her dad about the non-anemone in the tide pool, and look through the encyclopedia until they figured out what it was. If it was a new species, they could call the biology department at Yale University or even go behind the scenes at the Peabody Museum and look at specimens.

☽ Gevera Bert Piedmont ☾

However, what if the Peabody Museum's curators wanted to catch and mount the creature, killing it? Hyssop chewed her lip, thinking of Audubon and all his beautiful paintings of birds, done from taxidermied specimens. Better not to tell anyone and allow it to live, perhaps?

She thought she recognized her dad's work truck as she detoured yet again around a fallen tree. She was a little confused about where she was. So many trees had come down during the hurricane that the neighborhoods looked different. Hyssop rarely paid attention to street names, either.

She was so lost in thought about the hydra that she wasn't aware of her surroundings, and that's how they caught her.

The biker gang.

Charlie, Joanie, and Ted had Hyssop surrounded before she realized they were there.

"Skeletor," Charlie taunted, grabbing the handlebars of Hyssop's bike.

Hyssop was thin, but not that thin. She blinked at Charlie, whose eyes were small and ratlike behind his glasses.

"Where you been?" Joanie had short black hair and dressed like a boy. Joanie was mean, no matter how she dressed.

"Let me go," Hyssop said.

"You ever coming back to school?" Ted grabbed the bags from Hyssop's basket and started going through them.

"Don't touch those things."

"Stupid beach trash." Ted threw the bags. Shells and glass tinkled and smashed.

"You went to the beach?" Joanie singsonged, tilting her head side to side. "It must be nice to have every day off from school, huh?"

Ted moved behind Hyssop and took hold of the back of her bike seat.

"You know why I can't go to school."

"Oh, you're *allergic*," Joanie continued in the same high-pitched, singsongy voice. "You might *die*."

The biker gang laughed. Ted shook Hyssop's bike. She clutched the handlebars, staring at Joanie.

"Skeletor," Charlie repeated. "Cuz you can't eat."

"I can eat," Hyssop said sullenly.

"Nothing good. No sketties, no PB and J," Charlie stated.

"No chocolate milk!" Joanie exclaimed, her eyes wide with fake horror.

☽ Biker Gang ☾

"No ice cream." Ted shook the bike harder. Hyssop dug the white heels of her Converse into the damp pavement.

"No grilled cheese sandwich." Charlie narrowed his already small eyes.

She couldn't eat any of those things, true.

"You need to learn what you're missing," Charlie said.

Hyssop looked around in a panic. "No." She couldn't get off the bike; she couldn't get away.

Joanie twisted her fanny pack to her belly and extracted a wrapped sandwich.

Hyssop smelled peanuts. Her breathing hitched. "No, it's not a joke, please don't. If you only knew what it was like to be allergic to something. It's awful."

"It's plenty funny." Charlie stepped forward and grabbed Hyssop's thin arms.

"And delicious, don't forget delicious." Ted let go of the bike and put his hands on either side of Hyssop's head, holding it still from behind.

Joanie put down her kickstand with a practiced foot move and swung her leg over her bike. Hysterically, Hyssop noticed Joanie rode a boy's bike. Joanie unwrapped the sandwich: peanut butter, purple jelly, fluff, on white bread, cut diagonally, with the crust left on. A beautiful, thick sandwich, homemade with love, probably by Joanie's mom, who did not know what a monster her daughter was.

Hyssop clamped her lips shut and said in her throat, "nuh-uh, nuh-uh, nuh-uh" over and over.

"Open," Charlie commanded, opening his own mouth as an example. He needed braces.

"Nuh-uh."

"How will you know what you're missing? Joanie's mom makes the best sandwiches in the world. Why else do you think we're friends with her?"

Joanie gave Charlie a sideways look of near hatred before she pushed the middle of a sandwich half against Hyssop's closed mouth, smearing peanut butter on her lips. "Open up. Taste it."

"Nuh-uh." But it didn't matter. Peanut butter was touching Hyssop. It was too late. Her lips started to swell, and then her throat. Hyssop gasped, opening her mouth helplessly to get air, and Joanie shoved the sandwich in, folding it to make it all fit.

☽ Gevera Bert Piedmont ☾

The biker gang laughed as Hyssop spit it out and doubled over. Tears ran down her reddened cheeks as hives popped out on her face and neck. She grabbed at her throat and choked. The hives spread to her eyes. She lifted her face to the other kids, barely able to see them.

Joanie's mouth fell open. She already had braces. "Her eyes." Joanie backed up and hopped onto her bike, barely getting the kickstand up. Half the sandwich lay pristine in the road next to the scrunched-up, spit-out half. "We gotta go."

They fled.

Hyssop dragged her bike down the street to where she thought she had seen her father's truck, her vision growing narrower, her breathing heavier, her footsteps slowing, the shells and sea glass forgotten in the gutter. She did not make it all the way to the town works vehicles before she collapsed.

She gasped awake in the hospital and refused to say what had happened. It wasn't worth the hassle. Joanie wouldn't get in trouble for force-feeding her a peanut butter sandwich, nor would the boys for holding Hyssop down. Hyssop's heart was pounding from all the epinephrine, and her head felt swollen and unsteady, her skin itchy and two sizes too small.

"I don't remember," she lied in the car on the way home. "I didn't feel well and remembered seeing the town workers' trucks nearby."

"What were you doing in that part of town?" Her mother turned and looked over the front seat.

"I went to the beach but got detoured on the way back with all the trees down." Hyssop started to explain the wonderful black-purple hydra and decided not to. "To get sea glass and shells for Dad."

Her father's jaw hardened, but he said nothing, just kept driving.

"I'm sorry. I dropped the bags somewhere when I got sick. But the beach is all rearranged, and so much stuff washed up. I can find more, I'm sure. The tides won't come up that far again, and everything will still be there."

Would the hydra escape, or would it stay in the pool?

"You should stay home for a few days. The roads are dangerous," her mother said. "School is still out. I won't make you do any lessons."

☽ Biker Gang ☾

Hyssop scrunched her face. That meant the biker gang would be out and around, too. But she felt an urgent pull to see the black anemone again. "I'll be careful."

"I still don't understand how you got peanuts on your face."

"Some papers blew on me," Hyssop lied. "They must have been contaminated."

☾ ☆ ☽

Hyssop left home early, figuring the other kids would sleep late. Her dad's coworkers had returned her bike—they had recognized her, even though her dad hadn't been working with that crew. She wore a blue hooded sweatshirt because the morning was cool, but that wouldn't disguise her. Her bike's red banana seat and matching basket were distinctive, as was her skinny body.

The lower part of the beach was clean where the overnight high tide had scrubbed away Gloria's gifts. The scent of death had lessened, and fewer seagulls wheeled in the air. Footprints crowded the parallel rows of debris where others had beachcombed. Hyssop's heart sank. Maybe she could still find good glass and shells for her father.

But first, the tide pool. She searched the debris as she walked, finding another decent piece of driftwood to use as a poker. Other humans had been over here, too, and Hyssop worried about the anemone. Had someone taken it out of the tide pool? What if the Peabody Museum had heard of it and was writing a paper on it at this moment? Hyssop clambered over the rocks, slipping on the bladderwrack, heading to where she had last seen the black hydra.

Tide pools were usually rich with life. Sea urchins, sand dollars, starfish, mussels, seaweeds, crabs, sometimes a lobster, all sorts of small fish got trapped at low tide. Today, the pool looked empty. The rocks were stripped bare of mussels and barnacles. Of course, people ate mussels and even urchins, but usually would only clear a small area.

Hyssop's belly tightened, and her toes clenched inside her sneakers. Everything was gone. No darting silver killifish. And in the area where she had last seen the black hydra-bodied anemone, nothing. Just a flat place on the rock. At least she hadn't made a fool of herself telling her father about her discovery and dragging him here after a long day of work only to show him a bare rock and an empty tide pool.

She sat on the damp weeds. Her blue jeans immediately soaked up the cold moisture. Hyssop swished her poking stick

Gevera Bert Piedmont

through the water where the black hydra used to be. She tried to convince herself that no one had taken it; the returning high tide had swept it out to sea.

As she gazed away from the beach, far out toward the horizon, a bunch of tentacles writhed above the water's surface, like an enormous version of the small hydra. She blinked a few times until the illusion, the wish fulfillment, went away and banged the stick into the rock in frustration.

"I found one cool thing for once," Hyssop said to the empty tide pool. "And I couldn't even have that." She dug her heels into the slick weeds, popping the air bladders. She pushed the broken plants into the pool and tried to hit them with her stick.

The hydra crept from under a nearby rock overhang. It was almost three feet tall, half of that whiplike tentacles. The tentacles grabbed the broken bladderwort and shoved it into the hydra's mouth.

Hyssop's bottom lip sagged. A couple of tentacles stuck out of the water in her direction.

"Are you hungry?"

She tore handfuls of bladderwrack and handed it to the hydra, watching it eat.

"You're just a baby," she realized. "A hungry baby." A baby *what*? Hyssop turned her head toward the horizon again. Had she really seen those enormous tentacles lashing the morning sky? "You ate everything in the pool, didn't you?" Since yesterday.

Hyssop sat on the cold, wet rock and fed handfuls of bladderwrack, seaweed, and whatever she could reach to the hydra's tentacles. She reconsidered telling the Peabody Museum about this creature.

"I'll find something else for you to eat," she promised the hydra, pushing herself to her feet. As she walked, she shoved vegetation into the pool. Her parents had taught her the exact opposite, not to tear up the seaweeds, but this was a special case. The hydra had already denuded the pool of life.

As she searched for sea glass and shells, Hyssop filled another bag with bits of dead things, scrunching her nose at the smell. Crab pinchers, mostly, ripe and stinking, in one bag. Blue and green glass and unbroken shells in the other. It felt like others had already picked over the area, and footprints proved that point. Hyssop felt tired, a reaction to yesterday's allergy attack and treatment, and she still had to pedal home. Scooping up some seaweeds that didn't look too dried out, she tossed them

☽ Biker Gang ☾

in with the crab claws and trudged back toward the tide pool. She didn't crawl back across the rocks, just went to the edge nearest the shore and peered into the water at the bare sand. The hydra was nowhere in sight.

"I brought you something." She upended the bag. Rotten bits of crab drifted to the bottom. The plants floated, buoyed by their air bubbles.

The hydra moved faster than Hyssop imagined, darting from behind a boulder and advancing toward her through the sand. It had five thick legs, perhaps making it related to starfish and other five-petaled sea creatures. Its whiplike tentacles flailed and snatched the pieces of crab, seaweed, and other debris from the water. After it had taken everything, it waited, tentacles undulating in Hyssop's direction.

"I don't have anything else right now."

A few of the whip ends poked out of the water at Hyssop. She licked her dry, swollen lips, sensitive since yesterday's peanut butter fiasco. Whatever this creature was, today it was big enough to threaten her. The hydra could have drowned her if Hyssop had gotten in the water with it.

"I'm sorry. I'll try to come back later, or tomorrow."

The tentacles withdrew.

Hyssop walked a few steps away and turned back. The hydra was retreating.

As she put the bag of glass and shells into her bike basket, she chewed her lower lip and again reconsidered telling her father and the Peabody Museum. Whatever this giant anemone was, it was unique. It had grown in a single day from something the size of her hands to over half her height.

Tomorrow, it might leave with the tide.

Hyssop pedaled out of the parking lot and leaned to make the right-hand turn. The hydra needed food, and it wasn't getting any more in that small tide pool.

She decided to fill a bag with deadfall apples. Gloria had knocked so many off her mom's trees. The hydra didn't seem fussy. Hyssop could get back to the beach before the next high tide with the apples, and if the hydra seemed inclined to stick around, she would tell her dad that night.

Deep in thought, Hyssop hadn't been paying attention to her surroundings again. Workers had cleared much of the downed trees and storm debris, and she hadn't had to detour.

"Fat face!" Joanie yelled.

Gevera Bert Piedmont

Hyssop closed her eyes for a moment but had to open them to keep pedaling.

"Look at her face," Charlie taunted. "Skeletor with a fat face."

Her three nemeses rolled from a side street and ambushed Hyssop, surrounding her. She stopped.

"What happened to your face?" Charlie cocked his head. The late morning sun glinted off his glasses.

Hyssop sucked her lips into her mouth and stared at him. Could they really be that stupid?

"She's always been that ugly," Ted offered. His front wheel nudged Hyssop's leg.

"I got another sandwich for you," Joanie offered, patting her fanny pack. "Since you enjoyed the one I gave you yesterday so much."

Despair flooded Hyssop. They were never, ever going to stop. Next year they'd all be in high school, and the torment would continue for four more long years, but even then, Hyssop could not go off to college and escape them; she would have to stay home where milk and bread and peanut butter would not kill her, and these three and their assorted friends would be there too, forever plaguing her.

Her future stretched before her, with a gang of kids on bikes around every corner, just waiting with peanut butter sandwiches in hand.

She released her lips, blowing them out. "I found something cool on the beach after the storm."

Charlie scoffed. "Like what? A flower?"

Hyssop turned her head and stared through the glasses into his tiny eyes. "A dead shark."

"A shark?" Ted pushed his bike harder against her leg.

"No way." Joanie's hand tightened on her fanny pack.

"Yeah." Hyssop put her fist on Ted's front wheel and shoved it away. "I think it's a great white. A big one."

"No one else said anything. Everyone's been to the beach," Joanie argued.

Hyssop shrugged one shoulder and kept her eyes locked on Charlie's. "I was gonna go pull out its teeth or maybe take the whole jaw."

"No way," Joanie repeated. "We're gonna take its jaw. It's ours."

)) Biker Gang ((

"Do you know where it is?" Hyssop twisted Ted's wheel, and he almost fell.

"We'll find it." Charlie broke Hyssop's stare.

A one-shoulder shrug again. "Maybe. And maybe I'll get to it first."

Charlie and Joanie wheeled around to head to the beach, but Hyssop clutched Ted's bike by its twisted front wheel.

"Leggo!"

She tilted her head. "What's wrong? You don't like it when someone holds your bike and you want to leave?"

"Weirdo, leggo!" Ted pushed at her hand. "Hey! Joanie! Charlie! Wait up!"

Hyssop took a deep breath and shoved Ted hard enough that he and his bike tumbled over. Then she pedaled her own bike, hard, around the block and back toward the beach, knowing she wouldn't beat Charlie and Joanie unless they grew hearts and waited for Ted.

They did not grow hearts. They had thrown their bikes carelessly at the bike rack, unlocked. Hyssop arrived, her breath rasping in her throat, and took the time to lock her bike, snapping the hasp just as Ted arrived. She took off running, her long, skinny legs churning the sand as she crossed the dune to the beach proper.

Hyssop glanced to the right toward the tide pool and saw no one. Fresh scuffed tracks led left to where Charlie and Joanie walked at the edge of the headland as it curved, searching, pushing each other.

Ted came up behind Hyssop and shoved her, but she expected him and did not fall.

"Where is the shark?" He turned his head both ways. "I don't see it."

"Exactly," Hyssop said. "But they went the wrong way. It's hidden. That's why no one else has found it."

"Guys!" Ted yelled, waving his arms.

Hyssop grabbed at him. "You want to share with them?"

He subsided. "But I gotta share with you?"

"I found it. I didn't have to tell you all about it." Hyssop found her stick where she had dropped it earlier and headed toward the tide pool, her heart pounding. "I thought we could all be friends instead of you guys ragging on me all the time if I showed you something awesome."

Ted followed her and didn't agree.

☽ Gevera Bert Piedmont ☾

Hyssop walked in her own footprints from earlier, heel to toe. With every step, her heart moved further into her throat. She thought of the map of the rest of her life, of being tormented at every turn.

"How big do you think the shark is?" Ted said finally. "Do you think we could cut off the fins too?"

Hyssop nodded, no longer capable of speaking. She pointed to the tide pool.

"It's in the pool? Is it all rotten?"

She stopped at the edge, in her own footprints again, and Ted stood beside her. He was shorter than she was. Hyssop glanced left where Joanie and Charlie were now headed in her direction, still apparently arguing and pushing each other.

"I don't see it. Someone else must have found it." He leaned forward.

"It's in there." Hyssop's voice cracked. She swished her stick in the pool with one hand and placed her other hand gently on Ted's back.

The hydra darted from behind the boulder.

Hyssop shoved Ted into the cold water.

The hydra shot forward and enveloped Ted headfirst with its tentacles. A huge bubble rolled to the surface. Disturbed sand clouded the water. After a moment, Hyssop turned away and put the stick over her shoulder, waiting for Charlie and Joanie.

Something touched her foot, and she glanced down to see how much the hydra had grown. It was probably as tall as her shoulder.

It was stroking her Converse high-top with one tentacle with apparent affection.

Another pair of sneakers, blue ones, lay discarded in the sand beside torn scraps of material.

"Hey!" Joanie yelled. "Where's Ted?"

"He had a terrible reaction to some shellfish," Hyssop said blandly. "Come and see."

☾ ☆ ☽

Gevera Bert Piedmont *is a neurodivergent cyborg swamp witch living on the edge of a frog pond in Connecticut with her spouse, cats, and an impressive collection of rubber lizards. She is the author of* The Maw and Other Time-Traveling Lizard Tales, *the Mickey Crow paranormal series, coauthor of* Airesford *(the other author is an actual zombie), and editor of the* Necronomi-RomCom Cthulhu Mythos *duology. Her short stories have been published*

☽ Biker Gang ☾

in Love Beyond Death, The Fellowship of the Old Ones, Heart of Farkness, Through a Scanner Farkly, Doomscrolling, Wicked Sick, Something Woked This Way Comes, *and others. Her novel* Fat Monster *will be published by Nightmare Press in late 2024.*

Bert has an MFA in creative writing and belongs to the Horror Writers Association, Connecticut Authors and Publishers Association, and New England Horror Writers. Connect with her on Facebook @geverabertpiedmont, at geverabertpiedmont.com or obsidianbutterfly.com, or on her Amazon and Goodreads author pages.

A Home for His Fears

Anne Woods

It was the farthest north he had ever gone, and Mike knew it would end in disaster.

Normally, his mom didn't like the boys to go past the old Franklin place on their bikes, the beige one-story rambler with the gnome in the yard on the corner of Cow Hill and Anne. The face on it was so bleached the only distinguishable feature left was the black pupils of its eyes. The effect gave the gnome a wide-eyed appearance, the little clay figurine perpetually surprised at the activity going on around him.

More like surprised at how boring it is, Mike thought as he pedaled harder. His older brother Gary called Old Mystic "a nothing town," and Mike had to agree. He had the suspicion that someday, when he was grown, he'd look back at this time, and he wouldn't be able to remember a thing about it. It would just be a haze of summers and school days and little dots of holidays, all blended together like a thin soup. When anyone asked, he'd respond that his childhood was "fine," unable to recall whether it was a good or bad one in particular. The idea that the moments of his life were going to waste sent an anxious shot of adrenaline to his belly whenever he stayed on it too long.

Mike leaned forward. The road began a gradual climb up Pumpkin Hill, and his legs burned with effort. He felt a little panic in his chest as he fell behind. The other boys all had newer bikes with gears to help them, but Mike just had his older sister's single-speed with the banana seat. He tolerated the yellow color but had cut the tassels off the handlebars the first chance he got. The other boys were nice enough to say nothing at all when they saw it, though he figured getting teased for it would have been easier.

☽ A Home for His Fears ☾

Roger called out to him, half turning on his seat and almost tipping his Schwinn over in the process. "C'mon, man! You gotta see it!" He turned back around and righted himself, swerving away from a collision with the Johnson's mailbox at the last second.

Mike didn't have the room in his lungs to answer and just nodded. Even if he did, he wouldn't have said anything, too worried that he'd start begging them to turn around if he opened his mouth. That anxious feeling, the one that showed up out of nowhere this year on the first day of junior high, had settled deep into his chest that morning. He knew it would be there to stay until he went to sleep that night, lying in bed and looking at the glow-in-the-dark stars on his ceiling. He'd toss and turn, feeling guilty for being afraid, and ashamed that he couldn't even name what it was about. His mom had asked him at the breakfast table a few days ago what he was so worried about all the time. Mike had just shrugged, but what he really wanted to say was, "Everything, but why aren't you?"

He wished he could be like Gary, who worried about one normal thing at a time. Right now, it was his college applications. Last week, it was whether Jenny Hooper would go with him to homecoming. Gary never seemed to think there was a disaster around every corner, just waiting to ruin his life in the blink of an eye.

"C'mon Mikey!" called Roger.

The boys had paused at the crest of the hill. Mike pushed a little harder, his calves and thighs screaming as he pumped the pedals. His jaw ached from how tightly he held his mouth shut. He hadn't even wanted to go on this stupid adventure to begin with.

When Roger had appeared in the clubhouse that morning, claiming that something was up at the old house on top of the hill and they should all go check it out, Mike was reluctant. There could be (probably was) something dangerous in the house, but it was more likely something normal, like a rotted roof ready to cave in or spiders. Even if there wasn't, he'd spend the whole time they were there nervous about whether his parents would find out. They never yelled, but they had perfected the art of being disappointed, and it sent him spiraling on the occasions it was directed at him.

Mike didn't really believe the house was haunted, but the place sure looked like it could be. Roger claimed he had seen someone in the second-story window early that morning, as he sat in the back of his dad's Chevy on their way home from running errands. A ghostly figure grabbed at the rotting curtains and held a finger up to its lips to shush him as he stared. Mike was sure Roger saw something, but more likely it was a breeze lifting the curtains or a trapped bird flitting against the windows.

Mike didn't believe in haunted houses because he didn't believe in ghosts. He used to be uncertain about the tooth fairy, but then caught his dad slipping a fiver under his pillow one night after he lost a molar. The things that Mike worried about were the only scary things you *should* worry about. A sudden fire burning the house down, his dad losing his job at the factory. Getting tetanus from an old nail at the clubhouse. Taxes, a concept Mike was pretty unclear about but knew enough of to be overly concerned with. There were too many honest-to-God dangers to worry about things that probably (maybe?) didn't exist.

Pulling to a stop in front of Roger and Andy, Mike panted and then gave a thumbs-up, his hand shaking. They all took off in a rush, riding wavy lines down the middle of the street and laughing. Steve was at the front, looking serious as always, followed by Roger and Andy riding side by side. Andy was trying to see how close he could get to Roger before their spokes touched, occasionally misjudging the distance and sending the two of them careening away from one another like bumper cars. Mike brought up the rear and tried to ignore the feeling that the world was creeping up and just about to tap him on the shoulder.

Mike thought over Roger's story as they pedaled the last few blocks. The pavement had flattened out, and he was able to pedal idly, his heart rate slowing and his breath returning to normal. To Mike, the tale seemed suspiciously specific. Someone shushing Roger was an odd thing to make up a story about. Maybe someone down on their luck had found their way into the house. There had been more of them lately in town, holding cardboard signs saying *help plese* and other misspelled sentiments, standing at stop signs with cups at their feet, staring into each car as if it may be the one to save them.

"They're barking up the wrong tree in Old Mystic," Mike's dad had said. "The cops will just drop them off in the next town over." It was never the same people twice at the stop sign, a rotating cast of characters that all seemed to wear the same uniform of dirty jeans and a pair of sad eyes. Mike's dad would never look at them, keeping his eyes straight ahead, but Mike would look.

☽ A Home for His Fears ☾

He felt like it was the least he could do, to help them be seen, if even for just a moment.

Racing along the last block, they pulled to a stop in front of the house. The word *dilapidated* came to mind. Mike spelled it wrong two times in a row on the weekly spelling bees in English class, and he couldn't think of a better description for the place that sat before him.

He hadn't seen it in a while, but it looked just the same. The old house was two stories of flaking red paint, torn shingles, and cobwebbed eaves, a small front porch too shadowed for how bright the afternoon sun was. The filthy windows were covered in a layer of yellow grime like the old aquarium in the garage at his house. A screen door leading into the front swung back and forth on rusty hinges, slamming against the house with every pass, then bouncing enthusiastically open again.

See, thought Mike. *A breeze*. It was probably always just a breeze in these types of stories. The thought should have reassured him, but it didn't. He was chilled from the inside out standing before it. The sun only warmed the outside parts of him, the very top layer of his skin hot but everything else underneath frozen solid.

"She was right there." Roger pointed at the second-story window on the end. The sunlight reflected off the pane of glass, dark from the gray curtains just behind it.

A trick of the light, Mike thought.

A trick of delight, said another voice inside him. It sounded a lot like the one that spoke to him at 2:00 a.m. Although his legs felt shaky, there was something wonderfully delicious about being scared of a specific thing, a ghost in a house instead of whether there'd be a quiz on *Romeo and Juliet* at school on Monday or what it meant when his parents argued in hushed voices from behind their bedroom door, his mom coming out wiping red eyes on the sleeve of her favorite sweater. This was a safe kind of fear.

Mike looked at the rotting structure in front of him, could almost see the woman inside peeking up from the bottom of the window. This house would be an excellent place to store your fears for a little while. The walls may be falling down, but the bones were good underneath, the structure itself standing strong even in the face of a Connecticut winter.

"I don't see anything, man. Are you sure?" Steve pushed his glasses back up his face and looked up with narrowed eyes as if squinting would give him X-ray vision to see into the bedroom. His parents worked in a lab, though Mike didn't think they were scientists. Steve was always questioning everything and calling it "the scientific method." It drove Roger up a wall.

"So sure. Like, beyond sure. She was so spooky. She held onto the curtain with one hand and was like— " Roger mimicked what he had seen, shushing them all with his caterpillar eyebrows raised and one hand gripping an imaginary curtain, his mouth open just a hair to show the tips of his crooked bottom teeth.

"Have you considered the possibility . . . " Andy looked about the group with a smirk. "That you're just an idiot?" He burst into laughter, his mouth open and arms wrapped around himself. Roger pushed him, and Andy took a couple steps back, but he couldn't keep his donkey laugh inside. Steve cracked a smile and even Mike chuckled a bit. He wished he could laugh as big as Andy and not feel weird about it.

If only I didn't think so hard all the time, he thought.

"Maybe we should go inside?" said Roger, and the four looked at one another. It was obvious none of them wanted to, but each wanted even less to be the one to admit it.

"Yes," said Steve finally. Mike caught Andy's eye and was happy to see that Andy looked as reluctant as he felt. His laughs had died off, and he was staring at the ground. Mike was hoping they'd find the door locked, maybe poke around in the yard a bit, then get home in time to watch *Jurassic Park* on Friday Night Flicks. "We should probably investigate Roger's theory." Roger rolled his eyes as Steve put the kickstand down on his bike and headed for the space in the front fence where a gate had probably once hung. "Scientific process, and all that." He pushed his glasses back up his nose, and Roger followed behind him.

Andy mimicked Steve behind his back, sticking his tongue out the side of his mouth and crossing his eyes, then sliding an imaginary pair of frames up. Mike snorted and waved him off. They all walked behind Steve up onto the front porch, the steps creaking under their weight and the wood giving way a little with an alarming, soggy feeling. Mike could imagine falling through the porch, the sharpened ends of the broken wood tearing into his ankles, his foot burying into the muck and the insects below.

Infection, he thought. *Tetanus.*

"You coming, Mikey?" Andy asked.

Mike had paused at the front door as they all went inside.

☽ A Home for His Fears ☾

"Yeah . . . " he said. "Yeah." Mike didn't particularly want to go inside the house, but he certainly didn't want to wait alone on the front porch while everyone else did. Especially not this front porch, with the broken railing and the bit of lacy wooden trim that hung down. He glanced out at the street and it felt like he was peering from between a whale's jaws, the great teeth ready to close and carry him to the bottom of the ocean in an instant.

No, he would not be waiting out here, please and thank you.

The boys filed into the house and stood in the entryway, each displaying their own little nervous tics Mike had gotten to know over the years. Steve rubbed his hands on his pants over and over again, and Roger shifted from one foot to the other, a little dance that made a slight *shush* sound as his Chuck Taylors rubbed against the floor.

Andy was still, which was unusual. Andy rarely held still. Mike had lost count of the number of times he'd been sent to the principal's office for fidgeting in his chair during class. The last time Andy had cried out, "I just can't hold still, I just can't!" as he walked out, looking at Mike as if the boy could fix it. Mike hadn't slept for two nights straight thinking Andy was mad at him for doing nothing, until Andy showed up at his house that Thursday with the newest Spiderman comic like nothing had happened. For Andy, he knew, it hadn't.

"Should we go up?" Andy whispered, and even his quiet voice was too loud for the space.

Steve nodded, and held up a finger to shush the boys, then crept toward the stairs. Mike wondered if the woman waiting up there had had such a wide-eyed expression on her face when she stared at Roger.

The boys climbed the creaky treads to the landing and then continued to the second floor. They stepped into the hall. Mike knew they weren't as sneaky as they were hoping to be. Four young boys, stomping and coughing from the dust and twisting this way and that to try to keep their eyes everywhere at once, were about as subtle as an elephant. Especially in a house such as this one where the cartilage was long gone and bones ground upon bones. Every moment caused something to crack or squeak or let out some other little sigh of old age and protest.

The boys paused. There were four doors on alternating sides of the long hallway, a rotting red carpet rolled out on the floor between them like a dog's long tongue. Each door was slightly ajar, save the very last.

☽ Anne Woods ☾

Steve led, with Roger, Andy, and Mike behind him. Mike felt the heat of the other boys across his front, leaving the backside of him cold. It was too easy to imagine something coming out of the space behind him, pushing through the gold rays of sun that streamed through holes in the wall and the open windows in the rooms, lighting a million flecks of dust that refused to settle. Something that might slip a finger down his spine, or whisper something terrible in his ear.

A trick of the light, a trick of delight.

Mike turned just to be sure, but nothing was there. Not even a faint breeze of something just gone by. The hallway was empty; the stairs were silent.

"Look!" hissed Roger, pointing into the first open door. The boys crowded around and peered in.

A grand desk stood in the middle of the room, facing the doorway. It was dark wood with a green square on top, adorned with a small lamp and several rotting books. It reminded Mike of his grandfather, a lawyer down South with a sugar-coated accent and a barrel chest. He had died behind a desk much like this one last summer, a heart attack that left him face down and dead on a Tuesday afternoon. It was the first death Mike had ever known, and it made dying seem a more tangible thing to the boy, not some far-fetched urban legend but a real thing that could strike anywhere and anytime.

Light filtered through the window, illuminating the thick layer of dust coating all the surfaces. The room even smelled like Grandpa, cigar and leather and the slightest scent of sweat that people in South Carolina always carried with them. Not the acrid kind that seemed to come from his own body these days, but sweet sweat diluted in aftershave. A great leatherback chair sat behind the desk, swiveled to one side like the occupant had jumped up in a mad rush to be somewhere else. A grandfather clock ticked from a dark corner. Mike could hear it but couldn't see it. He was amazed that it still ran, after how long this house had stood empty.

The boys stepped back and exchanged a glance. Mike could see they felt it too, that sense that though the room was dusty and decrepit (another spelling bee word), they had only just missed someone leaving.

They continued down the hall, passing a bathroom on the right. Mike half expected to see the clawfoot tub still full of steamy water, a faucet drip drip dripping away, but it was empty, save a

☾ A Home for His Fears ☾

gray ring around the inside that marked where the water used to be. The filthy white octagon tiles on the floor were unbroken, but the tile behind the tub was shattered, a hole in the center large enough to fit his entire fist inside. The edge of the tub there was chipped, and he wondered what sort of accident was responsible for the damage.

A trick of the light and of violent delights, said the voice inside him.

Creeping, creeping so slowly he felt they hardly moved at all, they drew ever closer to the room at the end of the hall where Roger saw his ghost. Mike's heart was beating harder now, just as it did when he pedaled up the hill. He had the inescapable idea that he was on that hill again and just about to tip over the other side when his pedals would spin freely and he couldn't brake too hard without fear of flying off the seat altogether.

The third door was open wide, an ancient nursery long abandoned. In the middle of the room sat a crib with a rotted veil around it. A mobile spun idly in the corner over a warped changing table, a collection of circus animals and clowns suspended from each wire. It looked just like his baby sister's room, so real he thought that he might see Julie curled up and sleeping if he tiptoed over and peered over the side of the crib.

The other boys wandered down the hall uninterested, but Mike hesitated. On the floor lay a teddy bear, both eyes missing, just like Julie's bear. One eye had fallen off, and Mike's parents had worried she would swallow and choke on the other one, so they pulled that one off, too. Julie, too young to be disturbed by the ragged appearance of the bear, happily went back to gripping it in one sticky fist, dragging it about and occasionally drooling as she gnawed on its arms and legs.

Mike heard a noise from the crib, a faint rustling like a babe tossing and turning as it woke from a nap. He crept closer and could see a bundle inside it moving about, obscured by the sheer curtain that hung from the ceiling. A snuffling sound was coming from it, like a babe rooting about for a bit of mother's milk.

He reached the edge and brushed the curtain aside. He held his breath low in his chest. Mike reached slowly for the blankets, suddenly sure that when he pulled them back, he'd see his baby sister all pale and splotched in death, milk-white eyes staring back at him in confusion. He peeled the blankets back, needing to know. There was a child's onesie underneath, no arms or legs or head poking out, the whole torso wriggling like worms under a corpse's skin.

A skinny rat burst out of where the belly would be as Mike reached into the crib, hissing at him with a broken yellow tooth and black eyes. It dashed away, and the front flap of the outfit was thrown open. The rat had nested inside, stuffing the onesie with loose bits of paper and rags. In the center, naked and pink, lay a baby rat, surrounded by a mess of tissue and blood. Its brothers and sisters had probably been devoured, and only this one survived. Mike remembered hearing that animals did that sometimes. Blue veins pulsed just under the surface of its translucent skin.

"Mike?" Roger whispered from the hall. In disgust, Mike covered up the nest with the blanket and raced out to join them, trying not to picture a skinny rat watching him hungrily from the shadowed corners of the nursery.

The boys were standing in front of the last room, the only one with a closed door. They cast glances back and forth, none of them speaking but all with the understanding that sooner or later, one of them would need to be the one to open it. Mike avoided all their eyes, pretending to take an interest in the walls around him. A picture hung, the only one he had seen. It was a portrait of a young family, a seated woman with an infant on her lap, and a man standing behind her, one hand gripping her shoulder tightly. They had that thousand-yard stare that Mike always saw in old photos, the irises too white and their mouths smashed into thin, hard lines. Mike heard the turning of the doorknob and looked up.

It was Andy opening it, to Mike's surprise. Andy was almost as nervous a person as Mike, though he hid it better from everyone else. They talked about their greatest fears during backyard campouts, when Roger and Steve were snoring and the flashlight was off for the night. Andy always talked about getting stuck in the same town forever, growing old in front of the television with his mom in their two-bedroom ranch that reeked of cigarette smoke and heavy perfume. Mike told Andy about how sometimes his palms sweated and his heart raced, how he thought everyone was angry at him all the time.

Andy leaned around the door and peered in, his small, close-set eyes and his pointed nose vaguely reminiscent of the rat in the nursery.

☽ A Home for His Fears ☾

"It's empty," he said after a moment. He wasn't whispering now, and his voice sounded too loud in the house. Mike resisted the urge to shush him.

The baby is sleeping, thought Mike, then he shook the idea away.

Andy threw open the door and revealed a perfectly normal bedroom. A king-sized bed with an intricately carved wooden headboard filled most of the room, with a set of mismatched dressers against the walls and a small vanity with a stool set in one corner. The carpet was shaggy and out of date but clean, and the closet doors, the accordion type his mother hated in her own house, were closed but looked freshly painted.

The window where Roger had seen the woman was cracked open, the curtains billowing just slightly in the breeze.

"I knew it was the wind," said Steve, trying to slam the window shut and failing. It was stuck fast, open an inch or two and swollen from decades of rain. The boys began to chatter and interrupt one another, the giddy sort of talk kids share when they've all been afraid for no reason. Mike rarely had that sensation himself. The voice was always ready to chime in with a *but it could really happen the next time*, and that sense of dread would come rushing back in.

Mike looked about the room as they chattered at one another and laughed, but it was hard to focus on anything other than the headboard. He stepped closer to it, leaning in and peering at the delicate carvings. When he first spotted it, he assumed they were just artistic swirls and random designs to fill the space, but now that he was closer, he could see there were little scenes in each notch and rise of the wood. Crowds of people with horns on their heads, their arms raised and legs kicked out wildly this way and that. A pulpit and a preacher, an angry look on his face and a fist raised as he shrieked about the eternalness of damnation. A woman, on her knees and crying as the flames grew up around her. In the center, a man's stern face carved into the wood, his pupils raised in relief and watching everything around him.

A hand touched his back and Mike jumped, but it was only Roger. Mike noticed a bible on the bedside table, the pages waterlogged and stained, the front cover warped. A crucifix was next to it, a shiny maroon ribbon threaded through the top. The end of the metal cross was filed to a point.

Violent delights should be kept out of sight, the voice purred to him.

☽ Anne Woods ☾

"This place gives me the creeps, man," Roger said, and his eyes darted about. "Let's get out of here." The other boys were standing behind him, and they, too, seemed frightened, huddled together for safety. Mike did find it weird that the rest of the house would be so dilapidated but this room was still in perfect order. Some squatter had obviously maintained and lived in it; the bed looked slept in. Mike wondered what he would see if he went into the kitchen, if there would be a pan with the remains of scrambled eggs on the stove and a fresh loaf of bread on the counter.

The boys turned to go. The closet door opened. A woman in a tattered dress slipped out and stepped into the room. Her hair hung in greasy coils around her face, and dirt was smudged across the skin of her bare arms. Mike knew in that moment he wouldn't find that fresh loaf of bread on the counter, because she was too thin to have eaten properly in weeks. Her skin clung around each rib, the space above her collarbones so hollowed he could see the outline of every tendon in her neck. She brushed the hair out of her face with a skeleton hand, the bones of her fingers click-clacking against her skull as she did it.

Roger and Andy screamed and Steve worked his mouth up and down silently, and then they were off, bolting out the door and clattering down the stairs together. Mike's legs had ceased to work and he was frozen in place, staring down at the carpet instead of at the horror that rocked back and forth on thin legs before him. He had been wrong; it wasn't all clean. There was a patch here that looked like dried blood, the shag matted and crusty with something dark red. He thought he could smell it if he really concentrated. It was the scent of pennies and something rotten, roadkill on the shoulder when you had the car windows open in the summer.

The smell of your grandfather in the ground, his body melting to nothing.

The woman shuffled across the carpet closer to him. A pair of faded pink slippers were loose on her feet where the fat and muscle used to fill in the spaces between her toes. She stood silent in front of him. He didn't want to, but Mike raised his eyes and saw her.

Her face was drawn and her jaw hung open, swollen lips encircling her mouth. Between her teeth, he could see a blackened tongue poking at this tooth and that one as if it was trying to remember its purpose. Her eyes were sunk and wide. The skin

☽ A Home for His Fears ☾

of her eyelids had long retracted back, and he could see the tops of her eyeballs as they darted around in the socket.

"*Beb?*" she groaned.

Mike could only stare. His heart beat against his ribs so hard it hurt, each thump a painful reminder of his own frailty, how, just like this woman, he was only skin stretched tight over bones.

"*Beb?*" she said with urgency. "*Beeeeeeeeeb?*" She glanced at the door and back at him, running that worm tongue over her cracked lips. The others were long gone; he could hear them outside screaming to one another in the yard, though the buzzing in his ears obscured their words.

She shifted from one foot to the other almost nervously, watching him as intently as he did her. He could sense she was growing frustrated.

"*Beb?*" she asked again.

"I don't— " his voice cracked. "I don't know what you mean," he whispered, afraid this answer would send her into a fury where she scratched at his face with those thin, clawed fingers and pressed her swollen lips to his ear, screaming.

"*Beb. Beeeeebbb*," she tried again. As she said it, she held her arms up and entangled them, mimicked rocking a sleeping child in front of her chest.

"Baby?" he asked. "You . . . you want your baby?"

She nodded, her teeth clicking shut with every jerk of her head, the muscles on the sides of her skull thin and weak.

"All right. All right," he said to himself. He glanced down the hall, and she stepped back. He floated to the door and toward the nursery, his limbs tingling with fear so badly he couldn't feel the bottoms of his feet or the palms of his hands, like he had spent too long in the cold. She followed him until he got to the door, and then she stopped, eyeing the threshold.

Mike went into the hall. He could run, but maybe it would set her off, send her running after him, furious and violent, as her steps pounded down the hall behind him. He glanced up again at the photo and thought of the people at the stoplight begging *help plese*; he thought of Andy's eyes begging him to make things okay. Mike looked toward the nursery and moved closer to the crib. The skinny rat was still gone, but the baby was there, nestled under the covers among the grim remains of its siblings.

Mike could hear the woman down the hall calling, "*Beb? Beb?*" in an increasingly frantic voice, and he knew if he didn't stop it, she'd begin to screech. If he heard the noise, when he tried to run out the front door, he'd find himself trapped by the threshold too, staring out the windows as the cars and the other kids went by, shushing them to be quiet and *oh God* he'd be trapped in here with her for an eternity in the dark and the quiet.

Violent delights, said the voice, giddily. *Violent delights that come out at night.*

Mike scooped up the baby rat and the onesie. The nest gave the clothing some vague impression of a baby's torso, but it smelled of mildew and rat feces, and he felt desperate to wash his hands in water so hot it would burn. He walked back down the hall and stood at the door. He saw what the others probably did, that the room actually *was* as decrepit as the rest of the house, the wooden dressers stained and rotting, black mold crawling from the carpet up the walls to the sill of the window.

The woman rushed at him and greedily scooped up the bundle in her arms. He tried not to recoil as her fingers brushed him, the places where she touched him burning just under the skin. She cried tears that smelled like algae from a stale pond. She rocked it and cooed; the blanket squirmed under her touch.

"*Beb*," she said, over and over.

Mike turned and ran, slipping on the carpet in the hall. He dashed down the stairs, rotten boards cracking under the impact of his feet. He felt the faintest pull on him at the front door, a sudden sensation that he was running into a strong wind, but managed to burst through and erupt into the bright sun on the other side. He fell to his knees in the brown grass and put his hands over his ears and screamed, not caring about the scent of disease and filth that covered him.

The other boys gathered around and yelled his name, and all Mike could think was *Shhh, shhhh, beb is sleeping*.

(☆)

For Roger, Andy, and Steve, the memories of the house faded and became softer with time, until the day came that Mike listened, horrified, as they reminisced and laughed about it. He guessed the woman had never been real for them, just a closet door that happened to open at an inopportune time, their own imaginations filling in the blanks. Mike never shared what he experienced. When Andy asked at a campout years later, Mike said he was just too scared to move, that it had all been nothing more than a trick of the breeze through a stuck window.

A trick of delights, he thought.

☽ A Home for His Fears ☾

Mike couldn't share it with Andy. Not only would the boy not understand, but Mike *wanted* to keep the memory to himself. That was the way it stayed pure, so he could bring it up in his mind anytime his anxiety began to spiral.

If he ever lost it, all he had to do was bike up Pumpkin Hill to the house at the top and watch the second-story window. She'd peek out eventually, skeleton fingers clutching the thin curtain. Most times she'd be clutching the onesie, dancing and rocking it back and forth. But sometimes, her arms would be empty, and she'd raise one finger to her lips.

Mike would pedal away with a smile on his face, his heart thumping in relief.

Shhhh, he'd think. *Beb is sleeping.*

☾ ☆ ☽

Anne Woods *is a New England author with works produced through the Creepy podcast, Shacklebound Books, and Max Blood's Mausoleum. When she is not writing, she enjoys gardening and hiking through dark forests with her rescue dogs. Her stories and other information can be found at campsite.bio/thewriterannewoods or through her social media @thewriterannewoods on Instagram and @thewriteranne on Twitter.*

Ouch

Sasha Brown

The creature was almost to the Natchaug River when the three boys caught it. They surrounded it, straddling their bikes.

"Where you goin', glow-ass motherfucker?" said the skinny one with a cackling laugh.

"Home," said the creature.

"They won't take you back," said the leader, with a leather jacket and a baseball bat. "I messed with a baby bunny once, and its mother wouldn't take it back. It smelled like humans. Starved to death under the deck. Your freaky little friends won't want you back either, after what we do to you." Without warning, he swung the bat against the creature's head. Its long neck wilted sideways, and it let out a bleating moan.

"You ain't goin' nowhere," said the third, biggest boy. "Not 'til you make us fly."

They shoved it into a basket on the front of the leader's bike. It tried to climb out, so the leader hit it with the bat again. Its body was brittle in this world's heavy atmosphere, and the bat cracked its leg in the wrong direction. The boys wrapped duct tape around the creature, layer after layer, securing it in the basket.

"We saw what you did with them little shits," said the leader.

"Made their bikes fly," said the big one.

"Now you're gonna make our fuckin' bikes fly," said the skinny one. "Gonna be fuckin' rad."

The boys pedaled hard through the woods, but their bikes didn't leave the ground. The creature tried, but it was in too much pain; it couldn't concentrate. Finally, they pulled over.

"Bug-eyed bitch needs some motivation," said the skinny one, raising his fists. The creature held its hands in front of its

☽ Ouch ☾

face, and the skinny kid grabbed and wrenched its spindly fingers, bending them backward until they popped and splintered against its wrist. They snapped easily, like brittle twigs, and no blood came out. The boy held them there, looking into its eyes as if searching for something.

The creature groaned, wide-eyed. It had not known torture before. It hadn't known anger, either.

"You motivated now, you creepy fuck? You ready to make us fly?" said the leader, and the creature nodded. It was concentrating now. The bikes wobbled, hopped . . . and then soared into the sky.

"Woohoo!" cried the boys, pedaling through the night air.

The trees whipped by, and the creature reached out to one of them with its botanist's mind. An oak groaned, new growth splintering from its trunk, rushing out.

The big boy drove head-on into the new branch. Its jagged point entered his mouth and erupted from the back of his head. His bike wobbled and tumbled into the brush.

"What the fuck!" yelled the leader. "Did you fuckin' do that, you little alien creep?"

The skinny boy's wheels spun faster and faster, blurring. His hand moved involuntarily toward his front tire. "Make it stop!" he shrieked. "Help!" He grabbed his wrist and tried to pull away, but an invisible force yanked him forward until his fingers slipped into the whirring spokes. The wheel jammed; bloody fingers fell through the night; the skinny boy flew over the handlebars, clutching his ruined hand and screaming all the way down.

"You did this," hissed the leader. He raised his bat again, but he didn't strike. If he hurt the creature now . . . he was a hundred feet in the air and going higher.

Much higher. The Natchaug forest became splinters below them. The moon loomed huge as they crossed before it. Wisps of cloud hovered about them; it grew cold. "Bring me back . . . fuckin' down," panted the boy. "I'll let you go. Just take me down." But they rose until black space loomed above them, twinkling with brilliant stars.

There, teetering above the Earth, the bike flipped upside down.

The creature stayed duct-taped in its basket. The baseball bat fell into darkness, but the boy managed to grab the top bar of the frame. He hung there and gaped down past his feet. Dim lights gleamed below, matching the stars over his head. The void around him was wide and hostile. Empty fear in all directions. There was only the bike above him, and his white hands clutching the frame. His fingers on a metal bar, and nothing else.

How long could he hang? Already his joints hurt. He was sweaty with exertion and fear. One hand slipped, and he gave a frightened cry.

"Please," he moaned, as the pedals spun lazily above his head. "Please let me down. I'm so sorry. I've learned my lesson."

The creature, upside down, looked impassively at him.

Above, some of the stars grew larger, brighter, organizing themselves into a pattern. Lights. They had come back after all.

A deep hum surrounded them. The boy let out a pathetic sob. "They really won't take you back, you know. They'll think you're tainted. Broken. You could stay with me, though. I'll be nicer, I promise. I'll give you as much candy as you want. What do you say?"

The creature reached a crooked and broken finger out, and a light bloomed feebly at its tip. The boy whimpered, and his eyes crossed as he followed it.

"Ouch," said the creature, and touched him on the nose. Just a feather touch—but the boy shrieked, his hands slipped, and he plummeted away.

The bike rotated upright. The creature looked rapturously at the ship approaching with its fluctuating glow. It reached out with a mangled hand. Its broken leg throbbed; its pallid body was still taped into the bike basket.

"Home?" said the creature.

The ship hummed softly overhead. It bobbed in the night as though pondering. For a long time, nothing moved.

Then the ship floated away again, quietly, until its lights mixed with the stars.

☆

Sasha Brown *is a Boston writer, gardener, and dad whose surreal stories have been called "Creative! But in a bad way." He's in lit mags like* X-R-A-Y *and* Masters Review: New Voices, *and in genre mags like* Bourbon Penn *and* The Magazine of Fantasy & Science Fiction. *He's on Twitter @dantonsix and online at sashabrownwriter.com.*

Forever Children

J.P. Behrens

I tuck the covers under my body and over my head to hide from the monsters. The heavy quilt creates an impenetrable fort of fabric, imagination, and fear. As long as none of my body remains exposed to the cold New England night, I'm safe. My cocoon of safety fills with too much humidity from nervous breathing. The precaution is amended to allow my head to poke out, but my neck remains collared by the quilt to deter any bloodsucking fiends.

Sleep always wins the battle against alertness. Morning follows fuzzy nightmares. Nightmares that a quick shower and quicker breakfast obliterate before the bus for school arrives. But as the sun slides across the sky and dips below the horizon, night returns, and with it, the fear. Covers pulled tight against the low hum of a sleeping world, every creak convinces me something approaches, waiting for me to fall asleep.

When I hear the scratching at the window, I know it has arrived.

"It was just branches of the old maple tree brushing against the glass. The wind blew it just right, that's all."

"No, Mom. Something was trying to get in."

"You were just having a nightmare. You need to stop watching monster movies before bed."

That is always her answer, but how am I supposed to learn how to fight the monsters if I didn't do the research? In most monster movies, the heroes win, and I need to know how. I need to be prepared for when monsters get in. They always do, no matter what. That night, I double-check the window lock and watch the tree branches swing in the wind. The thin twigs of the nearest branch reach out, wobbling at least four feet away.

I hate that tree. Always have. It has a bulbous growth on its trunk that looks like the squat nose of a garden gnome. The

J.P. Behrens

old couple across the street have a small army of gnomes, trolls, and gargoyles decorating their yard. Most people think the statues look cute, but I always avoid their dead eyes. The tree bark healed in a strange way around limbs my parents trimmed to form two sunken, unblinking eyes that stare at the house. I don't want them to see me and visit in the night.

After Mom and Dad kiss me goodnight, I find my baseball bat within easy reach at the head of my bed. Sleep starts to drag me into the Land of Nod once all the edges of my covers are tucked and secured around me. Just as I am losing the battle against sleep, the scraping at the window returns. If I don't look, it can't become real, but I need to know.

The angle of the bed prevents a clear view, so I slip free and tiptoe over the chilly, old wood floor. Every step produces an ear-shattering groan from the floor in the deep silence of my sleeping home. As I reach the window, the silhouette of skeletal fingers rake the glass as if to scratch and claw a way through.

The tree's eyes stare through the window. The wooden nose flexes, and a craggy mouth tears a smile across the base of the trunk. I fall away from the window, run back to my bed, and pull the covers over my head. My rapid breathing chokes me into unconsciousness.

When morning arrives and my mother drags me out of bed, she finds both my clothes and bed soaked in sweat and urine. She doesn't yell, but I can tell she is disappointed. I decide that maybe it's a good idea, after all, to pause watching scary movies before bed. She agrees and changes my sheets.

That night, the scratching returns. I refuse to look out the window. A dim glow forms outside and commands my attention as if I am a simple-minded moth, oblivious to the danger. The glow congeals into an almost humanoid figure and touches my mind.

Join us! Be free of the fear. We will show you the night is glorious and full of beauty.

"What are you?"

We are the children of light. We are the children of night. We are the forever and the never will be. We are free.

"Can my parents come, too?"

NO! They are the rational that threatens. They are the have becomes and will be gones.

I back away. "I can't. My parents would miss me, and I don't want to leave them. I love them."

☾ Forever Children ☾

You will join us.

The light dims, and the night falls silent. No wind. No scraping. No lights. Still, the air is heavy with anticipation and expectation.

When morning comes, I rush downstairs. The house creaks and groans. Absent are the sounds of clacking plates in the kitchen, the low hum of the television, and the rustle of the morning paper.

My chest tightens. No coherent thoughts form. Tears burn as they break free and trace jagged lines down my cheeks. When the side door opens, I cough out a sob and find my mom setting a bag of groceries on the table. She rushes over and hugs me tighter than ever before.

"What's wrong? What happened? Are you okay?"

I tell her about the light and how it wanted me. I tell her how I said no, and it didn't think that would last. I tell her I thought it had taken her.

"That does sound like a terrifying dream. I'm sorry if I worried you. I just ran out to get groceries before work. I expected to be back before you woke up." She kisses my forehead. "You want pancakes?" I nod.

I calm down enough to ask, "Where's Dad?"

My mother freezes mid-whisk. "What do you mean?"

"Why isn't he here?"

"I don't know." Mom turns away and wipes her eyes. "I don't know why he left us, but we've managed for a long time without him. Does this have to do with your dream? Are you afraid you'll lose me too?"

What is she talking about? Dad said good night to me. Before any words form in my throat, she crosses the room in a blur and huddles me into another deep, warm hug. The hitches in her chest thunder in my ears. Tiny, warm droplets of water patter on my head and neck. I hug her back, tight, and choose to say nothing more. We remain there, together, wallowing in our sadness. How can I tell her that it's all my fault?

I try to ignore the lights, but their voices burrow.

Will you come to us now?

"No. I won't leave my mom alone. How could you do this to us?"

You will come.

I fall to sleep as tears soak my pillow.

☽ J.P. Behrens ☾

The house is cold and dark. Dust from my passing dances in the air amid the few beams of light leaking through pulled curtains. I race to check if maybe Mom slept through the morning. Her bedroom is dark and empty.

The furniture, pictures, fixtures, and knickknacks of a life are gone. Cracked walls and scuffed wooden floors greet me in every room. I pace through the house, searching for any evidence of a life shared, but find nothing. The doors are all stuck, and the curtains will only allow me to peek out. I see the world outside glide by as people walk past the ramshackle house and overgrown lawn. Neighborhood children cross the street to keep their distance, each daring the others to get closer, to knock on the door, to tempt fate. None do. I scream and rant. No one hears me.

The sun sets, and I go to the window to watch the pinprick dots of light cluster above the leering grin of the big-nosed tree. Across the street, several grinning garden gnomes, stone gargoyles, and mud-colored yard trolls stand witness, awaiting my answer.

"Can you bring my parents back?"

We can.

In all the books, fairies are tricky. "*Will* you bring my father back?"

They giggle. *We will if you join us.*

I whisper, "I will. But only after you bring them back."

The lights flare. A chorus of impish cackles thread through cold, winter winds full of dead, dried-out leaves.

It is done.

Dad's low snores rumble through our creaky, quiet house alongside Mom's relaxed sigh. No longer our house. *Their* house.

I slide the window open and let the lights blanket me.

Within the light, I see a child's bedroom room melt away and resolve into a home office. Toys, pictures, clothes, and half-started hobbies dissolve into a dream of never was. The child who was evaporates from the physical and intertwines with forever. A ghost of the child who was strikes out and imprints their lost story onto the nearest surface.

The bark of the tree shifts and cracks, telling the story of a boy once of the physical world who disappears into the eternal river of time bound by the realm of ancient rock and patient arboreal life. Oblivious to the story, the forever children seep back into the tree and resume their eternal games. The story spreads,

Forever Children

etched into the bark of every tree. A warning for those who know what to look for. However, those skills and magics are lost to the modern world. The warnings of myths and legends, fables and ancient teachings are taken as fairy tales and bedtime stories.

Some sensitive to the other world, individuals full of dreams and nightmares, will channel the histories of the hidden worlds and record them for all to read. Perhaps the forever children are sated and may never take another innocent soul into their realm. Perhaps the ancient powers will wither away and become grist for innocent stories that children drift off to sleep and dream about.

A scratch at your window awakens you to the truth. The forever people come, and no one will remember you after.

☆

J.P. Behrens *reads, writes, and practices kung fu. The rest of the time is spent with his family. Sleep is a wonderful fantasy he hopes to enjoy more one day. Visit him at jpbehrensauthor.com.*

Nathan's Night at Norwich

Rob Smales

Lightning danced across the distant night sky like the legs of some drunken spider god, outlining—a stuttery instant at a time—the huge pyramidal roof dead ahead. The hospital squatted beneath that roof, a Gothic mountain of brick and glass.

"I can't believe we're actually doing this!" Nathan sounded like a kid on Christmas morning.

I . . . did not. "Yeah. Me either."

Mom shot me a glance, returning her attention to the road as the thunder finally rolled. The wind pushing that storm our way was strong enough to rock the Jeep, and she didn't want to wreck in the hospital driveway, especially with us kids in the car. She still smiled, though.

"Well, at least *someone's* happy to come visit me at work."

It wasn't that I didn't want to. I just didn't want to as much as Nathan. The kid had a weird exuberance that should have seemed dumb—we were fifteen, for crying out loud, he wasn't some little kid—but there was something about it, about *him*, that was sort of . . . well, sweet. I'd never admit that, though, *especially* to my mom, who was so charmed by the kid she probably wanted to adopt him. Barring that, I think she'd be totes happy if he and I got married.

As if!

She parked by the huge, boxy building and killed the ignition. "Get your stuff, and let's get in there." She rattled the keys. "And get *all* your stuff. Once that storm hits, you're not going to want to come out to fetch anything."

In the backseat, Nathan held up his backpack, with its Sharpied message across the back: *My Other Backpack Is a TARDIS*. "Got everything right here. This is gonna be *great*! Thanks, Mrs. S!"

☽ Nathan's Night at Norwich ☾

"He's right," I said. "This is pretty cool. Thanks, Mom."

"All you had to do was ask." She faced me as Nathan kicked the door open and shot out of the car, eager to get the show on the road. She threw a thumb in his direction as his door slammed, grinning so wide she nearly split her head in two. "Anything to make your boyfriend happy."

I shook my head. "Don't even start that. Besides"—I gripped the door handle— "he's way more *your* boyfriend than mine."

I elbowed the door open—and the wind shoved it back into my shoulder. I fought my way out of the car—it's a good thing I *wasn't* trying to impress Nathan, because my loose Scunci disappeared into the gale and my coif was suddenly a lot more fright wig than red carpet—and I finally met the two waiting in front of the Jeep.

"Nice hair," Mom called. *Her* ponytail was intact, flapping straight out behind her like a flag.

"Thanks." Shouldering my own backpack, I made little *scoot-scoot* motions. "Shall we go?"

"Yes!" Nathan scurried up the front stairs without looking back to see if we were following. We were, laughing at his totally unabashed enthusiasm. We were all smiling as Mom worked a keypad set in the wall, the buzzer released the door, and we entered Norwich State Hospital.

Little did we know . . .

☾ ☆ ☽

At the nurses' station/front desk in the middle of the wide, vaulted main entry hall, corridors leading off to either side, Mom introduced us to Nurse Winston, her coworker for the night. Ms. Winston had steely hair and an expression to match, and didn't sound particularly friendly when she said, "I guess you can call me Amanda."

"So." She came around the counter-cum-desk, eyeballing us kids all the while. "You kids are writing a paper?"

That was the excuse Mom had cooked up for us being there. I opened my mouth to tell the story, but Amanda Winston looked scary serious and intimidating as hell, and my tongue wasn't having it; words completely failed to come out.

Nathan, though, had no such problem. "Yup! That's us. This is gonna be *so* cool! Lemme show you."

With that, he sat right down on the marble floor, unzipped the main pocket in his backpack, rummaged for a moment, and pulled out The Book. I looked at Amanda in something approaching horror, expecting her to start tongue-lashing Nathan for improper etiquette, or maybe dirtying the hospital floor with his teenaged butt, but she just stood there. I checked to see if Mom looked worried, but she only watched Nathan flip through The Book, a little smile on her face.

The Book. You could tell when Nathan talked about it, he was capitalizing the words in his head: never *the book*, always *The Book*. The Book was how he'd really started charming Mom.

☆

Kids at school knew Mom was a nurse, but most didn't know she worked at The Norwich State Hospital for the Insane. I didn't volunteer that information. People talked about that place a *lot*, especially kids, and most of it wasn't nice; I didn't need them taking jabs at my mom while poking fun at the local booby hatch.

Nathan found out on his own. Her being a nurse, he'd had questions when he'd met her. Him being Nathan, those questions were weird.

"Did you work on cadavers at school, like doctors on TV?"

He'd been trying hard to sound serious, though that excitement of his had been peeking through. I was pretty sure Mom had seen it, too. She'd smiled sort of uncertainly and said, "No, but I did have to take a whole bunch of anatomy."

"So, you know how the human body works?"

"Pretty much."

"Uh-huh." He'd unzipped his TARDIS-sloganed schoolbag and pulled out a Trapper Keeper stuffed with paper and bearing two words Sharpied across the cover: *The Book*. Plunking The Book on the kitchen table, he'd flipped through the pages, settled on one that looked like a list, and pulled out a pen.

"So." He'd sounded absolutely serious. "The Vulcan nerve pinch: real or horse hockey?"

"Wha . . . Uh, horse hockey?"

He'd checked a box and made a notation. "Hysterical strength?"

"You mean moms lifting cars off trapped kids, stuff like that?" She'd pondered a moment. "The jury's still out, I think. Some people definitely think it's a thing, and I've seen some stuff that leans that way myself. One out-of-control patient requiring six orderlies to subdue them—that's a half ton of orderly they're moving around—but I think that's mostly adrenaline and really not minding if they're hurting themselves."

☽ Nathan's Night at Norwich ☾

"Mh-hmm." Another check mark. Another notation. "Brown sound?"

Mom had blinked. "What's that? And what's this book of yours?"

It had been Nathan's turn to blink. "Oh! This is my big book of research." He'd spun it to face us and leafed through a few pages. You could tell from his expression he was proud. There were scrapbook-style pages with clipped articles and pictures pasted in, typed pages, and handwritten pages. A *Weekly World Mirror* headline flipped past: *Rat Girl Found in New York Sewer!* A few pages later, the *Weekly World News* proclaimed, *I Married Bigfoot—And We Have Three Kids!*

Mom had looked up at him. "You're really into those tabloid stories, huh?"

Nate had smiled. "Not just those. There are whole books about Bigfoot. But what I'm *really* interested in are the things right here in Connecticut, like the Glawackus or the Winstead Wildman. *Those* I can investigate on my own, try and separate the facts from the fiction. Talk to local experts. Like asking you about the Vulcan pinch and the strength thing. I asked an expert and got a 'pinch no' and a 'strength maybe.'"

Mom had nodded her approval. "So, you don't just take the *Weekly World Mirror* as gospel?"

He'd made a face. "No! You think I'm nuts?"

I'd winced at that, but Mom hadn't. "If you are, I'd be the person to tell, I guess."

"Huh?"

"Didn't Jane tell you?" She'd winked. "I'm a nurse at Norwich."

I'd held my breath as his eyebrows shot up. *No weird questions*, I'd prayed. *Please please pleeeeeease no weird questions.*

"So," he'd said. "What's it like, working in a laughing factory?"

☾ ☆ ☽

Now, he flipped through The Book to its thickest section, the one labeled *Connecticut*. He stopped in the middle, pointing to a sketch of something that looked like an Oompa-Loompa wearing a Mardi Gras head: a tabloid *artist's conception*.

"See, there are two main origin stories for the Melon Heads, and—"

"The what?"

) Rob Smales (

Nathan looked up into Amanda's puzzled face, eyes bright at the prospect of sharing his knowledge. "The Melon Heads. My *specific* area of interest is really cryptid origin research: the idea that within every legend lies a kernel of truth. You know, someone sees something they don't understand, so they sort of put their own spin on it. They tell their story, and it gets around, becomes popular, and then *boom*: you've got an urban legend. I want to find those kernels."

Thunder boomed, practically overhead, and he looked up at the vaulted ceiling. "It's like when ancient man heard thunder and said it was the gods fighting, or bowling, or whatever. They heard something, didn't understand it, so made up an explanation they liked and spread it around." He shrugged. "We think we're so civilized today, but we're still doing the same thing. Just hearing different noises and making different gods."

Amanda looked at this kid sitting on her floor with a scrapbook spread across his lap, wearing an expression of wonder. I didn't blame her. This was the most coherent explanation I'd ever heard Nathan give, and I had to admit, I was impressed. She shared a glance with Mom, and they both grinned.

Damned if Nathan's weird charm hadn't won out again.

"This kid's practically a scientist."

"Oh, don't get me wrong," Nathan said from the floor. "I'm looking for the kernel of truth, but I'm hoping that kernel is that the Galwackus and Melon Heads are real. That would be *so cool!*"

"Okay," said Mom. "Nutshell these *Melon Heads* for us. We can't stand around all night."

"Right." Nathan paused to organize his thoughts. "So, the Melon Heads are little people—just short people, not like leprechauns or anything—with big heads, who live out in the wilds of Connecticut—and Michigan and Ohio, but I'm strictly talking Connecticut Melon Heads here—who occasionally attack people, take them away, stuff like that. There have been sightings all over, and there are *lots* of origin theories for them, but there are two main ones. One is that they were a bunch of colonists, you know, like back in pioneer days, who split off from the main colony and went off on their own. Some say *driven off* because of witchcraft accusations, but whatever. The group was too small to be a real colony, and they turned to cannibalism to survive. Legend says they're still out there, but they got really weird from all the cannibalism and inbreeding."

He waved a hand.

☽ Nathan's Night at Norwich ☾

"I'm not really looking into that one because it was so long ago. It's not like there are written records at the library or anything. I'm here looking into the *other* main theory: a bunch of escaped mental patients who formed a sort of hillbilly extended family out there. With the same cannibal and inbreeding thing, of course."

"Of course," I said.

He ignored me. "The asylum thing's more recent, and there might be actual records I can look up. Now, most legends say the escapees came from an asylum that burned to the ground in the sixties, but I don't think so."

"The sixties?" Amanda frowned. "There wouldn't have been enough time for any inbreeding to show, I don't think."

"That's what I think." Nathan shoved The Book back into his backpack. "Bad diet could mess them up too, though. And lack of medical care—you know, broken bones setting wrong, infected cuts swelling up and going all gross—could make them look weird, too."

Amanda nodded. "That actually makes sense. I see you've thought this whole thing out. But— " She gave him a hand to his feet. "We *don't* live in the wilds of Connecticut. We actually have these things called *chairs* here. Maybe you've heard of them?"

Nathan blushed. "Sorry. It's just that I— "

"Get caught up in stuff. I noticed." She led him around behind the counter, motioning for me to follow. "Why don't you get situated here while Jane's mom and I do a quick rounds check."

She started to turn away, but paused. "You said the place they supposedly escaped from burned to the ground, so this can't be it. So what are you doing here?"

"That supposedly happened in the sixties, too, but I don't think thirty years is enough time for the inbreeding, the diet, none of that to do too much to them. That's like a generation, right? But there have been a lot of sightings around here over the years, and this *is* an asylum that's been here since 1904. Ninety years makes for a lot more generations than thirty, if they walked out of here when the place first opened, right?"

"Right. But what do you plan to find tonight?"

"Tonight?" He shrugged. "Nothing. But Mrs. S says this place is closing all the way down next year. Closing for good. When I *do* finish my research, if I write a book or something, I can at least say I spent one night in Norwich State before it was gone."

☽ Rob Smales ☾

The storm outside was suddenly reflected in her face: thunderclouds galore. She looked at Mom. "*Book? If?* Becca, I thought you said this young man was writing a paper for school?"

Mom didn't *quite* look like a deer caught in a pair of speeding headlights, but it was close. "Well, I, uh—"

"Oh, I can do that if you want, Ms. Winston." Nathan plunked his backpack on the nurses' station and fell into a chair. "It wouldn't be the first one, though. Actually"—he grinned rather sheepishly—"I think they're kind of sick of hearing about it."

She let that sink in a moment, then snorted an almost-laugh.

"Okay!" Mom looked relieved. "We're going on rounds. You can get settled in back there, but don't touch anything official looking, okay? We'll be right back."

I heard a *tick*, then a *tick-tick*, and looked at the ceiling. "Here it comes."

Mom, heading toward one of the corridors while Amanda went to the other, looked back. "Here what comes, dear?"

Before I could answer, the ticking went rapid-fire, expanding within the space of three seconds into a spattery roar as torrential rains suddenly pounded the windows, the roof, the very earth. Lightning lit the world, making outside brighter than day for half a second, and immediate thunder pounded down, the sky cracking almost loud enough to hurt.

"That." I waved the ladies a little goodbye. "Happy trails. We will be right here, okay?"

☾ ☆ ☽

Once they were gone, I staked out a corner of the wide nurses' station for myself, claiming a chair and putting my copy of *Tuck Everlasting* on the counter. Nathan was spinning in his chair, making *Star Wars* blaster sounds.

"You don't *really* think your Melon Heads came from here, do you?"

He caught the counter edge to stop his chair. "Maybe. I mean, it's possible, if I'm reading the sighting patterns right. They probably came from *somewhere* around here, and—"

"But my *mom* works here. She wouldn't . . . "

I'd expected his usual happy-enthusiastic reaction. Instead, he leaned forward, as serious as I'd ever seen him.

"No! No-no, it's got nothing to do with your mom. You guys are great. You're *both* great. This wouldn't have anything to do with *anyone* here today. I'm talking about like 1905, maybe

☽ Nathan's Night at Norwich ☾

1906. Most of this place wasn't even *built* back when I'm talking about."

"But you think those things are real? Those Melon Head people?"

I didn't know why this suddenly seemed so serious, but it did. I'd always kind of laughed off The Book. It was like a little kid believing in Santa or the Tooth Fairy: something harmless he believed in because he *wanted* to believe, that he'd grow out of someday. All that stuff he read and collected from books and tabloids—*The Weekly World Mirror*? I mean, come on!—had always seemed obviously, laughably made-up, comic books to read while in line at the supermarket checkout.

But here, now, I wasn't sure whether it was being in the mental hospital at night, or maybe the storm beating on the building making us seem isolated from the rest of the world, or maybe it was the seriousness of his explanation to Amanda, but it all seemed a little harder to shake off.

"I think," Nathan said slowly, thinking it through as he spoke, "that *something* happened a long time ago that started the rumor that eventually became the Melon Heads urban legend. It might have started here, but even if it did, it wasn't *here*-here, if you know what I mean. Does that make any sense?"

I nodded. It *did* make me feel better, and—this was kind of weird—so did talking to Nathan. It wasn't a romantic thing; I wasn't about to turn and throw myself into his arms like women did on *Days of Our Lives*, which Mom watched on her afternoons off, saying *Oh, Nathan, you make me feel so safe*, but he was . . . comfortable.

Mom and Amanda returned. Before they could say anything, Nathan hit them with one of his questions.

"Where's your security? I mean, isn't a night watchman supposed to be here or something?"

"Supposed to be," Mom said. "Cutbacks. It's not like this is a criminal facility, so when the funding started dying off, some of the first to go were on security."

Amanda nodded. "We still have a skeleton staff. You saw Brian, out in the guard hut. The guy who let you through the gate? But the mucky-mucks decided we nurses didn't have enough to do, so we get to track our rounds as *security sweeps*."

"There's no security here?" So much for feeling comforted; my voice was a little squeaky. "What if something happens? What if—" I caught myself before the words *some nutjob goes all*

Michael Myers on you could leave my mouth. "What if there's an emergency?"

Mom smiled, probably at my tone. "There *is* that skeleton security staff, and if anything *really* bad happens, the police are just a phone call away."

"How often does something really bad happen?" Nathan didn't sound squeaky at all. In fact, he sounded like he relished the idea.

Amanda smiled at that one. "Never. I'm not sure what you were expecting, young man, but this place is actually pretty boring—especially at night."

That was when, with a blinding flash of lightning and a crash of thunder, the lights went out.

☾ ☆ ☽

A voice—clearly mine—said, "Oh, shit."

"Jane!"

"Sorry, Mom."

Amanda's calm voice cut through the blackness. "Don't panic. The backup generators should kick in any second now."

The big plate windows bracketing the entry door were still visible as great gray swatches against the dark, but the rest of the world was gone, the storm not letting enough ambient light from town or even the streetlights out by the road to do much of anything in the cavernous reception hall. I waved my hand in front of my face, but only when it passed between me and those gray windows could I see anything at all.

"Yup." Amanda sounded more hopeful than confident. "Any . . . second . . . now."

The darkness sat there and kept us company while we waited.

"Well . . . shit."

"What are we going to do?" I said. I was trying not to sound afraid, but I'd never been a good liar.

"Don't panic," Amanda repeated. "I've got— "

With a *click*, a sudden brightness burst into being, a beam of light shining practically from floor to ceiling, the backsplash revealing both women and me all standing at various points about the nurses' station, hands slightly spread against the dark as if afraid we were going to walk into something though none of us was actually moving. I say *practically*, because the beam actually started about three feet above the floor, where it sprouted from the flashlight Nathan held beneath his chin, the upward-racing shadows turning his normally exuberant grin into a fairly hideous fright mask.

"—this," Amanda finished.

"Had it in my backpack," said the new Nathan face. "What happened to the generator?"

"Cutbacks," Mom and Amanda said in unison.

"Maintenance took a hit just like security," Mom explained. "There's barely enough staff there to handle the day-to-day stuff, never mind things we *might* need someday." Her voice dropped, muttering to herself. "But I am *definitely* making a goddamned complaint about *this*."

"There's a box mounted under the counter at either end," Amanda said. "There's emergency stuff in there, including flashlights. Why don't you put *your* light to work and get some for *us*, could you, Nathan? Besides, keeping it under your chin like that is starting to creep me out."

"I'm glad someone said it," Mom muttered, and I nodded.

Nathan fished the flashlights out and handed them over; in less than a minute, four brilliant beams carved through the blackness of the Main Hall.

"There," said Mom. "That's not so bad, is i— "

A scream tore its way up the throat of the corridor to the right. Mom started. Nathan's eyes bugged. I nearly peed my pants. Even Amanda's eyes widened a bit.

"Oh, dammit," she said. "That's Randy. And—oh hell—that means Billy Freeman is probably going to— "

A second scream slashed at my nerves, this one coming from the left.

"—join in." She made a face and looked at Mom. "Well, which do you want?"

"I'll take Randy." Mom flicked her light off and on, testing it. "I have a decent enough rapport with— "

"What's going on?" I didn't even try to keep the panic from my voice. "Is someone hurt? What— "

"We have two patients at the moment who are afraid of the dark." Amanda was checking her flashlight, too. "Terrified. What with the storm and all the thunder— " Another peal shook the building. "—most of the patients aren't sleeping well. Most of *them* probably haven't noticed the power is out, but those two, well . . . "

"They have night-lights," Mom cut in. "They would have been fine if the generator'd kicked in, but it didn't, dammit. The storm's bad enough; the patients will all be agitated—some of them for days—but all that racket will get them *really* worked up. We need to— " A thought struck her. "Nathan, pick up that phone right there and dial nine for an outside line. Do you get a dial tone?"

He snatched up the handset, stabbed the button, listened, shook his head.

"Oh, don't tell me." She grabbed the phone at her end of the station and repeated his process. Her shoulders slumped. "Terrific. The phone lines must be down. I—*feh!*" She slammed the handset back into its cradle, then looked at the floor for a moment, lost in thought. We all stood listening to the rain, the wind, and the pair of screaming lunatics. Finally, her head came up, and by the light of the flashlights, I saw she wore a small, tight smile. "Well, you two sure picked a hell of a night for a visit."

Amanda tapped her watch, then made a rolling, *Let's go!* motion with one wrist. "We've got to calm Randy and Bill down, or there'll be hell to pay for the rest of the week."

Mom nodded and they both set out for their respective hallways, though Mom did turn back just before she dropped out of sight entirely.

"Now, don't go anywhere, you two."

"Ha-ha," I said. "Funny."

She grinned, turned, and was gone, nothing but flickering light reflecting along the wall as her flashlight bobbed farther and farther away, and then that was gone, too. A moment later, there was the *clank-hissss* of a big interior door—a fire door, maybe—being released from that built-on footie-thing that was used to prop them open and allowed to swing shut, and the screams cut off with the door-closing *ka-thud*.

And Nathan and I were alone.

In the storm.

In the dark.

In the nuthouse.

☾ ☆ ☽

"So," Nathan said after a minute of listening to the rain and wind. "What do you want to do now?" He whipped his flashlight beneath his chin again, contorting his face in a way made even more hideous by the play of light and shadow across it, though, to be honest, it wasn't really any worse than his genuine smile had been. "Shadow puppets?"

☽ Nathan's Night at Norwich ☾

"No. And quit that. I'm *really* not in the mood for spooky stuff right now."

The light remained in place, only now words boomed out of the face above it in a cheesy, over-the-top cross between Dracula and the Count from *Sesame Street*. "But *now* is the *per*fect *time* for the *spooky* stuff! Ah-ha-ha-haaaaa . . . "

I shot him The Look—hey, he has a Book, I have a Look—and the laughter subsided, the flashlight dropping to point to the floor.

"Okay, fine. But don't blame me if—What was that?" He sat up, head cocked slightly in a listening pose.

"What was what?"

"I thought I heard something."

"In *this* storm? How could you hear—"

"There it is again. You didn't hear that?"

I started to reply; then a thought struck me. "I *told* you, I'm not in the mood for the spooky stuff right now."

"No, no." He stood, gazing off into the darkness mostly hiding the main doors. "I thought I heard a, uh . . . "

"A what?"

"Well, a knock."

He sat rock still, listening, while I digested that for a moment.

"I swear to God, if you're just messing with me—"

"I'm not. Swear to God."

We listened. I heard the rain rippling across the tarmac outside as the wind drove it this way and that. I heard air racing in and out of my throat, so I held my breath and listened harder. I heard the pulse pounding in my ears. My chest started to hurt, so I let the breath out and took another, intending to use *this* one to give Nathan that tongue-lashing he'd somehow not gotten from Nurse Winston.

The knock came, clear against the background hiss of weather; knuckles rapping, rapping at our chamber door, in a slow *one . . . two . . . three*.

That breath came out in a whispered "*Jesus!*" and we both whipped our lights up, beams fixed on the front entry door.

"Do you think—" I started.

"What should we—" Nathan began.

We both fell silent, staring at the big double door.

"You want to go get your mom?"

I shone my light into the corridor Mom had disappeared down, but I didn't even see the door we'd heard her close on the way; the darkness simply swallowed my flashlight's beam like a living throat.

"Nope."

"Well," he whispered. "Do you want to stay here?"

"Nope."

"Okay." He sighed. "Not a lot of options." He stretched his neck to the side and set his jaw—I think he was trying to look manly, but all he managed, really, was to look like he was trying to look manly—and edged around his end of the station.

I don't know how a whisper can cross with a shriek, but that's what I did. "Where the hell are you going?"

"To check it out."

"What about me?"

He turned his head slightly toward me, but never took his eyes from the door. "You wait here."

Oh, fuck that!

Before I'd finished the thought, I was edging double-time around my end of the counter, determined to catch up. We met in the middle of the lobby and moved toward the door together, a two-person knot with feet. We were almost there when the knock came again, startling us into a pair of doglike yelps. That close, though, I realized something I'd actually heard before but been too frightened to register: the knock didn't sound like knuckles on wood.

It sounded like knuckles on glass.

The window!

It must have hit Nathan at the exact same time because we moved as a unit, whipping about to aim our flashlights at the pane of glass on the near side of the entry door, the one right beside us. The double beam splashed off the glass, turning it into a mirror good enough that all I could see was us squinting in the sudden glare.

"We have to turn them off," Nathan whispered.

"No frickin' way," I whispered back.

"On the count of three."

"No!"

"One . . . two . . . "

The storm took things into its own hands, lighting up the sky with lightning so bright a hundred flashlights couldn't have competed. For almost a full second, it was bright as noon on a summer day out there. Our reflections disappeared as the mirror effect was completely wiped out, and Nathan and I screamed.

☽ Nathan's Night at Norwich ☾

A small man stood on the other side of the window, barely four feet away.

☾ ☆ ☽

The lightning faded, plunging the world into blackness. Nathan and I, ready (despite my own objections) to turn off our flashlights when he said *three*, had clenched when we screamed, pushing the buttons by accident, and though we'd been getting used to the dim lobby before, that blinding flash had sent our night vision packing. I couldn't even make out the gray of the window anymore, and it was right in front of us.

I backed up a step, then another, fumbling with the flashlight all the while. I'd never been a huge fan of the dark, but the darkness here *hid* things, *horrible* things. I wanted the light—*needed* the light—but couldn't find the damned button again. Now I understood why Randy and Bill had been screaming earlier; I was never going to be without light again if I could help it, and if that meant using a night-light, I was good with that. The damned button kept avoiding my seeking fingers and pressing thumbs. The frustration built in me like a scream, and I thought that was a fine idea, just a wonderful idea; a scream was just the thing this situation needed, so I squeezed the flashlight, strangling it even as I inhaled about as deep as I could so I could let out—

A hand found my boob in the dark.

I started, swallowed, gagged on my overfilled lungs in surprise, decided I was going to scream anyway, maybe in anger this time. The hand went away—then was back, pressing for an instant before disappearing again. The third time the five-fingered intruder landed, I finally heard the whispering.

"Take it easy. Don't turn it on; it'll just let them see us. Easy. I think we're okay."

Nathan, backing with me through the dark, blindly patting toward me in an effort to comfort me—hell, maybe just to find me. He'd probably be *mortified* if he knew he'd accidentally copped a feel—and that thought brought up a stifled laugh. It may have been hysteria, but a laugh's a laugh; his words started to register on me, and they sort of made sense: the dark wasn't just hiding them, it was hiding us as well, and that—

Waitaminute!

"Did you say *them*?" I whispered back. "Tell me you did not just say *them*!"

Rob Smales

"I saw three." My butt bumped the front of the nurses' station. Nathan stopped beside me. "The one right at the window and two farther back. What did you see?"

"I just saw the one." I'd stopped strangling the flashlight but still held it in both hands, working it round and round like a big plastic worry stone. "I saw the one at the window, and he was . . . "

He had a round head like a pumpkin with lumps and bumps on his face. One eye larger than the other, the small one squinted shut like Popeye—or maybe gone. Yeah, it could have been gone. Something about his shoulders, one higher than the other—was that a hump? Even his fist, raised to knock like that, looked twisted, like the fingers weren't right. The whole thing, the whole man, just looked . . .

"Wrong," I whispered. "He looked . . . *wrong*."

"They all did." I couldn't see his expression—I couldn't see *anything* yet—but from his tone, he didn't sound as frightened as I felt. He was afraid, sure, but there was something underneath, something familiar. He sounded almost . . . excited?

I gasped.

"You've got to be fucking kidding me! *Melon Heads*? Those are the *Melon Heads* out there?"

There was a thoughtful pause—it was only about *forever* long—before he said, "Yeah. I think they might be."

I groped, found his arm, and pulled him around to the back of the nurses' station with me. We squatted as far out of sight from those windows as we could get without going down one of those freaking terrifying corridors, and I covered the lens of my flashlight with both my hand and shirttail before turning it on. The "Riddles in the Dark" section might have been my favorite bit of *The Hobbit*, but it turned out that doing it for real sucked. The dim glow oozing between my spread fingers let me *almost* see his face.

"What the hell are they doing here?"

"Don't know."

"What do you mean, 'Don't know'? You're the expert, so what the hell are they doing here?"

"Maybe trying to get in out of the storm? Maybe coming home, like salmon when they swim upstream to the place they hatched from. That's the kind of thing I was hoping to find out someday. Or maybe . . . "

☽ Nathan's Night at Norwich ☾

He avoided my gaze—not the hardest thing to do when we could barely see each other anyway, but he was making an effort at it. A word danced around the edges of my mind, staying out of sight, though, to be honest, I had the feeling I really didn't want to see it. But I had to ask.

"Maybe what?"

"Well . . . All the legends agree on two things: One is that they attack people from time to time. The other is that they're . . . cannibals."

That was it. That was the word. He said it, and what I did next was pure reflex. I filled my lungs, opened my mouth, and bellowed a completely different word.

"*Mom!*"

☾ ☆ ☽

It took a while for Nathan to quiet me down again. There was a lot of murmuring on his part, a lot of babbling on mine, and he didn't seem to be making any headway until he . . . Well, he leaned in and kissed me.

That shut me up.

Mom had been poking fun at me for months, calling Nathan my boyfriend behind his back and stuff. I always shot the idea down, but she said it so often that sometimes I couldn't help imagining it. Those were the times I'd made a face while shooting the idea down. I'd heard the phrase, *It was like kissing my brother*; I didn't *have* any brothers, but if I did, I imagined kissing Nathan would be like kissing them. And it wasn't like I'd never kissed any boys—or girls—but Nathan, with his Book and weird sort of sweetness, I didn't imagine he'd ever kissed *anybody*.

But it wasn't like I'd thought at all. It was actually kind of . . . nice.

He just stared at me for the second or two it took for all that to run through my head. "You okay?"

I spread my hands—screw covering the light; they knew we were here. "What the hell was that?"

His eyes widened. "What?"

I touched my fingers to my lips, then spread my hands wider, the international sign for *What. The hell. Was that. Dude?*

He shrugged. "I couldn't think of anything else to do."

"Think harder next time."

"It worked, didn't it?"

I snapped my fingers in front of his face. "Focus! Cannibal heads right outside! What do we do?"

☽ 134 ☾

☽ Rob Smales ☾

He blinked. "Right! Uh . . . Well, I don't think they can get in through that glass. Psychiatric hospitals use polycarbonate. It's practically unbreakable."

"And that door's locked," I said. "Mom had to be buzzed in, remember?"

"Right! So, all we really have to do is sit tight and wait for the adults to come back so they can be in charge until the power and phones come back on."

He sat back on his heels, leaning his butt against the wall.

"Man, it's good to have a plan."

He was right. It was great to have a plan. And I really *liked* this plan.

. . . Unfortunately, I thought I saw a flaw in the plan.

"Hey, those buzzing lock things. They, uh . . . They work on electricity, right?"

"Duh."

"I mean, they're electromagnetic locks—like, the magnet is holding the door closed, right?"

He nodded. "I think so, yeah."

"And if there's no electricity for the magnet?"

Even in the gloom, I saw his eyes go wide. "Oh my God!"

We scrambled to our feet, bolted around the counter, and froze. We'd gone from plan to no plan; I didn't know about Nathan, but I had no idea which way to go. I suddenly couldn't even remember which way Mom had gone. I spun from one corridor to the other and back, and man, I *howled*.

"Mom! Mooooooom!"

Nathan glanced at me spinning and wailing and aimed his flashlight at the door. The right-hand door had a crash bar across it; my yowling mouth snapped shut when that crash bar jiggled slightly, and the door was pulled open a crack. Either the opener was being really sneaky, or they saw the light coming through the thin opening and knew they were bagged, but the door froze.

Nathan was already moving. His flashlight hit the floor as he leaped forward, grabbed the crash bar with both hands, planted a foot on the left door, and leaned back hard. There was a squawk, and the door slammed shut. He shouted over a shoulder.

"Get something!"

I looked left and right, saw only shadows and darkness. "Get what?"

"I don't know! Something to jam the door! Mop handle? Flagpole? Any—Uh!"

☽ Nathan's Night at Norwich ☾

The door jerked open a couple of inches before Nathan yanked it closed again.

"Anything!"

"There's nothing here! I— "

"Chair! Bring me a chair!"

The door bounced again, then again as I raced toward him, pushing an office chair, his flashlight on the seat and aimed at Nathan like a headlight. He was holding on, but he wasn't a jock or anything; he was tiring fast.

"Should I jam it under the handle?" I looked at the wheeled base. "Shit! This is the wrong kind of chair for that!"

"Do it anyway! Right between the doors!"

He took down his foot as I leaned the chair back and shoved it up under that end of the crash bar. The door jerked again, the crash bar caught the top of the backrest and popped the chair out of my hands—and half the backrest slammed back against that locked left door. The bar couldn't get through the backrest, the backrest couldn't get through the other door, and the Melon Heads couldn't get in.

There was a frustrated cry outside, high and ululating. A second voice joined in, and the door bucked hard. The chair held. The door bucked again, then again, quickly, and the chair slid sideways. It was almost entirely off the left-hand door when Nathan shoved it back into place, then spun about and had a seat. The door bucked again, jostling the chair, but Nathan simply spread his legs, planted his feet, and held his lock in place.

"Go." He pulled a shuddering breath and flapped a hand. "Find your mom. Or Amanda. Go find *somebody* while I hold them out."

He was telling me to do what I *wanted* to do—part of my brain wouldn't stop saying *go-go-go-run-run-run-go-go-go*—but I hesitated. This wasn't some dude I was leaving behind; it was Nathan. And he said he'd hold the door, but he looked terrified, and exhausted, and he wasn't some movie action hero or anything, he was . . . well, *Nathan*.

"Are you sure?"

"Nope." He took another breath, scooped up the fallen flashlight, and flapped the hand again—and the door bucked so hard it jerked the chair sideways despite his wide-spread Nikes. More voices joined the quavering wail outside, making maybe four or five. He dropped the light into his lap and gripped the sides of the seat with both hands, shouting, "Go! Go!"

Rob Smales

I sprinted back to the station, snatched my own light from the counter, and stood looking left and right, trying to remember which way Mom had gone.

"That way!" Nathan was pointing right. The door was still. Had the Melon Heads given up?

I looked back from the mouth of the corridor. "You sure about this?"

"Nope." I couldn't see his expression, but it sounded like Nathan was actually grinning. "But go anyway. I got thi— "

A shout rose up from outside, many voices working in unison, and the door was suddenly *pulled*. The chair half spun, taking Nathan with it, and the crash bar slipped free of the chair back. Nathan's feet had flown up, and he'd thrown his arms wide for balance. The door opened so fast it seemed to vanish. Rain pelted in, making a pattering ripple of wetness on the floor as a long, thin arm thrust in from the windswept darkness outside with hideous, popping jack-in-the-box quickness, and clamped onto one of Nathan's wide-flung arms. With a wordless shout of horror, the chair tipped, the flashlight fell, and Nathan was yanked out into the storm.

☆

I stood frozen. We'd had a plan again, of sorts: Nathan would hold the door while I ran to find Mom. Part of me still loved that plan, wanted to cling to that plan, and urged me to go find Mom. I'd never signed up for this. I was a kid, and the plan had been to fetch an adult to handle it. I could do that; I could go find an adult and let them handle it.

But this was Nathan, with his sweet earnestness and his Book, and he'd kissed me out of my panic because he didn't know what else to do and then told me to go on without him.

I crossed the lobby at a run.

Nathan's flashlight slowly spun on the wet marble, the tipped chair propping the door open. I scooped up the light, gave the door a kick, and burst out into the night, waving the flashlights about, trying to see where they'd gone. Something slapped my arm, and I jumped, screaming and turning and backing away all at the same time. It was a couple of yards of rope, tied through the doorhandle and whipping in the wind like Mom's ponytail had when we'd gotten out of the car, back when the world had made sense. That was how they'd overpowered Nathan's improvised lock: all of them pulling together like a flesh-hungry tug-of-war.

☽ Nathan's Night at Norwich ☾

"Nathan!" The wind scattered my voice while the rain slapped my face. I'd been outside for seconds, but I was already soaked. "*Nathan!*"

There was sound—too faint for words, but a voice—followed by a squeal more animal than human. I ran after it, away from the walkway and parking lot, cutting across the lawn toward the side of the building. I slipped in the grass and mud, shone my lights down to check the footing, saw a pair of gouges in the lawn just in front of me, deep and already filling with water. Nathan must have put his feet down, tried to pull back, but was yanked along, skiing through the mud.

Going the right way, I thought, and tried to run faster. The Norwich was entirely fenced in, and they'd taken him away from the gate, but the overall grounds were *huge*, and it wasn't like I knew my way around. If they got too far ahead of me, I'd never find them—and who was to say they weren't taking him to *another* gate?

I stopped, listening and trying to catch my breath, and shook dripping hair from my face, wishing I'd put it back up once we'd gotten inside. The rain was a constant hiss, beating against the ground and grass, the wind an accompanying rustle through the decorative shrubberies along the building.

"Nathan! Dammit, *Nathan!*"

Another wordless cry, closer this time. I whipped the lights about, but they were next to useless in the storm, showing me nothing but the rain falling for a couple of yards around me like a thick, wet curtain.

"Nathan!"

A grunt and a rustle—not the wind this time, but a rhythmic shaking of leaves—barely audible against everything else. I trained my lights on the shrubs growing against the wall—and one of them moved, a quick twitch while the others bobbed in the wind. I squeezed between them—and suddenly, there were people in front of me.

On the back side of the shrubbery, where no sunlight reached and no leaves grew, was a hollow space, almost a little cave. Wind and rain still made their way in, but the brunt of the storm was blunted by the thick foliage on the outside of the shrubs. In this natural little safe space, a half dozen small people crouched, elbows flashing as their arms worked, striking and yanking at a figure writhing and yelling on the ground in their midst.

☽ Rob Smales ☾

Nathan!

I shrieked. Whether the noise of the storm had covered my approach or they'd been too busy with Nathan to pay much attention, I took them all by surprise. They wheeled—and the nearest of them got my flashlight beams full in the face. Even scrubbed by the pounding rain they looked unclean, dirt and mud caking the bumps and excrescences peppering their skin, and I screamed one word, *"Help!"* though whether I wanted it for myself or for Nathan, I couldn't say.

They shouted back, probably in surprise, though the two with my lights in their eyes screamed loudest, drowning out even me. They threw their arms up across their faces, blinded at the sudden brightness and stumbling back. One fell against one of his mates—the one-eyed pumpkinhead who'd been at the window, I thought—while the other tripped on the figure struggling on the ground and went down, his legs tangled in Nathan's and landing on top of him.

Terrified, I tried to backpedal, shouting, "Run, Nathan, *run*!" but there was no grass behind the shrubbery, the naked soil churned into a mud slick by all their feet, and my own feet went out from under me. Unable to stop, I slammed into the tangled pair, the blinded one and the pumpkinhead, and while I managed to stay upright, they sprawled in the muck.

Seeing all this, the other three scattered, slippy-slidey, running out the other side of the flashlight-lit leafy cave in a way that would have been comical if I hadn't been so afraid of what they'd done to Nathan—or what they still might do to me.

"Nathan!"

"Jane! *Gaak*!"

"Nathan?"

But Nathan was struggling with the Melon Head who'd landed on him. He'd managed my name, but then the wiry little thing lying on top of him had flipped over and started strangling him, gripping Nathan's throat and leaning in.

"Leave him alone!" I swung one flashlight like a club and hit the lumpy head as hard as I could. The light went out with a *sprang* when the head of the flashlight popped off at the impact, the batteries sliding out and flying wide. The murderous creature fell sideways with a cry, and then Nathan, so mud-covered he looked like one of *them*, was struggling to his feet, kicking loose from those tangling legs and falling into me. We both would have fallen from the slippery footing if I hadn't fetched up against the solid brick wall of the Norwich.

The two cannibals I'd knocked down lurched to their feet. The one was holding up the pumpkinhead, but the pumpkinhead kept his eye trained on me. His oversized mouth dropped open, and he let loose that ululating cry we'd heard when they were working on the door. The cry was picked up immediately by two and then three other voices out in the night; he was calling back the ones who'd fled.

"Run!" Nathan and I yelled together, then we each took the other's advice and got the hell out of there.

I had the light, so I lead, running back the way we had come in an adrenaline-fueled sprint. The rain spacked my skin hard enough to hurt, but I didn't care. The wind whipped me with my own hair, but I didn't care. I didn't know the area, didn't know if there was anywhere to hide; all I knew was I wanted my mom, and she was in that hospital, and the door we'd come out of was the only way in I'd ever seen, so I was going there. Now.

"Wait!"

I stopped, nearly sliding into the wall on the wet grass. Behind me, Nathan lay on that grass like a runner who'd slid into home. The way he'd fallen, I could see that though they were thick with mud, those were definitely socks.

"Where the hell are your shoes?"

"They took 'em."

I helped him to his feet. "What?"

He shrugged. I opened my mouth to say that was the stupidest thing I'd ever heard, but movement behind him caught my attention.

"Uh-oh!"

He turned. Lightning flashed, illuminating a half dozen crouching figures emerging from the shrubbery. The one in the lead had a head like a pumpkin, and the strobing sky flickered in his single eye.

"Run!" I shoved Nathan into the lead, confident my sneakers would give me better traction, and I wouldn't be left behind. I glanced back a few times, but couldn't make out our pursuers. They could see me, though; all they had to do was follow the bouncing flashlight. Turning it off or throwing it aside would have been the smart thing, but I just couldn't do it. Fear may have given our feet wings, but I knew they were gaining on us. I could hear them getting closer, first their weird, high hunting cry, and then, as they closed the gap, grunts and shouts, words in some language that was definitely not English.

We'd been running for maybe half a minute, though it had felt like forever, and I'd started thinking we'd missed the door in the rain when my name came drifting out of the storm.

"Jane?"

"Mom!"

"Jane? Nathan?"

The grass and mud suddenly turned to sidewalk cement beneath our feet, and there was Mom, standing at the open door with her flashlight in one hand and the end of the door-pulling rope in the other.

"Where the hell have you been? This *not* the night for— " She finally got a good look at us. "What the *hell* happened to you?"

"Inside!" I all but pushed my mother toward the open door. "Inside now! They're coming!"

"What? *Who's* coming?"

"The Melon Heads," said Nathan, eyeing the rope. He likely hadn't seen it when they'd snatched him away.

"Ah-ha, very funny! What's— "

An ululating cry cut through the night, six throats giving voice to their hunger in unison.

Mom's eyes were huge. "What was *that*?"

Now I *was* pushing her. "Tell you in a minute, Mom! In! Now!"

I poked at the rope, but the knot was soaked and swollen, and I had no time to work it loose. All I could do was kick it out of the way so the door would close. Nathan shoved the chair back under the crash bar and took a seat again.

It hadn't been enough before, but it was the best we could do.

Mom was in full-on Mom Mode, asking questions but not waiting for answers. "What happened to you? Are you hurt? Nathan? Are you? What was that sound? Was that a person?" Her attitude shifted from *concerned* to *angry*. "I asked you a question! You answer me. What happened to you?"

The door rattled against the chair back. Mom gave a little squeak.

"People, Mom. Maybe they're Melon Heads, I don't know." They were, and I did, but she didn't need to hear that right now. "They tried to take us, and now they're trying to get in again, so if

☽ Nathan's Night at Norwich ☾

you have any secret Norwich nurse thing to do to *keep* them from getting in again, *please do it now*."

The door gave a *heave*, the kind that had been Nathan's undoing earlier. He was more ready for it this time, planting his feet and gripping the door as best he could, but he was exhausted. "A little help here!"

I braced the chair with him while Mom, uncertain what to do but trying to protect the children, put her flashlight on the floor and took hold of the crash bar itself. The door *pulled*, hard, but we were okay. It pulled again, harder, and then again, harder still, and I'd figured out what they were doing; they'd started working together in a *heave-ho-heave-ho* rhythm, throwing their body weight into it and generating a terrible amount of force.

Just as I figured it out, the worst happened. They *heaved*, the hardest one yet, and I slipped on the wet floor. My feet kicked Mom's legs out from under her as I sprawled across Nathan's lap. My weight pushed his feet out, splayed them too wide, and the chair spun out from under the crash bar, and the door flew open.

Mom, lying right in front of the breached door, saw Pumpkinhead and his crew for the first time as they surged forward. She scuttled back away from the door on palms and soles with a scream.

Not fair! I thought. *We should have made it! Not fair!*

Pumpkinhead reached the stoop, glaring at me with his one good eye. He stretched forth a hand to shove the swinging door out of the way—and the lights came on.

The Melon Heads flinched back, squinting and covering their eyes in the glare of the reception overheads.

Lights! my brain screamed. *Lights equals electricity, and electricity equals—*

I lurched forward in Nathan's lap, kicking at the floor to spin the chair just enough. My fingers hooked through the end of the crash bar, and I yanked for all I was worth. The door swung, the edge of it actually brushing Pumpkinhead's reaching hand aside as he looked away from the light. He turned back, saw what was happening, made a grab for the door, but he was too late. The door *thunked* closed with a satisfying, electromagnetic *click*. There was a furious cry, and the door rattled. It rattled again but didn't budge.

I scrambled off Nathan and went to Mom, still sitting, stunned, on the floor.

"You okay?"

Her face was pale. "Who . . . What are they?"

"I don't know," I said, taking her under the arm to help her to her feet. "Melon Heads?"

"But . . . those aren't *real*, are they?" Was she telling or asking? "They're just, you know, *Weekly World Mirror* stuff. Right?"

"Are they?"

"They're going!" Nathan was at the window, hands cupped around his face to cut out the glare. "They know they can't get in, and they're leaving! We've won!"

"Won what?"

We all turned to see Amanda stride into the room and put her flashlight on the nurses' station counter.

Mom said, "Where have you been?"

"Somebody had to get the generator working."

"You fixed it?"

Amanda shrugged. "I don't know the first thing about motors or anything, so I just did what my dad used to do to his Buick." She smirked. "I kicked it."

"Seriously?"

"Hey, it worked. But what happened in here? The floor's a mess! And that chair looks broken. And— " She squinted at Nathan. "And where are your shoes?"

☆

The police were wrapping things up. A half hour after Amanda got the generator working, the regular power had come back on, and with it, the phones. Mom had called the police to report the hospital broken into and her children assaulted—it seemed she'd finally unofficially adopted Nathan—and they'd sent out a car. The two officers had taken statements from everyone (though as soon as Nathan uttered the phrase *Melon Heads*, they'd stopped taking notes, one mouthing, *We got another one* to his partner over Nathan's head), then checked the property. They'd found evidence of squatters in one of the other buildings, one that had already closed from lack of funding, though they'd seen no sign of the squatters themselves.

"Looks like a group of homeless folks got caught out in the storm, then got confused as to which building they were staying in. You not having any lights, I can see how it could happen."

"But they broke in here," Amanda had pointed out.

"They were in a hurry to get out of the storm. It's a pretty bad one out there."

☽ Nathan's Night at Norwich ☾

"And kidnapping Nathan?" Mom asked.

The officer pointed to Nathan's filthy, mud-caked socks. "Mugging. If he'd had a wallet, they would have taken that with the Nikes."

They told us all to have a good night—*As if!*—and sloshed back out to their cruiser. I went over to Nathan, who huddled, grinning, under a blanket.

"'Go get your mom while I hold them out'? Really?"

"Hey, it almost worked."

"Well, it was brave. Really stupid, but brave."

His grin widened. "Oh, *that* was stupid? What about you coming out into the storm like that?"

My face grew hot. "Well, *someone* had to save your ass."

"You were *supposed* to go get your mom."

"Hey, I *saw* you get sucked out that door. I couldn't just leave you."

"So, what, that makes running out there after me s*mart*?"

"I couldn't think of anything else to do!"

"Think harder next time."

I had to fight off a smile at that. "So, what are you sitting over here grinning about?"

He drew the blanket in tighter. "Well, let's see: I got to spend the night in Norwich Hospital before it closed down, survived an honest-to-God Melon Head attack, and I was rescued by a pretty girl. I mean, it's not exactly an action movie, but for me it's great."

I could feel my blush deepening. "So, I rescued you?"

"Yup. Pretty much."

"And . . . And I'm pretty?"

"Yup," he said. "Pretty much."

Well, I couldn't leave it at that, with him having the last word and all, but I couldn't think of anything else to do.

So I kissed him.

☾ ☆ ☽

When asked what he does, **Rob Smales** *tends to answer, "I write words." When feeling particularly full of himself, he may go so far as "I write the words that occur to me at the time." Larger combinations of these words, affectionately referred to as stories, have appeared in nearly four dozen publications and anthologies, been nominated for three Pushcart Prizes, won a couple of readers' choice awards, and appeared three times in Ellen*

☽ Rob Smales ☾

Datlow's honorable mentions list regarding her Best Horror of the Year *anthologies.*

His most recent works include the novellas LaundryLegs *and* Spearfinger, *and he hails from Salem, Massachusetts, where you can bet he's currently writing something either funny or scary, but probably dark.*

He likes the dark.

Follow him @Robert.T.Smales on Facebook.

You Couldn't Steal a House in the Eighties

Agrimmeer DeMolay

I note that shifty look about you, know it well, since I too have it. I realize you resent the fact that you're a child and an aspie, living in a world not interested in your existence, but I assure you that I too was once a divergent urchin with similar complaints, which were more pronounced in an era predating smartphones and the audiences they allow for.

Since the '80s, I've wandered this continent coast to coast, and now I've returned to this corner of it to raise *yourself*. I've found this place to be the Shire of North America, full of nothing to do except for the trees and bushes. When I was your age, the big pastimes were roaming the woods, booze, and D&D, not in that order. On one special day, we did all three of those at once, but that's another tale. None of those cost any money.

What? Oh, I see your point. Yeah, well, a drink costs money for its purchaser, not its drinker.

Get comfortable. Focus on me, not out the window, please.
little you, slouched and slanted
shirt on backward
scent of garlic and onions

Now I'm the distracted one. I get tugged into the endless details. You know how those go, don't you, your shirt, your lunch. Wait, I mean mine. Focus.

This realm's only world-famous landmark was a university so elite that none of us could imagine attending it. Where there's no money, no festivities, and no grand landmark, one played role-playing games. We had no internet to speak of, an age before regular peoples' FICO scores and monetized behavior algorithms. We met in person, in a basement as windowless as any bomb shelter, many hours fighting orcs and ogres, solving

☽ Agrimmeer DeMolay ☾

puzzles, dreaming horrible dreams—for fun—the whole night like that.

Our characters were pushing deeper into, or under, a mountain, fighting every thinking being in our path, a violent melting pot, with our guys getting more injured with each bout. Currently, a pair of ogres were running toward "us."

I tossed a handful of dice onto the table. Once they stopped clattering over papers and wrappers, Donal scanned them all and declared, "Thirty-two." We agreed that it was good, for it was exactly enough damage to bring both ogres barely into the negatives, which meant unconsciousness. KO'd foes don't hurt you back. Success.

> bottle of cream soda
> poorly drawn map of a hallway
> an actual shillelagh

The dice mingled with all those objects. We began scooping up the colorful plastic gems. I found one on the floor and said nothing, not to steal it but instead to stop us from having to redo that encounter.

Evan Escher—who was known as EE to the group—let us know the straits he was in. "My guy still needs healing and food. Do yours? Why don't any of these bruisers have snacks on them?"

Donal replied, "Like pepperoni in their pockets, except they don't have pockets. Hey, maybe they *are* the pepperoni. There's wood back in the last room, enough for a fire."

EE was extrapolating something about where campfire smoke would flow off to while underground, and then he was on to something else—about diseases or food poisoning—but I missed most of his words because the crescendo to "Bohemian Rhapsody" burst from the speakers simultaneous to EE's spoken thoughts.

At that point, I noticed, after the whole night, that the room was not, in fact, windowless.

> the gloss of a tiny glass rectangle
> near the ceiling
> obscuring stars in an inky sky
> where midnight looks exactly like two or four

Excuse me, what did you just say? Oh, you're right. There is indeed a sameness with the windows. I was just commenting on your staring out this one, wasn't I?

Speaking of distractions, someone in the basement observed, "We seemed to have lost Mikal."

☽ You Couldn't Steal a House in the Eighties ☾

EE popped a whole potato chip into his mouth and then another while Donal stood and lingered by the billiard table. Donal placed its rack upside down on his head so that it framed his face. After a stony pause, he enunciated, "Yield."

This struck EE and me as advice that we ought to give ourselves a break.

EE asked, "Want to go for a walk?" It's something we often did when our homework was light, frequently with no destination.

Donal said he'd pass, but I raised a thumb. Donal's face held a mix of disdain and disgust as if we offered him hashish, or perhaps he was merely tired.

EE and I stepped outside. In the clear night, an almost-full moon hovered high above us as it lit curbs, parked cars, and roofs of houses. I inquired, "When did *that* happen?"

EE gave no indication that he knew what I was referring to.

As an aside, a bit of advice in life, watch where you place your antecedents. They're infirm and need guiding hands.

Anyhoo, he and I stopped by his house, which happened to be next door, where we grabbed small bottles of spirits and crammed them into our jacket pockets.

We stepped outside yet again. Few pedestrians were out and about besides us, marching zombies adhering to sidewalk routes. We hopped a fence into someone's backyard and made a beeline for the sleeping woods. Soon, there were no human presences besides us two. A potent moon kindly lit boulders, branches, and the spaces in between them where two teens could amble.

> two downed branches cross
> darkness deepens beneath them
> cloaking a surprise
> for a footfall

EE got his foot stuck in some pock. After releasing it, he complained about his ankle but kept up his pace just the same.

We each took a few swigs of our respective potions. EE's bottle slipped out of his hand and bounced along the earth, losing a splash of its contents. He scooped it up and took another swig. I couldn't discern any schmutz in the colorless light but instead imagined it. Soil mixing with brandy within his throat struck me as overly dependent behavior, and to communicate such disapproval, I kicked the bottle out of his hands.

His face froze in the argent light as a shadow thickened below his furrowed brow. He plucked up his flask a second time and

☽ Agrimmeer DeMolay ☾

examined it. "Don't be a dick." Heavens, all the instances when I've been given this advice, so simple and yet so unattainable. Like the grains of sand on the neck of his bottle, I brushed such wisdom off then as I do now, and we trudged on.

>the sound of twigs snapping
>while advancing
>but a long quietude
>when we pause
>no cricket
>no mosquito
>no wind

In the washed-out light, we noticed a rock wall, sleeping bubbles of stone that extended in both directions into countless acres. Without a word, we both scrambled over its solidity without dislodging any part of it, not that we were being careful.

I mused, "This wall could be older than our nation."

EE pondered and added, "When they built it, you think they had us in mind? Their ghosts are rolling over, 'You damn kids!'"

My mind dwelled on the image of just one such being.

>a given Mark Twain character
>his body made of smoke
>waving an ashen fist at us
>from his coveted hilltop

I said, "He can keep what's left of his rotting hovel, which never had a bathroom even when it was new."

"Look," EE seemed to reply.

I turned toward where he pointed, and I expected to actually see that translucent colonist, but instead noticed a two-story structure in the distance, its plywood and planks glowing in silver light. Someone had half built a house and then left it there like that, an unguarded treasure, or rather the *lair* in which said treasure would surely lie.

We tried the front door because why not? Luck was with us; it was unlocked. EE slipped in soundlessly, and I followed. The place's floors were more plywood. I feared that they'd creak, so I stepped in the spots where EE had.

That first room was dimly lit by a glowing panel in the far wall.

Was anyone there besides us? If no one else, then why tiptoe? We gradually relaxed our movements.

There was a low-pitched hum issuing from some unseen source, filling the air. A staircase of grainy wood to my right led

☽ You Couldn't Steal a House in the Eighties ☾

to an upstairs. Before me was a room that opened to my left and a passageway straight in front of me that extended into deeper darkness.

EE strode through the far archway and disappeared into unlit backrooms.

>	the smell of sawdust
>	pink tufts of exposed insulation
>	hammer, screwdriver, and boxes of nails
>	in the floor's center
>	ready for someone inclined toward creation

I lurched toward the glowing panel in the far wall, curious to learn more about it.

>	knobs, dials, buttons
>	a luminescent strip of subscript
>	incremental etchings, like a yardstick's

My hand gingerly touched a fat dial. In that instant, a booming voice issued from all around the chamber, "—a whale of a cake for a whaaaale of a dad, at your participating Carvel ice cream store, yup, and this year your Carvel dealer makes 'em loaded with fudge and nuts, and you can get Fudgie with an ocean to serve twenty people— "

Both hands frantically pushed buttons, turned dials until a tiny but resounding *click* silenced the booming Carvel god.

Now it was clear to me what the hum was: speakers. The panel before me was the control center for a built-in stereo.

I whispered to myself, "What the fuck." It wasn't a question.

I heard someone on the second floor say the same sentence, only louder, a man's voice and not EE's. His *was* a question.

EE appeared from behind a panel. He shot me a look which was, I'm fairly sure, also that very same question.

To answer without making more noise, I raised my right hand and pointed downward at my crown.

Then I heard footsteps above us. I could see that EE heard them, too, because he galloped out the door we had entered through.

I followed, but with my first step, I kicked over a box of nails, scattering them like caltrops.

I paused to consider the new mess, a tinge of guilt finally being felt. If I stepped anywhere, I'd shuffle more nails.

That's when I saw someone plodding down the plywood stairs.

☽ Agrimmeer DeMolay ☾
leather boots
legs wearing paint pants
a belted waist
the stock of a long gun
I stopped watching and started running.

Yes, yes, I could see how this story can be seen as inappropriate for you, but let me be the judge of that. It's my mistake to make, not yours. Take it on advisement, or as a lesson, or as trivia, whatever you want to take away from it. We're too far into it to stop now. The afreet won't fit back into the flask.

I made it out of the half-built house. Looking back, I saw lights popping on in the window of the room I had been in. I ran further, an antelope over fallen branches and trenches. Another window lit up, and yet another. The guy we had awoken—er, who *I* had awoken—was apparently searching the rest of the house for more of . . . "us."

I paused to catch my breath and found EE nearby. I clarified, "This night has been fantastical. What an absolute treasure."

"Precious! But you can't steal a house," EE pointed out.

The moon set. I trudged back into the woods. I couldn't navigate so well without helpful moonlight.

I don't know when I realized that I was separated from EE. Either I or he was lost.

I realize now that I couldn't find that house again even if I tried to. Once complete, in 1980-whenever, it would look like everyone else's. For decades or a century, it would more or less be the same structure before going the way of that ghost-colonist's hovel.

That night, I imagined the gun-toting dude as the ogre, but now I think the ogre was myself, since I was, in fact, an interloper and he the defender. I admit there was some amount of luck on my side not to get into worse straits.

Then, in the distance, I heard one loud crack. It echoed among the oaks and was swallowed by a silence that followed.

Hm? You demand there be a point to this story? Well, then. Heyheyhey, put that gaming gizmo down for a sec, will you? I'm almost there.

How can I articulate a point? Maybe I need to tell myself before I can tell you, eh?

I met a surgeon in a New Haven hospital sometime the next year. While looking at his clipboard, he said, "People are dying of boredom."

☾ You Couldn't Steal a House in the Eighties ☽

I asked him, "How?"

He swiveled toward me with a look of being interrupted. You see, I didn't realize he wasn't initially speaking to me, but he answered me anyway as he pointed down a hallway that smelled of rubbing alcohol, "That emergency room is filled with people who were bored, and so they drove too fast, partied too hard, drank too much, and went too far. They were bored until injured or killed. If they recover, then they might repeat the whole cycle." He shuffled away toward more important matters. He wasn't speaking for himself.

I have pondered what he meant, and that might be the meaning, the crucible of Connecticut. Lo, the varied ways we cure our—

        handheld game computer
            lighting up
         whooshing, whooping
  pulling the boy's mind into its screen

My own almost follows his.

Some discussions are wins, others not so much.

☾ ☆ ☽

The boy slouches on this bed. His eyes laser-focus on the device gripped in both hands; his left shoulder dodges as if flinching from a ghost.

The lad pauses and shuts his game, eyebrows raised. His father has almost exited the room. The small voice quickly inquires, "Did EE get away too?"

The adult freezes, still gazing toward the doorway. "That's not part of the story. That's not the point of— "

The young person, undaunted, asks, "What happened to him?"

The man slowly pivots toward the lad and swallows. "He moved to Florida."

☾ ☆ ☽

Agrimmeer DeMolay *grew up in the New Haven area and now resides in the Hudson Valley. He writes contracts and whatnot for lawyers. He grows poems for those who like them, as seen in* RHINO, DoubleSpeak, *and* Antipoetry Magazine.

The Withering

Kurt Newton

It was one of those bright, sunny days when the leaves on the trees were 3-D holograms, the green tinged with yellow as if the sky's contrast dial had been turned up to ten. Liam Holden and his friend, Roman Moody, were on their bikes, riding like every other sunny summer day. Today, they were on the other side of town where Roman lived.

"You like arrowheads?" said Roman.

"Sure," said Liam.

"I heard there's this old woman who lives on the other side of these woods who finds arrowheads in her garden."

"Where'd you hear that?" said Liam, riding in slow circles and figure eights around the stationary Roman.

"There's a path down the road that supposedly leads right to her house. I hear she also makes the best lemonade around."

"I don't know."

"You want a lemonade, don't you?"

"I could use a lemonade about now." Liam licked his lips.

"Well, c'mon, let's check it out."

Liam and Roman were twelve years old. They shared the same seventh-grade homeroom but not much after that. Liam came from a well-to-do family, while Roman's was just trying to make ends meet. When Liam moved into our Connecticut town last summer, he looked like every other kid at Woodfield Middle School. Roman stood out for all the wrong reasons. His ragged hair and threadbare clothes told the story of his family's economic status. But when they met up at the beginning of the school year, it was like none of that mattered. When Roman's younger sister was diagnosed with a life-threatening illness, Liam was the first to offer any kind of emotional support. He and Roman became good friends after that.

☽ The Withering ☾

The two turned their wheels and peddled to a spot on the side of the road where, if they looked at just the right angle, the stone wall broke and the trees parted.

"This must be it," said Roman. They left their bikes in the ditch and began walking.

Most kids never imagine there are places beyond the woods. It was a boundary one just didn't cross. The woods were like the sea—if you ventured too far, you'd get lost, or you'd drop off the face of the Earth. If for nothing else, it was wild, and something wild living in that woods could come and get you. At least that's what their parents warned them.

But after walking along a narrow path that sometimes appeared to dead-end, the two boys walked out of the woods into someone's backyard. There was a large, colorful garden, a well pump, and a small cottage made of stone, all bathing in the sun.

"Isn't this trespassing?" murmured Liam, wary of the quiet. He didn't want to disturb anyone if they didn't want to be disturbed. But Roman just smiled as if to say *I told you so* and continued walking right up to the back door. Liam hung back as Roman knocked. They were standing on a fieldstone patio overgrown with moss. There was a small, round iron table and several matching chairs. Nearby was a circle of stones—a fire pit—with the charred remnants of a recent burning. Liam was staring at the shape of the remains, trying to figure out what it was, when the door opened.

The homeowner wasn't the witchy hag Liam had envisioned but a kindly old woman with gray hair, round glasses, and a warm smile. She held a serving tray with a pitcher of lemonade and two glasses. "I've been expecting you."

She made her way to the iron table and set the tray down. "Don't worry, I'm not psychic. I could hear you coming through the woods. Please, sit. What brings you two fine boys here?"

"Nothing, ma'am," said Roman. He grabbed the lemonade and drank.

The old woman turned to Liam, her eyes magnified. "And you?"

"Curiosity?" Liam ventured, as if there were a correct answer. "My name's Liam. Pleased to meet you, ma'am."

"Hello, Liam. Are you not thirsty?"

Liam looked at the glass of lemonade. Beads of sweat had already formed on the glass's surface. "Oh, sorry. Thank you." He took a sip, then took two sips more. It was true what Roman had said: it was the best lemonade he'd ever had. It tasted like summer and green grass, cookouts and fireworks. At least, that's what went through his brain with each swallow, like snapshots of all the best things about summer taken from his memory. "Roman says you find a lot of arrowheads?"

"Yes, in my garden," the old woman said.

It was then Liam heard a scratching noise, and movement caught his eye. Furry bodies were climbing up the side of the house, chasing each other it seemed. At first, he thought they were squirrels, but the color was all wrong. "Are those cats?" he said.

"Yes, my two boys. Cochise and Geronimo."

Another furry body caught Liam's attention. This one was on the grass, however, and it moved slowly as if its legs were having trouble getting in sync.

"And that's Uncas, poor dear. He's not doing too well." The old woman made a whisper noise with her lips, and the two cats on the house dropped to the ground and came over to investigate. Uncas lagged behind.

All three cats were calicos. Each had a slightly different fur pattern. Liam held his hand low and rubbed his fingers together. Cochise and Geronimo ignored him while Uncas locked onto the movement and hurried its pace toward him. The cat pushed into Liam's hand and nearly fell over. Liam let out a nervous laugh.

"He thinks you're playing," said the old woman.

"What's wrong with him?" Liam scratched under the cat's chin.

"He's dying. Probably cancer. It happens."

"Oh. That's too bad. He seems happy."

"He will be."

Liam stopped scratching then. He was uncomfortable with the old woman's comment, as if death was the answer to the cat's problem. There were vets that could treat cancer in pets. But not everybody had the money to afford it, thought Liam. He sipped his lemonade and glanced at Roman. Roman merely shrugged his shoulders.

"You feel for the animal, don't you, Liam?" The old woman's eyes were on him, unblinking. Liam nodded.

"It's okay to feel things. But this poor soul . . . Come here, baby." The old woman bent, and Uncas ran to her as best he could. She picked him up and cradled him in her lap. The cat purred. "This poor soul is destined for something new. Isn't that

The Withering

right, sweetheart?" She held the cat up and nuzzled her nose against its whiskers. The cat tried to meow. Nothing but a squeak came out. "See, he knows."

Once again Liam glanced at Roman. He gave Roman a slight nod in the direction of the woods to tell him that they should get going. But Roman simply stared at him as if he didn't understand.

"You're not curious about the names?" said the old woman.

Liam thought for a moment. "I'm pretty sure I've heard of Geronimo before. Are they Indian names? I mean, Native American?"

"Very good. All three were chiefs, Uncas included. In fact, this land we're now sitting on was part of Chief Uncas's tribal territory. They only took from the land what was needed. And gave back when they could."

"You sure know a lot about Native Americans," said Liam.

"I should. Unlike your family, my family came from here. Our roots run deep. These are my ancestors."

Liam could swear the old woman was referring to the cats. And then he realized it was the names of the cats she probably meant. "Cool," said Liam. He gulped the last of the lemonade. "Well, we should get going." Liam went to get up and had to sit right back down. A wave of dizziness swept through him like a summer breeze.

"Don't you want to see the garden?" asked the old woman.

"Yeah, the garden," said Roman. "You should probably take a look at the garden."

It was hard for Liam to think straight. His mouth was suddenly dry.

The old woman leaned forward. "I'll make you a deal. If you find any arrowheads, they're yours."

Liam got to his feet and steadied himself. His brain was lagging, his body moving before it was supposed to. "Aren't you coming?" he asked Roman, the words leaving his mouth as if from an echo chamber.

Roman looked at him, again with the blank stare. "I've seen it already. It's your turn."

The old woman smiled and nodded. She stroked the little sick cat's fur. Even the cat stared at him with its dying eyes as if to say, *Go on, look*.

The entrance to the garden was about fifty feet from the patio. Liam began walking, drawn to the patch of growth.

☽ Kurt Newton ☾

He heard Roman speak to the old woman. "We're even now, right?"

"Yes, my dear boy. How is your sister doing?" There was a smile in the old woman's voice.

What an odd conversation, thought Liam. Perhaps he was imagining it. Perhaps he was imagining all of this and he'd wake up in his bedroom, the smell of bacon wafting in from the kitchen, his mother humming a song from the radio while she prepared his breakfast.

Halfway to the garden, Liam didn't know if it was the sun beating down or the thickness of the air, but he began to feel a little like he'd eaten too much sugar on an empty stomach. There were butterflies floating around his insides and it made him feel both jittery and tired at the same time. He turned. From a distance, Roman looked scared. He saw the old woman lift the sick cat, Uncas, off her lap and place it on the ground. The cat began to make a beeline toward him, the slowest beeline ever.

When Liam reached the garden, the sky's contrast dial had been turned up another notch. It was strange because the light in the garden was too bright, the colors of the flowers a kaleidoscope of brilliant purples and yellows, oranges and reds. At the entrance was a narrow path that wove its way around shimmering islands of sweet-smelling flowers and spice-scented herbs. There were tall, wooden stakes covered in emerald-green vines bursting with ripening vegetables. The furrows between the rows were rich with freshly tilled soil, the smell of sweet musk. To his amazement, the dirt was littered with arrowheads like thick chips of black and amber glass.

Again, he turned to look at Roman and the old woman, but he could no longer see the backyard. The tall plants blocked his view, almost as if they had grown in height since his arrival. The old woman had said whatever he found was his, so Liam got down on all fours and began filling his pockets with the arrowheads. One was so sharp it cut his thumb, and it began to bleed. "Crap," he said, sucking the blood from the clean slice.

He thought he heard a low drumbeat that sounded as if it was coming from the woods. Or it could have been his heart thumping in his chest. The drumbeat increased in tempo, and he saw movement out of the corner of his eye. It was poor, sick little Uncas finally catching up to him. The cat approached, stopping now and then to lick the blood that had dropped from Liam's thumb onto the soil. The drumbeat turned into a chant that

The Withering

turned into a howling in Liam's ears. It was a primal sound that now felt like it was entering every pore of his body.

A wave of goosebumps broke across his skin, and he began to shiver and shake as if the sun had been momentarily blocked. But there wasn't a cloud in the sky. Liam didn't know what was wrong with him, but he suddenly felt very tired. He laid down on his back, on the warm furrows, and let the sun's rays cover him like an invisible blanket. The chills subsided.

There came a distant sensation of tiny paws padding up the length of his body. Uncas sat on his chest, its dead eyes now swirling with a kaleidoscope of colors.

Liam couldn't keep his eyes open any longer. But even from behind his eyelids, he could see. Everything was alive—the plants, the flowers, even the ground itself—swimming with an energy all its own. The arrowheads in his pockets hummed like tuning forks. He heard the song of every tree in the forest and its millennia of spirits buried at their feet.

He felt the transformation begin, the cancer in his body withering like a dead vine only to be replaced by another that was brighter, stronger, more resilient. Most of all, he felt the excitement building in his heart, in his bones, in his feet, to once again rejoin his brothers and play like the warriors they once were.

☆

Kurt Newton *cites Dr. Seuss, Maurice Sendak, and Edward Gorey as his earliest literary influences. Add Saturday morning Looney Tunes, a healthy dose of* The Twilight Zone *and* The Outer Limits, *and a recipe for horror writer was in the making. Kurt's stories have appeared in over three hundred publications, including* Weird Tales, The Dark, Vastarien, The Best of Not One of Us, Space and Time, Black Infinity, Nightmare Abbey, *and* Cosmic Horror Monthly. *He is the author of three novels and four collections of short stories. He is a lifelong resident of Connecticut. Visit Kurt at kurtnewton.weebly.com.*

P.E.T.E.

Dale W. Glaser

Danny Cobb took a small lead off second base. Normally, he wouldn't dare risk being picked off, no matter how much Coach Emmons encouraged him from the dugout, for fear of bringing the wrath of his fellow eleven- and twelve-year-olds down on his head. But Danny felt confident. No one was paying any attention to him. They'd notice if he actually broke and tried to steal third, but that wasn't his plan. He just wanted a head start, a slight edge, and if he kept his movements small, he could get it. All eyes were on Pete Toomey, standing ready in the batter's box.

Pete at the plate gave Danny even more confidence. Throughout the entire season, Danny had never been on base with Pete up at bat. Now they were in the league championship, and in the bottom of the ninth, trailing 3–2 with one down, Danny had knocked a grounder to short that should have made for the easy second out. But the shortstop's throw went wide, and Danny had hustled to second on the error. Jason Valhern had struck out, setting up what could be the final at bat of the game: bottom of the ninth, two out, the tying run in scoring position. Top of the order. And, as everyone knew, Pete Toomey could hit.

The crowd was on their feet, cheering and yelling, a few voices urging the Tigers's pitcher, Brian Stirk, to throw heaters for strikes, drowned out by the parents and friends of the Roadrunners, not to mention the Roadrunners's dugout, chanting, "Pete! Pete! PETE! PETE!" Danny had played alongside Jason and Brian and most of the other boys for years, ever since T-ball, and he had worked hard and had fun, but deep down he knew he had no natural talent. Pete Toomey had come out of nowhere, arriving in town with his mother over Christmas break, starting sixth grade halfway through the year and showing up for Little League tryouts

☽ P.E.T.E. ☾

in the spring, where he blew everyone away, not only making the team but earning the leadoff spot.

Before Pete had moved to Easton, Brian had been the best player in the league, the one people could see winning state titles in high school, maybe even getting a UConn scholarship. It didn't hurt that Brian's father was a coach and had been since before Brian was even born. The fact that Pete overshadowed Brian only made Pete seem like that much more of a phenomenon and made it more fitting that the championship came down not just to Roadrunners versus Tigers but Brian on the mound versus Pete at the plate, a showdown for the ages.

The Tigers in the infield were tense, too tightly coiled for chatter, one out away from winning the trophy. Danny crept to his right, 170-plus feet away from sending the game into extra innings, prolonging the most magical part of a summer infinitesimally longer, and he wanted it so desperately. He ground the cleats of his left foot into the dirt while Brian went into his windup without even glancing back at second base. Danny was ready to push off and sprint as soon as Pete made contact with the ball, not if, but when.

Pete swung at the first pitch, the aluminum of his bat chimed, and for a heartbeat, he didn't move but only watched the ball hurtling through the air like a ghostly bullet, not in an arc high enough to shoot over the outfield fences, where the sightly rusty signs for the White Barn Coffee & Market and the Easton Pharmacy hung, but straight as a frozen rope, just over the webbing of the first baseman's glove as he went vertical to snag it. The ball cleared the infield but was going to fall in shallow right field, and Adam Gilman was charging in at it; Danny snapped back to himself and started to run like the devil was on his heels.

He rounded third, arms pumping, batting helmet slipping off the back of his head, and bolted for home. Tim Coyle, the opposing catcher, stood upright behind the plate, not covering it, not ready to catch the ball, so Danny knew he didn't need to slide. Danny stomped on home as he overran it, then immediately turned around, gasping, to watch Pete.

He expected to see Pete heading into second. Apparently, so did the Tigers, as Adam threw the ball to Robby Marshall at the top of the diamond, but Pete was already turning the corner at third. Tim stepped forward, bracing himself with one foot on home plate, holding up his mitt for the ball. Robby took half a second to orient his sights on where to throw as Pete, already running impossibly fast, somehow kicked in the afterburners and put on another burst of speed. Pete dove headfirst for home, kicking up a cloud of dust, as the ball zipped into Tim's mitt with a meaty *thwack*. Pete's hand found the surface of the plate before Tim could sweep his glove down and tag him, and the umpire was signaling safe repeatedly with energetic outward chops of his arms, and the game was over; they had won, Danny had tied it up, and Pete had scored to make it 4–3; the Roadrunners were champions. Everyone poured out of their dugout and gathered around home plate, jumping and high-fiving and shouting, and within a few seconds, Pete was up on his teammates' shoulders, and the chant had resumed again, "Pete! Pete! PETE! PETE!"

☆

The July afternoon stretched on into evening, the sun in no particular hurry to set, but it was truly late and beginning to grow dark by the time Pete and Danny finally headed home. Danny's parents and little sister Kellie had been at the game, cheering them on, with Danny's dad standing alongside other parents afterward, taking snapshots of the team posing with their trophy. His parents had taken Kellie home, trusting Danny to walk home with Pete after the end-of-season party at Mr. Pizza. The attendant sense of freedom and maturity had added to the enjoyment of the celebration, not that it needed it. Danny had scarfed down four slices of sausage and pepper pizza and downed two tumblers of Pepsi. He and his teammates fed quarters, supplied by Coach Emmons, into the jukebox to play Def Leppard and Whitesnake, and into Mr. Pizza's lone arcade cabinet to play round after round of *Centipede*. When the party had broken up, Danny had asked Pete if he wanted to go over to the Corner Cupboard, down at the other end of the shopping center, before walking home, and Pete had agreed.

Little League had introduced Pete and Danny, but they had bonded over comic books. Danny had made a joke at practice about a fastball special, not expecting anyone to get it, and Pete had grinned at him and said, "Like Colossus and Wolverine?" That had opened the floodgates as they started comparing favorites, and soon after, Danny invited Pete to walk with him to Corner Cupboard after school. The tiny convenience store, despite being otherwise unremarkable, had the best spinner rack in town.

While school had been in session, they had gone to the Corner Cupboard every Wednesday afternoon, but Danny and Pete hadn't made it there since summer vacation had started

☽ P.E.T.E. ☾

a few weeks earlier. They grabbed their favorites—*X-Factor*, *Uncanny X-Men* and *Classic X-Men* for Danny, *Fantastic Four*, *Thor*, and *Silver Surfer* for Pete—plus a couple of Yoo-hoos, paid, and headed for home.

Pete always read his comics while they walked, holding them in one hand by folding them back severely around the stapled spine. Danny had asked him once why he didn't try to take better care of the comics; by the time they were grown-ups, *Silver Surfer* #6 might be worth hundreds of thousands of dollars like a *Batman* or *Superman* comic from way back when. Pete had laughed and said he didn't think much about the future at all. Danny had let it lie after that. He and Pete had different lives; Pete lived in the Tara Apartments along Main Street, just him and his mom, while Danny's family lived in a Colonial at the end of High Ridge Drive, a well-manicured cul-de-sac about a quarter mile further back. Pete called Danny's parents "Ozzie and Harriet" in a tone that not only took in their model marriage but their whole middle-class lifestyle, and Danny would laugh at that despite feeling like he only partly understood the joke. Danny sometimes wondered if he had never been able to get Pete interested in X-Men because they were outcasts trying to find a place in the hostile world around them. Pete preferred the cosmic adventures that took place in far-off Asgard, or the Negative Zone, or the alien world of the Badoon Brotherhood.

Danny held his own comics gingerly between his thumb and forefinger, shifting them occasionally to not leave oily prints on the covers. While Pete read, Danny watched for cars and other hazards, but in a small town like Easton, both of those were few and far between, even now with the curtain of night falling and the streetlights buzzing. Mostly, Danny watched Pete. Danny liked the golden flecks in Pete's brown eyes, the swell of his biceps and the smoothness of his dark skin. Pete was beautiful to Danny in some ways he could describe and in others that he couldn't quite articulate and would never want to speak aloud even if he could. Some of Danny's classmates already had girlfriends, and Danny envied them for the experience, if not the specific girls they went out with. Sometimes Danny wished Pete was a girl, and sometimes Danny wished he himself were a girl so that he and Pete could be together, hold hands while they walked, even go as a couple to the Friday night dances at the town firehouse and hold each other swaying to the slow songs.

☽ Dale W. Glaser ☾

They were about to cross Holly Lane, on the other side of which was a single, long building housing ground-floor storefronts—Spokes the bicycle shop, Easton Florist, Zara's Baker—then Miller Street, and then the courtyards of Tara Apartments. Pete and Danny would cut across the grass to the back of the two-story brick units, and Pete would climb the stairs to his place while Danny kept going toward his neighborhood. They had done it countless times, and it was always around this point, walking along the chain-link fence with the green plastic slats that surrounded the electrical tower and transformer, approaching the corner of Main and Holly, that Danny would begin to feel an ineffable sadness, knowing that another walk with Pete was almost over. It hit him doubly hard today, now that the baseball season was over as well. He didn't know how he would make it through the rest of the summer.

A car swerved from Main onto Holly so fast that the tires squealed. The driver hit the brakes as soon as the car was fully on the side street, not out of concern to avoid hitting the boys, but as if to cut them off. Danny froze midstep, thinking for half a second it was a police car, given the size and shape, but then he registered that the hulking sedan was entirely black, including its tinted windows. Beside him, Pete dropped his *Silver Surfer* comic, tensing reflexively into a fighting stance, legs spread, fists raised.

Both front doors of the black car opened, and two adults Danny had never seen before stepped out. The driver was a broad-shouldered man with a shaved head, while the passenger was a slim woman with black hair pinned up in a bun. Both were wearing dark suits and mirrored sunglasses.

The man closed his door and took a step closer to Pete, saying, "It's over, kid. Time to come with us." His voice was hard and cold as granite.

"No," Pete said with quiet defiance, his fists creeping higher, from waist-high to even with his chest. "You better leave us alone."

"Us?" the woman repeated mockingly as she walked around the front of the car. She was carrying a steel briefcase. "We don't care about your little friend here. We just want you. Tell him to run along before he gets hurt."

"Pete, who are these people?" Danny tried to ask, but the words came out in a breathy whisper, like this was a bad dream where he was too paralyzed to scream. Whoever the adults were, they were terrifying, radiating pure menace. The man seemed emotionless, willing to do whatever violence was necessary to take Pete away with no qualms whatsoever, while the woman felt eager, like a compressed spring ready to explode, almost hoping that Pete would put up a fight so that she could lash out.

Pete ignored Danny, his eyes fixed on the man as he took another step forward. Pete slid backward a step. "Leave us alone, I said," he warned, "me and my mom . . . "

"Your mom?" The woman laughed cruelly. "Is that what she had you call her? Were you indulging her, or did you actually develop your own little delusional version of reality? Honestly, it's going to take so much taxpayer money to reprogram you back at Omega, and we're wasting more and more of it every second we're in this boonie little town . . . "

"Dr. Larkin is dead," the man cut in flatly. "Now you've got no one to cover for you, nowhere else to go, so come with us."

"She's . . . you killed her?" Pete asked. He sounded to Danny as if he were on the verge of tears.

"She signed her own death warrant when she ran off with you." The woman shrugged. She had taken up a position directly beside the man. She reached into her jacket, pulled out a gun and pointed it at Pete. "Get in the fucking car before I forget what a valuable asset Omega thinks you are."

"No!" Danny cried out, surprising everyone, including himself. He stepped in front of Pete, between his beloved friend and the muzzle of the gun.

"Stupid kid," the man growled, grabbing Danny's shoulder. "We told you to run along, and we won't tell you again." He yanked hard and shoved Danny aside. Danny sprawled on the street and felt the knee of his uniform tear as he hit the asphalt, bright pain blossoming from the impact. His X-Men comics fluttered out of his hand.

Pete gave a wordless howl, and Danny couldn't tell if it was for his sake, or for Pete's mom, apparently someone named Dr. Larkin, who Pete only called his mother, or if it was for something else entirely, deep within Pete's heart. Holly Lane was shaded by tall oak and maple trees, outside the reach of the nearest streetlamps, but Danny swore he could see Pete's golden irises glowing. The glow expanded until it was undeniable, not a trick of the light or Danny's imagination. It was as if Pete's eyes were high-intensity light bulbs, and Danny couldn't tear his gaze away from the searing, consuming white light haloed in pale blue above and deep magenta below.

Everything happened in a rush of chaos that prevented Danny from fully grasping the sequence or what was cause and what was effect.

The man yelled, "NO!"

The gun in the woman's hand fired with an earsplitting crack.

Pete's howl of agonized grief escalated to a shriek of rage, and the light in Pete's eyes exploded outward with the force of a firehose.

Danny felt a blast wave of heat radiating outward and threw his arm across his eyes to shield them from the blinding brightness, his skin hot all over. He heard the woman cry in a high-pitched wail, then fall silent. The steel briefcase she had been carrying clattered to the street, followed by the meaty thump of her collapsing frame.

A slightly different sound of bodily impact reached Danny's ears, and he risked a peek from behind his elbow. The man had tackled Pete, driving him backward and pinning him to the sidewalk on the west side of Holly. Pete thrashed his legs and twisted his arms with all his might but was overmatched by the larger-than-average adult, trained for a dangerous job. The man straddled Pete's chest with his knees on Pete's shoulders, one forearm across Pete's neck. "Save yourself the struggle, kid," the man growled through clenched teeth.

The man increased the pressure just below Pete's jawline, twisting Pete's head to the side. Pete strained against it for several seconds, trying to bring the man into his eyeline, then gave up and allowed his head to be rotated as far back as it would go. Pete bellowed and blasted another white-hot beam wreathed in blue and magenta electrical arcs, which sliced through the chain-link fence and vaporized the electrical transformer. A shower of sparks fountained out of the ruined stump of twisted metal and wires, then faded.

The area around them fell into the shadows of true night, with no streetlamps, window lights, or other sources of illumination to interrupt the darkness. Danny felt his heart in his throat, hammering hard enough to pulsate along his eardrums. On numb, shaky legs, he rose to his feet and crept toward Pete and the man, emboldened by the cover of darkness. The man leaned almost all his weight across Pete's windpipe, his other

☽ P.E.T.E. ☾

hand braced on the sidewalk. Pete's eyes were dimming, rolling back in his head.

Danny raised his leg and stomped his baseball cleats down on the man's splayed fingers, screwing his foot down as hard as he could.

The man roared furiously, tearing his hand out from under Danny's cleats with great effort and lashing out with a fist at Danny's knee. Blinding pain exploded as Danny felt the joint bend wrong, and he toppled down.

At the same time, Pete recovered enough to push the man up and off him. Pete sat up, looked at the black sedan on Holly Lane, and unleashed another white-hot torrent of destruction from his eyes. The middle of the car sagged and melted away, and the back end exploded in smoke and flames.

Out of the corner of his eye, Danny saw the man flinch against the force of the blast. The woman simply rolled like a ragdoll, lifeless. Her briefcase, deformed by the intense heat, sprang open as it was blown across the street, and folders of papers and photographs scattered everywhere. Danny spotted his X-Men comics swirling in the air, and his terrified, panic-stricken mind seized on them. He had to reach them, get them back, as if they were talismans that could somehow pull him out of this nightmare, turn back time to before the black sedan had cut them off in the street.

He crawled in an awkward tripod gait, the leg the man had punched all but useless. Danny passed the dead woman, trying not to look at the gaping wound, still steaming, where her right arm had been severed from her torso, the blood-soaked cross section of sliced muscle and cleaved bone and the exposed interior lung tissue. He reached the first comic, the cover torn in half, its edges singed. He grabbed for it but froze as he saw what lay beside it: a photo of Pete, younger but recognizable, stapled to a sheaf of papers striped in cream and pale green. By the flickering light of the flames, which had spread from the bisected chassis to the shutters and awning of Spokes, Danny scanned the printouts.

"P.E.T.E." ran across the top in oversized letters, followed by an omega symbol, drawn in rows of asterisks and spaces. Beneath that, the words "PLASMA-EMITTING TACTICAL EMBRYON," followed by line after line of technical data, abbreviations Danny didn't recognize and numbers he couldn't decipher, except for occasional self-explanatory fragments like "13,000°F" and

☽ Dale W. Glaser ☾

"LETHAL EXPOSURE" and "100% TERMINAL." But his eyes were drawn back again and again to young Pete's face and its hollow, haunted expression staring at the camera. Danny remembered glimpsing that expression on Pete's face when he and his mother, or Dr. Larkin, had first come to town, stealing fleeting glances at the new boy. But it had gone away, slowly but surely, replaced with the joy of catching the final out in a game, the excitement of following the Silver Surfer off to Rigel 3, the laughter when their algebra teacher, Mr. Hankenhof, had come to school wearing an outdated shirt from the '70s with such a wide collar that Jason Valhern called him Mr. Hang Glider Hof.

Whether he understood them or not, Danny knew these papers mattered, even more than the comics. He grabbed the folder full of Pete's life before they had met and hugged it to his chest. He heaved himself upright, leaning heavily on his non-useless leg, and turned around.

Pete and the man were squaring off. The man had his hands raised, Pete's were at his sides, and they paced in a wary circle. Danny had seen it before in the Saturday morning wrestling matches; whoever kept their hands up and their arms out was afraid, and whoever looked the most relaxed was confident they were going to win. The man reared up to his full height, arms extended above his head as if he were about to bring a sledgehammer down on Pete's skull. But it was all a feint, as the man immediately crouched and dove at Pete to tackle his legs.

Pete wasn't fooled. He let loose the plasma from his eyes in a blinding flash, and most of the man's body ceased to exist except for sizzling chunks of his bent elbows and one flaming shoe. The plasma beam struck the surface of Holly Lane and burrowed into the earth. Pete opened his mouth to scream, and more plasma issued forth, his face lost in a horrible nimbus, an angel of death with a smiting sword in an aura of blue and magenta, ripping the world apart. The two halves of the black sedan fell into the widening chasm, and Danny fell backward helplessly, slamming his tailbone on the street. Deep underground, thunder boomed, and somewhere down Main Street, a manhole cover clanged upward into the dark night sky, ejected by a geyser of flame. Others joined the chorus as the fire in the town's gas lines spread.

Finally Pete cut off the plasma, shaking his head ruefully. Danny became dimly aware of a low, orange light just beyond the nearest silhouetted buildings, an inferno of house fires rag-

☽ P.E.T.E. ☾

ing across town, surrounding them. Pete staggered toward Danny, who was crying and couldn't stop. The situation crystallized in Danny's mind: bottom of the ninth, two out, and Pete could hit, with an unnatural, uncontrollable power. Pete had killed the woman in the dark suit, murdered her, and he had also murdered the man, and who knew how many others in the past, how many more in the future?

Including Danny himself?

Danny had seen that if Pete decided to turn his obliterating gaze on anyone, there was nothing they could do about it. There was nothing for Danny to do but wait for Pete's judgment. But as Pete reached him, there were no pinpoints of hot death in his eyes. He sank to his knees. "Danny," Pete rasped. "Help . . . please . . . help me . . ."

Despite himself, Danny pushed himself off his back and sat forward. The skin around Pete's eyes and mouth was ravaged, cracked and blackened like overcooked meat, blood trickling to his chin. And he was crying, just like Danny was crying, tears glistening against the raw, red fissures.

Danny looked down at the papers in his lap. A dossier of printouts that quantified every element of Pete's strange physiology, line by line down to a sum total as a weaponizable monster, and a book of colorful drawings celebrating powerful mutants who lived and loved in spite of a world that hated and feared them. Danny raised his gaze and laid a hand against Pete's cheek.

"I will," Danny promised. "I'll help you."

Somewhere nearby, the sirens of a fire engine blared. Somewhere else, another gas line detonated, and the horizon brightened with flame. Danny and Pete helped each other to their feet and began to slowly make their way toward the edge of town, and whatever lay beyond it, together.

☾ ☆ ☽

Dale W. Glaser *is a lifelong collector, re-teller and occasional inventor of fantastic tales. He has published over forty short stories, plus various pieces of poetry, drabble and flash fiction, many of which were collected in Assorted Malignancies, published in 2023. His lifelong love of written words has manifested as a devotion to the English language almost exclusively, which is probably just as well because if he were to master any of the dead tongues that conceal ancient mysteries and invoke malevolent forces, we'd all be in trouble. He currently*

Dale W. Glaser

lives in Virginia with his wife, their three children, and a rotating roster of half a dozen or so pets. He can be found online at dalewglaser.wordpress.com.

The Ghost Girl of Rocky Neck

Benjamin Thomas

Tommy was running barefoot along the blue trail near Tony's Nose Overlook when his foot slipped and twisted sideways. He hit the ground and cried out. Rolling onto his back, knee bent and in his hands, Tommy sucked in air to try to push the pain aside.

"Jacob!" He called for his older brother while tears began to well.

The bottom of his foot was a rubbery mix of sweat, blood, and clumps of dirt. How far were they from the campground? Could he limp back on his own? Be welcomed by the scorn of his mother?

"Jacob!" He called again, but the trail was empty.

A dog barked from somewhere close. Tommy held his foot and tried to brush the dirt away. A woman came around the corner, laughing with a friend. Tommy scooted to the side of the trail to take up the least amount of space.

"Hey," the lady said. "Are you okay? Did you fall?"

He put his foot back on the ground and winced. "I'm fine. Thanks."

"Are you sure? Are you with your parents?"

"No. My brother's here. He's up there." Tommy pointed to where the trail rounded a corner and hoped Jacob really was somewhere nearby.

Not that he would notice if Tommy fell behind. His brother would be too busy chasing the older kids from a few campsites down. Ever since Jacob turned fourteen, he only focused on his friends or older people who could trade him a cigarette or a lighter or something cool that he could put in his room. Tommy, being four years younger, wasn't in high school, hadn't kissed anyone, and hadn't tried a sip of alcohol. Recently, Jacob started reminding him he was still just a kid.

☽ Benjamin Thomas ☾

"Okay," the woman said and, with a wary look at her friend, kept going.

Tommy started limping, leaving streaks of sticky blood on the rocks. He called his brother's name again, but no one answered. Jacob was probably at the end of the trail, down by the water or back on the beach with his new friends. What would he say to his parents if Tommy turned up alone? They were only allowed to hike the short trail on their own because Jacob promised to stay with him.

Voices came from around the corner. Younger voices, not adults or parents. Tommy froze. One of them was Jacob. He came back. Tommy couldn't stop himself from smiling.

Until the voices formed words and reached his ears.

"I don't know. He probably found something stupid and ran off. He's *so* lame. Every little animal or something, he's gotta go look at it."

One of the other boys laughed. "My dad gave me a gun to shoot squirrels."

"I have a BB gun too," Jacob said.

"No, a real gun. A twenty-two. Said I'm a good shot, too. Could hit a squirrel right outta a tree."

"No way," Jacob sounded marveled by this fact. They came around the corner, and Tommy couldn't bring himself to look at anything other than the ground. His foot ached, but he pressed it against the dirt and rocks in a solitary act of defiance. The pain caused his knee to shake. Jacob scoffed. "What the *hell* did you do, Tommy?"

That was another thing his brother had started doing: swearing. He would say the words randomly or when his friends from school were over and they were all hanging around by the pool, each one with a beer from their father's fridge in hand. Tommy came outside one time when they were doing this, and that was the first time he heard his brother say the f-word. The cuss sandwiched between *you better not . . . say anything to Mom or Dad*.

Tommy had gone back inside and turned on his Switch only to stare at the screen. *The Legend of Zelda* wasn't as much fun as when they were trying to figure it out together, each one taking turns and giving the other tips and pointers. Laughing when they messed up.

"Dude, seriously, what did you do?" Jacob asked.

☽ The Ghost Girl of Rocky Neck ☾

He was flanked by two boys from other campsites. One laughed while the other pulled out his phone and held it up. "Let me see."

Tommy shook his head.

"Come on, show me your foot."

Was this their way of including him? Making him part of the team? Tommy thought maybe, but somewhere inside, he knew it wasn't true. Nevertheless, he relented and awkwardly brought his foot up and rested it on his knee.

"Nice." The kid took a picture with his phone.

"This is why I told you to stay on the beach," Jacob said. "Now Mom and Dad are gonna go off. Good job."

"You were supposed to stay with me," Tommy said quietly. "Not just run off."

"No, I was supposed to be hiking. It's not my fault you can't keep up. You shoulda stayed on the beach."

"Then I'll just go back!" Tommy yelled.

One of the other kids put a hand to his mouth and faked surprise.

The one with the phone smirked. "Looks like he's gonna cry."

"Probably." Jacob rolled his eyes.

Tommy's stomach burned. He wanted to kick the kid in the shin and run, but his foot ached and his chest was tight, so all he did was turn and sprint back the way they came. Each time his sole hit the ground, the slice in his skin burned.

He brushed by other hikers, tears on his cheeks, and kept going until he reached the first part of the trail, a short but steep climb he now had to descend. He paused, waiting for a small group and their two dogs to come up. A few of them looked at him; one even hesitated slightly like he was going to say something, but didn't. When they were gone, Tommy turned to start climbing down when he saw a flash of white against a nearby tree. The trail was empty, but he swore he just saw a—what was that—a girl?

"Hello?" Tommy's voice shook. "Is someone there?"

But no one replied. There was just the faint sound of footsteps and a little bit of laughter.

☾ ☆ ☽

Back on the beach, Tommy's mother was furious. Several other people were watching her, listening to her shout at both of them. Tommy hung his head low while Jacob tried, and failed, to

Benjamin Thomas

argue that it wasn't his fault. That Tommy shouldn't have gone anyway, and how it wasn't his job to watch him all the time.

"This is why you should have let me stay home." He smacked his hands against his thighs. "I didn't want to come this year and you guys made me. So, this is your fault."

Their father stood up from his foldable chair and cleared his throat. "That's enough."

Tommy's mother finished cleaning his cut. She tied a bandanna across it and stood to say something to their father. Jacob sat and scowled at him.

They left the beach, his older brother's friends snickering from adjacent seats on a nearby log. Tommy looked over as one of them raised a fist to his cheek and mimicked him crying. Tommy's face turned red. They funneled into their parent's SUV, Jacob purposely shoving Tommy against the door.

"Jacob Miles," his mother shouted and slapped a hand on the hood of the car. "You want that done to you? Have me or your father shove you around so you see what it's like?"

"No." His voice was small.

"For Christ's sake, you should be thankful you have a brother. You realize how lonely it is growing up as an only child?"

Their father cleared his throat again, his way of awkwardly wedging himself into a conversation. "All right, Trace. He's sorry. Let's just enjoy the beach and then go get something to eat in town."

"Oh no. They aren't going to town. Not after that. We're going back to the camper."

"What?" Jacob exclaimed. "You can't ground us on vacation."

"Wanna bet, young man?"

Tommy slumped down on a towel, too scared to look at his brother and too bummed to look at his parents. A horn blared, and Tommy looked behind them. She was only there for a second, but Tommy swore he saw the girl from the trail.

☆

Tommy's mother and father sat outside their camper in the same folding chairs they used on the beach. Each of his parents was reading—their father a magazine and their mother a paperback book—while holding a drink in the other hand. Kids dashed by on bikes, and Tommy slumped back from the window and lay on his bunk.

☽ The Ghost Girl of Rocky Neck ☾

"This is your fault," Jacob said for the hundredth time since they had been locked inside. A timer on the microwave clock continued its countdown: a little over two hours left. "Why did you even want to come anyway? Those guys don't like you."

Tommy rolled over and folded his pillow over his head, wishing his mother hadn't taken the headphones and iPod he kept hidden underneath it. Or the tablet that hung around on the folded-down kitchen table. She couldn't have left something behind? Anything to drown out the incessant mockery coming from his brother's mouth?

He wondered if this was going to be the family's last trip to Rocky Neck. Tommy loved coming here. Loved looking over the trail maps with Jacob and their father, planning future hikes and adventures. He liked to pretend the maps were faded and old, and if he touched them a bit too roughly, they would tear.

Tommy curled his toes. His skin stung. The bandage—a real one, applied when they got back to the camper—was warm and sticky on the inside. He was starting to drift off, his eyelids heavy and foggy with the light gray color of a—girl? The camper door swung open; Jacob was on his feet. Tommy rolled over, squinting his eyes tight. Where did the—had he just seen someone?

"Finally," his brother said as he pulled on a pair of shoes.

His mother paused, her hand in their cooler. "Finally what? I still see plenty of time left on that clock."

"Ma, I'm not four years old. I'm fourteen, damn it."

The muscles in their mother's cheeks tightened. She put two bottles of beer on the table and gently closed the cooler. "You may be fourteen, *damn it*, but I'm forty. So, take your shoes off and sit back down because you just added another hour to your time. Got it?"

Before he could protest, she had readjusted the timer and was at the door. "Tommy, we're walking across to Jay and Patti's. You're still grounded, but if you need us, just open the door and holler, okay?"

Tommy nodded. When she was gone, his brother pressed his face against the door's window until finally grabbing his shoes and slipping them on.

"Where are you going?"

"Down to Kyle's." He glared. "Do *not* say anything."

"She's going to come back. Not to mention it's light out; how do you expect not to get caught?"

☽ Benjamin Thomas ☾

Jacob shut the bathroom door. "Tell her I'm in the bathroom."

"She can just knock on the door."

"Shut up, Tommy. It's your fault I'm stuck in here, so bite me and go back to bed, okay?"

Like that, he was gone. Tommy groaned and dropped back to his bed only to roll over and find himself face-to-face with the pale complexion of a girl.

He screamed, and she clasped her palm against his mouth. Her skin was frozen. As cold as ice. Tommy's chest pounded. His eyes swelled, and he wanted to scream again. Her skin was *wrong*. He could almost see through her.

When she slowly took her hand away, Tommy was nearly hyperventilating. She waited, a soft expression on her translucent face.

"You're a ghost. You're a ghost. Oh my God, are you a ghost?"

She prayer-pressed her hands beneath the side of her head as if she were lying down for an afternoon nap and nodded at him. Tommy jumped from his bed and stumbled backward until he hit the inside wall of the camper. He tried to calm his breathing. The door was only a few feet away, yet oddly, he didn't want to run through it.

"How—why—I don't even know what to say. Who are you?"

When she spoke, her voice was nothing but a whisper. "Hailey."

"Your name is—was—Hailey?"

She nodded.

He opened his mouth to ask something else when the door opened, and his father came in. His old man paused, an eyebrow raised.

"You all right, son?"

Tommy looked frantically from his now-empty bed and back to his dad. "*Yeah*—yes. Yes, I'm okay."

"Right." He retrieved more drinks from the cooler. "I know this isn't the way you wanted to spend an afternoon of your vacation, but you guys have to learn that your mother worries about you. She wants you to take care of one another." His attention focused on the bunk beds. The *empty* bunk beds. "Tommy? Where's your brother?"

Tommy's eyes went wide as his father looked around. "Jacob?"

☽ The Ghost Girl of Rocky Neck ☾

With his heart racing, Tommy brought a hand to his forehead to try and stop a confession from spilling forth. If he ratted out his brother, then Jacob would hate him even more. But he couldn't lie to his father. Oh God. Oh God. All thoughts of the ghost girl were gone . . . Until—there was a sudden thump inside the bathroom. Tommy froze. His father hesitated, then rolled his eyes.

"Say something next time, would you?"

When the camper door clapped shut, Tommy put a palm on the bathroom knob. *Okay. Okay. Okay.* He pulled the door open, and inside, sitting on the toilet smiling, was the ghost girl.

"You said your name was Hailey." She nodded and stepped out of the cramped camper bathroom. "What are you doing here? Are you going to kill me?"

She shook her head and then stopped, looked at him and shrugged.

"You're gonna kill me?!"

"Do you want me to?"

"Why would I want you to?" Tommy gawked. He paced back and forth, eyeing the door but unable to make himself run toward it. This was a ghost, after all! How many people could say they had seen a ghost? For real. He asked her again. "Why would I want you to kill me?"

Hailey raised her hand and pointed a finger toward him, the tip of which was smeared dark red. At first, Tommy didn't understand. But when she told him it was blood, his blood from the top of the trail, he shivered like ice had been dropped down his shirt.

"That's from my foot?"

She nodded. "I fell there too. I just didn't bleed; I tumbled."

He sat down at the camper's booth-like kitchen table. "What happened?"

"I slipped."

"You were walking, and you slipped?"

"Chased. Through the woods. I tripped and fell."

Tommy glanced at the door, just to calm his own mind that no one was coming toward them. He wondered where Jacob was and how long he would stay there. Would she vanish when he came back? He didn't know how to respond to Hailey's story, so he simply mumbled an apology.

She shrugged. "It's better. Now no one can chase me. Or say bad things to me anymore. It's just—it's better."

☽ Benjamin Thomas ☾

Jacob's voice rang through Tommy's head. *You shoulda stayed on the beach . . . Those guys don't like you . . . If you say anything.*

Almost as if she were reading his thoughts, nestled inside his head like a transparent larva waiting to hatch and feast, Hailey said, "I can make it better for you."

Tommy froze. Something crawled across his back and sent goosebumps down his arms. "How—how could you do that?"

Before she could answer, the door swung open, and Jacob bounded in. He looked at Tommy and the place where Hailey was—had been? A pang of sadness poked his heart.

Behind Jacob, two older boys from the other campsite came inside. One of them nodded. "Yo, is he all right?"

"Tommy?" Jacob asked. "Are you—did Mom and Dad come back?"

One of the other boys snickered. "I thought you didn't care if your parents came back."

"No—I—no, I don't. I just—Tommy, stop being stupid, Jesus."

He reached into the cooler and pulled out three bottles of beer. The other boys whooped. When they were gone, Tommy heard Hailey's voice in his head: *I can make it better for you, too.*

☾ ☆ ☽

That night, after his parents came back, sleepy and smelling like beer and wine and bonfire smoke, Tommy slid from his bunk, already dressed, his bare feet landing softly on the camper's floor. Jacob rustled beneath his sheets, causing Tommy to freeze. His heart pounded in his chest. The sound thumped inside his ears.

He picked up his shoes from the floor, refusing to wedge his feet inside them until he was out of the camper. His father snored suddenly and then sucked in air. This was it; Tommy was getting caught. His parents would find him sneaking out of the camper and lose their minds. He would be grounded until—except Hailey said it could get better.

Tommy eased the door open and stepped outside, the campground lit by pale moonlight. He slipped his shoes on and walked past tents and campers and smoldering embers ringed by stone. He followed the path until it reached the main area, then headed back toward the beach and Tony's Nose Overlook.

He wished he had brought a flashlight. Something to help him see in the dark. Lucky for him, the moon was bright enough to shape shadows and the outlines of rocks and trees. A branch snapped, and Tommy stood stone-still. Something rustled. A

☽ The Ghost Girl of Rocky Neck ☾

shrub. Leaves. There was no way he could wait; Tommy ran, and with every step, his foot pulsed with residual pain.

He was out of breath when he reached the trail. A rock cascaded down the side of the hill. Tommy looked and saw a flash of white between the trees.

"Wait," he called, but there was no one there.

Had it been Hailey? Was this where she fell? He climbed farther down the trail until his feet slipped on loose dirt. His knees hit the ground, a bolt of pain shooting down his shin. When he looked up, Hailey stood in front of him. Tommy could see the faint, blurry outline of tree branches through her skin and clothes. She leaned her head to the side as if studying him. The woods around them grew quiet, the ocean waves fading until Hailey leaned forward and suddenly said, "Boo."

Tommy screamed, and she laughed. Hailey skipped in a circle around him. After Tommy calmed down, tears running down his cheeks to form little muddy droplets on the ground, he followed her quietly down the trail. He asked where they were going, but she continued to hike in silence. When they reached the top, the edge dropped down, rocks cascading in a race to the bottom. Behind him, trees swayed against deepening shadows. "What do you—what do we do?"

Hailey pointed toward the ledge. Tommy, already dreading and knowing what he was looking at, leaned over.

"Fly," Hailey said simply.

"Fly? Like jump? Are you serious?"

"It doesn't hurt. It makes it better. Like a bath. It washes the dirt away."

The wind sliced through him like ice against his bones. Tommy stepped back and shook his head. "Won't I die? If I jump?"

Hailey shrugged. "I jumped. I'm still here."

"You're a ghost!" Tommy yelled.

A branch snapped. Hailey vanished as Tommy's brother broke through the tree line. His arm was cut, and he was sweating. Tommy stepped back, nearly forgetting the ledge behind him.

Jacob called his name. "Dude, what are you doing?"

Tommy couldn't make himself talk. He swallowed. Shook his head. His mouth would not form words. A flash of white appeared over Jacob's shoulder and then again near the trunk of a tree.

"Tommy," his brother said, stepping closer. "What are you doing out here? Are you okay?"

☽ Benjamin Thomas ☾

"Why are you here?" It was all he could ask.

"Because you woke me up when you were sneaking out. Who were you talking to?"

He thought of saying her name, of telling his older brother about the ghost girl of Rocky Neck State Park. But before he could manage the words, Hailey appeared a few yards away and slowly shook her head. Tommy knew it wasn't an option. She had come to him and no one else. Not to Jacob or his *cooler* friends. To her, *he* was the cool friend.

"I wanted to go for a hike."

"Near the edge of the overlook? Tommy, come here."

Tommy suddenly screamed, "What do you care? You have your new friends. Go play with them."

Jacob's lip curled, and he took another step forward. "What are you talking about? Those idiots from the other camp? Who cares about them?"

"You obviously do. They're the only people you want to hang out with."

"What are you talking about?"

Tommy took a step back; he felt the ledge beneath his heel and wished he were barefoot again. "Just go away, Jacob."

"Tom—Tommo—what's going on with you? Talk to me."

"You really don't care about them?"

Jacob shook his head. "Not if it means you're going to jump off a cliff. You're my brother, Tommo."

"But what if—"

"—no what ifs," Jacob said. "You're my brother. That's it."

Tommy, lip trembling, looked at the shaded wood behind his brother. There was no spectral girl. No ghost among the deepening shadows of the trees. Had he imagined her? He couldn't have. He had seen her. They had a conversation.

"Tommy, stop being weird and come on. Let's go do something. We can play games or whatever you want."

Before he could say anything, there was a chill on the back of his neck. Breath as cold as ice. Hailey's voice was in his ears. "Boo."

Tommy, startled and scared, jumped inland, away from the ledge.

Jacob rushed to him. "Jeez, dude. Are you okay?"

It took him a second to realize he was no longer standing on the edge, the ocean beneath him like a dark blanket ready to hold him close and never let go.

☽ The Ghost Girl of Rocky Neck ☾

"Yeah. I think I'm okay."

On their way back down the trail, Tommy asked his brother if he believed in ghosts. Jacob shrugged and leaped over a root. "Maybe? I definitely think it'd be cool to see one. You?"

"Yeah," Tommy said with a smile. "I do."

☽ ☆ ☾

Benjamin Thomas *is a multigenre writer from New England who spends far too much (and somehow not enough) time lying in the grass looking at the sky. His short fiction has been featured in a variety of publications, while his medical thriller,* Jack Be Quick, *is available from Owl Hollow Press. He's currently a narrative designer for the game developer Ion Lands, working on their forthcoming cyberpunk title,* Nivalis. *Get in touch at benjiswandering.com.*

Out There

Tom Deady

"Where are you boys headed?"

I looked up, already knowing who the voice belonged to. "Hi, Officer Griffin," I said. "We're going to Sunset Point to watch the meteor shower."

Sunset Point was the third-highest elevation in Farmington, Connecticut. Pinnacle Rock and Rattlesnake Mountain were higher, but we couldn't walk there from our neighborhood.

"Should be a great show. Don't go peeking into any of the cars up there," the officer added with a wink. "You might get a different kind of show."

I smiled at his brogue, then snuck a peek at Greg to see if he'd gotten the joke any more than I did. I knew kids went up to Sunset Point to make out, but I wasn't really sure what he meant. Greg's sly grin told me he knew *exactly* what Officer Griffin was talking about. Greg had an older brother and always seemed to know more than I did about *everything*.

"Hey!"

I turned to see Margaret speed walking toward us. *Shit*, I'd forgotten to stop at her house on the way. "I'm sorry— " I started, but Officer Griffin cut me off.

"Well, if it isn't Miss Herlihy," he crooned. "Gosh, if you're not the spitting image of your ma, right down to the beautiful, green eyes."

Margaret blushed. "Hi, Officer Griffin." She turned to me and Greg, and her smile faded. *"Boys,"* she said pointedly.

For some reason, I was glad she hadn't been there for his comment about Sunset Point.

"Enjoy the night sky, kids." Officer Griffin sauntered down the street in the opposite direction.

"I'm sorry, Margaret," I said, ignoring Greg's scornful look.

) Out There (

Her face softened but the color remained in her face, darkening the freckles that peppered her nose and cheeks. "It's okay, Pete. I just hope I don't accidentally push you off the edge of the Point." With that, she marched ahead of us.

Something about her was different: the way she walked, the way her jeans hugged her hips.

Greg punched my shoulder. "I'd like some fries with that shake," he said, waggling an eyebrow. It made him look mildly insane.

"Let's go," I said. "It'll be getting dark soon."

We made our way through town and cut across Greendale Park. There was a road that went up to Sunset Point, of course, but the trail through the woods behind the park, though steeper, was much shorter.

I'd climbed the trail a million times but never at twilight. The deepening dark made everything different. I don't mean it made the rocky trail more treacherous, though it certainly did. I mean, it made everything more . . . ominous. The shadows became figures hiding in the trees. The insects trilling and nightbirds calling became otherworldly. Then there was the way the silhouettes of the trees stood out against the darkening sky. I glanced at Greg and Margaret, but they seemed oblivious to the changes.

We gathered at the top of the trail, sweaty and out of breath, as the last light faded out of the western sky. I realized for the first time that we'd have to hike back down in total darkness and decided it might be better to take the long way.

"Where should we set up?" Margaret asked, looking around.

"I know the perfect spot," said Greg.

We followed him as he wove his way through the last of the trees to the clearing at the end of the road. There were already several cars there, the bassy rock music echoing strangely through the open windows. The smell of pot wafted our way on the warm breeze, and I heard laughter. I didn't think these people were here for the meteor shower.

More cars crept up the road, extinguishing their lights as they approached the parking area. We crossed the clearing, and Greg led us toward an outcrop of rocks I'd never noticed before. It jutted out beyond where the cars were parked and there was a small copse of pines huddled in the grassy area.

We left the gravel lot in favor of the grassy, pine-needle-blanketed woods.

"There," Greg said, pointing up.

☽ Tom Deady ☾

I followed his finger and could barely make out something in one of the trees. "What— " Then I realized what it was. Not a tree house, exactly, but a sort of platform built among the branches. What I imagined a hunter's stand would look like.

"How did you find this place?" Margaret asked, awestruck.

Greg nimbly climbed up to the platform, the branches of the pine forming a ladder of sorts. Margaret went next, and I followed.

"Robbie and his Neanderthal friends were talking about it one night," he said. "I found it a couple weeks ago."

The platform was about five feet by eight. Not big enough to walk around but spacious enough for the three of us to watch the meteor shower. I rubbed my hands on my jeans to rid them of pine sap, but it was no use; they'd be sticky for days. "Why would Robbie want to hang out up here?" I asked.

Greg grinned at me, then slid over a bit and pointed. In addition to giving us a beautiful view of the sky and our neighborhood below, the other side of the platform was a perfect vantage point for spying on the cars parked at the edge of the point.

"Pervert," Margaret muttered.

I laughed, knowing she'd probably take as many peeks in that direction as I would. "What if they come up here?" I asked Greg.

Robbie and his goons were no friends of ours, and I'm sure they wouldn't have taken kindly to finding us in their spot.

"Don't worry," he said easily. "Stitch got his license, and they'll be driving around in his shitbox Ford raising hell."

"Stitch Pruitt?" Margaret asked.

"How many people named Stitch do you know?" I quipped.

"But he's only in tenth grade," she went on. "How can he have a driver's license?"

"Because he's been in tenth grade for three years." I laughed.

"Look!" Margaret exclaimed, pointing at the sky.

I turned but saw nothing.

"What?" Greg asked.

"A meteor, dummy," she said. She crossed her legs and sat down all in one graceful motion.

I sat next to her; Greg took the other side. All eyes focused on the sky as indistinct music and laughter floated up from the cars below. I tried to identify the music . . . Night Ranger, maybe . . . or .38 Special.

☽ Out There ☾

For the next couple of hours, we marveled over the display the heavens were putting on. The shooting stars seemed to come almost nonstop and in every color imaginable. Watching them streak across the sky had my head spinning, contemplating the vastness of space and pondering other lifeforms that might be out there, light years away. Then Margaret slipped her hand over mine, intertwining our fingers, and all rational thought slipped away. I risked a look at her, but she was focused on the sky, though she was wearing a mischievous grin.

"What the— " Greg's voice pulled me back to reality just as I caught what had evoked his words. A meteor, this one yellowish-green, was moving slowly across the sky but growing bigger and bigger as it did. Then I realized why. It wasn't traveling *across* the sky; it was headed *toward* us.

"It probably just looks like it's coming at us— " I didn't have a chance to finish as the eerie yellowish light engulfed us, and the meteor crashed somewhere below us in the woods. The platform shook from the impact, and a cacophony of car horns filled the air. We tumbled backward and then scrambled to our feet.

"Holy shit," Greg said. Then he was moving toward the edge of the platform. "Let's go check it out!"

Margaret scampered after him, but I stood motionless at the edge of the platform, staring toward where the meteor had landed. My eyes were still recovering from the intense brightness, but I could still make out a yellowish glow.

"Coming?" Margaret poked her head over the edge of the platform.

"Yeah, I'll catch up," I said, turning back to the impact site. As my eyes regained their night vision, I saw motion, like lava spreading from the mouth of a volcano. *If lava was a shimmering yellowish-green*, I thought. Then I spotted a pair of shadows moving through the woods toward the glow. "Margaret! Greg! Wait!" But they didn't hear me. They kept running.

I climbed down from the platform, pausing when I noticed a bunch of people milling about the parking area. It looked like all the older kids were getting out of their cars, probably to check out the meteor. Then I heard them talking.

"Damn battery's dead; I told you not to use the radio."

"I can't even get a light on, never mind get the car started."

I shook my head and ran toward the meteor crash, following the path I'd seen Greg and Margaret take. Not bringing a flashlight suddenly seemed like a terrible idea. I stumbled through the heavily wooded path, the only sound my own footfalls. I stopped. No crickets. No peepers. No nightbirds. Just that thick, suffocating silence.

I considered turning back. I could wait for Greg and Margaret at the clearing and—

A scream ripped through the night.

I moved in the direction it had come from, ignoring the scrapes and cuts from the branches and pricker bushes that threatened to slow me down. It was Margaret's scream, I was sure of it, and nothing would keep me from getting to her.

As I crested a small ridge, my eyes adjusted to the darkness . . . but no, that wasn't right. It was somehow brighter. The light was coming from up ahead, but it was no flashlight producing that sickly yellowish glow. I paused, torn between my curiosity and my need to find—no, *rescue*—Margaret.

Another sound, not a scream this time, but something worse. Moaning. The kind bred only from extreme pain. I hurried toward it.

"Pete . . ."

"Margaret!" I moved to the sound of her voice. She was sitting on the ground, leaning against the trunk of a huge pine tree. From this spot, I saw the crash site a couple hundred yards down the hill. "Are you all right? What happened?"

"Help me up," she said. "We have to go."

I pulled her to her feet, her burning hands sending a stab of dread through me. How could she be so hot? "Where's Greg?" I asked.

Margaret burst into tears, falling against me, her arms snaking around my back. It would have been the moment I'd been waiting for if not for the cloying heat radiating from her body. I stared over her shoulder as she clung to me, the cold that rippled through me offsetting her fever. Something was happening. The greenish-yellow movement I'd spotted from the platform was inching toward us.

"Let's go," I said, looping an arm around her waist and pulling her back the way I'd come. I didn't want her to see . . . whatever it was.

We stumbled up the hill and over the ridge. I snuck a few glances back and was relieved to see we were keeping well ahead of the spreading substance. Margaret was mumbling incoherently, that nauseating heat coming off her in waves. I asked her about Greg, but her replies made no sense. Gibberish.

☽ Out There ☾

I'd somehow gotten us off the path. We were no longer heading uphill, but I didn't care as long as we stayed ahead of the glow. *Meteor juice*, I thought, and had to suppress the mad urge to laugh.

Margaret had lapsed into silence. Her fever was terrifying, and she was barely conscious, her head lolling against my shoulder. I almost cried with relief when we staggered through a thicket and reached the road leading down from Sunset Point.

Bakersfield Street was a steep, winding road between Sunset Point and our neighborhood. Looking down the hill, all I could see were brake lights from the cars that had been parking up there. "I guess they got them started," I muttered, wondering if the meteor could have screwed up the electrical systems or something. *The things we learn from horror movies*, I thought, and began trudging down the hill, holding on to Margaret.

It was a longer walk than I remembered, though I'd never done it staggering to hold up another person before. When we rounded the last curve, there were still a few cars stopped at the intersection with Commercial Street. Then I saw the red and blue lights flashing: there was a roadblock set up. It was likely to keep people from going along Bakersfield Street—then I noticed cars turning around that must have been trying to get up to the Point. Still, it looked like they were stopping each car on the way down as well. By the time we got to the cruiser, the rest of the cars were gone. I was glad to see Officer Griffin manning the roadblock. He had his back to me, sending off cars that were still trying to get up to Sunset Point. Thrill-seekers wanting to get a closer look at the crash. I waited until there was a break in the traffic and called, "Officer Griffin!"

The officer turned and grinned when he saw me. I thought it was odd—why would he grin when he saw me holding up someone who was clearly unwell? I shuddered; he'd already been grinning when he turned. As he approached, his expression remained frozen in place. I suddenly wished I'd crept through the woods.

Officer Griffin spoke through his grin. "Howdy, Pete. Evening, Margaret."

My plan when I'd seen the flashing lights had been to ask him for a ride. That plan had changed. "Um, hi, Officer Griffin," I said, wanting to get away from him as quickly as I could. "I'm heading home. See you later." *Why is he wearing sunglasses?*

"Hold that thought, son."

☽ Tom Deady ☾

His voice was stern, but that creepy grin was still plastered on his face. He stepped closer, and I took a corresponding step back, trying to make it look as though shifting Margaret's weight was the cause. The way the streetlight hit him, it looked as if his face . . . was moving. Like there was something under his skin . . . burrowing. "I really—"

Officer Griffin held up a hand like a stop sign. Something undulated on his palm. No, *in* his palm. I waited for him to ask what was wrong with Margaret, having already decided to tell him she'd had too much to drink, and I was taking her home. I'd blame it on one of the older kids who had been parked up there.

Officer Griffin, teeth still showing, glanced up at the sky. Then he raised both hands as if in victory. Or signaling a touchdown. "Did you see them, Pete? Did you *feel* them?"

The question took me off guard and I had no idea what he was talking about. "Who?" I blurted.

Griffin lowered his hands as he knelt in front of me. He swept his sunglasses off and leaned in close. "The . . . meteors," he said, quickly putting the sunglasses back on.

He wasn't fast enough, though. His reason for wearing them had become evident in that few seconds. His eyes, once a piercing blue—and by *once*, I mean only a couple hours earlier—were now a dull greenish yellow. *Had he stared too long at the meteors?* "Yes, sir," I said. "It was amazing. But I—"

"Yes," he said, getting to his feet. "Amazing." He turned back to the woods, staring off toward the meteor crash site.

I dragged Margaret away as quickly as I could, looking back over my shoulder to make sure he wasn't following. He wasn't. He was still staring into the distance as we headed home.

"Pete?" Margaret's voice was both raspy and groggy.

I altered my grip so I was holding her shoulders and could look at her. "Thank God," I said. "What happened? Where's Greg?"

Silent tears streamed down her face. "There was something out there."

"The meteor?" I wasn't sure if she was lucid.

She shook her head. "No, something else. I think . . . I think it . . . or they . . . came from the meteor."

"They?" I was confused. But at the same time, icy fingers wrapped around my spine. "Margaret, what did you see? And where is Greg?"

☽ Out There ☾

She swallowed. Licked her lips. Darted a glance over my shoulder. "Things," she said, her eyes blank. "They got Greg."

The cold fingers of dread tightened. "What do you mean?" Sirens sounded in the distance. I grabbed Margaret around the waist and started walking. I didn't want to be around if the police drove by. I didn't know why. "What got Greg?"

I felt her head shake. "I don't know. Worms, or snails . . . "

I flashed back to the glowing movement that had spread from the crash site. I'd taken it for some kind of liquid, but—

"They're going to get us all," she said, wrenching away from my grip and taking off down the street.

☾ ☆ ☽

"Pete, your friend is here!"

Mom's voice dragged me out of a sound sleep. I blinked at the bright sunlight streaming through the window. A glance at the clock radio told me I'd slept late. I was usually up early on summer vacation— Then the scenes from the night before played in my head like an old-fashioned film strip. Hanging out at the Point. The meteor shower. The crash. Officer Griffin. Greg. Margaret. I shrugged back a shiver and dressed quickly, bounding down the steps.

"He's waiting for you on the porch," Mom called from the kitchen.

He? I had assumed it was Margaret. The screen door screeched, and I stepped onto the front porch. Greg was sitting on the glider, moving slowly back and forth. He smiled when he saw me. *Or is he grinning?*

"Hey, lazybones," he said.

"What's up, Greg?" I replied, taking a few steps toward him. The front yard was bathed in sunlight, but his face was in the shadows of the porch, eyes hidden behind his *Top Gun*–inspired sunglasses.

He shrugged but said nothing.

I barked out a laugh. "I'm surprised to see you. Margaret said the alien worms got you last night."

Greg remained silent.

"Greg," I said, taking a step back. "Are you okay?"

"Sure," he said. "Why wouldn't I be?"

His voice was off. Robotic . . . but also sort of wavery, watery. "What happened to you last night?"

"Did you see them?" he asked.

Tom Deady

I took another step back. "Yeah, I saw. Greg, I have to go, okay?"

"Okay," he said, getting to his feet in a quick, fluid motion.

Then he was in front of me, that eerie dreamlike grin still there. He reached up and took off his sunglasses.

I staggered back, groping for the door handle. His eyes, normally a grayish blue, had changed. They were green. Sort of greenish yellow, actually. And they looked— I pulled my gaze away and stumbled into the house, pulling the screen door shut behind me with a banshee shriek.

"I guess we'll see you later," he said, and slid off the porch and down the sidewalk so gracefully he seemed to be made of liquid. I watched him go. For a minute I was sure something was wriggling under his tight white T-shirt.

I leaned against the door, trying to figure out what—aside from the obvious—was bothering me. I ran to the kitchen and grabbed the phone, dialing Margaret's house with trembling fingers. She answered on the first ring. "Hi, Pete."

I tightened my grip on the phone, fighting the urge to hang up. "Hey, Margaret," I said, trying to sound like I wasn't ready to jump out of my skin. "I, um, just wanted to see how you were feeling."

"Fine," she replied.

I waited, but that was all she said. "Well," I said, and tried to laugh. "You seemed pretty out of it last night."

"Oh, yeah," she said. "I feel much better now."

"Have you seen Greg?" I asked.

"No," she said.

"Oh, because last night, you said— "

She cut me off with a laugh. "I don't know what I said last night. I had a fever when I got home, and my mom made me go right to bed after taking some aspirin. I don't remember much after watching the meteors. Did you walk me home?"

I took a deep breath when I realized what had bothered me when Greg left. He had turned right, leaving the yard. But he lived down the street to the left. He was heading toward Margaret's house! "I need you to come over. Right now," I said, trying not to yell. Margaret started to say something, but I cut her off. "Take the back way. Hop the fence and cut through the Delucas's yard. Will you do that? Right away?"

"Sure," she replied warily. Then the line went dead.

☽ Out There ☾

I ran to the front door but couldn't see Greg in any direction. I bolted through the house, ignoring my mother's cries asking me what I was doing, and sprinted to the end of my yard. Margaret was just coming across the neighbor's yard, staring at their German Shepherd. Butch was going berserk, yanking on his wire run trying to get to Margaret.

"Margaret!" I called.

She turned and smiled—*or was it a grin?*—and walked to the fence.

"What up, Pete?" she said as she reached for her sunglasses.

☾ ☆ ☽

Tom Deady's *first novel,* Haven, *won the 2016 Bram Stoker Award for Superior Achievement in a First Novel. He has since published several novels, novellas, a short story collection, and the first book in his middle-grade horror series. He has a master's degree in English and creative writing and is a member of both the Horror Writers Association and the New England Horror Writers Association. You can find out more about Tom and his work at tomdeady.com.*

Many Deaths Before Dying

Warren Benedetto

The empty lot next to Eddie's house was the football field where Joe Montana threw the game-winning touchdown to Jerry Rice. It was the baseball diamond where Mark McGwire beat Jose Canseco in the most epic Wiffle Ball Home Run Derby in MLB history. It was where Rambo took down the Predator with a Nerf gun, and where RoboCop blew the Terminator's head off with a Super Soaker. It was my favorite place to hang out with my three best friends.

And it was the last place I saw them alive.

The four of us had known each other since we were toddlers. We lived in the same neighborhood, went to the same school, and played on the same Little League team. Eddie's house was our main hangout spot, partially because of the empty lot next door, but also because his mom kept the best assortment of snacks. Even better, his house had a finished basement with a ping-pong table and a Nintendo with its own dedicated television. He had all the best games, too: *Mike Tyson's Punch-Out!!*, *Metroid*, *Double Dragon*, *Contra*. He even had *The Legend of Zelda*, the one with the shiny gold cartridge that I coveted so much.

The empty lot was nothing special, but that's also what made it so special. It could be anything we wanted—a sports field, a war zone, an alien planet, or whatever else our imaginations could conjure. Some of my earliest, fondest memories were of the four of us running around in that lot, having squirt gun battles in the summer and snowball fights in the winter, then retreating to Eddie's house for Elio's Pizza and Fanta Orange soda.

The lot was mostly dirt, about the shape of a football field, with a row of dark green hedges separating it from the neighbor's yard. The ground turned into a mud pit when it rained, but it hadn't rained in weeks. That's why we were so confused

☽ Many Deaths Before Dying ☾

about the enormous puddle that had appeared there overnight. There were no sprinklers, fire hydrants, or water mains nearby. The nearest hose was coiled up by Eddie's front porch—it was nowhere near long enough to create a puddle in that part of the lot. And yet, inexplicably, there it was: a perfectly round circle of water, maybe fifteen feet across, with a mirrorlike sheen that reflected the cloudless sky.

"You're telling me you have *no* idea where it came from?" Marco asked Eddie.

"Dude, I swear." Eddie held up his fingers in a Scout's honor gesture. "Jack, tell him."

I nodded. "Yep. We were inside all night."

The previous evening, the four of us had been out in the lot until well after sunset, tossing a baseball around while listening to my Def Leppard cassettes on Eddie's boombox. We only stopped once it was too dark to see the ball anymore. Marco and Shah went home, but I spent the night at Eddie's, watching *Indiana Jones* movies on his VCR until 2:00 a.m. We were together the whole time.

"This sucks," Marco complained. "Now what do we do?"

The plan had been for us to play Wiffle Ball all afternoon, but the puddle was in the middle of our infield, in the exact spot where the pitcher's mound was supposed to be. It was so big that it even encroached on the baselines we had scratched into the dirt with the heels of our sneakers the day before.

"We could run around it," Shah suggested.

"Or through it," Eddie added. "We'll just take our shoes off."

I peered at the puddle, trying to examine it from different angles. "I don't know, guys. Looks pretty deep."

There was something about the thing that just felt *off* to me. The puddles in the lot were usually muddy and brown; the water in this one was perfectly reflective and oddly still, with a surface unbroken by mosquitoes or water striders. That was unusual—any standing water in our area was usually a breeding ground for insects. But not this one. It was like someone had left a giant compact disc in the dirt, shiny side up.

"It can't be *that* deep," Marco said. "It's a puddle, not a lake."

"Why's it so shiny then?"

"Don't ask me. Ask Mr. Wizard." Marco pointed at Shah.

Shah Patel was the genius of our friend group. While Marco, Eddie, and I spent most of our free time playing video games,

☽ Warren Benedetto ☾

Shah preferred hacking into government computer systems using his dad's dial-up modem. He couldn't *actually* hack in—he had no idea what he was doing—but that didn't stop him from running up exorbitant long-distance phone bills while he tried. His favorite movies were *War Games* and *The Manhattan Project*; he was a real "let's steal plutonium and make a nuclear bomb for the Science Fair" kind of kid.

"Hold this." Shah handed me the yellow plastic Wiffle bat he was carrying, then squatted next to the puddle to get a closer look. "Hmm. You sure it's even water?"

"What else would it be?"

Shah sniffed the air and then wrinkled his nose. "Not sure. Smells like— "

"Your asshole," Marco interjected.

"You would know," Shah shot back.

Shah wasn't wrong about the stench. I couldn't vouch for whether it smelled like his asshole, but it didn't smell like water. It had a noxious odor that reminded me of Mr. Birnbaum's chemistry lab: a mix of sulfur, ammonia, and . . . something else. Something sour.

Shah tapped his finger on his lips. "Maybe it's mercury."

"Like from a thermometer?" Eddie asked. "Where the hell would that come from?"

"A meteor."

"I'm pretty sure we would've heard a meteor hitting the ground next to my house, Shah."

"Hey." Marco pointed at the Wiffle ball I held. "Lemme borrow that for a sec."

"No. Why?"

"Just give it."

Marco tried to snatch the ball, but I dodged out of the way. Instead of reaching for the ball again, he feigned a blow to my groin—the kid was a notorious jimmy tapper. I immediately reacted, dropping the Wiffle ball and lowering my hands to protect my crotch. Luckily for my testicles, it was just a ruse, but it had achieved the intended result.

Marco snatched the ball off the ground and tossed it into the water. It landed right in the middle of the puddle. There was no splash. No ripple. The ball didn't bob or bounce. It hit the surface of the puddle and just . . . stopped, as if someone had pressed pause on the VCR at the exact second the ball had touched the water. Then, ever so slowly, the ball sank. That was strange too—it was hollow plastic. It should have floated.

"Whoa. That was weird, right?" Shah looked at us to gauge our reactions. "It's like some kind of non-Newtonian fluid."

Marco nodded thoughtfully. "Mm-hmm. Yep. That's what I was thinking too." He clearly had no idea what the hell Shah was talking about.

"Now what do we do?" I said to Marco.

"About what?" he replied innocently.

"About the ball!"

"Just go get it."

"And reach it how?"

"With the bat."

The yellow plastic bat in my hand was about three feet long, nowhere near long enough to reach the ball from where we stood. "It's not long enough, dumbass."

"That's what she said."

"Why don't you just walk in?" Eddie asked.

"Why don't *you* just walk in?" I snapped.

"Use the bat," Shah suggested. "See how far down it goes."

"You do it." I held out the bat to Shah.

"Oh my *God*," Marco groaned. "You're such a pussy." He grabbed the bat. "Gimme that."

My face flushed with a mixture of embarrassment and anger. Kids our age called each other pussies all the time, but I always took it personally; I couldn't help it. None of the other kids had a dad who was an actual goddamned war hero like mine was. He had saved like fifteen guys in his unit in Vietnam, taking out an entire enemy encampment while getting riddled with bullets and shrapnel, then carrying the wounded one at a time back to the LZ to be airlifted to safety. He had two Purple Hearts, a Bronze Star, a Congressional Medal of Honor . . . he even met President Nixon. My dad would never call me a pussy—he was way too old-fashioned to ever use a word like that—but I always felt like, deep down, he must be thinking I was. I listened to music by guys who dressed like girls. I was more into books than sports. I didn't like to hunt, fish, or do any of the things that he did with his dad when he was my age. Hell, I was almost a teenager and I was still afraid of the dark. I would never be half the man that he was, and I knew it. I think he did too.

Marco plunged the bat into the puddle to test the depth, sinking it as far as he could without getting wet. "Damn, that's actually really deep." He swirled it around. "I can't even feel the bottom."

"Just like your mom," I grumbled under my breath.

He pulled the bat from the water and shook it dry. "Ha-ha. So funny I forgot to laugh."

"Maybe it's, like, an old well or something," Shah said. "Or a sinkhole."

"That would suck," Eddie replied. "So much for ever playing Wiffle Ball again. Or anything else."

Marco handed the bat back to me. A wicked grin formed on his lips. "Dare you to jump in."

"Yeah, right."

"What's the matter? You scared?"

"No. Are *you*?"

Eddie began untying the laces of his Reeboks. "I'll do it."

"See?" Marco said. He clapped Eddie on the back like a proud father. "Eddie's not a pussy."

"Stop it," I growled through clenched teeth.

"Stop what?"

"I'm not a pussy."

"Okay. So, prove it."

I didn't move or say anything. My face felt like it was on fire.

After a few moments of waiting, Marco nodded. "That's what I thought. Pussy. Pussypussypussy— "

"Fuck you." I started to lunge at him, but Shah stepped between us and put a hand on my chest.

"Chill out, Jack. He's just kidding." He gave Marco a disapproving glare. "Right?"

"Right," Marco said. His tone was unconvincing.

While Marco and I were busy arguing, Eddie kicked away his sneakers and peeled off his socks, shorts, and T-shirt. He stood in his tighty-whities, swinging his skinny arms as if loosening his shoulders for a swim. "Who else is with me?" Nobody else volunteered. "All right, then," he said with a smug grin. "See ya later, pussies!" He sprinted toward the puddle and launched himself into the air, drawing his knees up to his chest for a full cannonball. "Cowabunga!"

I spun away and shielded my face in anticipation of a soaking splash. Marco and Shah did the same. But no splash came. Instead, there was a sharp slapping noise, the sound of an epic belly flop from a diving board. I turned back to see Eddie sprawled on top of the puddle, staring at the sky with a shocked, pained expression on his face. It was like the water had turned to solid Jell-O when he hit it. Then, just like the Wiffle ball, he began to sink. His arms flailed as the surface suddenly liquefied underneath him. An abbreviated scream escaped his lips before it was cut off by water flooding his mouth. And then he was gone.

Marco squealed with laughter. "Holy shit, that was epic!"

Shah bent closer to the puddle, trying to see past the reflective surface. He looked up at us, his brow furrowed with concern. "Think he's okay?"

"Relax," Marco said, his laughter tapering off. "He'll come back up."

We waited for what was probably ten seconds, but it seemed like forever. Finally, I broke the silence. "He's not— " My voice caught in my throat. I swallowed hard, then continued. "He's not coming up."

"He will," Marco answered. "Eddie! Come on, man! Quit screwing around!" He laughed again, but I could hear panic fraying his voice.

Shah snatched the bat away from me and thrust it into the puddle. "Eddie! Grab on!" He moved it around, trying to find Eddie's grip. "Come on, dude! Grab the bat!"

"Do you feel anything?" I asked. My heart was pounding in my chest. I had a very bad feeling about what was happening.

Shah plunged the bat even deeper, submerging his arm up to the shoulder. "Nothing," he grunted, his voice straining. "He's not— "

Suddenly, Shah was jerked violently forward, plunging face-first into the puddle. His legs kicked wildly at the dirt as he was dragged into the water. Despite his struggling, there was no splashing, no splattering—it happened as silently and smoothly as if he had slipped into a pool of shadow. The puddle barely rippled.

Marco stared at the spot where Shah just had been. "Guys?" His previous bravado had evaporated. He sounded scared. "Guys, come on."

"We need to get help," I said quietly. But I didn't move. I felt rooted in place, as if my feet had bonded to the Earth's crust. I was frozen solid, utterly paralyzed with fear. Shah hadn't just fallen into the puddle. He had been *pulled*. By what, though? The only thing I could think of was an alligator. But were there alligators in Connecticut? And even if there were, how had they gotten into the puddle? And where had the puddle come from in the first place? And why was the water so deep, and so weird? None of it made any sense.

"Shit!" Marco cried. "What do we do?"

I didn't respond.

"What do we *do*?" he asked again, his voice rising with panic. When I still didn't answer, he looked back at Eddie's house, searching for some sort of solution. His eyes lit up. "The hose! Let's go, gimme some help!" He pulled me by the arm, finally breaking me from my trance. I ran after him as he sprinted across Eddie's yard to where a long, green garden hose was coiled up beside the front porch. "Pick it up!" he ordered.

I gathered heavy loops in my arms as Marco unscrewed the hose from the pipe. Once it was free, we carried the messy tangle of rubber over to the puddle. Marco sat and began wrapping one end of the hose around his ankle.

"What're you gonna do?" I asked.

"I'm going in." He twisted the hose into a knot and pulled it tight.

"No!" I felt tears welling in my eyes. "You can't."

"You want them to drown?"

"No, but—"

"Then help me!" He limped to the edge of the puddle, dragging the heavy rubber hose behind him. "Count to twenty. If I don't come up by then, pull me out." Before I could protest any further, he took a deep breath and stepped into the water. He dropped like a lead weight, instantly vanishing under the mirrored surface.

"Oh my God," I mumbled. "Oh, fuck." I let the hose play through my hands as it uncoiled, ready to pull Marco out as soon as twenty seconds had elapsed. I counted as fast as I could: "One-Mississippi-two-Mississippi-three-Mississippi—"

The hose began to slip through my fingers faster . . . and faster . . . and faster. My skin burned from the friction of the rubber zipping across my palms. It seemed impossible that the puddle could be deep enough to consume dozens of feet of hose, but it was.

"Marco!" I tried to close my hands around the hose, but I was almost jerked off my feet by the force of whatever was pulling it. I had to let it go or risk getting yanked into the puddle myself. Just as the final coils of the hose unfolded, whatever had grabbed it—*had grabbed Marco*—stopped. I tentatively gripped the hose and hauled it hand over hand out of the water. It came

☽ Many Deaths Before Dying ☾

out easily. Too easily. After about a dozen feet, the end emerged. It was cleanly severed.

"Marco?" My voice was barely a whisper. The tears in my eyes spilled over. The hose slipped from my fingers and fell to the ground. The severed end flopped into the puddle. There was no splash.

A quick flash of movement in the water made my heart trip in my chest. I felt a swell of hope at the possibility that my friends were surfacing from the depths . . . followed by a surge of unspeakable horror at what I saw instead. It was something so alien, so incomprehensible, so *other* that I struggle to describe it in terms anyone can understand. It reminded me of the hind leg of a grasshopper—long, skinny, barbed, jointed—but twice as long as my arm and made of something that looked like black glass. At the end was a churning cluster of smaller appendages that moved like the mouthparts of a crab. They had the ghostly translucency of white quartz crystals, but they were as dexterous and multi-jointed as my own fingers.

The nightmare limb breached the surface of the puddle and extended in my direction. I stumbled backward, tripping over my own feet and falling on my back. Two more identical limbs emerged beside the first. They pressed into the ground by my feet as the creature began to lift itself out of the puddle. With a desperate cry, I drove my heels into the dirt, propelling myself away from the water as fast as I could. Then I rolled over, scrambled to my feet, and ran.

I ran past Eddie's house, down Grape Street, and all the way to my house on Peachtree Lane. Throwing the front door open, I sprinted across the kitchen to the phone on the wall and dialed 911. The operator thought I was making a crank call, but after a few minutes of pleading, I was able to convince her to send the rescue squad to Eddie's house. Then I hung up the phone and ran back the way I came. By the time I got to the lot, sweat soaked and gasping for breath, the police were there.

But the puddle was gone.

All that was left in the lot were Eddie's sneakers, socks, and T-shirt, exactly where he had tossed them. There was no sign of Eddie, Shah, or Marco. Just like the puddle, they had vanished.

I explained to the police exactly what happened, but they didn't believe me. How could they? A disappearing puddle? Water that doesn't splash? A trio of giant grasshopper legs with alien finger-mouths? I sounded like an insane person who had rented too many horror movies from West Coast Video.

Instead, the police had a much more realistic theory: the boys had run away from home. They assumed I was covering for them—albeit badly—by concocting a crazy story to account for their disappearance. The cops could never explain *why* the boys might have run away or where they might have run away to, but it didn't matter.

For the next twenty years, that was the official explanation. It's what Shah's parents believed when they moved back to India, what Marco's mom believed when she hung herself in the garage the next summer, and what Eddie's parents believed when they died in their sleep from carbon monoxide poisoning a few months ago.

After Eddie's folks were gone, a wealthy investor bought their land and knocked down their house so he could build a new mini-mansion on the property. With the addition of the empty lot next door, the new owner had enough room to add a tennis court, a putting green, and even an in-ground pool. It was during the excavation of the pool that a new clue to my friends' whereabouts was found. The construction workers hadn't dug up any bodies or bones, or anything gruesome like that. But a dozen feet underground, in the exact spot where the puddle had been, they made an unexpected find: a large cave with a puddle of strange, silvery liquid. And, beside the puddle?

An old Wiffle ball.

A yellow plastic bat.

And a tangle of rotten garden hose.

Some of the cops who had investigated my friends' disappearance were still on the force, so they immediately recognized the significance of the discovery. They contacted me and implored me to drive the four hours from my apartment in Pennsylvania so they could question me once again about what had transpired that day.

I crashed at my parents' house on Peachtree Lane while the police conducted their investigation. My dad had passed away a few years earlier, but his commendations were still proudly displayed in a case on the mantel, along with the famous photo of him shaking hands with Nixon after receiving his Medal of Honor. There was also a plaque with his favorite quote engraved on it, from Shakespeare's *Julius Caesar*: "Cowards die many times before their deaths; The valiant never taste of death but once."

☽ Many Deaths Before Dying ☾

There was no question that my dad had died only once. But me, on the other hand? I had tried following in my dad's footsteps by joining the Army after high school, but I couldn't even make it through basic training. The closest I ever got to a Medal of Honor was winning the Saturday night darts championship at my local bar. And I was still afraid of the dark. I was the coward Caesar warned about, dying again and again every time I let my fear stop me from doing the right thing.

The police forensics team spent the better part of a week poking through the dirt and clay for any other evidence that might provide a clue to my friends' whereabouts, but in the end, they found nothing. They closed the case again and told me I was free to go. But I didn't. Instead, I drove my rental car to the lot where my friends had disappeared.

With the investigation complete and with construction yet to resume, it was easy for me to access the lot without anyone noticing. I ducked under the police tape, then slid down the steep side of the muddy hole to the entrance of the cave where the bat, ball, and hose had been found. It was a low, flat space, maybe twenty feet across, with a domed ceiling striped with sedimentary rock. The excavation had collapsed one side of the cave, turning it into rubble and exposing it to the open air. Even in the dark, the puddle inside was just as shiny and strange as I remembered.

As I stared at the water, I thought about what happened that day, about how the lot that had been such a source of joy for us had turned into such a nightmare. I thought about Joe Montana and Jerry Rice, about Mark McGwire and Jose Canseco, about Terminator and RoboCop. I thought about Marco, and Eddie, and Shah. I thought about my father. If I had been more like my dad, maybe my friends would have still been alive. Not a day went by where I didn't wish I had gone into the water after them. Maybe I couldn't have saved them, but at least I wouldn't have had to live with the fact that I didn't even try.

After a few minutes of standing in silence, I sat down on the rubble at the edge of the puddle and took off my sneakers. I removed my shirt and pants, folded them neatly on the ground, and then placed my shoes on top, along with my wallet, car keys, and flip phone. Then I closed my eyes, held my breath, and stepped into the water. It was warm, so warm that it barely registered as being wet. It felt comforting, almost womb-like. It surrounded me, cradled me, embraced me. As I allowed myself to sink into the Stygian abyss, I felt calm. Peaceful. Content.

☽ **Warren Benedetto** ☾

Then, something grabbed my leg.

I should have been scared. I should have been terrified. But I wasn't.

For the first time in my life, I didn't feel any fear at all.

☾ ☆ ☽

Warren Benedetto *writes dark fiction about horrible people, horrible places, and horrible things. He is an award-winning author who has published over two hundred stories, appearing in publications such as* Dark Matter Magazine, Fantasy Magazine, *and* The Dread Machine; *on podcasts such as* The NoSleep Podcast, Tales to Terrify, *and* Chilling Tales for Dark Nights; *and in anthologies from* Apex Magazine, Tenebrous Press, Scare Street, *and many more. He also works in the video game industry, where he holds more than forty patents for various types of gaming technology. For more information, visit warrenbenedetto.com and follow @warrenbenedetto on Twitter and Instagram.*

Fluke

Joe Russell

keze87: its eyes were pretty much jelly. like at this point they were leaking out of its head
keze87: you could see the empty sockets
keze87: the meat of the sockets was weirdly soft too. kind of plush? the orifices were a fuckin maggot farm by the time i got to it, i saw them wriggling around in there
keze87: there was foam all over its muzzle, i wasnt sure if it was spit or like
keze87: liquefied organ

freddyvsjasonvsme: Oh my gawd
freddyvsjasonvsme: Do u think it had rabiez???

keze87: nah just decomposing
keze87: ive seen roadkill before but never this intact a body at this stage
keze87: shit was STRAIGHT flukefied
keze87: wanna see the pic i took?

freddyvsjasonvsme: UH WHY DA FUQ R U EVEN ASKING ME THAT
freddyvsjasonvsme:?!?!?!?!?!?!?!?!?!
freddyvsjasonvsme: YES!!

keze87: k 1 sec

Keze was my best friend, and he was a fucking genius.

☽ Joe Russell ☾

He was thirteen, like me, and lived in Connecticut, like me. He loved gross shit, like me, and we talked every single day. And he was the coolest, most creative motherfucker in the state. I wanted him to write a book of all the stuff in his head: Cronenbergian body-horror monstrosities, urban legends that could've been instant classics. Gore that'd make your skin crawl.

He spoke about it because he enjoyed it, and I know that because he spoke about it like it got him off. The way that boys our age talked about finding their dads' issues of *Playboy* under the bed. I'd get home after school, check my email to see if he'd messaged me during the day, and boot up AIM so that we could talk in real time until my brother Brody wanted to call his girlfriend or mom wanted to check her email or something.

I pronounced it in my head like *keys*. But it could've very well been *kez*, or *kesey*, like *One Flew Over the Cuckoo's Nest*. We lived on opposite sides of the state, me in New London and him somewhere up by the Berkshires, where it butts against Massachusetts. Where there's only green and dirt and a single shitty paved road to connect it all. Lots of time to spend with yourself and your own brain, I guess.

> **freddyvsjasonvsme:** I wish we had more roadkill here :/ Sometimes I see squirrels but never anything as big as possums
>
> **keze87:** yeah its whatever here

He seemed so grown-up, having seen *Cannibal Holocaust* and read the parts of *American Psycho* with the hookers, and chatting with him felt like being under his tutelage. There was *my* fucked-up, which was childish and pedestrian, and there was *his* fucked-up, which was actually worth something. What Keze enjoyed and what Keze came up with and what Keze *was*: it was scary because it was no-bullshit. It was thinky and convoluted and real and raw. I felt embarrassed telling him that I loved Chucky and *Riki-Oh*. He could give me a real education.

AIM pinged again. The picture. I downloaded it and kept talking to him as it loaded, filling in strip by fleshy strip.

> **freddyvsjasonvsme:** Does a post-fluke corpse go thru decomp normally
> **freddyvsjasonvsme:** Or does it fuck w/ your

☽ **Fluke** ☾
innards? Like make them degrade at different speeds

    I gave him some time to think. I'd defer to whatever answer he gave. The possum sounded gnarly, and I wanted to see it—I re-pinned back my hair, getting the stray strands out of my face, and leaned in close to the screen until the peachfuzz on my face stood up with the static, until each pixel became its own shitty little glowing box of meaninglessness. Zoomed out again and there were those jellied eyes that Keze mentioned. Patches of fur matted with blood and bile, the fluids spilling out and darkening the dirt around it.

    No doubt about it. This possum was dead as fuck.

> **keze87:** it eats away at organs one by one
> **keze87:** literally
> **keze87:** see its intestine? its been gnawed on

    Sure enough, in the picture, there had been chunks taken out of an innard that, according to Keze, was its intestine. Probably a fox or something.

    To us, though, it was the Fluke.

    The Fluke was this creature we'd made up together. We'd both seen the *It* miniseries and Keze was working his way through the book, and the Fluke was like Pennywise but—and this is how Keze worded it—not total kiddie shit. Though I didn't tell Keze I was scared to walk by sewer grates for six months after watching it.

    But the Fluke wouldn't have been anything without Keze. It was mostly based on all the shit that Keze saw around his house. Roadkill. Deer with chronic waste. It functioned like a disease, a poison, a prison: you saw the Fluke and you couldn't stop seeing it. It'd take over your body and walk around inside you and degrade your insides until your skin rotted. We talked about it like it was real, like it was something to watch out for and protect ourselves from.

> **freddyvsjasonvsme:** Stay safe out there XD

> **keze87:** you know me bro
> **keze87:** always prepared

☽ Joe Russell ☾

"Delilah." It was the middle of algebra. The voice was a whisper.

"I don't have the answer," I whispered back. I kept drawing. "Ask someone else."

"*Delilah*," again, pushier, with the bump of an elbow to my side and I realized who it was: Ruby Schneiter, who sat next to me. "Mrs. Hammond's here."

I looked up to see our teacher standing over us, her glasses hanging down on that strangleable string around her neck, her arms crossed and her shoulders squared. "Delilah, I've asked three times for you to come up to the board. We're on number sixteen from last night's homework. I'd ask if you were following along, but you're not even looking at your worksheet."

"Oh, sorry."

Mrs. Hammond leaned down and snatched my paper. "What is this?"

I'd tried drawing the possum from memory, recreating the picture that Keze sent me as best I could. Limbs splayed out, fur thick and sticky with dried blood, claws scraping the dirt as if trying to crawl away from whatever was ripping its guts out. Tiny circles gathered at the edges of the mouth represented each bubble of foam.

And into the picture, into that memory, I'd injected the Fluke. It loomed over the corpse, a possum-shaped shadow with its fangs bared and dripping.

It was pretty good, actually. I wished I hadn't drawn it on lined paper.

"Delilah. What *is* this?"

What is this? Well, what the fuck is anything? What a stupid fucking question. *What does it look like?* I wanted to say. But instead, I told her, "It's a dead possum."

The class broke into murmurs, nervous giggles, "what-the-fucks." I heard a broken-off huff from Ruby, and when I turned my head, she had her lips pressed together, her hand to her mouth, and her eyes urgently contacting the cluster of girls in the corner. Mrs. Hammond had removed Ruby and sat her next to me for talking too much and the rest of them were still at it, the girls putting their heads together like a football huddle, their pink torsos blending into one another, a couple pairs of eyes peeking up over their glossy heads.

"Do you think that this is appropriate for school?" Mrs. Hammond leaned closer.

☽ Fluke ☾

I looked between her eyebrows. At the sparse, graying hairs that almost bridged over her nose. "Probably not."

"Then why am I finding it on your desk?"

"Because I drew it."

More laughter.

"Don't be smart," said Mrs. Hammond. I knew what she meant, but it was a stupid fucking way of phrasing it. Didn't they all want us to be smart? Wasn't that the point of school? "I'll be calling your parents and letting them know you took a trip to see the guidance counselor today for drawing this. Please take the hall pass and go. I'll be keeping—oh, God—"

She stood upright and held her finger up like she wanted me to stop talking, even though I wasn't saying anything. She turned her face into her elbow and hacked an ugly, wet cough. A death-rattle cough, like she was going to eject her lungs right out of her mouth.

The guidance counselor, Mr. Santiago, asked me a lot of questions and didn't really seem to want me to talk. Did I want to hurt myself? Did I want to hurt others? Did I have a plan in place to do either of those things? Had there been anything difficult happening in my life recently—divorce, loss, a bad test grade? Were there any weapons at home? No, no, no, no, no.

It wasn't even a human in the drawing. It was a possum. But they were really on the lookout for anything in that vein, anything mildly fucked-up: the violence of a fox nosing along ripe erupted intestines wasn't the violence of a pencil drawing; it was the violence of the Trench Coat Mafia. Mr. Santiago found nothing of note and sent me back to class, but I went into the bathroom and stayed there until the lunch bell rang.

☆

From: keze87@hotmail.com
To: dputs@yahoo.com
Subject: it

on part ii chapter 9. adult beverly part so at first it was boring (talking about divorce) but its getting way better. just finished the part where she sees all the blood and her dad punches her in the stomach which just highlighted how dumb the pennywise parts are. idea: pennywise coulda taken a chunk out of bev and no one sees it but her so she can't even treat it

☽ Joe Russell ☾
and then the wound becomes infected but it
just looks like normal skin. parts with the dad
were way more brutal by comparison
keze

    Keze sent the email around one thirty this afternoon. He was available at weird times: times when I and everyone our age were supposed to be at school or asleep. He didn't seem to *have* things like school or homework or limits on his computer time. I knew a little about what his life offline was like—his mom wasn't living at home, and his dad was at home way too much.

    Keze said his dad sucked, but all dads suck. Mine sucked because he wasn't around often enough. He worked at a glass manufacturer, manufacturing glass. Mom worked full-time with the Coast Guard. So it was just me and Brody most of the time, and Brody had basketball practice in the winter, track in the spring, and soccer in the fall. A lot of our communication was me giving Brody my allowance in exchange for him renting R-rated movies for me at the Blockbuster. I didn't even know how Keze managed to find and watch the stuff he did.

    Keze's dad would sometimes demand his attention, but never to spend time with him. Just to yell at him. It made me grateful—for my parents' distance, for my brother's services. When we first started talking, Keze's dad worked as a groundskeeper at the local campsite, but they fired him, and now he just sat at home, slowly losing his sunburn and the dirt under his nails. Keze stayed in the basement all the time, so they didn't have to talk or even look at each other. His dad drank lots of vodka that, according to Keze, smelled like shoe polish, which means it was the really cheap shit.

    By the time his father was fired, Keze and I had talked about piercings gone wrong from forum horror stories, piercings gone right from *BMEzine*, serial killers, monsters, guts and gore. But the most scared I'd ever been when talking to him was one night when he told me he'd had a shot of that cheap vodka. It was the only time I'd lost sleep over our AIM conversations.

    I'd come home, and if Keze was with his dad, I'd see his away message—the same quote since the first day we started talking on AIM, the same quote that was there waiting for me when I got home from school the day I talked with Mr. Santiago, a line from *Hellraiser* about tears being a waste of suffering.

    Still, I messaged him.

☽ Fluke ☾

freddyvsjasonvsme: Dude I got sent to the guidance counselor's office today. For drawing the Fluke and the possum. My math teacher flipped *eyeroll*

Barely thirty seconds later, he said,

keze87: fuck that
keze87: guidance counselors are fucking narcs. drones at the asshole factory
keze87: anything you say can and will be held against you

freddyvsjasonvsme: Believe me I know. My lips were sealed
freddyvsjasonvsme: Fuck him and fuck my teacher. I hope her stupid allergies kill her LOL
freddyvsjasonvsme: Theyre well on their way anyway I really hope we get a sub. She's never usually this insane, maybe the sickness is going to her brain

It was fucking kismet, then, that I typed—

freddyvsjasonvsme: Or maybe the Fluke's claimed its first human victim

Because Keze—and this made me warm inside, warm and jittery, like a car starting—said:

keze87: holy shit
keze87: dude youre a fucking genius

☾ ☆ ☽

I first met Keze in a chatroom called FUKKED UP IN CT [LINKZ HERE]. It was exactly what it sounded like—locals chatting about shock videos, arranging meetups, swapping download links. Not snuff films or, like, dark web vids that were made just to be illegal. More like rotten.com kinds of stuff. Mostly people asking for the Columbine basement tapes. There were always graphic photos of corpses, though. GIFs of dangerously and disgustingly kinky sex. Budd Dwyer's suicide. I didn't click any of the links. A guy fucking himself with power tools was just as scary for the *fucking* part as it was for the *power tools* part, even if it was "kinda low-res sorry guys."

I greeted the legions of A/S/L-demanding d-bags with the stupidest intro possible:

> **freddyvsjasonvsme:** Hai guys :) Im new here, 13, an1 else want 2 talk???!?!!?

And with the onslaught of "hey"s that followed, there he was in my private messages. Bright, like the hazard-orange of a bio-waste warning.

> **keze87:** im taking u at ur word and believing youre 13 because theres no way an actual pedo would send a message like that
> **keze87:** but pro tip dont give away your age, theres a lot of sickos on here
> **keze87:** in a bad way. not in a cool way
> **keze87:** plus no one takes you seriously

> **freddyvsjasonvsme:** Ummmm how do u know Im not a pedo???

> **keze87:** cuz you just sent the online equivalent of a white van labeled free candy. even the most shit for brains pedo in the world wouldnt try that
> **keze87:** you type like a faggot
> **keze87:** r you gay?

I'm a girl, I'd typed into the chatbox. My fingers hovered over the Enter key.

It'd be a practical choice, I thought, to say nothing. If I told the truth, he'd have brought out the kid gloves. It's what guys do. What they think they should do. Spare the ladies from the truly nasty shit. It'd have been way harder to prove myself—what was I, a forever-Bev, always operating at a deficit?

So I self-preserved. I tapped *backspacebackspacebackspace* until it wasn't even a thought in my head anymore.

☽ Fluke ☾

"Hey," Ruby said the day after my visit with Mr. Santiago. "I just wanted to say that was fucked-up. What Mrs. Hammond did. It's like, literally a free country."

It was the last ten minutes of class, and we'd been given time to get a head start on homework. I'd done maybe half a problem before turning to my new project: a field guide on Fluke-possessed humans. *It knows you're onto it*, Keze had said. *That's why it freaked out and sent you away. It knew that you knew.* I'd only written the stuff that we'd discussed so far.

I shrugged. "It's fucked-up, what I drew."

"Oh." She looked at me. Not quite judgmental. More just curious. Open. "Then why'd you draw it?"

She'd knotted the hem of her T-shirt at the waist with a hair tie so that it showed a bit of her stomach. Not enough to get her dress-coded. Sometimes, I caught her tying her shirts up or rolling her skirt waist at her locker before class.

I shrugged again because I wasn't sure how to explain myself.

Ruby went back to drawing a photorealistic eye in her notebook.

"Delilah," Mrs. Hammond called from her desk. She didn't look up from what she was writing, but when she was done, she handed me the slip of paper. "This is a behavioral report. It goes home to your parents, just to let them know that the guidance counselor had to speak with you for . . . what happened yesterday. Have them sign it and return it to me."

When she opened her mouth, there was phlegm stuck to her teeth. It made them shine under the classroom lights—there was a string of it, suspended, between her upper canine and her back molar. She urgently reached for a tissue from the box that had become a permanent fixture on her desk and sneezed wetly into it.

I went back to my desk and recorded her symptoms dutifully.

Keze and I had talked more about it after I brought up the idea. Or—he'd talked, and I'd listened.

> **keze87:** when it comes you can hear it
> **keze87:** a tapping on the windows. on the walls
> **keze87:** its true form has long spindly limbs but moves like a shadow. or like dark energy,

☽ Joe Russell ☾

> its noncorporeal, identifiable only by the effect it has on its surroundings

I was tuned in. Alert, my eyes two little surveillance beams. The stakes were life or death and it sharpened my mind like a whetstone. Attuned me to every little thing. I jolted when the April winds skimmed the tree branches from outside against the glass. I began to fear the chalk scraping on the blackboard.

It was thrilling, the constant fear. It gave me a purpose. A mission.

And it was something that bound me to Keze, even offline. We weren't the Losers' Club because, as Keze had so insightfully pointed out, we weren't fucking losers. Our club didn't have a name because that was for babies, and we weren't third graders. But we had a creed and a goal and two members and that was all we needed, and all of those things belonged to us and us alone. My classmates were sheeple. Stupid. They wouldn't have understood.

> **keze87:** look for a sallowness of the skin: rashes or pockmarks
> **keze87:** a difference in the voice
> **keze87:** slurred words, especially as it adapts to human speech

Mrs. Hammond wasn't the only one with spring allergies, but they were hitting her really hard, and she refused to take a sick day. She dripped like a storm cloud; her eyes were perpetually glassy, waterlogged with tears, and she kept blinking them back. Hives erupted along her arms and neck. It made her irritable, meaner not just to me but to everyone, snapping at simple requests to use the bathroom and keeping us after the bell to finish up our review when she used to just let us leave.

> **keze87:** has there been a change in gait?
> **keze87:** the fluke is probably still learning to walk inside a bipedal host
> **keze87:** let me know if she seems to lumber or stagger everywhere or seems unsteady on her feet

☾ ☆ ☽

☽ Fluke ☾

"That doesn't look like math," Ruby said to me one day as she leaned over to see what I was writing.

She'd begun to chat with me more often, sometimes before and after class, but she still sat with her friends at lunch: a herd of girls who would actively go out of their way to tell other people that I was weird and they shouldn't hang out with me, though "weird" was probably the nicest they got about it.

"It's not." I'd repurposed my math notebook—I recorded Keze's questions in it before school and answered those questions in bullet-pointed notes during class to bring home to him. I'd noted that Mrs. Hammond wore heels every day, which would've been an additional impediment for the Fluke as it learned to walk on two legs.

"What is it?"

"Marilyn Manson." I pointed to the little doodle I'd made of *Holy Wood*'s cover.

"No, the writing." She reached over and pointed to my notes. The sketch I'd made of Mrs. Hammond's pumps. "That."

"Oh. Nothing. It's nothing."

"It looks like you're taking notes on Mrs. Hammond."

"My . . . mom's a doctor. She was curious about her symptoms." This was a lie. She did some kind of admin bullshit.

"Doesn't your mom work for the Coast Guard?"

"How do you know that?"

"My brother's at the academy right now."

I vaguely knew that she had an older brother. He was a senior when Brody was a freshman. "Well, she's. A doctor. For the Coast Guard."

She sat quietly for a second, letting Mrs. Hammond's rough drone of a voice drift through our conversation on a current of bacterial air. "I didn't know that was a thing."

After the final bell, Ruby paced her steps to catch up with me as I walked out of the building. I didn't say anything and she didn't say anything—we just walked next to each other, her sparkly sandals keeping time with my chunky skate shoes. Brody didn't have practice today, so I met him outside the doors to the middle school.

"Bye," Ruby said. She walked off in the opposite direction. Brody made a face. "Who the fuck was that?"

"No one." I wished it were true.

☾ ☆ ☽

keze87: youre gonna shit yourself when you

☽ Joe Russell ☾

hear what happens at this part when theyre in the sewers

keze87: i didnt email it to you because i wanted to save it

freddyvsjasonvsme: ????? O.o

keze87: dude the kids all have an ORGY
keze87: its like 12 pages long too its part of this whole thing where if they do that they become adults and then pennywise doesnt have any real power over them because he only cares about kids
keze87: page 1031 if you want to check it out

freddyvsjasonvsme: God. Somehow that's more fucked-up than the interdimensional killer clown

keze87: how are the notes going btw

freddyvsjasonvsme: Great, I even have people helping me XD
freddyvsjasonvsme: The girl who sits next to me has been a great scout

keze87: oh fuck no
keze87: dude. no.
keze87: is she hot? if shes hot and nice to you, its a trap. all girls want to do is play games with you because they know theyve got all the power in the situation
keze87: its better to not even get involved at all. whatever she knows about the fluke and about the shit we talk about, she cant know any more
keze87: shes probably a massive bitch anyway

freddyvsjasonvsme: Yeah, you're right
freddyvsjasonvsme: I was thinking today, actually, could we look at how the kids defeated Pennywise?? As inspiration for the lore??

☽ **Fluke** ☾

keze87: nah
keze87: those kids were fucking dumbasses
keze87: youre not gonna kill an evil inter-dimensional spider clown with a gay little slingshot

freddyvsjasonvsme: Wasnt the point of the slingshot that they believed in themselves and that made it real
freddyvsjasonvsme: Bc it was silver

keze87: do you even hear yourself right now
keze87: we should be prepared and think about what kinds of weapons would ACTUALLY come in handy

freddyvsjasonvsme: Haha yes ok should we decide on some of its weaknesses? Maybe some kind of exorcism chant in Hebrew or Sanskrit, a deeper cut than Latin

keze87: IMG_275.jpg
keze87: check it out
keze87: its my dads lol

It was a hunting knife.

☾ ☆ ☽

I have one picture of Keze. Not on purpose. He had a bunch of dead things in his room, lining the walls in thick-glassed jars—squirrel fetuses and cow brains, shit where I don't even know how he got it. He took a picture of one of the baby squirrels for me, and the bottom half of his face was reflected in the glass. His chin was pointed and thin, with a sullen mouth and big earlobes, all warped by the curve of the jar. He was wearing what I think may have been a Rammstein shirt. That was all I could make out of him: when I picture him, even now, there's an empty, shifting gray-green-blue mass where his eyes should be.

The photo is printed out and on my bulletin board. Mostly because of the squirrel.

☾ ☆ ☽

Keze kept talking about the hunting knife. The hunting knife became hunting knives, plural, became his dad's shotgun, became

☽ Joe Russell ☾

a picture of his dad's shotgun. He sent it to me, and I didn't want to look at it, but I let it load anyway, a grainy photo of it in the shed, just lying on the workbench, surrounded by random hand tools. The garden hose was a green coil in the corner of the photo, and the white light of the sun came through the high window. I wasn't sure when he'd taken the picture.

> **freddyvsjasonvsme:** Dont tell me you have the gun right now LOL

I was not laughing out loud.

> **keze87:** i know where it is
> **keze87:** if i need it

☾ ☆ ☽

Over the next couple weeks, his messages became sporadic—not in the sense that we never talked anymore; we still talked every day. But he'd send emails for me to discover at weird times. Late at night, when we should've both been sleeping. Midafternoon, when we both should've been in school.

As Keze ebbed, Ruby flowed. It started quietly, with eye contact whenever Mrs. Hammond hacked into her elbow. Or stumbled in her heels. Because it kept happening, and she kept getting worse. She always needed a few seconds to absorb anything we said, and I never got called out for doodling anymore because she didn't have the awareness anymore. Her eyes were wet and her nose was red, and I was surprised they hadn't just escorted her out of the building at this point. But it made her act fucking weird—she used to have a chocolate-chip granola bar every day at homeroom, but I never saw her eat anything anymore. I saw her take a sip of water sometimes but even that stopped.

And so April dragged on. On and on. We hit the twentieth, and you'd think that the ghosts of Eric Harris and Dylan Klebold were haunting the place—our teachers were so nervous, so aware, so tense. Mrs. Hammond finally collapsed. I wasn't there for it because it was during my PE period, but I saw her in the nurse's office on my way back from class. I caught some of the conversation: the EMTs were on their way, but she was probably just going to wait until she could go home herself. She was too lightheaded to drive.

"My friend had math with her third period, and she saw it," Ruby said during dismissal. She never sat with me at lunch, but

☽ Fluke ☾

she'd walk with me after school every day, saying goodbye at the big double doors. The ambulance was gone. "It was weird. Like, *weird* weird."

"Define weird."

"Like—when she was unconscious, she was talking. In her sleep, I guess. She just said some weird shit." Ruby's light hair curled around her shoulders. I'd only seen sheep in real life a few times, on a class trip to a farm or on a road trip with my family, and their coats were never purely white; they were beige, blond, platinum. Her hair reminded me of them. "She was whispering . . . *it's got me*. It's got me, it's got me, over and over. Like she was in the fucking *Exorcist*."

"I have to tell you something," I blurted.

We were in the doorway. Ruby paused. "Oh, yeah?"

And while I was waiting for Brody, I spilled. The Fluke. Not much about Keze, because I worried that he'd be pissed. But I told her that I'd made up the Fluke with a friend, and it was just for fun, nothing serious, and I made myself sound so above it all. Math is so fucking boring and lame. So it was a way to pass the time. That kind of thing. I hoped it sounded cool. And she just nodded and accepted it.

Keze was offline that afternoon. And that evening. And that night. But the next morning, I woke up to a wall of text in my email inbox:

> From: keze87@hotmail.com
> To: dputs@yahoo.com
> Subject: i feel like were onto something. you and me. were different. we know what they dont. and we see what they cant. people walk around all day with their fucking eyes closed they walk around like theyre dead like their headss are down stuck in the dirt like theyre hollow but you and i can see above it and throughit and we know. dont be scared but i had another shot of vodka and i think it makes me more aware. it brings down the filter and its like the veil comes down with it. there are things in the universe that we odnt know and cant explain but we stand in the threshhold i can tell that were on the verge of understanding.
>
> IF SOMETHING HAPPENS TO ME: I AM AT 81

☽ Joe Russell ☾
GRANGER LN IN CANAAN CT. YOU ARE THE
ONLY ONE I CAN TRUST.

When I got to school, I greeted Ruby as soon as I saw her. It felt like a betrayal.

☽ ☆ ☾

I had a dream where I met Keze and I bashed his head in with a rock.

He dropped onto the dirt road—we were on a dirt road, lined by black pines—and the blood spilled from his head. But his skull didn't quite cave, and I had to drop onto my knees to finish it. The blood was shining, sticky blackness on my hands and the rock and his head, and he twitched under me. It wasn't like *Riki-Oh* with its rubber guts or the red paint blood bursting out of Bev's sink. And the bone just kept *cracking*, this disgusting, wet, heavy cracking, and then he went still.

It was dark in the dream, and his face was turned away from me, so all I could see was his short hair, his bare arms splayed out. My face stung. I wanted to cry. Why did I do that? Why would I ever do that? What had possessed me?

I saw something bulge underneath his skin at the forearm. A moving target, nano-twitchings like a muscle spasm, but unlike a simple spasm, it was prominently semispherical, a bubble just under the surface. I raised the bloody rock again and was about to bash it like a cockroach and then I woke up.

☽ ☆ ☾

"What is this?" Ruby loved asking that. She pointed to my *House of 1000 Corpses* poster— "poster" was a stretch, really, it was four pieces of 8.5-by-11-inch paper with a quarter of the design printed on each one, taped together to form a complete picture. One of Dr. Satan's experiments glared, its white face broken by the black line of sloppy DIY attachment, thin but severe, like a paper cut.

I'd invited her over. It was her fault. She walked out of class with me, out of the building, and she always went the opposite way from me. And we were about to split off in our usual directions when she stopped. Brody was at track and would be for a while, and she was just waiting, so I didn't have much of a choice when I asked if she wanted to keep walking with me.

When we got home, she asked why my house was so fucking small if my mom was a Coast Guard doctor, and I told her that her house was probably fucking small too, and she was like, *yeah, it is, but I didn't say my mom was a doctor*. She was mean, but it was a way of being mean that told me she knew me. Cared, almost. A way of being mean that cut you in the exact places you were hurting. Which was a kind of caring, anyway.

"Um—it's a movie. That I really like."

It made my stomach squirm to answer her—I felt excited. I felt repulsed by how much I liked her curiosity, letting her into my room, into my life, letting her see the things that Keze would've had me close off to all the "braindead fucking sheeple normals."

"Huh," she said.

I stacked her up to her friends in my head. Her clothes were the same baby blues and pinks as them, the same soft velour. Her voice singsonged, like the others, but she didn't believe it, didn't mean it, not like the others. She read the title aloud carefully as if she were pronouncing a greeting from a foreign-language guidebook. I listened for disgust but found none. No good disgust, no bad disgust.

I'd learned that. With Keze, I'd learned that. There was the normal kind of disgust, or at least the typical kind, which was the bad kind: simple, naked aversion. The kind you feel upon seeing something you never want to look at again. But there was also the good kind of disgust. My disgust. Keze's disgust. The kind that draws you in, demanding and pungent. Like smelling gasoline.

And like I said, none of that came through with Ruby. Her wide, sheep face was blank and observational; her docile, little mouth pursed neutrally.

"What's it about?"

"A family of serial killers. They, like, kidnap these guys and their girlfriends and torture them and kill them and stuff." I waited for her to respond, and it took her a few seconds, all spent looking at me like she was expecting something.

"That's it?"

"It's, um. Y'know. Kinda grindhouse-y." A word I'd learned from Keze, to make any of my favorite movies sound smarter than they really were. "Like, the actors are all really hammy, and the story is really contrived and dumb, and the script is kinda ass. And the violence is totally fake. A guy gets skinned, and it looks like he's covered in red paint, and one of the killers wears his skin as a mask, and it's totally just rubber . . ."

"So it's a bad movie. You like a bad movie."

"No. I mean, yes. I mean, that's what I like. The sort of, um, movie violence. Stupid violence."

☽ Joe Russell ☾

Stupid violence. Boy violence. It was kind of a rush to tell her about it. Ruby Schneiter in her little pastel henley and track pants, with her gray-blond Sheri Moon Zombie curls, baptized in blood. This room was full of things that I'd deemed too off-putting for the people around me. What Keze said only we could understand. Ruby seemed determined to understand them. It made me nervous.

"Huh." I had no time to analyze the tone of her voice. Her face. She was already onto something else—my bulletin board, with its picture of the jarred squirrel. "Who is that?"

"It's a dead squirrel."

"No. The guy in the pic. Is he your boyfriend?"

"What!" My cheeks got hot. This was stupid. This was stuff that girls liked—even, deep down, Bev girls. The only way to win was not to play. "No!"

"Delilah Putnam, you have been holding out on me." She leaned in. "Who knew? What's his name? He looks older. Is he in high school?"

Ruby. Soft, safe, mean Ruby. I wanted to be able to tell her anything. "I don't know. He's—my friend. He goes to another school. He's our age."

"What school?"

"Not in New London. We met at, um, summer camp. And we were in the same . . . we weren't in the same cabin, but we were in the same, like, group, but he was in the boy's counterpart to the girl's cabin I was in— "

"You are suuuuch a shitty liar." She giggled. "So cute. How'd you really meet?"

"We, um, haven't. We met on AIM. We chat and email. But we've never—I've never, like, seen him. In real life."

I didn't even know his real name. It was normal online—he didn't know mine, after all. Bringing that into the cold light of reality exposed it. Exposed me. I felt stupid. But she didn't seem to care; when her eyes widened, the shock in them held traces of interest.

"Okay," she said. "Now you *have* to tell me everything. I wanna know all about him."

Just us girls, I thought. *Just us Bevs.*

☾ ☆ ☽

"So, Delilah." Kelsey-Ann (she went by both and got really pissed when we had a sub who called her Kelsey) folded her hands and put them in her lap and leaned over the cafeteria table. Her

☽ Fluke ☾

lunch, lukewarm chicken nuggets and a fruit cup, remained untouched except for a few leaves taken from her wilted side salad. "I've heard, like, so much about you. I was wondering when Ruby would drag you over to sit with us."

"I told them about how cool you are. And about Keze," Ruby's voice was reassuring, but everything else about the situation wasn't—the smiles on the other girls' faces were tight, like they knew if they opened their mouths too much, laughter would escape. "I mean, I don't have any online friends. When I'm on AIM, it's always with people I know in real life."

"I thought you were a dyke, to be honest," Madison, sitting between Ruby and Kelsey-Ann, said. "How do you know you aren't talking with some random forty-year-old?"

"She's got a picture of him," Ruby said. Gasps all around.

"Ruby!" I said.

She turned to me and her face was still so neutral, so perfect and neutral and nice and full of nothing that it made me angry.

"It's not—*of* him. He's in it. But it's not of him."

"So it's like that," Andi-with-an-*i* said. "Do you guys have cybersex?"

I didn't respond.

Kelsey-Ann turned to Madison. "Even Delilah got a boyfriend before you."

"You are such a *bitch*," Madison said.

I thought about Keze saying the same thing about Ruby. I looked at Ruby. "Why did you ask to hang out with me?"

"Oh my God. Did you think . . . ? That's really cute." Kelsey-Ann always giggled after she said everything. There was nothing to laugh about.

I stood and turned on my heel and ran to the girls' bathroom, then sank into a stall and cried.

The door swung open, then closed. I let the last hiccup catch in my throat and clenched my jaw to avoid making any more noise. I wanted it to be Ruby. Even after what she'd said and did, I was hoping she'd come in, knock on the stall door, tell me that she didn't mean it. That she told those girls off and she wasn't talking to them anymore.

But it was just Mrs. Hammond. I knew it even before I peered through the narrow slit between the bathroom door and the stall divider. The sound of her heels clacking, quick, on the tile, the ragged breathing.

☽ Joe Russell ☾

She sounded as if she was in a hurry. She stood at a sink, hunched over, and hastily turned on the water. She swallowed gulpfuls of it, wheezing throughout—slurping and wheezing, wheezing and slurping, gurgling dryly with each cough.

And then she stilled. Braced her hands on the rim of the sink, on either side, and gripped it tight, the muscles in her hands straining. The echoing conversations from the hall, kids going to and from their classes, coming back from lunch, petered out until there was silence.

I saw it, I swear to God. Even today, I'll swear to God I saw it: the hair at her nape was parted, revealing the skin, and I watched as her flesh moved. Bubbled. Like there was something crawling around underneath it. Like in my dream. And then, as quick as it came, it went away.

☾ ☆ ☽

I came home ready to tell Keze all about my day. Ready to self-flagellate, too: *You were right. Girls are bitches. I should've trusted you.* But he was offline, and there was a new email in my inbox that made my chest feel tight. No text in the body, just a subject line:

From: keze87@hotmail.com
To: dputs@yahoo.com
Subject: MEET ME IN CANAAN

"Brody." I pounded on my brother's door with the side of my fist. "I need a favor."

He turned up *The Slim Shady LP* to drown me out.

"Brody," I shouted, "it's serious. Like life or death. You can pick the frozen pizzas we get next time we go to Costco."

Brody ignored me, even though he loved sausage and peppers on his DiGiorno's, which I hated.

"And I'll make dinner for a month—"

Eminem was my only answer.

"And I won't complain when you bring your friends over, and I'll do the dishes and mow the lawn and take out the trash—"

The music turned down. The door swung open.

"Jesus. Really? You could've just stopped at doing the dishes," Brody said. "What do you need?"

"I need you to drive me two hours across the state."

"It's a school night, fucktard."

I reminded him about the dishes and the lawn and the trash and the pizza. He got his stuff.

☽ Fluke ☾

It took about two hours and fifteen minutes because we got lost on some back roads and stopped at a rest stop to get snacks, but we arrived in Canaan by nine o'clock. It was dark and windy, even though it was almost May. He dropped me off in the general vicinity of the address; I told him I'd meet him back there in a few minutes and headed out with my flashlight, trudging over gravel and pine needles and old leaves in sneakers that were absolutely not made for it.

There, impossibly, on the dirt road—a dark, fuzzy lump. I knew it was the possum before I saw it. Fluids still bubbled across its maw like soap scum, the body still wet, its spilled innards still glistening, like it'd died a day ago and not been here for weeks. I poked it with a stick because that's what you do with dead things, poke them with sticks, but it didn't make me feel any better. It just felt like poking a dead possum with a stick.

Keze's house was down a small side road. I had to shine the flashlight on the wooden street sign, the tilled-up dirt around the base of the stake suggesting it had fallen and been replanted too many times to count, and the address was what he'd told me. The black outlines of the trees gapped around the house. Just patches of grass and more dirt to form a pathetic imitation of a lawn.

The door was open: not just unlocked, but slightly ajar, like the house's occupants had left in a hurry and forgotten to close it behind them. "Keze?" I called. "It's Del— "

I realized it wouldn't mean anything. He didn't know my name. I probably didn't know his.

"It's me. I saw your message."

The television was on but not switched to any channel, silent and static, lighting the grody carpet around its base. My hand surveyed the inside wall of the foyer for a light switch, finding nothing. I stepped into the darkness with my flashlight shining a single beam ahead, feeling my sneakers step over old magazines and envelopes that'd been blown by the wind off the entryway counter, until a thin, cold chain dragged across my face—finally, a lamp. I pulled it.

My stomach heaved with the chips I'd gotten at the rest stop, bilic acid bubbling up, salt-and-vinegar sickness. The living room was messy. The armchair where Keze's dad must've spent hours drinking himself into a stupor was knocked onto its side. Stains bled out onto the rug. I couldn't tell how fresh they were or what they were composed of. The couch cushions were thrown onto the floor, and between them, the gun from Keze's photos.

As I squatted to check out the envelopes, all overdue bills, I heard it:

Tap, tap, tap.

I paused. It was behind me.

Tap, tap, tap, tap, tap.

"Keze?"

Tap, tap, tap, louder this time, the taps coming more rapidly. There didn't seem to be anything in the windows. My flashlight reflected back from the glass.

"I'm here."

Tap, tap, tap, tap.

The tapping crescendoed to an incessant battering on the windowpanes, *taptaptaptaptap*, battering hollowly on the insides of my ribs like a marimba. I closed my hands around my ears and huddled as if to brace myself, but it was still there, like it was coming from my head: *tap, tap, tap*, from the treeless lawn.

☆

Joe Russell *is a horror writer based in central Connecticut. His interests include extreme horror, experimental formatting, and internet fiction in all its forms. His work explores the extent to which what unfolds online is "real life," how the ways in which we communicate online impact how we relate to one another, and, naturally, how best to turn his characters' innards into their outards. Like his narrator Delilah, he does a lot of thinking about horror that is not just scary but actively unpleasant, repulsive, and distasteful to its readers and viewers, and why it actually rules. His influences include William Gibson, Porpentine Charity Heartscape, Clive Barker, John Darnielle, and the anonymous writers and redactors of the Hebrew Bible. "Fluke" is his first published short story and hopefully not his last.*

When Joe is not writing, which is more often than it should be, he's working as a paraeducator. And when he isn't working as a paraeducator, he's probably cooking, doing the crosswords, or working his way through every James Bond novel. The best so far is The Spy Who Loved Me. *He also posts reviews and short stories on his website, joerussellwrites.neocities.org.*

Doug's House

Judith Pancoast

My father gave me a shiny, red, brand-new ten-speed Miyata bicycle for my fourteenth birthday at the end of June 1984, and that opened the door to my summer—a summer filled with good things, one very bad thing, and a mystery I haven't solved to this day.

We lived in the blink-and-you-miss-it township of Winchester, Connecticut, a teenage girl's no-mans-land. From September to June, a bus took me out of town to a regional high school, and in the summer, I stayed stuck at home. My school friends all lived in other towns except for one girl, Bertie, who lived on the other side of Winchester Lake, which might as well have been the moon. Her summer job at her grandfather's farm stand allowed her to work on her tan while selling peas and such. Meanwhile, I puttered around the nooks and crannies of our gloomy, old house like a bored ghost—sweeping, dusting my mother's Hummels, and washing the old, chipped china plates we used for our meals.

The sun never shined through our windows in the summer, so I'm not kidding when I describe it as gloomy. Before she left, my mother hung filmy, yellowing yard-sale curtains, and what light filtered through them highlighted the front room in a haze of French's mustard peppered with dust motes. Every spring, I took them down and washed them, and as much as I wanted to, I never threw them out. Maybe if I kept things the way they were when Mom lived with us, she'd come back.

Have you ever noticed how every home has its particular smell? For example, my grandma's house in New Hampshire always smelled like cookie dough. I don't know if our house had a smell because you never notice your own, do you? Not unless someone else tells you about it, and no one ever visited. If it did

Judith Pancoast

have an aroma, I imagine it smelled like musty cinnamon buns. My mother loved cinnamon buns.

The temperatures soared that summer and our small table fans didn't do the trick, so I kept the windows open in the hope of a slight breeze making its way in. No matter how many showers I took, a sheen of sticky sweat covered me. It seemed I was constantly swatting at some buzzing insect that invaded through one of the holes in the screens.

My father forbade turning on the television during the daytime. He insisted that I read, keep house, or work in the garden. Of course, he'd never know if I did watch television, but I'd been born with an integrity gene that kept me from disobeying his rules.

When the chores were done, I'd often take a glass of extra-sugary Country Time lemonade and sit out in the one ratty aluminum folding chair, reading my library book, the queen of all the sunburned grass I surveyed.

Everything changed when I got that bike.

Dad said I could ride it wherever I wanted in town as long as I wore my helmet, learned the biking rules of the road, and kept up with my chores, so on day one, right after he went to work, I flew out of there like a bat out of hell and rode up to nearby Highland Lake.

The day shone. The sun shimmered on the water, the air smelled fresh and clean, and the breeze coming off the lake made the ride that much more comfortable. As I pedaled past the cottages that dotted the shore, I saw children playing in the shallows while their mothers kept a careful watch. Families gathered on the public beach and visited the seasonal ice cream and sandwich shop at the nearby motel. On the opposite side of the road were green and yellow meadows speckled with wildflowers—they looked like the Monet print my mother had cut from a calendar and hung in our bathroom—and an occasional house. Despite the beautiful location, there were no McMansions back then, just nice, middle-class homes that were affordable for the locals.

I'd like to say the wind blew in my long hair, but the helmet made that impossible. Still, all of this peace and beauty calmed my addled teenage brain, and I felt like a real nature girl riding around the perimeter of the lake.

That night, however, my otherwise sedentary lifestyle caught up with me. Every muscle in my body spasmed and I

☽ Doug's House ☾

couldn't sleep. For the next few days, I limited my riding to shorter jaunts, but eventually I built up my stamina and my muscles. In a week I felt ready to ride out to West Road and Lake Winchester.

My father and I never went up to Lake Winchester, so it surprised me that there were far fewer cottages there. The vibe said "rural" in contrast to the more touristy and populated Highland Lake area. I didn't see any people except for a young woman in the yard of a sad-looking mobile home on the opposite side of the road from the lake. She hung out her laundry while a toddler skittered around her. Hardly any traffic went by, just one old rattling pickup. I began to feel like I'd ridden into a *Twilight Zone* episode, and just as I wondered if I'd come to the cornfield where all the people were buried, I went around a bend in the road and saw Doug's house.

How did I know Doug owned the house? Easy. Wooden letters about two feet high spelled D-O-U-G right over the front door. That snagged my imagination and got me wondering about the type of guy who would announce his name across his home like it was a department store. Other than that, the small cottage looked normal, if a bit run-down. The saggy front porch needed work, and a coat of paint wouldn't have hurt either. A perennial garden cried out for an afternoon of weeding.

I wanted to know more, so I vowed to make it a mission to ride to the lake daily, hoping to catch a glimpse of the mysterious Doug. That day, I rode past Doug's house to the farm stand and hung around with Bertie. We listened to *Thriller* on her boom box and compared notes on *'Salem's Lot*, which we were both reading. The afternoon sped by, and when I glanced at my Swatch and saw it was nearly five o'clock, I hightailed it home in time to make dinner for Dad.

After several days of riding by, I'd begun to think that no one lived in the cabin, Doug or otherwise, when one day I came around the bend and saw somebody heading down the front path toward the mailbox. I slowed my pedaling as I got closer, and the guy came into focus. Not very tall, he didn't walk so much as waddle, even though he looked to be of average weight. He wore a blue-and-white-checked flannel shirt despite the heat, and a pair of green Boston Celtics basketball shorts. By his appearance and the way he carried himself, I judged him to be a teenager.

He turned to head back to the house as I coasted by, his hands empty of mail. He didn't notice me, and I didn't dare stop and talk to him, but now my curiosity edged up a notch. Next time

☽ Judith Pancoast ☾

I'd stop, just to chat. He looked pretty benign . . . what harm could it do? I wanted to know about those big letters.

On a hunch, I rode back at the same time the following day, and sure enough, I caught him waddling out to the mailbox. This time, I coasted up on the other side of the road and stopped. He looked up, startled when he saw me.

He appeared older than I'd first thought—maybe thirty—and his open, guileless face bore all the hallmarks of Down Syndrome. That didn't bother me. My favorite aunt, Heather, also had Down's, and I loved being around her.

I smiled and said, "Hello."

He broke into the biggest grin, and I swear the sun jacked up its high beams at the same time. He ran a hand through his short, sandy-brown hair, and bounced a bit. "I'm Doug."

I laid my bike down in the grass and crossed the road. "I'm Meg." I extended my hand, which he shook with enthusiasm.

"This is my house," said Doug, pointing up at the letters.

"I figured that. I ride by here every day and see your name."

"Yeah. I did that."

"It's pretty cool."

He stood there for a long moment, smiling and staring at me without a trace of self-consciousness. Then, as if breaking from a trance, he said, "Uh, I can't invite you in. Nobody goes inside unless Mama knows them."

"Does Mama live with you?"

He shook his head emphatically. "No, no, no. She had to go live in a home in Hartford."

"So you live here all by— "

He jumped in before I could finish, as though defending himself. "I'm okay here. I can take care of the house."

"That's great. Well, I guess— "

"Do you like the lake? You can sit by the water if you want to. It's okay with me."

He pointed to the neat, sandy little stretch behind the house. I saw a couple of loungers and a weathered, gray picnic table where he probably enjoyed some nice times with his mama before she went away. I knew what it felt like to have your mama leave, and it sucked.

"That would be nice, but I can't today. Maybe on another day. I have to get home and do my chores."

"I like Michael Jackson."

☽ Doug's House ☾

"I do, too. But I do have to go now, Doug. I'll come by again tomorrow if the weather is nice."

He waved right in my face, turned, and went back into the house. Finished with me.

After my father left for work the next day, I completed my chores in record time and took off for Lake Winchester.

I came upon Doug's house just as he headed for the mailbox. This time he stopped and looked around, scanning the road right and left. When he saw me, that big grin broke, and once again the sun got even brighter.

"Meg!" he shouted and ran into the road. "I was looking for you."

It's a good thing I had already braked because I almost ran him down.

"Woah there, Doug. Wait a sec." I got off the bike, laid it carefully on the ground, and guided him back onto the lawn.

"I need to get the mail." He reached into the box, pulled out a flyer, and turned away.

"Where are you going? I thought you wanted me to visit you!"

"Uh-huh. I just need to put this in the house. Be right back." He waddled off, singing to himself (an out-of-tune version of "Beat It"), not a care in the world.

I waited. And waited. And waited some more. Finally, I peeked through the front screen door. I saw a small living room with a colorful, hand-knitted afghan slung over the plaid sofa. There were plenty of knickknacks on every available surface, and things looked pretty dusty, just like my house.

"Doug! Are you alive in there?"

From beyond the living room door, I heard him say, "Yup."

"I'm out here waiting for you, remember?"

A few more minutes went by before he came out, carrying the board game Trouble. I didn't ask what else he had been doing that took so long. Aunt Heather did stuff like that all the time. Absolutely no concept of time or the fact that people were waiting for her.

Doug held out the game. "Want to play?"

"Sure. That would be fun!"

We walked around to the picnic table by the water and spent the next hour playing Trouble, and he beat me every time. I didn't let him win, either. He just played well, even though a few times I ended my turn and caught him gazing out across the lake,

Judith Pancoast

somewhere else completely. When that happened, I said, "Earth to Doug, Earth to Doug!" and he snapped back as though he'd never been away. Once I could've sworn he whispered the word "creature" under his breath, but I wasn't sure, so I didn't ask.

When I left, he gave me a giant, squashy hug.

"Come back tomorrow. I'll let you win." His open-mouthed smile revealed that he had quite a few missing teeth. That endeared him to me all the more.

"Okay, I will. I promise."

He abruptly turned and marched into the house like he'd forgotten I was there again.

I went back the next day, and the day after that, and it became a routine. Believe it or not, we had a lot in common. In addition to enjoying Michael Jackson, we both liked Elvis, black-and-white horror movies, and playing games. He had some old puzzles that featured the Universal Monsters—which were too cool for words—but he never wanted to put together the one that depicted The Creature from the Black Lagoon. He said it scared him. I should've paid more attention to that.

I delighted in our burgeoning friendship, enjoying his sense of humor and his wild imagination. (Although I don't think he knew about imagination; I think he believed the stuff he told me, like the fact that his girlfriend would soon give birth to three puppies, all different breeds. He had already named them.) He kept me on my toes, and I looked forward to our visits and enjoyed the fact that to anyone who saw us, we'd make an oddball pair. Me, a tall, skinny, awkward girl, and shorter, waddling Doug. I didn't care. I couldn't possibly feel sad around him.

One day, Doug said, "Mr. Haskell is taking me to see Mama today."

"That's great! I bet she can't wait to see you. I'm sure she misses you very much."

"Yeah. Like your mama misses you."

That came out of nowhere. I stopped packing up the Trouble game and stared at Doug. By that time, he knew I lived with my father, but I hadn't mentioned my mother to him at all.

He continued, "She loves you."

I put the lid on the Trouble box and sat down on one bent leg on the picnic table bench.

"Doug, I haven't seen my mama in a long time."

"She loves you, though." He stared at me with those deep-brown eyes, the color of Hershey's kisses.

☽ Doug's House ☾

I let out a short, bitter laugh. "I don't think so, Doug. She took off when I was five and never looked back."

"She loves you."

I might've sounded a little mean; I couldn't help it. "Can we please stop talking about this? My mother doesn't love me. She walked out the door with her suitcase one day, and I haven't seen her since. People who love you don't leave."

"Not true. My mama had to leave and she loves me. Your mama loves you."

He was insistent, almost as if he knew it for a fact, and that bothered me so I let the subject drop.

I began wearing my bathing suit under my clothes for my visits so I could go swimming. Afterward, we'd sit side by side in the loungers, me reading a paperback mystery and Doug with his *Star Wars* novelizations. We developed a habit of companionable silence that seemed to satisfy both of us, sitting there relaxing while the constant waves lapped the shore. I nodded off more than once. I'd wake up and catch Doug, frozen, with his eyebrows scrunched in concentration, staring across the lake as though keeping watch for something. He kept his thoughts to himself, and it made me nervous.

This is the way things went for the next month or so. If the weather cooperated, I did my chores and rode up to Doug's. Sometimes I'd visit Bertie, too, and I tried to talk her into going to see Doug with me but she didn't feel comfortable with that.

She said, "I didn't think anybody lived in that ratty, old shack. Not a lot of people live on that side of the lake since they caught that guy down there."

"What are you talking about?" I munched on some peas straight from the pod.

"My grampa told me there was a bad guy who lived down there. Grampa wouldn't say what he did, but he's in jail now anyway. I guess the word spread and a lot of families moved away and couldn't get anybody to buy their houses, so they're just sitting there, rotting. You should tell your dad about Doug."

I didn't think my father would understand, and he'd probably forbid me from visiting Doug again. I figured what he didn't know couldn't hurt him.

My father owned a small auto body repair shop and came home late every day, worn out. He rarely asked me about my day. Once in a blue moon, after dinner, he'd ask about the books I read and expressed relief that I could get to the library by myself now that he'd bought me that new bike "that cost me an arm and a leg; you'd better take good care of it and always use that lock I got you," but he never said much more. I could've been entertaining the Night Stalker all day long and he wouldn't have been the wiser.

We got a spell of heavy rain at the beginning of August that lasted five days. The lakes were threatening to overrun their banks, fast-flowing streams of water headed past our house toward the storm drains, and I swear I saw Mrs. Kelleher's chickens from up the road zooming by on a surfboard one morning. Where I'd been used to it before, now being in the house by myself all day made me crazy. On the first sunny morning, I couldn't wait to get back over to Doug's. I pedaled as fast as I could, but when I came around the bend, things felt different.

He wasn't outside waiting for me when I coasted to a stop in his driveway at the usual time. Everything felt still. The oddest thing, though, was that flyers were sticking out of the mailbox. Doug, who only got junk as far as I knew, never let mail accumulate. He loved getting those flyers and he looked over every single one before throwing it away.

I pounded on the front door. "Doug! Doug! Are you in there? Doug, are you okay?"

He didn't answer, so I walked around to the back and found him sitting at the picnic table staring out at the sparkling water, which was exceptionally brilliant in the sunshine after the storm. The wavelets reached his bare feet.

"Doug! There you are! I was worried."

He turned toward me, his face puffy and worn. He looked as though he hadn't slept in several days. "Hey Meg," he said in a small and unenthusiastic voice.

The sand, still wet from the storm, squished under my feet as I approached him. Detritus washed up from the churning of the lake littered the shoreline, including a battered, yellow child's pail and tangled wads of lakeweed. "Hey, are you okay? I'm sorry I haven't been here. I couldn't ride my bike in the rain."

He glanced toward the lake and quickly back to me. "I'm okay."

I sat down across from him. "I missed you. What have you been doing these past few days?"

"I don't wanna tell you."

☽ Doug's House ☾

Doug had never said anything like that to me before. Considering his tendency to be a chatterbox, I couldn't imagine a thing he didn't tell me.

"What do you mean? Dougie, you know you can tell me anything. It's okay."

"I don't wanna scare you."

My breath caught in my throat. I hadn't expected that.

Now he stared out at the water again. "Maybe you should go home."

I pounded my hand on the waterlogged wood and he flinched. "Doug! What the heck is going on? This isn't like you at all. You have to tell me what's up."

He turned back to me, those chocolate-kiss, almond-shaped eyes now red-rimmed. "The creature is back. He's *back*. Something happened during the storm, and it woke him up."

"The creature? What creature?"

"You know, the creature from the movies. The fish man. He doesn't live in a lagoon. He lives in the lake."

"Doug, that's not real. That's just an actor in a rubber suit."

"He is real. I see him. He comes out sometimes after a storm. He's back now."

This guy expected his imaginary girlfriend to give birth to puppies. There would be no convincing him that his latest flight of fancy couldn't be real.

"If he's here, you need me. I can help protect you."

"No, no, no. I'm the one who is supposed to protect you. I am the man of the house."

"Okay, you can protect me. But I'm not going. Two are better than one when facing an enemy anyway. Now, go get the Trouble game. My skills are getting rusty."

Doug had a way of pinching his lips together when ticked off, and I saw that now as he rose from the table in a huff. "Okay." He clomped up the back steps.

He retrieved the game, taking less time to do it than I thought possible for him. I had to keep calling his attention back from the lake while we played, but I still lost anyway. Whatever he had seen out there, it stuck in his head and would not go away. My best shot would be to distract him and try to get things back to normal, and that's just what I did until the day came when he didn't mention the creature at all.

The "dog days" of summer were upon us, a time of exceptional heat and humidity when people moved more slowly

Judith Pancoast

in a haze of mugginess. We'd been taking our quiet time in the loungers when I glanced up and saw a wad of chalkboard-gray clouds moving in from the west, portending a thunderstorm. After a few days of being landbound—at Doug's insistence—I'd hoped to take a swim that day, but now I had to be quick. I stripped off my shorts and top, expecting Doug to admonish me any second, but he didn't. He just continued looking at his book as I waded out in the water. A swath of lakeweed wrapped around my ankle and I let out a little yelp, realizing that his talk of scary fish-men had truly spooked me. Luckily, he didn't hear me. I made a half-hearted paddle for about ten minutes and headed back to the shore in record time.

I'd settled back in the lounger, applying Coppertone, when he announced that he wanted cookies. Knowing it would take him a while to fetch them, I grabbed a book from my bag and dove in. The few rays of noontime sun that weren't yet occluded by the clouds beat down on me, warming my cold skin, and the rhythmic waves lulled me. Before too long, I'd fallen asleep.

I dreamed of lakeweed wrapping itself around me in a rubbery embrace, covering my face, and pulling me down into the murky water. Then I found myself buried in sand, grains falling into my open mouth as I tried to scream.

An orchestral clap of thunder forced me awake, and blinking, I coughed the imaginary sand away. Through the blur, a shocking fishlike countenance came into view not six inches from my face. Green fish eyes stared into me while the odor of rotten trout rode the creature's panting breaths as his round mouth opened and closed, opened and closed. His razor-like claws raked across my belly. This was too outrageous to be real—I couldn't be awake, despite the cold rain pounding down on me. The dream had just shifted again.

I screamed as you always imagine you would in a horror movie, trying to break out of the nightmare of his frigid, scaly body climbing on top of me, scraping my skin. Try as I might, I could not wriggle out from under him. No, I wasn't asleep. Somehow this was a real thing, an actual half-man, half-fish with the weight of six feet of mud pressing down on my body.

I heard a howl of rage and saw Doug charging down the back stairs, wielding a silver sword that flashed in a strobe of lightning, and as I felt the fish-man's rubbery lips latch on to my breast like some horrible, malformed baby, my brave friend plunged the blade into the heaving back of the creature. It screamed, sound-

☽ Doug's House ☾

ing like a thousand saws twanging at once, and rolled off me. As soon as I got free, I grabbed my shorts and T-shirt and ran. Doug grunted, the knife plunging through scales and crispy fish skin as the monster continued to wail. I couldn't wait around to see what happened. I just couldn't. I jumped on my bike and rode off as fast as I could, thunder, lightning, and torrential rain be damned.

Somewhere in the back of my mind, I knew I still slept on the lounger, Doug placed Oreos on a tray just so, and the diamond-studded lake provided my lullaby. This is what I believed until I got home, ran into the bathroom, and saw the bloody scrapes covering my face and body. I fell to the linoleum floor and wrapped myself into a tight ball, and that's where my father found me, shivering and raving about the creature, hours later when he arrived home from work.

At the emergency room, my father told the nurse I'd taken a bad spill on my bike, and my continued ramblings about some horror-movie monster attack earned me a CAT scan. After determining that my brain didn't sustain any damage, they sutured the deepest cuts, gave me a sedative, and sent me back home with my dad. Under the influence of Xanax, I spilled the entire story of the summer to him. To say he was ripshit is putting it mildly. He wanted to go out to Doug's house and murder him that night, but I played the "little girl" card and convinced him that I needed him to care for me more than he needed to go throttle Doug.

Dad put a closed sign on the front door of the shop the next morning and made me go with him to the little cottage at the bend in the road on Lake Winchester. On the way over, I kept telling him that my injuries were not Doug's fault, that he'd been trying to save me, but my story sounded insane, and I don't blame my father for not believing me.

Coming around the bend, we saw police cars idling on the side of the road, their lights flashing, and people in uniform everywhere. Yellow crime-scene tape cordoned off the backyard.

Dad pulled over.

"You stay here. I'm going to go find out what's going on," he said, as I stared out the window, fruitlessly scanning the area for Doug. I was only too happy to stay in the truck. Just being there and seeing the scene made my stomach churn, and when my father headed back toward me with a police officer, I opened the door and heaved all over the grass. Dad rushed to pull my hair back as I continued to throw up. When I finished, he wiped my face with his handkerchief and put his arms around me, holding me tight to his side. He whispered, "You need to tell this officer what happened to you."

Before I could open my mouth, the officer said, "Hello, miss, I'm Officer Andrew Russell. Your father says you sustained those injuries here yesterday afternoon. Can you shed some light on what went on?"

I ignored him. "Daddy, I don't feel good. Can't they just talk to Doug?"

"Well, sweetheart, see, that's a prob— "

Officer Russell interrupted. "I'm sorry, miss, but there's no one named Doug here."

I pulled away and looked around. "Well, where is he? This is his house, can't you see?" I motioned toward the big letters. "He was here yesterday when everything happened."

The two men exchanged a serious look which froze the hollow of my stomach. "What's wrong? Is Doug okay? He saved me. He has to be okay!"

Neither of them said anything, which upset me even more, making me demand to be heard.

"Tell me that Doug is okay!"

I practically saw the "idea" light bulb over Officer Russell's head. He said, "Miss, could you please describe Doug for us?"

Eager to prove my case, I said, "Sure. He's a little shorter than me, maybe five-foot-six, and he has dark blond hair with a little bald spot on the crown. And, you know, he has Down Syndrome."

Officer Russell nodded officiously and said, "That sounds like the man in the pictures in the cottage." When he opened his mouth to say more, my father jumped in.

"Let me tell her, won't you?" he said. "You can see she's upset. Let me have a minute or two with her alone, and then I'll call you back over, okay?"

The officer nodded and walked away while my father helped me climb back in the truck, went around to the driver's side, and got in.

I started shaking again and couldn't stop. "Daddy? What's going on?"

"Sweetheart, you see, well . . . " He turned and gazed out the window. "I don't know how to say this, but Doug, the guy who lived here, he hasn't been here in a couple of years."

☽ Doug's House ☾

"What? That's not true. He's been here all summer. I've spent time with him nearly every day. There must be some kind of mix-up."

"Did you ever see or know of this Doug before?"

"No, Daddy, how could I have? I never came out here until you gave me the bike. I only just met Doug in June."

He shook his head slowly, wringing his hands. Then he took a deep breath and blurted it out.

"Megan, sweetheart, Doug Doherty has been dead for two years. His mother smothered him in his sleep when she learned that her brother had committed her to a residential care facility. She had dementia, you see, and her brother wrested power of attorney from her. He planned on putting Doug in a home as well."

"What? That's impossible!"

"It's all true, Megan. The man you spent time with had to have been someone impersonating Doug."

I couldn't believe my father's crazy theory. "Daddy! Listen to yourself! Do you actually think someone with Down Syndrome played an elaborate trick on me all summer?"

"Well, I have to admit, that does sound kind of— "

"Or do you think I'm nuts? That I imagined all this? What about the creature that attacked me? I'm sure you think I imagined that, too. Next thing I know, you're going to put *me* in a— "

"Hold on a minute. Just calm down." He took my hands in his. "See, this is the part that's even stranger. There *is* a dead *man* on that beach, and he's been stabbed several times, just like you told me Doug did to the creature."

I listened.

"Turns out this man—a convicted rapist—lived in another cottage on the lake before he went to jail. They released him on parole last week during that big rainstorm we had."

Now it made sense.

"Oh my God. Dougie said he knew the creature, that he'd seen him before, and he said he came back during the storm. Do you think that's who he meant, Daddy? That he saw that guy as a monster, and then I did, too?"

My father just kept shaking his head. "I don't know, Meg. I'm still trying to wrap my head around you spending the summer with a man who's been in his grave for two years. Did anyone ever see you two together?"

I wracked my brain, but I couldn't recall one incident of anyone ever walking or driving by during our visits. Like I said earlier, there weren't a lot of people around Lake Winchester that summer.

"No, I guess not."

"Well, it's a mystery to me. But someone killed that man, and the police want you to go down to the station, make a statement, and get fingerprinted."

"I didn't do it! You know I didn't! How could I have done it? Where would I have gotten a knife?"

"The police say it matches a set of silverware in the cottage. The brother has been renting it out, but the family that had reserved it this year canceled at the last minute, so it's just been sitting here empty."

"No, Daddy, it hasn't been empty. Doug was here."

My father looked at me and sighed. He was quiet for a few minutes, then shrugged and nodded his head once. "Well, maybe he was here. Stranger things have happened. And if he was, I'm damned glad of it."

Officer Russell accompanied us down to the police station and I got fingerprinted, even though I knew that when they tested the fingerprints on the knife they'd be a match for Doug's, and that's exactly what happened. No one could explain it. That silverware had been used and washed a lot of times during rentals of the property. Whatever prints Doug once left on that knife should have been long gone.

☆

My father gave me away at my wedding twelve years later, and soon after, he was diagnosed with stage-four lung cancer and passed away quickly. Losing him crushed me, but my new husband was my rock. I'd met him while studying to be a teacher at UConn. He was from upstate New York, and that's where we settled and raised our family.

A few years ago, we took the kids up to my old stomping grounds, and though I've never told them the story of that summer, we drove up to Lake Winchester just to look around. The area has been developed quite a bit. There's a new public beach where some of the older cottages once stood, and a mini-golf course, restaurants, and several nice hotels surround the lake. As we drove around the perimeter on my old bike route, I thought for sure that when we came around the bend there wouldn't be a trace of the summer of '84.

"Look, Mommy, it says DOUG on that house. What kind of guy would put his name on his house in big letters like that?"

☽ Doug's House ☾

"Huh," I said, my throat tightening when I saw the cottage. Instead of just the porch, the entire house was sagging, but it stood there after all those years.

I managed to choke out the words. "I don't know, sweetie. Maybe someone larger than life, like a hero."

☾ ☆ ☽

Judith Pancoast *was born and brought up in Waterville, Maine. At the tender age of five she conceived her first short story, about a swivel chair that would take its passenger on a ride to hell. Unfortunately, she could neither read nor write at the time, so the story remains untold to this day. Judith attended the University of Maine in Orono just like Stephen King did, but, unlike Mr. King, she majored in music. She deferred fiction writing to focus on songwriting for many years (and was nominated for a Grammy Award) until fate intervened and no less than Mr. Mojo himself, Joe Lansdale, invited her to collaborate with him and his son, Keith, on the stage musical adaptation of his novella* Christmas with the Dead. *During this process, Judy shared a few of the short dark-fiction stories she had been writing on the sly and Mr. Lansdale encouraged her to continue writing and submit stories for publication. Her stories have appeared in* Northern Frights: The Journal of Horror Writers of Maine, Dark Horses: The Magazine of Weird Fiction, *the* Manor of Frights *anthology,* Scary Snippets *anthology, the online zine* Half Hour to Kill, *and* The Dark Tome *podcast. Judith is a proud member of the Horror Writers Association.*

She is also the author of a non-horror, heartwarming Christmas novel based on her song, "The House on Christmas Street."

Judith lives in Connecticut with her husband and three rescued pets—two cats and a dog. Her two adult daughters are gainfully employed in the entertainment business. Visit her at judypancoast.com.

It Happened Deep in the Woods

Tom Moran

On the first day of summer vacation in Moosup, the streets were alive with the bustle of joyous children celebrating their newfound freedom from school's rigid confines. The tiny speck of the town sat just off Interstate 395 in the Quiet Corner of Connecticut. Bisected by the Moosup River, which powered the village's massive textile mills in more prosperous times, the village was the proud home of one of the country's few V-J Day parades. Like many of Connecticut's mill towns, Moosup struggled after the closure of the factories after the Great Depression gutted the economy, until Griswold Rubber and Kaman Aerospace brought industry back to the old mill complexes a decade or so later. A working-class town, Moosup had its fair share of petty crime, like theft and alcohol-induced shenanigans, but it always exuded a bit of Rockwellian charm with its picturesque main street and welcoming neighborly denizens. Moosup truly was a town in which everyone knew each other.

While most children were whooping and riding their bikes, enjoying the warm, breezy weather, Timmy Simms and Rodney Cliff were engaged in an intense game of *Castlevania*. Well, it was actually Timmy who presently gripped the controller in sweaty hands as he struggled to beat the wickedly difficult Grim Reaper boss; Rodney, less skilled in the art of Nintendo, relegated himself to the cheering section as he watched his friend play.

"Whip the sickles! Whip the sickles!" Rodney shouted as he crushed his pillow in an anxious bear hug.

"Duh . . . what does it look like I'm trying to do?" Timmy replied.

"Now, JUMP."

"Damn it!" Timmy yelled as his character died. He tossed the controller in frustration.

"Whoa, take a chill pill, Timmy! You break that, you're buying it."

☽ It Happened Deep in the Woods ☾

"Sorry." Timmy picked up the joypad and wrapped it in the cord before turning the NES off.

"Rodney, your little friend is here!" Mrs. Cliff called from the bottom of the stairs. The boys understood that "little friend" was her code for their buddy Pete Bradford. Pete was a latchkey kid; his father had run out on the family when Pete was only four, leaving Pete's mother to raise him alone. Mrs. Bradford worked two jobs: during the day at Griswold Rubber and in the evenings as a bartender at the old Moosup Hangout. This left Pete to fend for himself. Although a good kid and loyal friend, Pete was rough around the edges and often found himself in trouble with the local police. After Mrs. Cliff caught him smoking in the garage, she banned him from entering the house.

The boys bounded down the shag-carpeted stairs, ignoring Mrs. Cliff's obvious hands-on-hips disapproval as they passed her and exited through the front door.

"Figured that I'd find you nerds hiding inside," Pete said. Dressed in a white Poison T-shirt over a white long-sleeved tee and a faded pair of Levis, his shoulder-length brown hair hung in greasy curls. He stood next to his prized possession: a bright teal Mongoose BMX bike. Pete had earned the money for the bike the previous summer by doing odd jobs around town . . . and selling a bit of weed to the local teens.

"We would have been outside, but we knew your mom was probably working the streets, and we didn't want to embarrass her," Timmy replied, grinning.

"Watch it, Simms," Pete said, smiling, as the trio slapped hands.

Pete pulled a semi-crumpled cigarette from behind his ear and placed it between his lips as he searched his pocket for a lighter.

"Seriously, you're going to light up here?" Timmy asked. "If Rodney's mom catches you again . . . "
"You gonna tell on me, Simms?" Pete put the cigarette away. This had become Pete's catchphrase every time Timmy tried to keep him out of trouble.

"Hey, Rodney . . . I was just down at the 7-Eleven, and I overheard these two guys talking. Steve Trendeau's father was let go from Kaman Aerospace, and the family is leaving town."

"For real?" Rodney asked, his excitement palpable. The Cliffs were not just the only Black family in town, but they were also one of the most well-to-do. Mrs. Cliff worked as a nurse at

☽ Tom Moran ☾

Day Kimball Hospital, and Rodney's father was a supervisor at Griswold Rubber. Although not wealthy by conventional standards, the Cliffs were "Moosup rich." Both his skin tone and perception as being a rich kid made Rodney the target of many of his classmates, the worst being Steven Trendeau. Luckily for Rodney, Steve was terrified of Pete, and Pete was more than happy to defend his friend.

"Now, if we could just get Eamon O'Neil's family to leave, the world would be a better place," Timmy chimed in.

Pete's expression darkened. "With any luck, that asshole will pick on the wrong person and end up dead in a gutter."

Eamon was two years older than the boys, despite being in the same grade. The town bully, Eamon was constantly on the prowl for younger children to beat up or humiliate. Not being one to ever back down or shut his mouth, Pete had a particularly rough time with the ingrate, having been at the receiving end of his beatings several times. The last one had left Pete with a broken arm.

"I got the new *Castlevania* game." Rodney tried to lighten the mood. "We could grab my Nintendo and head over to Timmy's house to play."

"Yeah, that's a big no," Timmy said. "My dad was out drinking late last night, so he took a sick day today. I'm not going near my house until Mom comes home."

"It doesn't matter anyway. I think I've got something that will pull you two geeks into the sunlight for a bit." Pete lowered his voice as if to emphasize that the information he was about to reveal was top secret.

"What do you got?" Timmy asked.

"What if I told you guys that I might know where Carl has been hiding out?"

Rodney and Timmy's mouths fell open in unison.

"I would say that you're full of shit," Rodney retorted.

"And you'd be wrong! I was hanging around the old railway trail, and I saw his mother drive up and park at the end of the path. She was acting really suspicious, like she thought someone might be following her. Anyway, she grabbed a couple bags of groceries out of her car and set off on the path. I followed her a while until she veered off the trail and into the woods just past the dam. Now, who would Mrs. Brundage be bringing groceries to?" Pete smiled triumphantly.

"Did you tell the police?" Timmy asked.

☽ It Happened Deep in the Woods ☾

"Hell no! You think that they'll listen to me if I don't have an exact location? We need to figure out where he's camping first."

"Wait . . . *we*?" Rodney asked. "You're not suggesting that we ride out to the middle of nowhere to find a killer? I tried to avoid that guy *before* the murder charges!"

"Yeah, I'm with Rodney. That sounds wicked dangerous."

"It doesn't need to be. I saw which direction she was headed. We'll just hide our bikes and hoof it until we find the spot. As soon as we know where it is, we hop back on the bikes and call the police. Think about it—we'd be heroes!"

Timmy and Rodney exchanged glances, unconvinced.

"I'm going whether or not you two pussies come with me. So, what's it going to be?"

Pete had had his own brushes with local law enforcement, and Timmy wondered if his friend didn't see this opportunity as a "get out of jail free" card. Still, the idea of being the kids that led to the apprehension of Carl Brundage had its appeal. He looked at Rodney.

Rodney's heavy sigh said it all.

☾ ☆ ☽

Moments later, the three boys raced down River Street on their bikes and turned down the old dirt path that was once the railbed for the New York, New Haven, and Hartford Railroad. Shut down in the '60s, the eight-mile path wound from Moosup through the surrounding forests and the neighboring town of Sterling before continuing to Rhode Island. Local kids from both towns used the dirt path as a bicycle and dirtbike highway between the two villages, and the surrounding woods provided an abundance of space for unsupervised drinking, smoking, partying, and other mischief.

These days, there was little evidence of the rail line that ran through the forested area; with the exception of a couple dozen or so ancient, teetering utility poles and the occasional rotting railroad tie, the path was fairly clear of man-made obstacles. The surrounding trees had grown over the stretch and canopied it with their branches, creating a dark, cool, gloomy atmosphere.

It made perfect sense that Carl had chosen this remote stretch to lie low.

For the first part of their trip, the boys stayed uncharacteristically quiet, and Timmy found their silence unnerving. Carl Brundage existed as a boogyman to the kids of Moosup. Town legend had it that he was born from an incestuous relationship between his mother and her much-older uncle. Rumor claimed that Carl was not only a bit limited cognitively, but certifiably insane as well. Over his short thirty years of life, he had alternated stays at The Norwich State Mental Hospital and Brooklyn Corrections. Officially, he had previously been jailed for burglary, assault, statutory rape, public intoxication, and corrupting the morals of a minor when he jumped the fence of Moosup Elementary School while naked and high. However, Carl had been suspected of the murder of his cousin since last fall when the man was found beaten to death in his trailer. When the police recently made public an arrest warrant for the miscreant, he disappeared. Plainfield police had appealed to the public for any information on his whereabouts, but so far no one was talking.

Although Pete's plan sounded simple enough, Timmy recognized the danger they could find themselves in. This wasn't sneaking into Mr. Laplantier's yard, where the worst that they could suffer was a scolding. No, if the rumors were true, this little excursion could be deadly . . .

Rodney dodged a rock as he pulled up next to Pete. "If we find him, how are we going to get in touch with the police?"

"We'll head to the Sterling Post Office and call from there," Pete said. "It will be quicker than riding back home."

Timmy consulted his Casio; he had to be home in two hours. "If I don't get home by four, my dad will kill me."

"We should be back long before then," Pete said. "And, even if we're not, we'll be heroes! Your old man can't be mad at that!"

Timmy felt the tight ball of anxiety in his stomach grow a little larger. Pete obviously didn't know his father very well.

For a moment, Timmy thought he heard another bike approaching behind them, but when he turned around, that stretch of trail was empty.

This mission was starting to spook him.

The boys approached Brunswick Avenue and Pete turned left and onto the Glen Falls Bridge before skidding his bike to a stop. His friends joined him on the old truss bridge overlooking the roaring Moosup River and frothy Glen Falls.

"Okay, we're almost to where I saw Carl's mother walk into the woods, so we're going to need to be careful from here on in. I say that we ride in and stash our bikes right before the path leading up to the top of the ledge. That way, if we have to leave in a hurry, they'll be right there."

"What if he spots us?" Timmy asked.

☽ It Happened Deep in the Woods ☾

"We'll just have to be careful not to get too close. If he sees us, we run back to the bikes and ride out of here."

Rodney leaned back on the banana seat of his Schwinn and shook his head. "Why do I feel like this is a terrible idea?"

"Hey, if you two geeks want to run off home, that's fine by me. I'm going in."

Timmy felt like he should protest, should convince his friend to just call the police and let *them* find the killer, but he stood silent.

"So, you guys in?"

"I'm in," Rodney said.

"Me, too," Timmy responded.

"Let's do this." Pete hopped back on his bike and peddled to the trail entrance while his friends followed.

The air in this section of the path seemed thicker, and the scent of wet mud mingled with the musty odor of decaying leaves and a subtle spice of pine. The trail was wider, but the previous week's heavy rains had left it riddled with deep, muddy ruts and puddles that gripped their bicycle tires and made travel slow going. Sweat ran from Timmy's forehead and into his eyes as he pumped his legs to pedal through the slop.

"Up here," Pete whispered as they approached the thirty-foot-wide channel between two towering walls of glistening bedrock, where the massive stone had been blasted to make way for the rail line over a century ago. Forty-foot ledges of pure rock loomed above this fifty-yard-long section of the trail, the trees that grew on their summits curling over the breach and blocking out much of the sun. Pete hopped off his bike and walked inside the brush line at the base of the narrow dirt furrow that curled up the terrain to the top of the ledge on the left.

The other boys followed suit, laying their rides down in the shin-high brush next to Pete's.

"What if someone comes along while we're up there and steals them?" Rodney asked.

Pete unsnapped his camouflaged sheath and slid out his survival knife. The massive blade had been a gift from his mother after he became obsessed with the latest *Rambo* movie, and Pete never left home without it. Approaching one of the many maple saplings that lined the path, he used the knife to hack a few down. "Here, put these over the bikes to hide them."

Rodney and Timmy laid the brush over their bikes.

Tom Moran

"Okay, let's go." Pete strode up the steep dirt incline that led to the top of the massive ledge. Timmy and Rodney followed. When he reached the summit, Timmy peered over the edge, becoming dizzy when he saw the massive drop to the path below. The boys remained silent as they moved along the trail that meandered through the trees and brush, penetrating into the untouched forest. Beams of sunlight cut through the thick leaf cover, dappling the leaf-strewn forest floor in shifting pools of light.

As they drew closer to the river, the brush grew thicker, and the boys used it as cover as they crouched and walked from one patch to another. Suddenly, Pete froze and held his hand up to motion for the boys to stop. Timmy and Rodney crowded around him behind a tangle of honeysuckle, pricker vines, and shoulder-high saplings.

About thirty yards ahead was a small clearing beneath a bunch of towering pine trees. Just inside the brush line stood a weathered, blue tent. Before it was a small campfire constructed from fist-sized stones, its contents charred and blackened. Crushed beer cans and empty food containers littered the area around the makeshift campsite.

"Look," Pete mouthed, pointing at the tent.

Sitting on the ground next to the tent were two grocery bags from the Better Valu supermarket.

"So, we found him. Now, let's get out of here," Timmy said. Although they were concealed by the brush, he couldn't help but feel exposed.

"Do you think that he's in the tent?" Rodney scanned the woods for any sign of the man.

In his young life, Timmy had been in some situations that were quite dangerous. There had been close calls with cars when he was riding his bike, and the time that he fell through the ice when playing on Moosup Pond. Heck, he had even had a hunter nearly mistake him for a deer when he was out in the woods last fall. Still, none of these made him feel as frightened and close to death as he felt now. Just a few dozen yards away, a murderer slept.

"What are you pussies up to?" shouted someone from behind them.

The boys wheeled, their eyes wide.

"Oh, Jesus, no . . . " Rodney muttered.

Standing in the path, a shit-eating grin smeared across his pale, freckled face, was Eamon O'Neil. He wore cutoff jean

☽ It Happened Deep in the Woods ☾

shorts, a faded New York Giants shirt, and had his long, straight, red hair pulled back into a tight ponytail. Timmy remembered hearing someone behind them earlier, and he realized that Eamon had been following them the entire time.

"I asked you a question, dweebs." He stalked forward.

"Eamon, shut the hell up," Pete seethed as he glanced back at the tent to make sure that Carl hadn't appeared. "He'll hear you!"

"What did you say to me, shithead?" Eamon snatched Pete by his T-shirt and shoved him to the ground.

"You asshole, keep it down. Look! It's Carl Brundage's camp."

"What?" Eamon shouldered past Rodney and peered across the clearing. "How do you know it's him and not some homeless man?"

"Pete saw his mom bringing him groceries," Rodney said.

As Pete picked himself up and brushed himself off, he shot Rodney a glance and shook his head. "It's him. Now, why don't you shut up before you get us killed?"

For just a moment, Eamon's blue eyes widened and his homely features projected fear. Then, like a cloud, it passed, replaced by a mischievous smile. "Well, I'm not afraid of that freak. Let's see if he's home . . . "

"Eamon, no— " Pete began.

Without warning, Eamon turned and punched Pete squarely in the face.

Stunned, Pete crumbled to the ground, his nose gushing blood.

"What did I fucking tell you, Bradford? Shut your mouth!"

Rodney, panicked, tried to calm the bully. "Seriously, Eamon, we just want to get out of here before— "

"Hey, Carl? You in there, you crazy bastard?" Eamon screamed.

Timmy helped a still-stunned Pete to his feet. "Eamon, don't."

"Caaarlllll, you inbred motherfucker. We know that you're in there!"

"Oh, hell no." Rodney turned to run, but Eamon grabbed the back of his shirt and pulled him into a one-armed chokehold. "Where you goin', boy?"

"Seriously, Eamon . . . this isn't a joke! We need to get out of here," Timmy begged.

☽ Tom Moran ☾

Eamon ignored him. "Carl, your mother owes me some money from last night. You need to pay up."

Ahead, the tent swayed gently in the breeze, but nothing else stirred.

"You pussies . . . he's not even here."

No sooner had the words tumbled from his lips than the tent stirred. The boys watched, frozen in horror, as someone slowly unzipped the door flap and stepped out into the clearing. It was Carl Brundage. Dressed only in a pair of stained white briefs and work boots, his sinewy, muscular body was covered with crudely drawn tattoos, once black but now faded to sewage green. His trademark flattop Mohawk was overgrown and matted against his head, and the beginnings of a beard covered his square jaw. Wincing against the bright sun, he scanned the area until he saw the boys.

"Oh, shit," Pete whispered.

Carl smiled, and it was slippery and pure evil. Reaching to the ground, he picked up a machete and gripped it tightly. With a primal scream, he hoisted the weapon above his head in thick, tattooed fingers and charged at the kids.

"Fuck!" Eamon released his grip on Rodney and turned to flee, shoving Pete to the ground as he passed. "Have fun with Carl!" he called as he ran off through the woods.

"Go!" Pete screamed as he scrambled to his feet.

Like something from a nightmare, the half-naked maniac charged across the clearing in a full sprint.

The boys didn't need to be told twice; all three took off into the surrounding woods. Rodney, the smallest and fastest of the trio, soon took the lead with Timmy right behind him as they sprinted through the trees, oblivious to the branches that slapped at their faces and pulled at their limbs.

Timmy chanced a glance behind him and panicked when he found no sign of Pete.

"Rodney, where is Pete?"

"I thought that he was right behind us!" Rodney leaped over a fallen tree.

Timmy, not quite as fleet of foot as his friend, caught his toe on the shattered nub of a branch and landed awkwardly, twisting his ankle. *Oh no*, he thought as he took another step and felt his ankle buckling as shooting pain radiated up his leg. "Rodney!" he called out.

☽ It Happened Deep in the Woods ☾

Rodney continued his flight, and Timmy watched, helpless, as he was swallowed by the woods.

Pausing to catch his breath, he heard a horrific, prolonged scream of agony from somewhere deep inside the woods. Timmy's flesh erupted in goosebumps as he realized that it might have been Pete.

Panicked tears filled his eyes as he hobbled down the dirt path and looked for a place to conceal himself. Finally, he came to the spot he was looking for. Just off the main trail, up a short incline, was a small, rocky cave. The boys had discovered it last summer and had considered using the cramped den as a makeshift fort but they found the spider-infested confines less than hospitable. Wincing as his wounded leg throbbed, Timmy managed to climb the hill and drag himself through the overgrowth and loose stone and into the damp recess. Shimmying to the back of the structure, Timmy tried to get comfortable, but the jagged rocks that formed the cave walls dug into his back and butt. He noticed with disgust that broken beer bottles, crushed cans, and used condoms littered the dirt floor of the cave. Finally, pulling his knees up to his chest, he settled into his hiding spot and listened.

For a moment, the only sound was the afternoon breeze rustling through the trees. Then, the unmistakable crunch of someone running through brush.

His bladder ached for release, and Timmy cried as he emptied it where he sat.

"I know you're hiding," came the sinister voice. "Why don't you just come out so we can talk?"

It occurred to Timmy that if Carl had been living in the woods for the past couple weeks, he probably knew the area better than they did. If that was the case, he would know about the cave. If he discovered Timmy, the boy would be trapped.

"Where are you?" the low, gravely voice came, this time closer.

Timmy tried to stifle the sobs that wracked his body as he heard his pursuer crashing through the surrounding foliage. Glancing down, he noticed a huge wolf spider just inches from his toes, and he froze as it crawled onto his Adidas and up his pant leg. He stared at the creature, his eyes bulging, as he fought the impulse to brush it off, to scream, to run.

"Come out, you little shit," came Carl's voice from below the cave, a couple yards away.

☽ Tom Moran ☾

His heart beating in his throat, Timmy clutched his knees in the fetal position, holding his breath as he waited for the danger to pass. He listened as the whoosh of footsteps receded further and further away from the cave.

Thank God, Timmy thought as he released his breath. However, before he could relax, the alarm on his wristwatch sounded. The piercing digital tone reverberated through the cave, its volume amplified by the echoey acoustics.

Panicking, Timmy tried to cover the face to muffle the sound, but the damage had been done. From outside came the sound of footsteps fast approaching. He mewled as he scrambled to find a weapon to defend himself with. Hands trembling, he picked up a fist-sized stone and broken bottle neck.

"I hear you," came Carl's voice as he approached the cave entrance.

"Hey asshole!" It was Pete's unmistakable voice from further away.

The footsteps stopped; Carl shrieked like a wounded animal.

"That's right, you inbred pussy. Over here!"

Pete's drawing him away, Timmy realized.

For a moment, silence; then the footfalls retreated as Carl gave pursuit.

As Timmy crawled from his hiding spot, he felt his eyes tearing again, but this time in gratitude. Pete had just saved his life and, in the process, put his own life in danger. He felt nauseated as he realized that, out of the three of them, Pete was the slowest. What if Carl caught up with him?

There was no time to consider; he had to get back to the trail and get help before Carl returned. Timmy dragged himself across the floor of the cave and out into light. He searched the ground around the entrance and found a tree limb he could use as a makeshift crutch. Moving as quickly as his injured ankle would allow, he made his way through the woods and in the direction that he hoped was the end of the trail. He moved toward the rumble of the Moosup River. As he struggled through the sometimes-dense foliage, he continued to scan the woods for any sign of his friends or of Carl, but with the exception of a few birds and squirrels, nothing stirred.

Finally, he saw a sunlit breach between the trees ahead as he picked up his pace and made for the opening. He squinted as

☽ It Happened Deep in the Woods ☾

he stumbled from the trail and into the clearing just across from the old Glen Falls Bridge.

"Timmy!" someone shouted from across the bridge.

He turned to find Rodney pedaling toward him.

"We need to get help!" Timmy begged. "Pete's still in there . . . he saved me." As he spoke, the dam restraining his emotions broke, and his words poured forth in a wave of sobs.

"The police are coming," Rodney said, breathless, as he pulled up next to his friend. "I got away and got some guy up the street to call."

As if on command, the sound of police sirens drew closer in the distance.

The two boys huddled together as several police cars tore down Brunswick and pulled into the clearing.

☆

While one of the police officers interviewed the two boys, several others cordoned off the entrance to the trail. A small crowd gathered around the area as word got out and curious onlookers wandered down Brunswick Avenue to crane their collective necks to see what all of the commotion was about.

About a dozen officers and a police dog had entered the woods about twenty minutes earlier, and so far there had been no news about Carl or their missing friend.

A tall, thin, blond-haired cop with a thick push-broom mustache approached the boys, and they immediately recognized him as Officer Hanley. Hanley had been their elementary school's DARE officer a few years back, and the boys knew him well. "Timmy, Rodney . . . how are you two holding up?" He put a reassuring hand on Timmy's shoulder.

"Have they found Pete yet?" Timmy asked.

"Nothing yet, but they're looking."

Suddenly, loud, incomprehensible shouting erupted from somewhere deep in the woods. Deep, agitated voices bellowed commands, and a high-pitched scream responded. A dog barked. A collective hush fell over the crowd as the rubberneckers strained to hear. They gasped as the rapid pop of gunshots rang through the air before all fell silent again.

Officer Hanley's radio buzzed to life. "2101, we've got a 10-54 and a possible DOA. We're going to need at least two ambulances, maybe three."

"Copy," a different male voice responded.

Timmy and Rodney made eye contact, both thinking the same thing. "Pete . . . " Rodney said.

Noticing the boys' obvious distress, Hanley said, "Listen, why don't you two follow me to my car and sit down for a bit. I have a couple cold Mountain Dews, and you can get out of this heat."

The officer started to lead them to the patrol car when there was suddenly a commotion at the entrance to the trail. As they turned to look, two officers emerged from the tree line; in between them was Pete. His Poison T-shirt was gone, and he had scratches on his face and hands and dried blood on his nose, but other than that, he was alive and well.

"Pete!" the two screamed in unison as they broke away from Hanley and raced to their friend. The three boys embraced, each shedding tears as the stress and horror of the day overwhelmed them all.

☆

The next morning, Timmy awoke early from a fitful sleep plagued with dreams of spiders and murderers and made his way downstairs. Mom stood at the sink in her bathrobe, having taken the day off to support her son. "Good morning, Timmy. Would you like some eggs this morning?"
"Sure, Mom . . . thanks."

Word about the killing spread like wildfire in a drought across the small town. While searching the woods, police stumbled on the mutilated body of Eamon O'Neil. Apparently, the bully had not been as fortunate in avoiding Carl's wrath. The officers who made the discovery agreed that it was the most heinous and violent crime scene they had ever encountered. An autopsy later revealed that Eamon was stabbed over seventy times.

The dog led the search party to Carl's camp, where they found the fugitive packing up his tent to flee. When officers drew their guns and ordered him to surrender, Carl exploded, screaming that he was being framed, that he was the victim of a massive conspiracy. When he turned suddenly to grab something from inside the tent, the officers opened fire. Carl initially survived the shooting only to die later in the hospital.

Most of the news Timmy heard from his parents when they had finally returned home; the more lurid details came from Rodney and their friends.

His parents, although relieved that he was unharmed, were none too pleased that the boys had undertaken such a foolish

☽ It Happened Deep in the Woods ☾

and dangerous mission, and the severity of his inevitable punishment was still a topic of discussion. If Timmy was being honest, he wouldn't mind a lengthy grounding; he had experienced enough adventure for a while.

Timmy sat at the table and saw that his father had left the morning paper behind with his breakfast plate and empty coffee cup. Surely, there would be something about the murder and shooting. Dragging it over, he unfolded it, revealing the bold headline.

Murder Suspect Shot Dead by Police After Killing Local Boy

The article was accompanied by a huge, full-color photo, and Timmy scanned it for details. It looked to have been taken in the woods, and it featured two detectives at the crime scene. In the background, one of the plainclothes officers stooped over a bloody, sheet-covered body. One of the feet protruded from beneath the shroud, revealing a dirty Nike Air Max.

Timmy sucked in a breath; the body obviously belonged to Eamon O'Neil. As much as he loathed the bully, it was still shocking to see someone who had just been alive lying there like a hunk of meat. *That could have been any of us* . . . he realized.

In the foreground, another detective held a clear evidence bag with a bloody knife in it.

The caption below the photo read: "A detective bags up the suspected murder weapon."

Timmy felt his face grow hot and his stomach tighten as he leaned in closer to the paper to get a better look, hoping that he was somehow seeing it wrong.

The weapon in the bag wasn't Carl's machete; it was a camouflaged survival knife.

Pete's knife.

If the body in the background was Eamon, and the murder weapon found by the body was Pete's survival knife . . .

Timmy felt sick as he lowered the paper, folded it back up, and slid it back in front of his father's spot at the table.

Perhaps it was a misunderstanding. Pete had told the police that after he had drawn Carl away from the cave, he'd run through the woods and had hidden beneath an uprooted tree until he heard the police talking. He'd never mentioned anything about losing his knife. And where had his T-shirt gone?

With his mother busying herself at the stove, Timmy rose from his seat and crept out into the living room. Grabbing the

☽ Tom Moran ☾

phone receiver from the cradle, he dialed the familiar number and waited. After three rings, someone picked up.

"Hello?" It was Pete.

"Hey, Pete . . . it's Timmy."

"I'm surprised that you're not grounded from the phone," Pete joked.

"My mom doesn't know that I'm on it." Timmy felt his mouth go dry as he tried to formulate the question. "Hey, did you see the paper today?"

"Nah, not yet. Hold on . . . my mom left it on the counter. Did we make the news?"

"Just check out the article."

There was some rustling in the background, the whisper of unfolding paper. "Oh, look at that! A nice big . . . " Pete trailed off.

"Pete, that's your knife, isn't it?"

For several painstaking seconds, there was silence.

"Pete?"

"You gonna tell on me, Simms?"

Timmy felt the tears welling up as he realized that, no matter how he answered, his friendship with Peter Bradford wouldn't survive. "No," was his simple reply. And he meant it. Whatever had happened in those woods, it wouldn't take away the fact that Pete had risked his own life to save him. And Eamon had made it a point to torture his friend any chance he got; could Pete *really* be blamed for taking advantage of a terrible situation? As much as Timmy would try to convince himself that nothing had changed, that Pete was still a good guy, he realized that he would never be able to look at his friend the same way again without thinking of Eamon and his grisly end.

"Thanks, Timmy. You really are a good friend."

"Thank *you* for looking out for me, Pete."

"Guess I'll see you in a couple years when you're off restriction," Pete tried to joke, but it fell flat.

Without another word, Timmy hung up the phone, buried his face in his hands, and cried.

☾ ☆ ☽

A high school teacher by trade, **Tom Moran** *lives in Connecticut with his amazing wife, Billie, three mostly grown-up children, four dogs, and over 250 tarantulas and spiders. Although he was actively writing and illustrating in the early 2000s, having published the novel* Acquired Taste$ *and the illustrated novella* The Problem with Mickey, *Tom eventually took a hiatus to focus*

It Happened Deep in the Woods

on caring for his menagerie of arachnids. For the past decade, he has maintained a successful YouTube channel and podcast devoted to the care of spiders, while continuing to write almost exclusively for his reading classes. However, after finding a box of his old publications during a trip to his attic, he once again got the itch to get his sick little stories out to the masses. You can currently find him on his author YouTube channel @TomsHorror.

Between Sharp Teeth and Lady Slippers

T.L. Guthrie

Safe in the long branches of a red oak tree, Sam hid with skinned knees tucked up tight to her chin, watching the monster go through her things. Mom always said that it wasn't polite to touch other people's stuff without permission, but the monster touched whatever he wanted.

"Sam!" her mother yelled, stepping into the doorway of their new house. The trim was painted the same bright red as the leaves in her tree, but the front door was white. "Samantha!"

The monster walked down the ramp of the moving truck with all Sam's boxes stacked on the furniture dolly. "Where is she?"

Her mother didn't seem to notice that his mouth was full of sharp teeth, perfect for eating little girls. Sam hid at the edge of the yard where it butted up against the forest surrounding their new property. She would have gone farther, but she worried that the monster might turn his attention to her mother. Once, she ran away, and the monster threatened to slurp her mother up strip by strip if Sam ever did it again. She was too scared to go far.

"She took the dog out," her mom said. "Buddy got into something dusty and was tracking it everywhere."

"That damned dog," the monster spat as he pulled the dolly up the three steps to the porch. The house was big—two stories and wider than it was tall. It looked like a big box, with neatly spaced windows marching in perfect symmetry on either side of the gabled front door. The painted windowsills were white like the front door, but the horizontal paneling of the house was gray.

Sam wished it would burn down. It was her fault they were here. The monster had warned her to keep her mouth shut, and she'd messed up. Just like he'd threatened, the monster made sure that she lost everything. They'd packed up all they owned

☽ Between Sharp Teeth and Lady Slippers ☾

and moved to the middle of nowhere, Connecticut, where there wasn't anything but trees and farms. Now there was nothing to keep him away from her except the red leaves of her hiding spot.

"Be nice," her mother scolded the monster as she moved out of his way in the door. "Sam! Buddy?"

Sam turned to look into the woods when she heard something coming her way. It sounded bigger than Buddy, and she put her feet underneath her on the branch in case she needed to move. Were there bears in Connecticut? She only knew about Tennessee.

Everything went quiet in the canopy as the noise drew closer, except the distant, melancholy call of a whip-poor-will. Most of the birds, at least, she recognized: sparrows and warblers, cardinals, the occasional jay. The only one that she didn't know sounded like a mix between a creaky door opening and a meowing cat. Sam held her breath, feeling very alone. It was dumb to be scared, but she was.

Buddy burst through the underbrush, pink tongue flopped out on one side, looking nothing like a bear. The golden retriever lifted his paws as he pranced through the scrub, a squeaky basketball clamped in slobbery jaws. He'd loved that basketball since he was a puppy, just like in the movie he was named after, but sometimes Sam thought he'd have been a better Lisa Frank than a Buddy. She'd only been six when the monster said he'd hurt the puppy if she didn't pick the right name. Buddy still felt safer than Lisa Frank, but she wondered what it would be like not to worry about the safe choice.

"Buddy." Sam laughed, stupidly relieved. She jumped out of the tree when he didn't acknowledge her, and the dog scrambled to the side with a yelp, startled at her sudden appearance. Sam dove to grab his leash before he got out of her grasp. It burned her hands as it pulled, but Sam got her fingers into the loop of nylon before Buddy yanked it away from her. He dragged her through the brush, but soon he realized who it was, and then he was on top of her, covering her face with sloppy licks.

Sam sputtered through squeals, trying to push him away, but he was relentless. Buddy was the one thing that the monster hadn't managed to take from her, and Sam didn't go anywhere without him.

"Are you Sam?"

Surprised, Sam turned her head toward the voice, pushing Buddy's seeking mouth out of her face. There was another girl there, moving through the brush toward her. She had smooth brown skin, still bronzed from the summer, and dark hair pulled back from her face in a black braid down her back. Her clothes were simple and handmade but clean. Sam sat up, dusting the leaves off her own shirt. The other girl was wearing pink shoes like petals—lady slippers, like in her mom's old flower bed—and Sam was a little jealous of them.

"How did you know?" Sam climbed to her feet, brushing off the seat of her pants and adjusting the leash around her wrist.

"Buddy told me," the other girl said. "I'm River. He said you need help."

"I thought you were a bear." Sam breathed out with relief.

River laughed. All the birds that had fallen quiet when Buddy arrived laughed with her, an ocean of unexpected sound that echoed strangely off the trees. "No. I am many things, but a bear is not one of them."

Sam saw nothing in the leaves, but she knew the birds were there. She could feel them waiting to see what River would do. Sam wanted to wait, too. It was exciting, like being at the top of a roller coaster. She stuck out her hand to shake, like she saw the grown-ups doing all the time. "Do you live close?"

"Kinda," the other girl said. She pointed at Sam's hand. "What's that for?"

"Just to say hi. I don't want to be rude, and you're my neighbor." Sam's cheeks went pink with embarrassment. Well, maybe she wasn't grown-up enough yet. "I don't know how you do things around here."

River eyed her long enough that Sam started to pull her hand back, but then the other girl grabbed it, quick as a snake. Her palm was rough, but so was Sam's, only Sam's was also dirty with bark and sap from climbing trees.

"Want some cheese balls?" Sam patted down her pockets to find her snack. She found it on the ground where she'd jumped out of the tree, along with Buddy's basketball. "I had them in my shirt pocket, so they shouldn't be squished."

"I've never had cheese balls."

Sam noticed how short the other girl was. River only came up to her chest. Her mom had been saying Sam was going through a growth spurt. Maybe she'd be one of the tall sixth graders this year. Sam held the snack out to share, letting River go first.

"Why is there a monster at your house?"

☽ Between Sharp Teeth and Lady Slippers ☾

Sam froze. The monster had warned her not to talk, under threat of destroying everything she owned. In the beginning, Sam had been sure her mother would stop him, but her mom never noticed any of the bruises and scrapes, missing toys, or ripped-up books. Maybe she really did believe Sam when she said she was just clumsy. The monster made her a pretty good liar. None of her other friends had ever asked, and the burden of knowing was heavy. There wasn't much else he could take away except her mom and Buddy. If she wasn't careful, he could hurt them all, but . . .

Something desperate unfurled in her chest. "You can see him?" Sam whispered.

River looked at her sideways before popping another cheese ball in her mouth and crunching it mightily. She raised her chin. "Of course I can. He's in my woods."

Sam laughed. River looked like a queen on her throne. "Oh, your woods. I'm sure he'll apologize right away."

"He won't," River sounded as serious as Sam felt when she thought about the monster. "He is the kind that takes and hurts and crunches bones. You should stay with me in the woods. I can help you get rid of him."

A spear of anxiety lanced through Sam's gut, leaving an ache like a wound. "I can't. It's not that simple. He's got my mom. And we're just two kids."

"You're just a kid. I'm something different."

As the two girls shared the snack, Sam decided that while River might be a little weird, she still wished that River was right. Here in the trees, Sam felt safe for the first time in ages. She could almost remember the last time she'd been really, truly happy. A long time ago, before her mom and the monster got married, she found out that he was evil.

River asked to help with the monster three more times that day. After Sam said no the fourth time, River didn't ask anymore. It felt unexpectedly bad, like Sam had failed somehow, but River didn't act that way. She just pointed out all the birds in the trees around them, the ones that Sam hadn't even seen before. The creaky door bird was called a gray catbird, and it had a brown stripe under its tail and black eyes like shiny pebbles.

For her part, Sam told River how she liked cartoons about kids with no monsters the best and how she hated when the monster made her watch the scary ones with his arm around her shoulder. Sam didn't mean to; it had just been so long since someone listened that it slipped out. But the angry snap of River's black eyes sent her stomach flopping with fear, so Sam changed the subject to all the snacks that her mom kept in the kitchen, a topic that was of great interest to her new companion. Buddy adored them, wallowing around on his back in the leaves, squeaking the basketball until both girls collapsed in giggles.

Sam was having so much fun that she forgot about the monster until she heard him calling for her from the edge of the yard. He sounded furious, like the night Jenny's mom called to ask about the long, finger-shaped bruises around Sam's arm. If she made him that angry again, she had no idea what he might do.

Sam jolted to her feet. "I gotta go," she blurted out, fear tightening her chest.

With Buddy's leash in hand, Sam bolted for the house before River could say anything. She didn't want the other girl to see how scared she was, and Sam didn't want to see how disappointed River was that she was doing what the monster said. She'd worn bruises for weeks under her clothes after Jenny's mom called. She couldn't do that again, not if she wanted to climb trees with River like she'd promised.

"Mom?" Sam opened the back door. She picked sticks out of Buddy's fur and tossed them on the porch. The monster didn't like Buddy getting things dirty.

Instead of her mother, the monster came around the doorway into the kitchen. Sam drew up short, pulling back on Buddy's leash. At first glance, the monster looked like a perfectly normal human being. He was tall, head and shoulders taller than her mom, and built broadly with wide shoulders that drew his shirt taut across his back when he was angry. His hands were big, too; Sam once saw him pick up and throw a basketball at Buddy with just one hand. His face was all sharp angles, meant for frowning. Sam would rather see him frown. Seeing the monster smile always meant something bad was going to happen.

Most of the time, like now, the monster wore jeans and a shirt that buttoned in the front, and he usually rolled the long sleeves of the shirt up to his elbows. Underneath the button-up, he wore a T-shirt, but underneath that, where smooth human skin should be, the monster had leathery scales and hard, knobby horns all over him. Instead of normal human teeth, the monster's mouth was full of long, sharp triangles with jagged edges.

☽ Between Sharp Teeth and Lady Slippers ☾

He bared them at her now in a smile, his eyes as sharp as those teeth. It was not a good smile. Sometimes, when no one else was around, he threatened to bite her fingers off one by one, just to see what she would do. This smile held that threat without needing to say it. Sam curled her hands around Buddy's leash, the best she could do to keep them both safe.

"Where have you been?" the monster snapped. Buddy growled when he stepped forward, and his smile disappeared in an instant at seeing the dog in front of her.

"We went for a walk," Sam said, her voice small. "To keep Buddy out of the way. I tried to clean him off on the porch."

"Get rid of him." The monster took another step toward her but retreated when Buddy growled again. "Out!" he shouted at the dog, pointing toward the porch. Buddy barked, and he would have lunged at the monster's outstretched hand, but Sam hauled on the leash and pulled him backward, hitting the wall next to the door. On the table next to her, one of her mother's vases wobbled. Sam hurried to steady it.

"I'm sorry," she said. "I'll fix it, just— "

The monster's hand clamped over hers. Sam knew better than to struggle against his vice grip. If he made any bruises she'd be in extra trouble, just like with Jenny's mom. She wedged herself between Buddy and the monster, shoving the dog away from her impostor stepfather.

"Why would you do this, Samantha?" the monster asked, his voice low. Sam shivered, a chill racing down her spine at the ice in his tone. Just when she was positive he was going to hurt her, the monster flung her hand back at her and swiped the vase off the table in one fell swoop. It shattered on the floor so abruptly that Buddy stopped throwing himself against her legs. Sam stood stunned, trying to make sense of what had just happened. She looked at the monster, but he just smiled back at her, that same wide shark grin.

"Lie, Sam. Make her believe it was you, or I will break her neck so that she's awake when I cut her open." He stepped away to the entrance of the kitchen and raised his voice so that her mother was sure to hear. "Sam? Samantha! What did you do?" He sounded scolding as he knelt next to the broken pieces of her mother's vase.

"Babe?" Samantha's mom called from the hallway. "Is everything okay? What's—oh no," she said, as she stepped into the doorway. "What happened? Is anyone hurt?"

T.L. Guthrie

"I'm all right," Sam whispered, mostly for herself. She did not want to see her mom cut open.

"I don't know," the monster said, his head down as he gingerly picked up broken pieces of ceramic off the floor. Out of her mother's sight, he held the biggest piece like a knife. "I heard something break so I came to see."

"What happened, Sam?" her mother asked.

What happened, Sam? What was she supposed to say? Samantha hesitated, frozen like a deer in the headlights of her mother's gaze. He had a knife. Was it hard to snap someone's neck? After a second, her mom's face softened. "Hey, it's all right," her mom said. "It's just a vase. We can get another one."

"It wasn't me," Sam blurted out, knowing even as she said it that her mom wouldn't believe her. She looked back at the monster so that she didn't have to see the disbelief in her mother's eyes. He was watching her with a tight smile. If she hadn't been so scared she might have been angry, but her mother had her back to the monster and Sam knew how strong his hands were. What if he really did snap her mom's neck?

"Sam," her mother scolded gently. "Tell me what happened."

"He knocked it off the table on purpose," Sam whispered. "He was mad because Buddy barked at him and I'm afraid he's going to hurt somebody."

"Samantha," the monster said, straightening to his feet. He shouldn't have been able to hear her. "What are you talking about? I wasn't even here in the room. You know better than this."

Her mother looked back and forth between the two of them, then settled on Sam with a frown. "Sam," she said. "You don't have to lie. You're not in trouble."

Sam stared at her. She hadn't expected to be believed, but for her mom to take the monster's side right in front of her hurt more than she thought it would. Why couldn't her mother listen? Sam wanted so badly to keep her mom safe. She'd done a really good job, but she was so tired of holding the truth behind her back. Sam wanted her mom to believe her, like River had. She didn't want to lie anymore. But the monster shifted behind her mother, raising his hands onto her shoulders, and Sam's breath caught. "You're right. It was me," Sam lied, before anyone got hurt.

"All right." Her mom put a hand on her shoulder, and Sam's stomach sank like a stone when she swallowed the lie. Why was

☽ **Between Sharp Teeth and Lady Slippers** ☾

it so easy to believe Sam was the bad guy? Sam wasn't the monster. "Well, let's just get it cleaned up for now. Take Buddy outside so he doesn't hurt his paws, then come back and we'll clean up."

Beaten, Sam took Buddy back out the door, listening intently to the soft murmur of her mom and the monster talking in the kitchen behind her. She was petrified to leave after what she'd done. She had to find a way to get them all out. Her mother wasn't safe, but Sam didn't know how to convince her. Telling the truth hadn't gotten her anywhere. The monster was right. Sam did know better.

"Sorry, Buddy," she said as she unclipped the leash. Buddy licked her hand like he understood, and Sam's lip quivered as she buried her hand in the soft fur of his neck. "Go find River," she whimpered to him. "Tell her I said I was wrong. I do need her help."

Shooing Buddy away was the hardest thing that Sam had ever done, and it hurt her feelings that he bolted away into the woods without looking back. She slouched her way back into the kitchen. Most of the ceramic shards were cleaned up. "I'm going to go find a broom," her mom said, heading for the hallway. Sam stood by the door, alone with the monster again. Her relief at seeing her mother warred with queasy terror as she left.

"You thought you were smart, didn't you?" The monster grinned at her. "You never learn. Why would anyone ever believe you instead of me?"

"I'm sorry," Sam said, tucking her hands behind her back. "Please don't hurt anybody."

The monster laughed, the sound rolling out like thunder in the empty kitchen. "No promises, Sam. I'm feeling very hungry. Maybe tonight is the night."

Sam thumped against the door, her palms pressing against the wood panels. She wished she could push herself all the way through and out the other side. She wished that she was back in the safety of the red oak tree. His laughing made her want to scream. Tears welled in Sam's eyes, but it wasn't until her mother appeared back in the doorway, broom and dustpan in hand, that they streaked down her face.

The monster was bending over the last of the ceramic pieces like nothing had happened. Sam imagined she could still hear him laughing. Her mother swept up the broken pieces and threw them away. Sam wondered if that was what would happen to her, too.

T.L. Guthrie

Buddy didn't come home for dinner. Sam stood on the back porch and called until her throat was hoarse, but most of her words were lost in the whipping wind. For a while, she watched the clouds boil in the bruised sky and the leaves tumble over each other in the yard, but eventually she had to leave the bowl by Buddy's plastic igloo. She wasn't giving up. There just wasn't anything else she could do.

The monster spent all of dinner grumbling about how long it would take to rake up leaves in their new yard. Sam spent most of it staring at her pizza and not eating, hoping that his talk about leaves meant he wouldn't hurt anyone tonight. If he did, would it be her fault?

She wondered where River lived. Sam tried to remember where the closest house was to theirs, but everything looked the same once it turned into woods and farms. It couldn't be too far away, but if it wasn't, where was Buddy? Did River really live in the woods? Could she actually help with the monster? Sam couldn't understand how they were supposed to kill a monster on their own.

What if Buddy stayed away because he liked River better than her? Sam didn't know what to do without him, and she was worried about Buddy being out in the storm. She always felt safer when he slept on her bed. Without Buddy to protect her, she didn't really know what to do, but Sam knew she had to do something. So, when she cleaned up her mess from the table, she grabbed the only thing she found by the sink—a fork—and shoved it in her pocket.

The stairs up to her room were miles long when Sam climbed them and left her mom behind. Her room was full of boxes; the mattress and box spring sat on the floor with the bed frame propped up against the wall. Sam opened her window so that if Buddy came back, she might hear the jingle of his collar. And then she sat at the window and looked at the fork, turning it over in her hands. It wasn't much of a weapon, but it was the best one Sam had ever had. She was scared that she might have to use it.

When bedtime came, Sam found a blanket and curled up on her bare mattress, listening to the wind and distant thunder. She was too tired to cry, and too afraid to worry whether the monster had chosen tonight.

☽ **Between Sharp Teeth and Lady Slippers** ☾

A loud thump woke Sam in the middle of the night, prickling her arms with goosebumps. She wanted to believe it was from the chilly, wet air coming from her window, but she couldn't convince herself. It was thunder. It was nothing. The hair on the back of her neck rose as she heard another thump. No, it was something heavy coming up the stairs toward her room. Sam's heart pounded so loudly she was sure that the monster would hear it.

A long, scratching scrape accompanied the next thump, one step closer to her bed. Long claws ripped through the floral wallpaper in the stairwell, tearing it away like notebook paper. Tonight, the monster wasn't even pretending to be human. Sam shoved her hand under her pillow and snatched up the fork. It seemed very small.

"Ssssam." The whisper slithered through her open doorway like a snake, fangs exposed and ready to bite.

Two more thumps on the stairs brought the monster to halfway, and that's when panic shot Sam upright in the bed. Holding her breath, she slipped over to her door and eased it closed. Another thump came from behind her as she scrambled in the dark, sobbing as she flailed for the wooden chair to her desk.

Her hand swatted into the back of the chair, knocking it over onto the floor with a sharp crack. There was a beat of complete silence before the rush of running feet pounded toward her door. Sam lunged with the recovered chair, using her full weight to wedge it underneath the doorknob as it turned in the monster's hand. There was no lock on her door, but the chair held for the first vicious shake of the knob, and then through the shudder as he threw himself against the other side.

"Samantha," the monster commanded. He wasn't trying to be quiet, wasn't afraid of waking her mother, and that scared Sam the most. "Open the door, little girl. I am still hungry, and you smell so sweet."

"Go away," Sam whimpered. She didn't want to be this close, but she was scared that if she moved, the chair would slide away. "Please, please go away."

"Your mother was delicious," the monster cackled. He scratched at the door, tearing into it, and little slivers of debris bounced through the crack underneath. The chair would not keep her safe forever, but Sam couldn't move. Her mother was gone. If she believed him. Did she believe him?

Dust rained on Sam's head as the door shook and held, shook and held, beneath the furious battering of the monster on the other side. Sam could hear the panting frustration of his grunts as he failed to reach her, and she knew it was only a matter of time before he succeeded. She might have stayed there, frozen, if the hissing call at the window hadn't drawn her attention.

Sam had no idea how River climbed all the way up onto the gable outside the window, but the girl was there, black hair glistening against her skin where the rain plastered it to her head. There was barely enough light to see the outline of her against the weather outside, but Sam was sure it was her. River needed to leave before she got hurt.

"River," Sam whispered, her breath coming in little gasps. "You can't be here; he'll hurt you, too. Please, you have to run."

River tilted her head, and her eyes reflected green in the dark. "Let me in, Sam."

"No! I said you have to go!" The door banged behind Sam, almost flinging her off the chair. Something in the frame splintered. "He's going to get in, River. He'll hurt you!"

"No. He won't."

"Who are you talking to, Sam?" the monster growled. For a moment, his violence subsided. Sam held her breath as he listened. It was stupid, but maybe he'd think she wasn't here anymore. Then the monster laughed, that horrible rolling thunder. "Your bones will snap like little sticks," he teased through the door. "I will make sure you're alive to feel most of them."

"Let me in," River urged. There was no fear in her voice. "Sam, trust me. I can do this. I can help you."

"Sam, trust me," the monster laughed as he battered the door. Leaning the full weight of her small body against the chair, Sam clamped her hands to her ears to think. The fork was cold against her temple. The door wouldn't hold much longer, and she had to decide what to do. Sam wasn't interested in letting the monster hurt anyone else. Resolution flooded through her: River wasn't coming in; Sam was going out.

Two more times the monster threw his massive weight against the door, and two more times the chair held, although it bucked against Sam's small body. The splintering got louder behind her each time, the frame creaking and groaning underneath the monster's claws.

After the next lunge came, Sam flew across the room to River. "Don't come in," she said to her friend, holding her hand out the window. "We have to go."

☽ **Between Sharp Teeth and Lady Slippers** ☾

River hauled Sam out the window by that one hand, far stronger than her kid-sized body should be. "I won't let him hurt you," she said. Her voice sounded bigger too, and Sam thought again to the way that her eyes had reflected the light.

"I have a fork, but I'm scared," Sam whispered back to her, looking back at the window at the sound of the chair scraping on the wooden floor.

"Don't be." River took her hand and leaped from the gable down into the yard, pulling Sam along. They fell, but they didn't hit the ground hard. Sam's bare feet slid on the wet grass.

"What are you?" Sam asked her, because now out in the rain she could see that her friend glowed, and that her shadow on the grass was far, far longer than it should have been. Even though she didn't think River would hurt her, she was very glad for the fork in her hand.

"Someone that believes you," River said. She turned toward the house at the sharp crack of a door bursting open. The monster roared with rage. "Go into the woods. Buddy is waiting," her friend said. "You don't have to see this."

"What are you going to do?"

"I'm going to fight," River looked at Sam. "And I'm going to kill a monster."

Sam stared at her friend long enough to decide she was telling the truth. She looked back up at the window, hearing the destruction taking place inside her room. Her mother might still be in there. She couldn't just leave.

"We," Sam said to River, brandishing her fork. "We're going to kill a monster. Together."

"No, Sam." River turned to her, putting two warm hands on Sam's shoulders. When had she gotten so tall? "It's time for you to go. Let me protect you like you've protected them. This isn't your responsibility."

Tears pricked at Sam's eyes. She had waited so long to hear someone say that. She threw herself into River's arms, holding her tight. "I'm sorry that I made him mad, River."

River knelt down to eye level with Sam. "None of this is your fault. I'm going to make it right. Go find Buddy. He said to call him Lisa Frank."

Sam laughed, pulling back to look at River's reflective eyes. This was what the truth felt like. It had to be. "I believe you."

☽ T.L. Guthrie ☾

T.L. Guthrie *is an invasive species located in the Oregon Willamette Valley in the Pacific Northwest of the United States. Originally discovered in the Appalachian Mountains in the 1980s, Guthrie was transplanted to the Pacific Northwest in 2010 for reasons unknown and continues to thrive there unabated with family. They can be found focused primarily around short works and novels of strange science fiction, fantasy, and horror. Follow them on Twitter @ tl_guthrie.*

Incident at Elderhill Farm

John Opalenik

"It's just over the hill here," Steve called over his shoulder as he pedaled his bike toward the old farmhouse and attached meat-packing plant. "Trust me, guys. It's going to be like we're playing *Goldeneye* or something!"

Elderhill Road wasn't the kind of road that kids rode bikes on often. It was a long way between houses with no sidewalks and a thirty-five-mile-per-hour speed limit that most drivers took as a suggestion. The road stretched for miles, and aside from the old farmhouse, there wasn't anything besides houses, fields, and little patches of forest sitting there to remind people of what the town once was, a hilly woodland nestled in a valley in the middle of Connecticut.

"It would be cooler if it was like a game of *Perfect Dark*," Kyle shouted into the wind.

"It's the same exact game." Steve pulled up his bike next to Kyle and kicked it playfully.

"No way!" Kyle protested. "The graphics on *Perfect Dark* are way better, and even if you're saying it kind of plays the same, *Perfect Dark* has aliens in it."

"I'd rather be playing *Doom*," Charles stated flatly. While the other boys preferred the high-paced action of the other games, Charles couldn't help but find the dark, frightening imagery of *Doom* alluring.

Charles took two pumps from his inhaler and pedaled fast to join the others in front of the farm. Although he'd rather be home with the air conditioner on high and the blue glow of his computer screen as the only light source, he had to admit this place was perfect. The empty parking lot led to two rocky dirt paths on each side of the structure, built into the side of a hill. The back of the roof was only two feet off the ground, easily

John Opalenik

climbable. That roof had different levels, angles, and sections, which led Charles to believe that the building had started small and been added onto over its decades of use. Still, he also knew that Steve and Kyle would look at it and see perfect places to hide, take cover, and jump off during a paintball match. The sign on the front of the building read, "Elderhill Farm: Serving Connecticut for over 100 years."

"Dude. This place is crazy." Kyle ran up to the front window and cupped his hands against the glass to peer inside.

"I know. Isn't it crazy how big the door to the freezer room is in there? I guess it has to be to get a whole cow through. My dad came here to have them deal with the deer he shot when he took me hunting last month. I was walking around the place while he was paying, and when I saw it, I couldn't stop thinking about how awesome it would be for paintball." Steve left out the fact that he then went outside; the sight of slaughtered animals hanging, ready to be turned from corpses into food, both made him nauseated and filled him with a sadness he didn't want to admit was there.

Kyle peered inside. The concrete floor looked indestructible, as if it had always been there. The room was dark except for the fluorescent light blinking in the display where cuts of meat would have been sitting if they were open today. The stillness made it feel like the building should be silent, but the persistent hum of the freezer made the building feel like a living thing, vast and carnivorous.

"We shouldn't leave our bikes out front. People driving by will see them and know what's up," Steve announced.

When Charles tried to walk his bike around the right side of the building, Steve stopped him, saying that the right side of the building contained an open animal pen, and they ought not bother the animals. Instead, they were walking their bikes up the steep path to the left of the building when Kyle noticed a path through a patch of tall grass leading to a small pond, maybe thirty feet across.

"Do you see that?" Kyle gestured to the pond. "Looks like the sort of fishing spot that would be perfect for farmers on the weekend. I'm surprised they aren't here."

"Stop worrying," Steve insisted. "They all drive big pickup trucks. If they're coming, we'll hear them a mile away, and we can just hide out for a few minutes and sneak away."

☽ Incident at Elderhill Farm ☾

"Now that you mention it, there are a lot of good hiding places around here," Charles observed.

"Yeah. So you better watch out once the paintballs start flying!" Kyle playfully jabbed Charles with his elbow.

Always the leader of the group, Steve cut in. "Before we can start, we need to finish checking the place out. We don't want to step on a loose nail on the roof or something."

Steve, Charles, and Kyle walked the roof, occasionally pushing down harder with their sneakers to see if there was a weak spot in the rough, black shingles that made up the slaughterhouse's roof. While it seemed solid, Steve noticed a beehive hanging from an overhang far on the opposite side of the building from where they'd started. Each agreed that side was out of bounds. The last thing they wanted was to come home covered in beestings.

After climbing down from the roof, Charles looked at the trees surrounding the farmhouse. "Are the trees going to be out of bounds?"

"Yeah. Out of bounds," Steve confirmed. "It's a great spot to take cover, but then we'd have to decide how deep into the woods is too far and it would be too much."

"Woah, look at those!" Kyle pointed to the dirt by the forest's edge. "Bullets."

"Shotgun shells," Steve corrected.

"Oh . . . " Kyle's voice trailed off for the ten seconds it took for him to regain his confidence. "Either way, it looks like the farmers did a lot of shooting here."

Charles squatted and examined where the red and green cylinders with metal caps lay. "I think they were firing in all directions."

"Dude, you're just quoting the movie *Predator*." Steve started laughing. "Don't get me wrong. That movie was badass, but if they were shooting in every direction, there'd be bullet holes in the farmhouse, and the only ones I see are right there." He pointed to the tree line where a ten-yard stretch of trees had been riddled with shotgun blasts.

"Maybe a pig got loose or something?" Charles offered.

"Yeah, right!" Kyle started laughing. "You really think they'd start blasting like that if Charlotte got out?"

Charles sighed. "You really didn't pay attention back in third grade, did you? Charlotte was the spider. The pig's name was Wilbur."

☽ John Opalenik ☾

"Still . . . wouldn't they just let it go?" Kyle tried to prove that despite his botched literary reference, he was still right. "I don't think they'd shoot like that unless it was at something dangerous, not just a pig."

Charles got darkly excited and jumped on the chance to counter Kyle's assertion. "Boars are so dangerous! I read about this time that a farmer got stuck in the pen with a boar, and it used its tusks to— "

"Okay. Enough guys." Steve cut in, hiding the fact that he couldn't stand gore. That's why he pushed their group toward video games like *Goldeneye* and *Mario Kart* instead of *Doom* and *Mortal Kombat*. "It doesn't matter. We just won't go out . . . " His voice trailed off as he noticed something up the one trail wide enough for a truck to make it up. "Do you guys see that?" Steve pointed to a shape in the distance that was a shade of red that might have blended in if it were autumn and the leaves were changing color, but in the middle of summer, it stood out.

"Dude, let's just play paintball. We don't need to go into the woods," Kyle protested.

"Aren't you even the least bit curious about what might be out there?" Charles countered, halfway hoping it would be something creepy.

"You can just wait here," Steve asserted. "Charles and I are going to go check it out."

The second Steve said that, Kyle knew there was no way he was going to sit there while his two best friends went off on their own adventure. They'd exaggerate and make it sound like it was so cool, and he'd feel like he missed out. He cursed under his breath and followed them up the rocky trail into the dense New England woodland.

As they moved farther up the trail, the thick canopy made it look like it was getting dark out even though it was noon on a Sunday, and the red structure began to take shape. A little further, it became clear that they'd found an old shack ravaged by both the passing of years and by dozens of bullet holes. From a distance, it looked like nobody had gone near the shack in years, but when they got closer, they saw boot prints in the mud that rain hadn't washed away.

"Oh, dude. What's that smell?" Kyle pinched his nose closed.

"Maybe this is where the farmers used to take a crap before they got plumbing." Steve chuckled at his own joke.

☽ Incident at Elderhill Farm ☾

"No. It doesn't smell like that. It smells like roadkill or something. Maybe this farm is doing some *Texas Chainsaw Massacre* stuff and hiding it here." Charles raised his paintball gun, ready to coat any chainsaw-wielding maniac with paint.

"What are you going to do with that?" Kyle sarcastically asked, his voice nasal and high-pitched from pinching his nose. "You going to paintball the killer into submission?"

"I was going to aim for the eye and then run." Charles hefted the paintball gun proudly. "Then I'd tell the police to look for the guy with one eye and a face full of paint."

"You know." Steve tried to ignore the stench so he could sound serious. "It's really cool that you're the one kid whose mom lets him rent R movies, but all that *Texas Chainsaw Massacre* and *Doom* talk is why kids at school think you're weird. You know we'll always have your back, but if we get put in different classes when we start high school . . . I don't know. You've just got to watch out for yourself. Don't do anything that'll put a target on your back."

Charles tried not to show how much of a gut punch Steve's admonishment was while he figured out how to respond. He wanted to say that no, they wouldn't always have his back. That Steve would make the football team freshman year and be too good for him, and that soon after that, Kyle would get a girlfriend. Kyle was handsome and funny and didn't get zits every time he ate fast food the way Charles seemed to. Soon Kyle would ask some girl out, and he'd start spending all his time with her, and that would leave Charles alone with nothing to keep him company but the very things that Steve said were the reasons people thought he was weird. That conversation was inevitable, but he wasn't ready to have it today. "Whatever. Let's go see what stinks." He couldn't help but hit back in a small way, though. "I'll go first. I may be weird, but at least I'm not chicken."

He pushed the paintball goggles over his eyes and crept forward using hand signals he'd copied from movies to direct Steve and Kyle to follow him.

Steve set down his paintball gun, took out the pocketknife his father had given him the first time they went camping, and followed close behind Charles.

Kyle stood a few feet back with his paintball gun held low in one hand while the other continued to pinch his nose closed.

The doorway into the shack was no longer a perfect rectangle, as the wide spread of buckshot had widened it and morphed it into a deformed oval, and whatever door had been there was now nothing but splinters on the ground. When Charles stepped inside, he saw what he first took for a stone altar, but when he got closer it looked more like one of the slabs of concrete used to build the slaughterhouse floor. He wondered if the farmers had somehow gotten the waist-high slab of concrete in through the doorway or if they'd dropped it there and then built the shack around it; either way, it had likely been there since that part of the slaughterhouse had been built.

"Look at all the footprints." Steve pointed with the tip of his pocketknife. "People come in here regularly, but it looks like they haven't done anything to repair all the damage."

"What's this? It looks like when they roll up forks in napkins at a fancy restaurant." Charles nudged a rolled-up cloth with the barrel of his paintball gun. The black fabric unraveled, revealing something embroidered into it with golden thread. Charles felt like he had to know what it was or the mystery would keep him up at night. He unrolled it all the way. The cloth turned out to be about a foot long and two feet wide and the embroidery wasn't writing, but instead a rudimentary tree that looked like an ancient cave painting. The tree itself was stitched in the gold he'd seen earlier, and the root system that stretched down just as far was a deep shade of red that he almost couldn't see against the black fabric.

Kyle finally barged into the shack and unpinched his nose. "Oh, it actually doesn't smell as bad in here." He paused when he saw the embroidered symbol. "What is *that*?"

"I don't know, but I'm going to take it so I can look it up at the library later." Charles rolled it back up and shoved the cloth into one of the cargo pockets on his black pants.

Steve stepped toward the door. "If the smell isn't coming from in here, it's got to be behind the shed. Let's go."

Steve and Charles stood at the front together as the rancid smell intensified; it reminded Steve of a combination of overripe bananas and that one summer his dad tried to make a compost pile. It made his eyes water. When they made it to the crest of the hill, they looked down into what appeared to be a patch of swampland just twenty yards into an otherwise dry forest. A stream flowed from the top of the mountains, through the swamp, and into the pond they'd noticed earlier, and this piece of land about thirty feet beyond the shack appeared to be the one area where the stream spread out into a pool that could have been a foot deep or deeper than Kyle's swimming pool. By the time Kyle caught up to them with his T-shirt pulled up over his nose, they realized what was blocking the flow of the water.

The rotting skeletal remains of what must have been dozens of animals from the farm lay partially submerged in the patch of swampland. A skeletal lamb's leg and hoof rose out of the water like a submarine's periscope. A bloated, rotting cow floated on its side. A pig had been there for so long one would struggle to tell where its body stopped and the landscape began.

"Dude! What the hell?" Kyle pulled his face out from under his T-shirt and turned away just in time to vomit his ham-and-cheese sandwich all over the precarious path leading back to the shack. When he finally stopped gagging, he gasped, "Why did the farmers do that?"

"Maybe this is where they throw out the bodies after they slaughter them." Charles offered, but it felt wrong even saying it. It *had* to have something to do with that shack and the symbol embroidered on the handkerchief.

"I don't think so," Steve countered. "I'm no expert, but I think there's a lot of meat left on the bones that they could've used. Baby back ribs. See?" He pointed to the cracked ribs protruding from a floating pig.

"Dude, don't say that." Kyle gagged. "I'll never eat them again. Do you think the animals were sick, so the farmers shot them and left the bodies out here? Is that why it smells so bad?"

"No, that's the methane from bacteria growing," Charles replied. "I read in a book that—"

"Not now, Charles!" Kyle interrupted. "God, you're so *weird* sometimes."

"Look," Steve stammered, his usual confidence wounded. He pointed to a young lamb still alive and weakly trying to paddle its way through the muck to get to dry land. "We have to do something . . . right?" He and Charles looked at Kyle simultaneously.

"Me? No way. Why me?"

"You're the tallest. Don't worry. We'll hold your belt so you don't fall in," Steve explained as Kyle cautiously inched down the steep incline.

The boys fashioned a harness out of Kyle's belt and Charles's backpack. Steve and Charles held on tight with their feet dug into the mud as if they were preparing for a tug-of-war. Kyle reached out to the poor animal as it waded toward him and wondered if grabbing it by the head or by one of its forelimbs

John Opalenik

would be better. As the lamb's movements slowed and it let out a cry that was equal parts pained and exhausted, Kyle started to think that it wouldn't matter soon enough.

Suddenly, the slick patch of muck slid from beneath his sneakers and he pitched forward, ready to do a belly flop into the mixture of pond scum and animal remains. Kyle squeezed his eyes shut and prepared for the splash, but it never came. Steve and Charles had dug in their heels and held him by their makeshift harness.

"Guys! Pull me back," he shouted.

"Come on, Kyle. You're so close. Just grab it, and we'll pull you both back." Steve grunted as he struggled to keep his friend out of the muck.

"I guess I could try." Kyle looked down, expecting to see the dying lamb, but instead saw a bubble six inches across growing on the surface of the water. Just when he thought it would burst, a slit crossed its center and opened, revealing a huge eye staring right at him. He turned his head and saw the lamb jolted back to its former writhing self as a dozen appendages that looked like the chitinous claws of some giant crab, but with the flexibility of tentacles, wrapped around and through the lamb and pulled it under. "Guys, get me out of here! Something's in the swamp eating these things."

The boys had never seen Kyle so scared. They started pulling right away as the greenish-brown muck coalesced into a more solid form just beneath their friend.

As he started to rise slowly, Kyle looked back at the giant eye that stared at him until it burst like a pimple. When the pus drained away, it revealed a circular maw with dozens of sharp, hooked teeth ready to pull him beneath the surface and out of this world.

The mouth and the slime it sat upon rose slowly, savoring the fear that dripped off his face in the form of both sweat and tears. Just as he began to let out a scream that would convey the terror that words could not, he felt his body being pulled backward with a violent speed that sent him reeling onto the dry land at the edge of the swamp.

"Dude! What the hell was that?" Steve shouted as Kyle stared back, too scared to form words.

"It looked like something out of a *Swamp Thing* comic, except not awesome," Charles stammered. His eyes grew wide

Incident at Elderhill Farm

when he saw more crab claws breach the water. They were easily as long as the boys' legs. "It's coming!"

Steve grabbed Kyle by the shirt and dragged him upright. "Come on. We've got to get to our bikes and get the hell out of here." Once he knew Kyle was on his feet and able to move, he turned and ran down the path toward the farmhouse. He was the only one who was into sports, and he outpaced them quickly. He hoped he could get to their bikes first so he could use his speed and maneuverability either to distract the abomination chasing them or to help his friends escape.

Charles glanced back and saw that the creature had the texture of a boiling vat of fleshy pink jelly, with appendages ranging from tentacles and claws to limbs that looked far too human growing and melting back into its mass whenever it seemed to need them. It had multiple mouths that stretched and tore as it roared before reforming into one large maw capable of swallowing a person with only a little bit of tenderizing that its rows of teeth were more than capable of doing.

Suddenly, a thick rope of slime with a giant hand that looked like chewed bubble gum shot forward toward them. It hit Kyle in the back and started pulling him backward with a violent shake that dropped him to the ground.

Luckily, it had latched onto his backpack rather than his flesh. Kyle wrestled out of the backpack and scrambled forward as the monstrosity chewed up the backpack and spit it out when it realized the leather and plastic container didn't hold any morsels of meat.

Before he could get up, the ooze slithered forward and reared back behind Kyle with one massive mouth that could crash on him like a wave of teeth. He turned just in time to see it tower over him. Kyle raised his hands in a futile defense when he heard a familiar pop and saw the creature's single basketball-sized yellow eye burst like a wet balloon as a volley of three pink paintballs hit it. He turned around to see Charles holding up his paintball gun proudly.

Kyle picked himself up and ran toward Charles. "Just like you said, 'Aim for the eye and run.' And now it's time to run!" The two took off down the trail, avoiding loose rocks since a twisted ankle would be a death sentence.

As they got closer to the slaughterhouse, Kyle pointed out that the carnivorous slime was slithering through the woods to the right of the trail, cutting off the path around the right side

John Opalenik

of the building where Steve and their bikes were. "It's blocked, man. We've got to go around." They broke off to the left side and clambered over the roof.

Kyle's long legs carried him faster than Charles could keep up, and he got to the roof first. His mind still reeled with the terror of what pursued them, and he forgot about the beehive. His sneaker stomped close enough to it that the area right behind him exploded with a cloud of bees. For once, Charles was grateful that he was the least athletic of his friends and turned right up the steeper incline of the roof to avoid running headlong into what could be hundreds of beestings. He had almost made it to the peak of the roof where he would be able to see their bikes and the way out when a weak spot in the roof gave out beneath him, and he fell into the slaughterhouse.

☆

Steve made it to the concrete slaughterhouse and tripped when the path changed direction sharply. He picked himself up and looked to his right, where he saw the half-liquid form of the creature that hunted them rise out of the little fishing pond he'd noticed earlier. He wondered if it was a second creature or the stretched-out form of the same one. When the boiling mass of flesh generated a set of spiky spider legs the size of street signposts and lunged for him, he dove onto his stomach and decided that, either way, he needed to get to the bikes. Not taking the time to pick himself up, Steve crawled forward, hoping he'd make it to the parking lot before it could attack again.

He saw his bike, a bright blue Huffy, waiting for him on its kickstand. Steve jumped onto the bike and pedaled to the edge of the road, where he could either turn left and find his friends or turn right and get the hell out of there.

☆

Wet, rotten wood slowed Charles's fall but also cut his forearms as he shielded his face from the onslaught of debris, and then there was a fraction of a second with no sensation except the air blowing past him. He landed on something rough and fleshy before bouncing off onto the unforgiving concrete. He opened his eyes and found himself in a pen, surrounded by the pink flesh of half a dozen pigs, as startled as him. Charles couldn't help but remember what he'd read about what a boar's tusks could do to a person. He eyed the back of the pen and saw cows and a few sheep. He stood up slowly, hoping that a sudden movement wouldn't set them off, and backed away while simultaneous-

☾ Incident at Elderhill Farm ☽

ly pulling the cloth he'd found earlier out of his pocket to press against the deep gash on his arm that might need stitches if he ever got out of this.

One pig snorted aggressively in his direction, and as he turned to make a run for it, a horrific squelching sound came from above as the creature, the color of spoiled meat, poured itself through the hole Charles had fallen through and into the pen with them.

A spiky tendril shot from the formless mass and impaled the pig that snorted at Charles before the end of it spread out into a crescent-moon shape and pulled backward, cutting the pig in two. When the blood splashed onto Charles's face, he didn't care about provoking a pig attack anymore. He turned and ran for the metal bars that kept the pigs trapped inside. A cacophony of squeals, bones crunching, and wet squelching noises invaded Charles's ears as he climbed over the bars. Charles looked back at the death trap that he'd nearly escaped, lost his grip, and fell on the other side of the bars. He saw a tendril slithering out of the carnage toward him and prepared for the worst.

"Charles. Get on the bike!" Steve shouted as he and Kyle rolled up to the opening where the animal pens met the parking lot, each on their own bike and Steve balancing Charles's bicycle next to his. Charles saw a few beestings on the right side of Kyle's face and forearm, but somehow he made it out.

Without a hint of hesitation, Charles rolled over the concrete ledge onto the ground. He picked himself up and grabbed the bike. The spiky tentacle lashed out, followed closely by the writhing mass of flesh, claws, and teeth. It rushed forward faster than any of the boys could pedal but stopped just short of the concrete ledge, quivering with a hesitation that it hadn't shown the entire time it hunted them.

"Why did it stop?" Kyle asked, not expecting an answer.

"Look." Steve pointed at the embroidered cloth with the tree symbol on it that Charles dropped when he rolled out of the animal pen. The creature wouldn't cross it. "Do you think it's trapped in there now?"

"I don't think so." Charles ominously pointed to the hole he'd made in the ceiling and the roiling mass of flesh and slime already slithering its way out. "Let's get out of here!" He grabbed the cloth and stuffed it back into his pocket before he took off on his bike with the others.

☾ ☆ ☽

John Opalenik

The three nearly made it past the edge of the farmland when Steve stopped his bike.

"I know that was really messed up, but we can't stop here." Kyle waved for Steve to catch up. "We have to get back home."

"We can't just run." Steve's face held a sense of grave determination. "We'd lead it right back to our neighborhood."

"What are we supposed to do? We're just kids on bikes with nothing but paintball guns and a pocketknife," Kyle argued.

"We also have this." Charles held up the black cloth that somehow saved their lives.

"Oh great! A handkerchief. I guess that's good since a big carnivorous snot is going to kill us." Kyle's eyes darted back and forth between his friends and the farm, where the sound of more animals being consumed, cows he thought, had suddenly stopped.

"No. Charles is right. That symbol on there stopped it. We can use that." Steve turned his bike back toward the farm and faced the ever-changing mass of flesh and slime, which had worked its way onto the street to chase them down. "That freezer is like a bank vault. Only one way in, and the door is thick and metal. We could draw that symbol on the concrete floor right in the doorway to keep it in."

If he wasn't about to get killed, Kyle would have laughed. "Sorry. My little sister has all the sidewalk chalk."

"No. It's all right. They have a chalkboard behind the counter to post their specials." Steve started to feel more confident. "I can draw it off while you guys break in, find the chalk, and get the freezer door open. Then hide somewhere while I lure it into the freezer. As soon as I get out, we slam the door and draw that symbol on the floor right behind the door. Boom. It's trapped."

"This isn't one of our video games, Steve. You can't take one for the team and then your mom just makes us pizza bagels after," Kyle explained. "If this doesn't work out exactly the way you said, then you're not coming home."

"I get that." Steve nodded. "I just know that if we let that thing loose, it's going to follow us right back to our neighborhood, probably get us anyway, and who knows how many other people on the way."

"If you're going to do this, take the cloth. It saved us before. Maybe it can help you." Charles handed the black cloth to Steve. "You're sure you want to do this?"

☽ Incident at Elderhill Farm ☾

"That thing's been trapped there for who knows how long, and we let it out. This might be our one chance to make things right." Steve started pedaling back toward the farm. "We have to try."

☾ ☆ ☽

Steve pedaled toward the creature slowly, conserving his energy for when he needed it most. He knew that he had to get as close to it as possible before changing directions. If he turned too early, it would easily cut him off. The creature seemed to realize that slithering along the hot asphalt didn't give it as much maneuverability as before, so it sprouted its giant crab legs again. He got close enough that it started forming a pseudopod that could lash out at him, and he quickly turned left, leaving nothing but a skid mark where the tendril landed.

He stood on the pedals, pushed hard to get up the hill quickly, and prayed that the thing chasing him was the same as the thing that came out of the pond. If not, he'd be sandwiched between two monsters with nowhere to go. Luckily, the pond remained still, and he could turn onto the flat land behind the building where he could build up some speed and have room to maneuver. He wove on his bike as the crab-clawed creature chased him. Soon, it had closed the distance enough that it could try to grab him. Steve didn't have much time.

A snotty tendril lashed out and snagged the rear wheel of his bike, forcing it to stop abruptly as Steve flew headfirst over the handlebars.

Steve didn't have time to think about the bumps and bruises he'd gotten on his landing. He had to go for the door and hope Kyle and Charles had enough time to do their part. The creature had already begun to surround him, so he ran up the back of the roof toward its peak. When he looked over the top, he didn't see Kyle or Charles; either they were already inside, or they weren't even close. Steve looked back one last time as he gripped the edge of the roof and lowered himself down enough to drop the rest of the way without hurting an ankle. He landed and crumpled into a heap by the front of the building. Before he could pick himself up, he saw that the window had been broken. The large freezer door had been left ajar, and half of the tree symbol from the handkerchief they'd found was drawn in the doorway. Steve looked at the daunting task ahead of him and climbed inside.

When the horror that hunted him poured over the edge of the rooftop and onto the pavement, it was more liquid than solid

John Opalenik

but quickly sprouted octopoid appendages ready to drag itself in any direction it needed to, but instead, it paused. Steve had hidden behind the open freezer door and it sprouted another dozen eyes and something that might have been an ear to find him.

"I'm over here, dickhead!" Steve shouted as he leaned the upper half of his body out from behind the door and extended a middle finger toward the monstrosity.

It sprouted short, chitinous legs and scuttled toward Steve, keeping low to the ground at first and then rearing up and extending its front legs into giant crab claws when it got close enough to try to grasp at him. Part of Steve wished he still had his bike so he could outmaneuver it and get out of the freezer as soon as it followed him in, but he realized that even if he had the speed and maneuverability afforded to him by his reliable Huffy, he had to buy enough time for Kyle and Charles to draw the rest of the tree symbol and be ready to slam the door the second he got out.

A crab claw the size of a stop sign thrust forward and snapped at the air just behind him.

Steve changed direction to put a row of hanging pig corpses between himself and the mass of claws and teeth. The claw seemed to grow bigger as it thrust toward him. It snapped a pig in half, and when the creature slithered over the half that fell, the corpse disappeared behind it, leaving only a hideous smear that made it abundantly clear to Steve what would remain of him if he couldn't get out of the freezer.

Steve looked back just long enough to run out of space in the freezer, and he slammed shoulder-first into an unmoving concrete wall. The dark thought of what would happen to him if he couldn't get out in time suddenly felt more real when he looked up and saw the creature reared up so high that only about a quarter of its body remained on the ground. Its entire underside was an oval mouth with rows of teeth that spiraled inward like a chainsaw, and beneath the mouth were arms with hands that looked like a man's if they were made of meat-flavored jelly, ready to grab him and pull him inside.

He reached into his back pocket for the cloth that could save him, but there wouldn't be nearly enough time. Steve prepared for what he hoped would be a quick end, like a video game where you were either up or down, never maimed, disfigured, or left to spend one's last moments staring down at where your legs used to be.

☽ Incident at Elderhill Farm ☾

The distinctive popping sound of two paintball guns firing as fast as someone could pull the trigger cut through the hideous slurping and growling sounds the creature made, and suddenly, the shapeshifting slime stopped.

A pustule the size of a basketball grew and then popped on the creature's back, revealing a single eye that stared at Charles and Kyle, who stood holding two empty paintball guns. They couldn't shut the door. They'd be killing their best friend. Charles got down on the ground and hastily tried to complete the symbol in chalk. Kyle looked over the abomination and tried to make eye contact with Steve just to show that he hoped their sacrifice meant something. Instead, he saw Steve rolling something up into a baseball-sized wad.

"Kyle. Catch!" Steve lobbed the pocketknife with the black cloth wrapped around it over the monster that separated them and then ran for the edge of the freezer.

Despite not being as good at sports as Steve, Kyle caught the wad, and it immediately started to unravel in his hands. The creature flinched and scuttled back just far enough for Steve to do a baseball slide out of the freezer and slam the door behind him.

The weight of the thing they'd trapped slammed against the door, and all three of them pushed their bodies against it to keep it from opening. "Get the latch closed!" Kyle shouted.

Steve got into a wide stance and pushed his shoulder into the door like he was back at football practice. "Never mind the latch. Why isn't the tree thing you drew stopping it, Charles?"

"I don't know. I drew it right!"

"Think of something. This door isn't going to hold for long!"

As if it understood what they were saying, the creature slammed even harder into the door, and Kyle fell forward onto the tree symbol and skinned his knee on the ground. Suddenly, the slamming stopped.

"Why did it stop?" Kyle grabbed his shin and examined the wound on his knee.

"The blood." Charles pointed to the blood smeared on the lower half of the symbol. "The roots of the tree on the cloth are red. Maybe it was blood."

"Dude. That's so gross." Kyle nearly gagged.

"Let's get the hell out of here." Steve stepped away from the door, ready to turn and run if the thing in the freezer resumed its attack. "We've got to tell our parents about all this."

☽ John Opalenik ☾

"We can't do that. Our parents will call the cops, and they'll cover it up, just like in the *X-Files*," Charles argued. "What we've got to do is figure out what this tree symbol is and what the people at the farm know about it."

As they made it out of the building and into the daylight, Steve realized that Charles was at least partly right. Whether the cops could handle it or not, the boys would never know what they'd encountered or if they were truly safe from it. The monster under the bed would be real for the rest of their lives. "Maybe we can take that handkerchief to St. Dom's. I heard the priest there used to be an exorcist or something, and if he doesn't know, we can take it to CCSU and find a professor of symbology or something."

"Is that even a real word?" Charles tilted his head doubtfully.

When Steve picked up his discarded bike and, exhausted and injured, they started pedaling back to their neighborhood, Kyle chimed in. "Whatever we do, can we *please* go back to my house so I can change my shirt and play some *Goldeneye* first?"

☾ ☆ ☽

When they got back to their neighborhood, Charles looked at the cut on his arm and realized that Steve's or Kyle's mom would make him go to the ER and get stitches and that his mom wouldn't be able to pay for the hospital bill on her tips from the local diner she'd worked at since she was only a few years older than Charles. Instead, he rode his bike to Serafino's Pharmacy and used the money from his paper route on a package of butterfly bandages and a tube of antiseptic. There would be a long, ugly scar, but at least they could keep the house.

He returned home, put on a black hoodie over his T-shirt to cover his wounded forearm, and opened his sketchbook to draw what he'd seen. Charles hung the drawing next to other creatures he'd sketched from movies and video games, leaving his research hidden in plain sight, but when he tried to put pen to paper, he realized that he couldn't capture it, not *really*. It wasn't the constant dark shape of the shark from *Jaws* or the pink muscley mass of one of the demons in *Doom*. It was everything and nothing all at the same time. He couldn't draw the creature, only parts of it that existed when they were needed and melted back into its mass when they weren't. The end result was a collage of eyes, tentacles, claws, and teeth, which, when he thought about it, wasn't inaccurate. He wrote down its capabilities and attacks,

☽ Incident at Elderhill Farm ☾

making them sound like they were from a video game, just in case his mom was more curious than usual.

Charles wasn't sure what he, Kyle, and Steve were going to do with the information, but he knew that if he didn't figure out what they'd seen, it would eat away at him in a different way. Not chewed up and swallowed, as he'd narrowly avoided being, but slowly digested from the inside out.

☾ ☆ ☽

All of the boys slept unquietly that night. Every time Kyle closed his eyes, he saw the basketball-sized yellow eye staring back at him and couldn't help but dwell on how close he'd come to being devoured by the kind of monster he'd convinced himself didn't exist after his mom told him he was getting too old to ask her to check the closet before going to bed. He argued that he was still just a kid, but when his mom pointed out that Kyle's little sister never asked her to check under the bed, he knew there'd be no convincing his mother to let him be a kid just a few years longer.

Steve stared at his bedroom ceiling and thought about when he and his dad brought the deer to Elderhill Farm. He felt disturbed enough seeing pigs hanging from hooks, drained of blood and frozen, but now realizing that the people his dad was talking to had kept some sort of monster locked away in the woods for who knows how long, he wondered what other secrets they kept and what they'd do to keep them.

The shadows cast by the back porch light through Charles's bedroom window danced as the wind made the branches of the trees writhe. He had to get up and pull the shade down to block out the world and the frightening things it contained. As soon as he retreated to the safety of his bed, he heard a knock at the front door. He looked at the clock; it was time his mom got home from closing up the diner for the night, so he checked the door and saw her standing outside with her arms full of groceries. "Norma ordered too much frozen stuff and didn't have room to keep the frozen wings from the MLB season opener special, so she gave them to us. I guess we'll be having chicken for dinner for the next couple of nights . . ." Her voice trailed off, ambivalent about how generous Norma had been since Charles's father left. "Come on. Help me get these in the freezer."

Charles and his mother rarely spoke after she got back from a night shift, and he liked the quality time. He felt bad lying about having a normal day, but he wasn't ready to tell her about

John Opalenik

what he'd seen yet. That day would come when he knew more and when he had proof.

When he returned to his bedroom, the window had been opened, and harsh black Sharpie had been scrawled over the bottom of his drawing of the creature he'd seen. It read, "Return to Elderhill Farm. We have so much more to show you."

☆

John Opalenik *is a horror writer and educator from Connecticut. He is the author of The Primeval series,* The Blue Beneath the Mountain, *and the short story collection* Among the Willows and Other Strange Tales. *He's had numerous short stories published in anthologies and zines. He lives in central Connecticut with his wife, son, and dog.*

Keep up to date on future releases and events at johnopalenik.com and @johnopalenik on Instagram and Threads or on Facebook @ john.opalenik.

Made in the USA
Middletown, DE
08 July 2024